I0672132

Trinity House

Timothy R. Keen

READING
MONKEYS

ISBN 9781947265189

May your fountain be blessed, and may you rejoice in the wife of your youth. A loving doe, a graceful deer— may her breasts satisfy you always, may you ever be intoxicated with her love. Why, my son, be intoxicated with another man's wife? Why embrace the bosom of a wayward woman? For your ways are in full view of the LORD, and he examines all your paths. The evil deeds of the wicked ensnare them; the cords of their sins hold them fast. For lack of discipline they will die, led astray by their own great folly.

Proverbs 5: 18-23

Timothy R. Keen

Table of Contents

PROLOGUE

It all happened so fast. I was sick with Covid-19 and quarantined in the rectory, watching the Easter service streamed to my computer. It was almost worth the fever, headache and shortness of breath to not be in church on Sunday morning. I don't recall when that ever happened before, on Easter no less, one of Pastor's biggest events. It was my job too but not on that particular Sunday, thanks to the coronavirus. I was drinking chicken broth, wrapped in a blanket, lying on the sofa, when a weather alert streamed across the bottom of the television. A tornado had been sighted a few miles from Modoc and everyone was to seek shelter. Just then, an alarm sounded from the center of town, howling like a banshee. Modoc had installed a tornado warning system a few years previously.

Should I go to the church's basement, contaminating god-knows how many of the congregation with Covid-19?

We had already lost several church members to the pandemic. I didn't want to kill anyone, so I wrapped myself in the blanket and went to the bathroom, settling down in the bathtub to wait nervously. We take tornadoes seriously in Oklahoma. I was suddenly cold, teeth chattering from the fever.

My phone rang in the other room, so I got up to get it. It was probably Pastor checking on me. Shivering, dragging the blanket with me, I found the phone and answered his call.

"We're in the basement, Lady," he said.

"I shouldn't join you because of the Covid virus," I

answered, then added, "I'm going to get in the bathtub."

A pause as if he were thinking. "Good idea. That cast-iron tub is a perfect tornado shelter. Just climb in and cover yourself with your Yoga mat and a blanket, just in case."

"I'm going right now—"

*   *   *

I woke up in a hospital bed, a plastic tube in my arm, in a lot of pain. A nurse entered the room to check on me, fiddled with something I couldn't see, and I mumbled that I had the Covid virus. She nodded and hurried away. I fell asleep. I woke again, this time in a room with curtains blocking my view, dying of thirst and hurting everywhere. It felt like I had been run through a meat grinder. There was a cast on my right arm and something was wrapped around my head. My right leg felt as if it weighed a ton. I tried to raise up to see what was going on but couldn't move. Just as well because my headache was worse than before the tornado had struck.

I remembered my phone call with Pastor. *Where was he?* The congregation had gotten safely to the basement and would have survived the tornado that destroyed the rectory and probably the church building. It must be because of my having Covid. Sure. It would take a few days to get everything sorted out because my phone had been lost in the wreckage. Pastor was probably waiting in the hospital to visit me.

I slept and when I woke up, Macbeth Lunatic was standing next to my bed, wearing a mask, nervously shifting his stance.

"Where's Pastor?" I mumbled.

HYPOCRITE

It took thirty years or so for me to realize that I'd lived my life as a robot, an unthinking person, an automaton that calculates the path of least resistance and follows it. I'm not a real person. Some women would describe me as a personal prostitute; at best I am a hypocrite because I'm lazy but not like someone who doesn't take out the trash; instead, I'm one of those physically appealing women who stops thinking the minute she meets a man who looks like a good candidate to take care of her. Boys were already hanging around in junior high, like flies to honey, drawn by my blush blonde hair, small upturned nose, and precipitous physical development. I always assumed that sexual appeal was an advantage, a fortuitous physical characteristic that would catapult me into the upper echelon of society. I was encouraged to be a good student because, according to my mother, older men liked educated women and I was definitely supposed to marry an older man. Young men were unreliable and hadn't proven themselves yet.

I was never particularly interested in boys—or girls—so I never practiced the fine arts of romance and sexual entrapment. It had never been necessary.

My parents decided that the best place to find a good husband was college, so I packed my suitcase and moved into the women's dormitory at the University of Iowa, close enough to home to return on weekends. My mother was very pleased when I chose English Literature as my major. I did read a lot and still do, so I enjoyed it and did well. It wasn't until my senior year that I learned that my degree qualified me to be a school teacher. I was starting to worry about my future because I hadn't found a serious, good looking, older man to marry yet, and I was certainly not interested in looking for a job, especially not as a school teacher. I was spared the ignominy of employment or returning home with no husband or job when I finally met the perfect man, in the library.

Pastor Church was a man on a mission to save the world from Hell, one soul at a time. That got my attention. I had never met anyone with such a well-defined purpose for his life, and he had a plan. Religiosity for Pastor was like a bird's nest-building skill. He had been raised in a devout Catholic home and learned the basics from his parents, like praying and believing, the same way birds learn which twigs and grasses make the best nests. He had added to this basic toolbox and switched to Evangelical Protestantism as the optimum path to save the world. He probably would have become Hindu if he'd lived in India. I'll bet that a bald eagle could build a hummingbird nest if it really wanted to, which is why Pastor is the spiritual leader of a nondenominational church rather than a Catholic priest. He had been raised on transcendental beliefs and learned how to direct other peoples' superstitions to help them live better, happier lives. Pastor was a peddler of cheerful fantasies, delusions of the present and the future. He didn't worry much about the past.

It's funny I used a bird nest metaphor because I was probably suffering from empty-nest syndrome when these events took place. Our youngest son had graduated from community college the previous year and moved into an apartment of his own, right here in Modoc. I don't see him much though because he works long hours as the assistant manager of the Homeland Food store. His older brother had moved to Oklahoma City to attend college and never returned. I only see him at Christmas but he calls on Mother's Day and my birthday.

Pastor tried to brainwash Seth and Joseph, but it didn't take because they inherited a commonsense gene from me. Even if they had been superstitious, his tyrannical approach to raising children would have turned them against God after eighteen years. I was proud of them. Of course, Seth's departure left me alone with Pastor, with no one to distract him.

I wanted to scream when I woke up next to him every morning, dreading another day suffocating from his dogmatic world view. Being alone with him most days, nothing interesting to keep me busy, had made me realize how much I detested Pastor Church and everything he stood for. It had taken twenty-three years to arrive at the inevitable conclusion that agnostics and evangelical Christians don't mix. We're like oil and water.

Being a mentally lazy person, I'd had no opinion about religion when I met Pastor so I adopted his beliefs. It was like new underwear. After a couple years, however, the bra chaffed and the panties were too tight, so resentment grew, kept at bay for a while by the business of raising two boys. It was becoming difficult to pretend being a good little minister's wife, especially considering my ongoing affair with Macbeth Lunatic. I wasn't in love with Mac, but there was something between us. He was my only friend. Despite, or because of, our relationship I often felt like a prostitute—servicing Pastor and looking forward to spending intimate time with Mac. I should have been ashamed.

In the final analysis, I was a hypocrite. My life was meaningless, a vacuum without substance, a void hidden behind the social facade I'd haphazardly constructed, a veneer woven of lies, deception, repressed emotions, unexpressed hostility, self-delusion. The worst part is that I didn't feel any guilt, not even for having regular sex with my husband and a married man at the same time. How could anyone mistake me for a morally upstanding person, the wife of a preacher?

I certainly didn't.

WOMANIZER

I'm not proud of what happened, even if Lady insists that it wasn't my fault. Just don't take her too seriously. I'll tell it like it is and let you make up your own mind. We have to go back a few years to get to the beginning.

Things would have turned out differently if I hadn't met Missy. I was stationed at Fort Sill, about a hundred miles from Oklahoma City. I worked in grounds maintenance, installing new landscaping, cutting grass, trimming trees, stuff like that. I worked hard and learned how to keep a big place like Fort Sill looking good on a budget. When I got out of the Army, I was a landscape maintenance professional. I was also a married man because I met Missy Farmer while serving my country.

Missy was studying nursing at the University of Oklahoma. I was only a couple of years older than her, but you'd have thought she was still in high school from the way she acted. So innocent and naive. I was young and thought I was god's gift to women, so it was pretty easy to get to know her. She was cute and had a nice figure. We dated a few months and got engaged because it seemed like the thing to do. But I kept seeing other women. Those other girls were for fun. Missy was serious. She was a Christian. We were going to have a family. I had no interest in religion, not that I hated it or anything. I just never thought about it. It was important to her, so I started going to church with her. We got married in the church she'd attended all her life. Her whole family was religious, but not as much as her. It was like there was this whole family and town waiting for me and it felt good. Anyway, when I got out of the army, she quit nursing school because she didn't like the sight of blood and besides, she was going to be my wife. So, we moved to her hometown, Modoc, Oklahoma and her father loaned me ten-thousand-dollars to start a landscaping business. He made sure I understood it wasn't a wedding present.

I was accepted by Missy's family and the people of Modoc without a second thought. Good people. I made a point of making them proud, repaying the loan within a year, attending church, being good to Missy, getting involved in charities, being a good father and provider. That was all in pubic.

In private, I continued drinking like I'd never gotten out of the army. I was an alcoholic—correction, I am an alcoholic—but I didn't know it back then. No one knew about my drinking except my fellow secret drinkers, upstanding men and women like myself.

The birth of our daughter, Trinity, was a turning point. Missy had found a purpose in life. She also had a post-partum decrease in her libido whereas mine continued undiminished. It was easy to find women with a taste for alcohol and sex, however, so Missy's new attitude wasn't a problem, only an inconvenience. I restricted my dalliances and liaisons to women from church, who had as much to lose as me and thus kept our affairs private. We didn't see anything wrong with doing that because we weren't emotionally involved. We were just having fun, blowing off steam through a healthy hobby, like bowling.

I've heard that change is often slow and occurs unnoticed, but I can honestly say that everything about my life changed when Missy and I attended a Wednesday bible study at Trinity House. The church had been suggested by a friend of hers who swore that the pastor spoke to every Christian, whether evangelical or fundamentalist. That's why Missy had insisted I join her. She leaned more towards a literal interpretation of the Bible whereas I think that something was probably lost in translation and God's Word should be taken with a grain of salt. We never argued about it, but it was a subject that came up all the time. You can guess why my interpretation was more liberal.

At any rate, Missy and I both fell in love with Trinity

House, but for different reasons. She couldn't stop talking about the coincidence that our daughter shared a divine name with the church. She was further inspired by the preacher, Pastor Church. I could relate, with a name like Macbeth Lunatic.

What got my attention about Trinity House was Pastor Church's wife, Lady Church, who stood by his side at the entrance after the meeting and said goodnight to everyone as they left. I felt something when her hand briefly held mine in a soft, cool grip while her blue eyes examined me closely. I was fascinated. Missy left the church she'd attended all her life as if they'd become communists, giving her family no more reason for her sudden departure than that she liked Pastor Church's way of presenting the Lord's words. I went along without complaint, thinking about Lady Church and what the future held for me. We fit into the new church like hand in glove. Maybe two hands into a pair of gloves.

It took a while to get Lady into bed, but I'd had plenty of practice with religious women. It was made easier by the presence of a guest bedroom in the church, used by ecumenical visitors from around the country who gave guest lectures on topics of concern to all Christians. Pastor was a thoroughly modern minister with as good a grasp of the Bible as anyone I'd ever heard talk. At any rate, by the time I finally got Lady into the guest bed, we had become friends. I really liked her and sometimes forgot to seduce her when we were alone. This relationship went on far too long and I should have seen the warning signs of our breaking my rule against becoming emotionally involved. I'll get back to that, if she doesn't.

Missy and I had attended her old church for ten years, volunteering for various charities and church programs without recognition for our efforts. After all, Jesus said we should do good works without expecting reward. So, when we joined Trinity House, I volunteered to take care of the poorly maintained landscaping at my own expense. I didn't expect to be publicly applauded for such a mundane task, only to have my efforts recognized by the church's board and participate in landscape maintenance discussions.

*   *   *

That was then and this is now.

I'm not being uncharitable when I say that Dim Light is an idiot. He went to college for a couple of years and got an AA degree in sales, so he was somehow qualified to be a church elder. He was responsible for building maintenance, which put me in the position of being his underling, at least in his mind. Dim might be a good insurance salesman, but he's a poor manager, and he doesn't know anything about building and grounds maintenance, not that he cares. I'll let him speak for himself.

"Well, Mac, we need to have this new sound system working by Easter. We can do that, can't we?"

"I'm not an electrician, Dim, so I can't speak about the wiring. We should have someone take a look at it before we do anything."

Dim scoffs and says, "You know enough about electricity to figure this out. It's only a sound system. Not much more than buying a new stereo. What's it going to cost us?"

I'm glad Dim admits that this will not be covered by our non-existent contract for landscaping, but I'm not happy about going outside my comfort zone—electrically speaking. "Fifty-dollars an hour because I don't know what I'll find. An electrician would be able to give a better estimate because they know what to look for."

Dim whistles, trying to impress me with his indignation, and says, "That's a little steep, Mac. How about a flat fee of one-hundred dollars?"

I pretend to be considering his counteroffer before saying, "Hire an electrician and it will be done properly and you won't have to worry about the quality of the work."

"You drive a hard bargain, Mac, but okay." He winks at me and adds, "Let's not get carried away."

I say, "Sure," knowing I'll pay an electrician to do the work. That's how Dim is.

Melissa Tight joins us, saving me from further conversation with Dim. Melissa is very sexy. We'd had a one-night stand with no return engagement because she suffered from vulvodynia, a painful vagina. I'm thinking about our last encounter when she greets Dim and me.

"What are you boys up to?" she asks, looking at me longingly. She wants it but is afraid of what sexual intercourse would mean.

I smile and answer, "It's tight, Melissa. Easter is going to be difficult but Dim and I have a contract."

She smiles seductively and says, "Don't give up, Mac. You never know what might come up."

I know one thing that's coming up. She knows it too, giving me the look, the one that says how badly she wants to have sex with me. The look she'd been giving me for months.

A couple days later, I take the issue of the sound system to Pastor, asking him to overrule Dim's decision and get an appraisal from an electrician before continuing with the project. He trusts Dim. I am flabbergasted. *How could anyone trust an insurance salesman?*

I feel like Job at this point, beset by problems beyond my control. Like Satan is having a field day with me. A few days later, Lady approaches me while I'm pulling weeds around the rectory.

"Is this a bad time to talk?"

She does that, wanting to talk when I'm working. Before I can answer her question she continues.

"What's your opinion about abortion?"

I look at her, forgetting the weed held in my right hand. "I guess I'm in favor of letting people live, but I'm not sure a few million cells are a human. I guess that when an embryo looks like a person, it should be treated like one."

"That's a fetus. I guess you..."

Lady needs me, so I stand up and lead her into the church, to the guest bedroom. She's unusually aggressive, leaving me exhausted. I fall asleep in her arms and don't get home until late. Missy doesn't question my story about pulling weeds in the dark.

THE REAL THING

I always stood next to Pastor after service, to thank everyone for coming to church. That's how I met Macbeth Lunatic. I knew what he was the instant I shook his hand. People like him can't hide it. It's in their eyes. He was undressing me and imagining fondling my breasts before our handshake ended. If the greeting had lasted another moment, he would have imagined me on the floor, forcing himself on me, not that he would have had to rape me. I wanted him, thinking of the guest bedroom in the church. I imagined his hands on my breasts, gripping my buttocks, caressing my groin. I was excited and he knew it. His congenial nod conveyed his consent to our making love at a later date.

Note my use of the phrase "making love" rather than "having sex," Mac's phrase for satisfying his yearning for a quick orgasm. I would teach him the meaning of "making love," even if he didn't know it at the time.

I fell head-over-heels in love with Mac that first day we met, even if I didn't know it myself. The rest was inevitable. But it wasn't physical, even though Mac is a good-looking man. His high forehead is topped by thick, dark-brown hair, brooding brown eyes gazing over a narrow nose, and full lips begging to be kissed. His small chin only serves to emphasize his intelligent brow. He is also a very reliable person, who doesn't waver in his attention to details. I've never met anyone except Mac who reads the fine print in a contract. I know he's a womanizer; after all, that's how we met, but that's not his fault. For him to forego having sex every day would be like my pretending to believe the transcendental nonsense Pastor was pushing. He would implode just like I did…but that comes later.

Back to the story. I could see that Missy Lunatic wasn't satisfying Mac the first time I laid eyes on her. She was a virgin, despite having given birth to a daughter; like in the story of Jesus and the manger, it was a virginal birth. Their daughter was even called Trinity. How fitting.

All this happened ten years ago. I was only thirty-five, and I was what men call *hot*. The concept of making love rather than having sex kept me from going after Macbeth Lunatic as if he were a Christmas present. I had never even thought of having an affair before meeting him but this was different. It was destiny and couldn't be denied. I hadn't felt this way in my entire life, definitely not when I'd met Pastor, not even when we had sex the first time. I was more excited at meeting Mac in church than when Pastor had taken my virginity. I craved his touch. I was going to enjoy this experience more than anything I'd ever done in my life.

I played with Mac, who no doubt had thought I would be an easy lay. I taught him how to treat a woman. His respectful language couldn't disguise the lust in his heart, which prevented him from meeting my gaze for more than six months. Trying to get my attention, he performed small favors, like filling the wood box every day on his way to work. I watched while he worked around the church, giving him the satisfaction of knowing I was aware of his presence, touching him occasionally, making it clear that I would be his when he earned the privilege. He worked hard to meet my expectations. I made him languish in the shadow of what I offered, touching, brushing against him, and finally a peck on his cheek. I thought I would faint when my lips touched his flesh. He felt it too. His hand instinctively reached around my waist but was quickly withdrawn. I wished it had completed its trajectory and pulled me against him. Moments like that became more common, each occurrence amplifying how much I wanted him, while signaling that he wasn't yet man enough for me. He understood and improved, until neither of us could wait any longer to consummate our love.

I can't find words to describe what it was like, when Mac

and I finally made love. All I can do is describe it. Pastor was out of town, attending a nondenominational conference on how to use social media to spread the Message. Mac had just finished loading his mower on the trailer and I offered him a glass of tea on the porch. He jumped at the chance, knowing what was coming, what I was offering. We drank the tea and I casually broached the subject.

"I'm not sure how to say this, Mac, so I'll just say it. I've grown fond of you and I would like to sleep with you, but that isn't possible…"

"I feel the same way, Lady, so why don't we just go inside and satisfy whatever it is that's taken a hold of both of us?"

I was about to faint as I nodded and, shaking in my sandals, led him into the rectory. Once the door was closed, he took me in his arms and kissed me gently. I melted into his lips, or maybe it was his head. I don't know, but I don't remember anything else until I climaxed, the best orgasm of my life. This was the real thing.

Over the ensuing years, I suspected that Mac was having other affairs—after all, he hit on the preacher's wife—but I didn't care because I was his best girl. I could see it in his eyes; even in public, in church, he couldn't hide his feelings. He was mine, whether he knew it or not. And I was his. Until death us do part. There were some uncomfortable and ironic side effects to being Mac's best girl. For one thing, I was jealous of Missy. He and I had discussed their marriage, and I knew that he didn't love her even though he wouldn't admit that he loved me. That didn't help because I didn't like sharing Mac with anyone.

There was another issue, more important than Mac's having other girlfriends: I had learned, after ten years of being married to Pastor, that I was never going to become a Christian, and I couldn't make an emotional commitment to an idealogue. Mac had told me that he'd become involved with religion through Missy and, being who he is, had accepted it as his own philosophy. That's one of the things I love about him. He doesn't do anything halfway, like me.

One day when Pastor was attending a bible conference in Dallas, Mac and I were alone while he was cleaning up around the rectory. He took very good care of the rectory because he wanted to be near me. I'd even kidded him about it. He'd joked that he never knew when I would be in the mood. We had in fact made love earlier that day, but not in the bed I shared with Pastor; after our first time, Mac and I always used the guest room in the church.

"Why are you so sure the Bible describes the relationship people have with the universe? I mean, most of humanity thinks very differently. How do you know that you're right and they're wrong?"

He stopped raking the clippings and looked at me the way he does now, as if I were the only person in the world. "You should know, Lady. Pastor talks about that all the time. Weren't you listening?"

I shook my head. "I want to hear your opinion."

He thought a minute and said, "I don't understand it very well, despite Pastor and Missy and others explaining it to me. That's why I accept it on faith."

"Accept what on faith?" I asked, edging closer, so that he wanted to reach out and touch me.

He was having trouble concentrating, so I gave him a mocking smile and suggested, "Whatever they tell you?"

Certain he had found the definitive answer, he grinned at me, pointed his finger at my chest, and said, "You're a clever one Lady, using your college degree to try and trip me up. Suppose you explain what you're getting at before I answer? How about that?"

That was fair, I suppose. "Well…let me see…" I cleared my throat and began, "No one knows what's going on with the universe, life, death, why bad things happen, why some people seem to be so lucky. Science has discovered some basic principles, explained by physics and biology for example, but scientists don't pretend to have answers for problems we can't see or touch. That's why their ideas are reasonable. Don't you agree?"

He was thinking again, but his head was shaking slowly as he quipped, "I don't know that I agree with that. Scientists say plenty that they can't prove. Pastor calls it speculation. Missy calls it doubletalk with big words."

I didn't want to defend scientists, who had overstated what they could prove often enough to justify criticism. I would do better by focusing on the bottom line. "Sure, but that's not what I'm talking about, Mac. I'm referring to the big unknown—no one knows what happened billions of years ago, or even if there were billions of years. We don't know about the distant past or places that are far away, like other galaxies. So, if scientists have theories based on observations, and change them all the time, why do you think there's a guy sitting on a throne of gold, choosing who lives and who dies? And this guy never changes his mind?"

He stopped raking again and faced me before confidently replying, "Pastor talked about that. We do change our beliefs and they even come in different forms because of our uncertainty about exactly what God's plan is. That's why there are Fundamentalists like Missy, Evangelicals, Catholics, even Muslims and Hindus. The point isn't that one of these religions is correct, it's that they're all searching for the truth. God has chosen not to reveal His plan to us, so we have to try and figure it out on our own."

Mac wasn't as stupid as some people thought, but he was misled. I approached him again and risked touching his arm, before saying, "But all this groping about for the truth is based on nothing but wishful thinking, wild and crazy ideas invented by lunatics—"

Mac chuckled and I joined him.

"Many great scientific discoveries were made by men who were treated as lunatics by other scientists during their lives."

There was no point in pursuing the topic. Pastor and Missy had too great an influence on his thinking. Mac isn't stupid but he doesn't care about metaphysical theories that have no bearing on his life. He accepts whatever someone else tells him. The problem as I saw it was that he could easily accept a belief system that wasn't only meaningless, but also potentially hazardous to his own health and safety. I would definitely be a better influence on him than Missy with her Fundamentalist beliefs. The simple fact, which infuriates me to this day, is that some people can't face the unknown universe, the vicissitudes of life with billions of other people committing random acts, and thus they turn to superstition. I didn't think he was one of them, even if he pretended to be.

I knew all about Missy and her marriage to Mac because

she was quite a talker, especially with someone she didn't see as a threat, like the pastor's wife—me. Unaware that she was confessing to a rival, she'd informed me that she and Mac had a platonic relationship as brother and sister in Christ. I'd been supportive while inwardly conflicted; she wasn't competing for Mac's affection, but I was envious of her because I wished Pastor and I were nothing more than brothers and sisters in Christ.

My mind wandered as I followed Mac around the garden, never venturing more than a few yards from him. I was awakened from my trance by his voice, chiding but playful. "You know, you sound like you're becoming an atheist, Lady. That could be a problem, what with your being married to a minister and all…"

I trusted Mac, so I confessed my feelings. "I'm an agnostic. I don't need to believe in a person who runs the universe. Not knowing how it works doesn't make me want to stop living or become a hedonist; it actually gives me a calm feeling, like I'm one with the whole universe. I'm as big as eternity." I wanted to say more, like how I didn't understand why he could have so many girlfriends and remain a devout Christian. He was a hypocrite like me, but it was easier for me to accept because my ethical system recognizes that people make mistakes, especially in personal relationships. It was imperative that I correct my error whereas Mac could go on living with the wrong woman for the rest of his life, never admitting it even to himself.

He nodded knowingly and said, "Your secret is safe with me. I like the way you put it though: One with the universe. Eternal life. We have more in common than either of us might have thought."

We continued talking while he worked, until he reluctantly packed his garden tools. I followed him to his truck, where he said, "I wish I could stay and never go home again…that's not what I meant—"

"I moved closer to him, scanning the area for any observers, and risked a peck on his cheek. "I feel the same way. Now go home and play house with Missy."

His head ducked, his lips against my ear, whispering, "You too, but don't play too hard."

INFIDELITY

I suspected that Mac was having an affair with Melissa Tight, the young, very sexy choir director, but I had never suspected what Vanity Blunt was going to reveal. She'd always struck me as a world-wise woman because she made no secret of her early career as a model and film actress. Vanity was gorgeous. In her fifties, her blonde hair appeared natural and there wasn't a wrinkle on her face. She must have felt I was a kindred spirit because of my blonde hair and, like I said, I was blessed with a nice figure and appearance, which I've maintained through the years. At any rate, when I expressed interest in her idea for a church garden, she became chummy. Next thing I know, she's telling me about having a fling with Mac five-years ago, when he and I were already in an intimate relationship. I got little consolation from knowing I was his best girl, because we were still together, whereas their relationship had only lasted a couple of weeks.

Despite having no idea why women felt compelled to confess their innermost secrets to me, I enjoyed the position of authority I found myself in, like the king's regent. I was the preacher's wife—Pastor's wife. As disgusting as that was in reality, I played it up, encouraging open conversations; never promising to keep what I heard to myself, I nevertheless felt as if I'd taken a vow of privacy. Another side to my position as confessor was that I learned about everyone's religious beliefs. I passed this information to Pastor, filtered appropriately because of my implicit vow of confidentiality.

Vanity Blunt loved talking as much as Missy Lunatic. She had met Mike while still an actress, a career that ended when she wouldn't do a full-nudity scene and was sued by the producer for breach of contract. Mike had been attending a meeting of the National Bar Association at the Orange County conference center in Los Angeles, where she was participating in an acting workshop. The way she described falling in love reminded me of meeting Mac. Wanting to hear about a successful love affair, I encouraged her to continue. Her story didn't sound too different from my own or Missy's. There was one difference, however; despite Mike misrepresenting his law practice in Modoc, turning out to be a chauvinist, full of shit (her words), and an egotist, she loved him. They were very happy.

She liked Trinity House because Pastor was a good speaker and didn't spout fundamentalist dogma. Mike liked being on the church board. We laughed about that and I told her that Pastor saw the congregation as his flock. We had become best friends.

I wanted to share Vanity's revelation with Mac, but I had to wait until the weekend. Not having felt his hands on my body for more than a week, I had to settle for standing close enough to smell him as he unloaded some chemicals from his trailer.

"I had an interesting conversation with Vanity Blunt. Have you two ever met?"

He shook his head, never breaking eye contact. "No. Just in church and at church gatherings. Stuff like that."

So that was how he did it, justifying his inappropriate behavior to himself—stuff like that. I was angry enough to say, "Have you had any other girlfriends besides me?"

"No," came the lie from his lips.

I was livid. I wanted to force him to face the fact that he was an adulterer as defined by his own moral code, a belief system I no longer accepted.

"I find it hard to believe that you flirted with and then seduced me, Pastor's wife, but haven't had an affair with any of the other healthy, attractive women available in Trinity House."

Mac was speechless, his eyes turned away to avoid admitting his infidelity.

Righteous anger swelling in my breast, I continued. "You are an adulterer, Mac. You have been having an extramarital, sexual liaison with at least one married woman for almost ten years. This is something I know for a fact because I am your mistress."

"What do you want?" he mumbled.

"Do you recall our conversation about being at one with the universe?"

He nodded.

"I am certain that the universe doesn't care if I'm an adulteress. I'm also certain it doesn't care if you are an adulterer—my interest is personal."

After a long delay, he said, "Personal?"

I was so angry and frustrated that I just said it. "Did you have an affair with Vanity Blunt after you and I started seeing each other?"

His face turned so red that I thought his head was going to explode before he finally answered, "We might have got together a couple of times. I don't remember..."

"Well, she certainly remembers!" Not finished, I added, "Don't you ever cheat on me again, Macbeth Lunatic, or you'll find yourself praying to your deaf god for the Rapture because that's the only way you'll escape my wrath."

The pain in his eyes made me want to apologize but I didn't relent. After more than a minute, looking at the ground, glancing at me, he mumbled, "I'll try. I don't want to lose you."

Still angry, I retorted, "You'd better do more than try Mac because I've had it with your bullshit. Don't ever lie to me again!"

I stomped away before he could respond, hiding the tears flowing down my cheeks.

FUNDAMENTAL BELIEFS

Pastor had a difficult job. Knowing how hard it was to maintain a semblance of peace within Trinity House, I did everything I could to keep these sanctimonious, superstitious fools attentive to the progressive, Christian educational system Pastor was implementing. As ridiculous as this objective appeared to me, it served to focus these miscreants' limited attention span on whatever core beliefs they shared. The biggest problem confronting Pastor was that his congregation's core beliefs were a moving target. It wasn't like in the days before social media, when a minister had some control over his congregation's sources of information.

The Fundamentalists were the biggest problem. These were the most superstitious members of Trinity House, desperate for an immediate answer to every insipid question that crossed their minds. They needed closure and they needed it right now. Missy was a fundamentalist. She had spoken to me several times about QAnon and the deep state.

When questioned, her eyes rolled as if she were having a seizure and she mumbled, "They're out to get us, Lady, unless we prepare for the war against the legion of Satan."

I never bothered to respond because I'd been hearing similar crazy stories from about half the women I spoke to in the congregation. Fundamentalism was no longer about believing the universe was created in seven calendar days; it now included a satanic cult preparing to take over the world. The battle of Armageddon described in Revelations was too ambiguous for the digital age. They had their answer delivered in equivocal but precise detail, shared periodically by QAnon. It was imminent. They were living in the end times. It didn't matter that none of the rest of us were.

The fundamentalists were perfectly represented by Dim Light, a certifiable idiot, and his superstitious, voodoo-believing, oversexed Latina wife, Melina. He was an insurance salesman and she sold houses. She was doing well. They always sat near the front of the church so that she could take center stage to perform her show. She danced, spoke in tongues, swayed back and forth, and sometimes fell to the carpeted floor, shaking as if having an epileptic seizure. Dim would watch with concern but never check to see if it was the real thing.

The evangelicals are a slightly less-volatile group; just as superstitious, they nevertheless have functioning prefrontal cortices and are capable of thought. They don't exercise this ability very often however, instead repeating the mantra that America was becoming hedonistic and socialist, and soon they wouldn't be able to go to church to sing hymns in a vain effort to feel as if they actually liked the person sitting next to them. Mike and Vanity Blunt were exemplary evangelicals within the Trinity House congregation. They believed whatever would maintain their status within the community because they couldn't face the uncertainties of life without supernatural support. They were lost souls like Mac.

I hadn't realized how much Pastor had come to rely on my intelligence gathering and analysis until he asked for my opinion about what he described as a developing crisis within Trinity House. I shared what I knew without breaking my foolish sense of propriety.

"Trinity House is a microcosm of America. Half the people I talk to are convinced that Donald Trump is the Messiah, fighting the great beast in the end times. They don't care what anyone says about Revelations or anything else. They know the truth because they heard it from a reliable source on the internet. They are brain dead. The Evangelicals are tired of Covid-19 and just want life to get back to normal. Their attention span isn't much longer than the Fundamentalists', but they aren't as easily stirred up."

"I don't think I have your full support, Lady. You sound

like a cynic—"

I cut him off, "You asked me what I've learned from the superstitious fools you condescendingly refer to as your flock, Pastor. Well, that's what I've learned."

He started to chastise me for my unkind but realistic assessment, thought better of it, and asked, "Are there any leaders among the conservative members of the congregation?"

"Conservative?"

"The Fundamentalists."

"I don't know if I'd call them conservative, Pastor. After all, these are people who follow QAnon and worship Donald J. Trump. Aren't conservatives supposed to be people who don't want to rock the boat..." Pastor was aware of the shift in my opinion since the election of President Trump in the 2016 election. He was still on the fence.

"They are waiting for a new messiah," I added.

He finally replied, "That's what I've gathered as well."

Pastor had been the leader of Trinity House for twenty years and now he had to deal with a new generation of believers, who were tired of his thoughtful but unprovocative message. They were the more gullible of the social media crowd and they wanted action, which he was unprepared to supply. He was concerned about the church splitting—that's how he had founded Trinity House in the first place.

The Messiah had become the Pharisee.

JUST LIKE OLD TIMES

Sometimes Lady goes too far, like when she accused me of being an adulterer after she'd learned about my affair with Vanity Blunt. Lady is an example of just how low a person's self-esteem can sink when they don't walk in Jesus' footsteps. She as much as admitted that she was a hypocrite, playing sacred hymns on the organ, smiling during Pastor's sermons, standing next to him to greet the congregation, all the while thinking it was a farce. It was Lady who should be ashamed. It doesn't matter that she runs and hides, calling herself an agnostic, unrepentant, willing to act like she's married to two men if that pleases her. Missy is my only wife and always will be. I'm only having a good time with Lady, just like I'd only had fun with Vanity. I am not an adulterer. *Maybe Lady felt like one and was transferring her guilt to me?*

I can't believe I let her trick me into admitting that I didn't want to lose her. For the love of God! I'd sounded like a lovesick puppy. I definitely was not lovesick, just ask Melissa.

Melissa Tight. Now there's a sweet child of Jesus. After our one-night stand, she'd been distant while letting me know she was still interested. Like the time I was in the office, replacing a bad electrical outlet.

"Just like old times, isn't it, Mac?" she asks, brushing past me.

I know what she means. The bedroom is just down the hall. Oh man I want to take her down there and get some sexual relief because Lady has been giving me the cold shoulder. "I'm ready anytime you are," I say, hoping for the best.

She wants it. I know she does, but she shakes her head, a few loose strands of light-brown hair waving like grass in the wind. "I'm okay for now, but don't go anywhere."

Then I put two and two together. Lady was becoming clingier than before, acting like she was my wife whereas Melissa didn't want to have a roll in the hay. Pastor had hired her with the Board's approval, but I'm willing to bet that he's having an affair with her and probably paying less attention to Lady. I share the results of my detective work with Melissa. "You and Pastor are hooking up."

She doesn't bat a long eyelash, dark-green eyes meeting my gaze as she replies, "We get together in my apartment, sometimes overnight—"

"His quick trips to Oklahoma City," I add. "I wouldn't mind spending the night at your place. It would be a lot better than ducking in and out of the guest room here." I nod towards the hallway.

She comes close enough for me to smell her mint chewing gum, leans towards me so that her breasts press against my chest, and whispers in my ear, "Pastor is more than a sexual partner. He has a dream and I'm part of it. We're going to transform Trinity House into a megachurch."

Her soft lips rub against my ear and I want to drag her to the other room and ravage her the way I know she wants me to. My arm slips around her narrow waist. She doesn't resist, but I suddenly recall Lady's threat. Instead of doing what nature demands, I kiss her passionately. She bites my lip painfully and I recoil.

"What was that about?"

"I didn't ask you to kiss me as if we were going to the guest room. We are not. If you want to retain any chance of getting together in the future, you're going to have to wait until I'm ready."

"What's going on?" I plead.

"Pastor is more of a man than you Mac because he doesn't think with his penis. A spiritual man like Pastor needs to have a clear mind if he's going to hear the Lord's voice, so I'm keeping him satisfied while his cynical, uptight wife ignores him. I don't believe that Lady Church is a Christian anymore, if she ever was."

Lady had complained about Pastor's insistence on nightly sex—until Melissa had joined Trinity House. *What he's doing isn't that different from me. The kind of affairs we're both involved in aren't about having a family. It isn't adultery.* Still stinging from Lady's harsh words, I don't defend her but keep my arm around Melissa's waist, pulling her against me.

"How do you know I'm not as spiritual as Pastor?"

She presses against me, arousing me to the point where I can't think. Knowing my state of mind, she says with her lips caressing my cheek, "You cut the grass, Mac. Pastor is fighting to keep Trinity House from splintering along the Fundamentalist-Evangelical fracture, which threatens to destroy everything he's worked so hard to accomplish. I'm part of his effort, defending God's people from the darkness, from ignorance, through music."

She knows I'm sexually aroused, so she gently presses her lips to my neck while her hands dance around my body. My groin is suddenly warm from the uncontrolled release of pent-up sexual desire I hadn't acknowledged even to myself.

She knows what happened. "Do you feel better now, Mac?"

I avert my eyes, ashamed to meet her gaze.

"You are such a child," she says and leaves me standing there, the warm sensation quickly turning cold.

UNEXPECTED NEWS

I stared at the digital display on the plastic dipstick, blinking several times, not believing my eyes.

"PREGNANT," was the extent of its vocabulary, although I was certain it could have said something else, like maybe, "NOT PREGNANT."

PREGNANT.

I did the math in my head, an easy math problem. I hadn't had sex with Pastor in three weeks whereas Mac and I had gotten together several times during the previous weeks. Pastor wore a condom but I didn't insist Mac did because it didn't feel natural. I looked at the word again and laughed. Well, this was pretty natural, the natural result of having unprotected sex when you're still menstruating. I must have lost count. Or my mind.

I had been pregnant before—twice in fact, once for each of our sons, Seth and Joseph. Pastor and I had taken no precautions when we'd first gotten married because he wanted to have children whereas I accepted pregnancy as part of being a woman. I'd enjoyed the experience both times, but I hadn't wanted to spend my life pregnant, so I'd insisted on birth control. I took the pill and he wore a condom until my fortieth birthday, without a single unexpected pregnancy. The experience of raising two boys had been more hands-on fun for me than for Pastor and, to be honest, I wouldn't have minded doing it again—with Mac this time. I'd met his daughter, Trinity, who was obviously his offspring in both appearance and behavior. I liked her because I could see how close they were, nothing like Pastor and his sons.

My initial elation was dampened when I gave it some thought. Keeping Mac's baby would inevitably lead to a divorce from Pastor because I wasn't ready for some kind of *modern family*. Either Mac would divorce Missy or I would become a single, unwed mother, an option threatening employment. I had to be prepared for any of these possibilities before I talked to Mac about my discovery because, despite how I felt about him, how I knew he felt about me, we'd never explicitly declared our mutual love and affection. The outcome was too close to call.

This was yet another example of my not wanting to make decisions. For example, if I'd been more involved with college life, I might have met someone to fall in love with, instead of marrying Pastor as the last man standing my senior year. More than one of my college friends had asked why I was marrying a devout Christian, much less a minister. I should be ashamed to admit, more than twenty years later, that I'd simply shrugged and said, "Why not?" I'd lived with the consequences of my ambivalence, which included two healthy and independent sons.

My personal opinion is that people get too excited about apparently important life decisions, which inevitably lead to unexpected and unwanted outcomes within a few years, no matter how carefully considered beforehand. Maybe that's why some people get married several times. My behavior wasn't a result of stupidity but only acceptance of the reality of who we are. I learned that from reading a lot in college.

COVER STORY

I'm sitting in church and thinking that Pastor is pretty much the same kind of man as me, no better no worse. He's standing up there behind the pulpit talking about the sanctity of the marriage vow, how God meant for a man and a woman to enter into such a sanctified contract. Sanctimonious is more like it if you ask me. He's talking about young people getting married without having premarital sex. I agree with all that, which doesn't make me a hypocrite, because I wasn't a Christian when I met Missy, after having plenty of premarital sex. You can be sure that she made sure our daughter understood that God frowned on carrying on like the girls on TV. Real women don't have sex with guys they aren't married to, she'd insisted. I agree with that sentiment.

I look at Lady, sitting at the organ all high and mighty, proud of herself, an adulteress looking down her nose at me because she thinks I'm one too—I mean an adulterer. Then I realize what's stuck in her craw, what makes her an adulterer but not me. She's in love with me. I sure don't feel the same about her. That's it. She got emotional and that's why she acts like we're married, but I'm smarter than that and I've never let emotions creep into our relationship. But that doesn't mean that I'm going to cut it off, why should I? Jesus will forgive me for being a sinner. We're all sinners. Knowing what I'm doing and admitting that I'm a sinner is what makes me not an adulterer, by not praying for Jesus's forgiveness, Lady has become an adulteress and that's her decision. She sure isn't a Christian.

Melissa is giving me the eye right there in church, in front of the whole congregation, sitting in the choir box, waiting for the Christian-rock group she formed to perform after Pastor finishes his sermon. What she really needs is for me to drag her off the podium and give her what she wants. After goading me into embarrassing myself, she thinks she's got me over a barrel, but I don't see it that way. If Pastor was satisfying her, she wouldn't be looking at me the way she is. She wants it, by god, she wants it bad, but it wasn't adultery because I didn't have any feelings for her other than wanting to get her into the guest room, better yet get an invitation to her apartment like Pastor.

His sermon is about adultery and premarital sex. I figure it doesn't apply to an adult woman like Melissa or he wouldn't be so set against it. Maybe what he means is that we should avoid it if we can, but it's not a sin, and besides she was asking Jesus for forgiveness every day, just like me.

Missy is watching Pastor as he talks about the plight of unwed mothers, nodding as if she had personally experienced it with our daughter. As far as I know, Meredith never had a boyfriend in high school. She was in the choir and taught Sunday school. I figure Missy is sympathetic towards unfortunate mothers whose daughters had been tricked by Satan, so I throw some "Amens" in there along with her, to show my support for Pastor's message. I'm glad it doesn't apply to me.

I can see the smug look on Lady's face because I'm sitting next to Missy—my lawfully wedded wife, not like that tramp Lady who is nothing more than my mistress, whether she wants to admit it or not, satisfying my sexual needs, talking to me about things I can't talk to Missy about, like Missy's lack of sexual desire and her fundamentalist beliefs, not to mention whatever it is that had kept Lady and me together for ten years, no, we're not together, we are not a couple because that would be adultery. Everything changed when Melissa showed up and gave me a glimpse of the pleasure her youthful body could deliver. Sitting there in church, I can't get the image of her full, firm breasts out of my mind, her body writhing in ecstasy as I ravaged her, moaning with pain and pleasure. It had only been afterwards that she'd told me about her sensitive vagina, but now I doubted the truth of her excuse. She had been focused on Pastor and I had been nothing more than a distraction, a one-night stand.

Pastor finishes the sermon and Melissa's band begins performing their cover of *The Hope Inside*, by Colony House, which gets Missy and the other fundamentalists on their feet, expressing their joy at being one with the Lord. It's a good song and the band, led by Melissa, is doing a great job, so I stand up to join the worship. The band is drowned out by people singing along, shouts of spiritual ecstasy, some folks speaking in tongues, others translating. I get it, why Dim Light wants the sound system upgraded as soon as possible. The cost had been approved by the Board and it would improve the spiritual experience for everyone.

I can't fully enjoy the Lord's presence because Lady, sitting at the organ with a hypocritical smile on her face, is watching me, judging me, challenging me to share the joy of being one with our Savior, but I can't take part in the experience being shared by Missy and the other congregants because Lady is watching me, sequestered behind the organ on the dais. I know what she's thinking because she isn't a fundamentalist, an evangelical, not even a Christian, people she thinks of as superstitious fools.

The band plays another hit song. The congregation shares the spiritual experience, feeling the Lord's presence, except for me. I am being watched by an unbeliever who thinks she has a hold over me because of the years we've shared, making love— no, not making love—having great sexual experiences, but she's wrong. I got her flowers and firewood and trimmed the shrubs around the rectory because it was my job, not because I wanted to be with her. And even though I like the way she makes coffee, and how she always comes outside to talk to me about important stuff as much as the weather, it's not because I have any feelings for her. Lady is an arrogant fool if she thinks I love her.

I am not an adulterer.

OUTPATIENT

Listening to Pastor talk about premarital sex and the tragedy of unwanted pregnancy convinced me to talk to Mac about my situation, although I hoped he would see it as our problem. I wanted to make up with him after our argument, so I interrupted his examination of the electrical box. He was deep in thought when I entered the utility closet, looked up and smiled briefly, then frowned and turned back to his work.

"What's wrong, Mac? Are you still angry because I said we were both adulterers? I think you're just confused about our relationship because, believe me, I sure am, but we can't ignore each other. We've been together…" His face hardened and I left my sentence unfinished.

"That's the difference between us," he began, pointing his screwdriver at me.

"What are you talking about?"

His head was nodding proudly as he continued, "You think we have a relationship, but I don't."

"Don't what?" I asked, unsure what he was referring to.

"We are not in a relationship, never were, never will be, just a sexual affair without even romance, pure sex, that's all it ever was. So, I'm not an adulterer because I don't have any kind of relationship with you, Lady. Sorry to disappoint you."

I didn't know whether to laugh or cry at his foolish manifesto. He wouldn't respond well to either reaction, so I tried to clear up his muddled thinking.

"Did you come up with that all on your own?"

"I have a wife and she's not you, so we don't have any kind

of relationship. Is that clear enough for you?"

I took the screwdriver from his extended hand and responded as calmly as I could. "Everyone has a relationship Mac, even people who only see each other at the grocery store. I think what you mean is that we aren't in a romantic relationship. Is that what you meant to say?"

A pregnant pause.

"Well, are you saying that you and I don't have any feelings for each other?"

He nodded.

"I don't know where you came up with that idea because I can give you plenty of examples of our feelings for each other. Do I have to—"

"No you can't," he interjected. "You've been fooling yourself for ten years, about our...our relationship, thinking it was romantic when all it ever was, could ever be, was sexual because we're both married."

"Then why was I the only one to discover that you were an alcoholic and help you quit drinking? There's nothing sexual about that. Missy hadn't even figured it out and she was living with you."

"Well—"

I cut him off. "Why have you been bringing me flowers on my birthday for eight years, in the middle of winter? The fact is that we are very fond of each other, which is why you do such a good job cleaning up around the rectory, bringing firewood, doing odd jobs. That's why I make your favorite coffee whenever you come around, and go outside to talk with you no matter the weather, why I want to spend an entire night with you so bad it hurts, why I don't want to—"

I didn't finish the sentence because I was afraid of his reaction to what I wanted to share with him. I threw the screwdriver to the floor, turned, and with tears flowing down my cheeks, fled from the only man I'd ever loved.

The next day I drove to Oklahoma City to get a medical abortion. It was Tuesday. I told Pastor I wanted to go shopping, which I did occasionally so he wasn't suspicious. I spent the two-hour drive asking myself questions that I should have posed years before.

Why had I remained married to Pastor, after realizing that I didn't love him and was fundamentally opposed to his core beliefs? I am mentally lazy, both intellectually and emotionally. I had plenty to eat and a safe place to live, nothing to worry about. I was young when we met and impressed by his age and charisma. I must have thought I would adopt his ideology since I had none of my own; and become what he wanted, a young minister's wife. I had fulfilled my obligations but without much relish. There was nothing wrong with Modoc, which I found to be a pleasant community with mostly agreeable neighbors, nor was I repulsed by my duties as Pastor's wife. It came down to something as simple as my not being superstitious. I hadn't thought about that when Pastor and I got married, assuming that our minds would meld into one, an idea I had expressed to him. But it turned out that we were fire and ice, with respect to belief in the Christian deity, which I just couldn't wrap my head around.

Why had I fallen in love with Mac? That was the real question, the reason I was driving to Oklahoma City to have a medical abortion. I suppose upon reflection that my relationship with Mac was the only real thing I'd done in my life. It had been instigated by hormones and so was at least partly done on autopilot. It was an emotional experience, an adventure undertaken for no purpose other than it felt good. Mac was right that we had no *official* romantic relationship but dead wrong about our not being so fond of each other as to constitute a strong emotional bond. The excitement I'd felt when we first met had only increased over the years and our silly fights had no effect on my feelings for him. Mac was my emotional companion, and I wasn't going to let him go just because he was as conflicted as me about our relationship. We would work out the details and live the rest of our lives together, even if we had to create a scandal to escape our unhappy marriages.

Why had I let myself become pregnant? Oh my, that was the most difficult question of them all. Pastor used a condom because his belief in the sanctity of life wasn't as all-encompassing as the Pope's. An unconceived child didn't need to be protected. I had been having sex with Mac for almost ten years with no protection at all. I had always been aware of my ovulation cycle and avoided getting together with him when necessary, but I had become complacent. I loved him so much that I never insisted he wear a condom, didn't want him to because I wanted our flesh to press together, the sensation worth the risk, but I had been playing with fire. It's also possible that I subconsciously wanted to get pregnant from Mac, to carry his child in my womb, proving how much I loved him, and then raise it with him, watching the fruit of our love grow into someone like him. But I was older now. Had I become pregnant when I was in my thirties, I would have carried it full term and proudly announced that it was Mac's child. That would have been a scandal. Having a baby at forty-five wasn't safe. I may have conceived a child with Down's syndrome, which is why I'd wanted to talk to Mac, but we'd both acted like fools and the subject hadn't come up.

Patches of snow, denuded trees, frozen ponds, partly obscured by the fogged car windows, reminded me of the meaningless cruelty, machinations, and miserable life of Richard III from Shakespeare's play. This was indeed the winter of my discontent and, for some reason, I knew it was going to be a very unhappy season for everyone at Trinity House. When summer eventually came, I would be content with Mac at my side. Don't ask me why I felt so confident about my future, especially with a man who didn't think we had a romantic relationship.

The women at the clinic were very supportive, explaining in detail what a late-term abortion was like, even though I was in the first trimester. It was the law. After this horror show, I signed the papers to express my informed consent, and was led into an examination room, where a woman doctor verified that I was pregnant and talked some more about the important decision I was making. I restricted my responses to head movements, with monosyllabic answers when required. After several hours I was given a pill, a cup of water, and another warning about possible side effects that could impact operation of a motor vehicle. I said I had taken the bus. We all knew it was a lie, but our conversation met the statutory requirements of the Oklahoma legislature.

I had cramps, like from indigestion, while shopping for spring clothes that would get Mac's attention, so I didn't eat anything. I found just the right combination to show him that I wasn't a fat old woman, but just as exciting as Melissa Tight, the music director—I didn't like the way Mac looked at her during church. She was young and very attractive. I had a lot of work ahead of me to compete with someone like her. Knowing Mac, I was certain he'd already gotten in her pants.

The return to Modoc was as disturbing as the drive to Oklahoma City. I cried most of the way, thinking about what I'd done, killing a baby, nullifying a life I could have shared with Mac, without giving him the chance to have an opinion. By the time I pulled into the driveway, I hated myself for not being what Pastor had expected of me because, lacking personal goals or desires, I should have been strong enough to pursue his. I had failed him. That was strike one. After falling in love with Mac, I should have made my feelings clear to everyone and straightened out this mess, but I hadn't. Strike two. I should not have gotten the abortion. That was the perfect opportunity to prove that Mac and I were in love and belonged together. Even with a fifty-fifty chance of having a handicapped child, it would have been worth it because it would have been our child. Mac's and mine. That was strike three.

My mind was made up by the time Pastor greeted me at the front door of his house, a residence in which I no longer felt welcome. I wasn't going to compromise anymore. I was not a Christian and never would be. I loved Macbeth Lunatic and always would.

The cramps were pretty bad, so I excused myself and went to the bathroom. I made sure to clean up the blood stains after my long shower in hot water, trying to wash away my guilt. At least I didn't get dizzy or feel sick.

GUILTY CONSCIENCE

I needed something to distract me from thinking about what I'd done, what I had become, but mostly to make up with Mac. My relationship with Pastor had changed after the abortion and during the drive home. I no longer thought of myself as his wife but only his housekeeper and prostitute; either position would have paid better if I'd done it professionally. At least the bedroom duties seemed to have lessened lately, with all of Pastor's trips to Oklahoma City to consult with other church leaders. I briefly wondered if he had a girlfriend, maybe a prostitute, whom he visited on his trips, a wonderful idea but one unlikely to come to fruition, not with Pastor's religiosity. He must have noticed the change in my demeanor because he suggested a solution one day over dinner, baked salmon with rice and broccoli.

He thanked me for preparing such a tasteful and healthy meal as he piled tartar sauce on the thick filet, obliterating the seasoning. Pastor liked strong flavors, but he appreciated the healthy meals I put together, which had kept him almost as slim as when we'd married. The niceties out of the way, he helped me find a solution to what he thought to be my biggest problem.

"You know, Lady, you have so many talents that are going to waste, like your organizational skill and the way you talk to people so easily. I wish I could get members of Trinity House to open up to me the way they do with you."

I appreciated his recognition. "Thank you, Pastor. I'm only doing my part in keeping the church running efficiently. But what are you referring to? Do you have something to say?" I had started speaking to him impatiently after my abortion.

He winced at my harsh tone, probably attributing it to whatever he was about to address, had some rice, and continued, "You should get involved with a project, something within Trinity House or possibly Modoc at large; you must feel alone, now that Seth and Joseph have moved out, leaving you with nothing constructive to do all day, and I don't like the idea of you spending all your time sitting around the house, planning meals and cleaning."

I refrained from responding to his chauvinistic analysis of how I spent my days and focused on his main point, which reminded me of something Vanity Blunt had suggested.

"You know, Pastor," I began, emulating his condescending tone, "Vanity and I were talking the other day about planting a vegetable garden, the products to be distributed to a food bank, with excess sold at the farmer's market to earn a little money for the church. I think it would be challenging and fun to take responsibility for something like that. Vanity expressed no interest in doing it, you know how she is."

I'd called his bluff. He wouldn't go for it because he didn't like the idea of investing the church's resources in activities not directly related to saving souls.

"I don't know if that's a good idea," he responded.

I shrugged, knowing how to placate him and achieve my own objective. I would use my honed prostitution skills to cajole Pastor into agreeing to the plan, with the bulk of the labor being supplied free-of-charge by Mac, who would succumb to my sexual prowess and acquiesce. It would be presented at the next Church Board meeting and passed unanimously. Pastor was right about my organizational skills.

There was something else on Pastor's mind, something that didn't involve me directly. He hemmed and hawed, talking about how Melissa Tight and he had been working on the church's musical outreach program and their plan for upgrading the sound system. I read between the lines: Pastor was carrying on with Melissa Tight, distracting her from collecting Mac as a trophy.

GLASS CEILING

I can't stay mad at Lady, even though she's wrong about us having an emotional relationship. We're just friends. Anyway, she has a project she wants to talk to me about, so I meet her behind the church. It turns out she wants me to volunteer my time and my tractor to plant a vegetable garden, all for a good purpose, encouraging my agreement with a fresh pot of coffee. I love her coffee. It was going to be an acre, a reasonable size for a church garden, planted with seasonal and perennial vegetables to supply our unfortunate neighbors with more than basic nutrition. She's worked it all out. We discuss it and reach a compromise. We're enjoying being together so much that we slip into the guest room to make love—I mean, have sex—afterward.

We're laying in the bed, her arm draped across my chest as if it had been there forever, when I think of something. "Do you know anything about my becoming an elder? Maybe I shouldn't ask, there's probably an oath of confidentiality or something."

She shakes her head distractedly, pulls herself onto my chest, sighs, and says, "Not when it comes to you, Mac. I became the Church Board's permanent secretary after several years of Pastor trying to decipher the notes written by members of the congregation. The subject of your promotion came up and was discussed for about fifteen minutes. You have supporters and detractors. The Board is split, so the decision not to make you an elder was based on the ambiguity of your commitment to the tenets on which Trinity House is based."

She shushes my unspoken complaint with a finger on my lips and continues, "The fundamentalists support you whereas the evangelicals are skeptical of your qualifications because they are elitists. I don't know if you're aware of the socioeconomic foundation of Trinity House..." Her words trail off and she kisses my chin, then my lips, waiting for a response.

I clear my throat, which is a little dry after making love—having sex—and do my best to finish her thought. "I get it. The college educated folk are evangelicals while the working people are fundamentalists."

"Why do you think that's the case?" she asks, kissing my nipples, caressing my cheeks with her fingertips, so that I'm having a hard time thinking.

She doesn't fool me, not for a minute, wanting to somehow show that my beliefs aren't based on the Word of God. "You have to stop baiting me, Lady, at least with dry breadcrumbs like that. You know I don't bite."

She kisses me hard, her firm breasts pressing against me, arousing me the way Melissa does, but it's real with Lady—who I am not in love with. She finally comes up for air and says, "Their college educations let them build a more complicated story Mac, but it's just as full of holes as the Fundamentalists'. At any rate, you aren't a Fundamentalist like Missy because you have an open mind, which is why we're lying in this bed, about to make love again."

I let her inaccurate statement go because I'm thinking about something more important. "So, I guess it's my fault. I didn't ask about becoming an elder and I sure as hell didn't do whatever was required, the way Dim Light and others did."

She's rubbing against me now, knowing how to get my attention after so many years together—that's not what I mean—as she says, "I checked the records and Dim didn't do anything to become an elder, other than attend college for a couple of years. You will never be an elder, even though you are already responsible for landscaping and building maintenance. They like to have a college man in charge, even though Dim Light is incompetent. I'm sorry..."

It isn't supposed to work that way in Trinity House, where Jesus is the master, not Dim Light, Mike Blunt, or even Pastor Church, all of them college educated. Apparently, the board is an elitist college-boys club to which I haven't earned entry. I find my tongue and, empowered by Lady's gentle rubbing against me, express my displeasure. "Maybe I should stop being their lawn boy. That would get their attention—what do you think, Lady?" I'm thinking that maybe I don't want to help with the church garden, even if it means disappointing her. I'm about to share the bad news when she starts getting aggressive.

She's panting as if we're already making love as she answers my question. "I just want to be with you, Mac. I don't know what I would do if you weren't here, cutting the grass, cleaning up, bringing me firewood and flowers. I can't give you advice because I am hopelessly in love with you."

No one had ever said that to me, especially not a beautiful, college educated woman like Lady. My resolve is weakening and I stammer, "I may go along with the Board for now, so that we can work together on the garden project. We'll figure it out after that." I should straighten her out, about being in love with me, because she's the only one of us who loves the other. I let it go.

Lady nods as she finally accomplishes her immediate goal and sits upright. She's rocking back and forth as she says, "The only thing that matters is that we're together, Mac. Everything else is inconsequential."

Making love—I mean, having sex—with Lady is probably a lot like speaking in tongues, at least for me. I begin to babble meaningless phrases about loving her and never letting her go when she does something that's never happened to me before. I have an orgasm first but I can't get away because she's at the wheel. Unable to tell pain from pleasure, I'm frantically rubbing her breasts, begging her to stop before she kills me. It seems like an hour before she shivers, goosebumps covering her breasts, and falls forward. After several minutes, she lifts her head and gazes into my eyes.

"I love you Macbeth Lunatic and I will have you to myself, as my husband, no matter what it takes."

Still not recovered from her sensual assault, my brain fuzzy, thoughts blurry, I mumble, "No one has ever loved me like that, Lady, but do you know what you're saying?"

She suddenly sits up, a self-satisfied smile brightening her unwrinkled features. "Until death us do part."

Maybe we are more than friends.

MEDICAL EMERGENCY

I hadn't meant to get carried away with Mac, declaring my love so forcefully, but I'd felt so empowered when he had an orgasm before me, even if only by a few seconds. Mac had always lasted longer than me, leaving me panting in pleasure until he finished. He'd probably thought he was a stud and thus not in a serious relationship with me. By outlasting him and not stopping when he climaxed, I'd unintentionally reversed our dominance roles; in his mind, he was now in the subservient position. I had broken Mac like a young stallion. He didn't argue with me any more about our relationship, especially when I brought him to his knees several more times. Yep, Mac was all mine now, so I assured him that I'd find a way for us to be together, one that wouldn't leave him feeling guilty, ruining the future we were going to share.

I noticed the change during Sunday evening service. Mac wasn't looking at Melissa like a lovesick puppy, instead focusing his attention on me, which I rather enjoyed. It wasn't just that she was so much younger than him, they had completely different interests.

Mac was not musically inclined; in fact, he remembered the words to very few of the hymns we sang in church. And he didn't clap his hands much, being out of time with the rest of the congregation when he did. And Mac absolutely, positively, beyond a shadow of a doubt, with god as my witness, did not have emotional experiences in church and under no circumstances would he be overcome by the Holy Spirit and speak in tongues. Fainting from such an encounter would be like his winning a Nobel Prize.

Therefore, I was shocked when he started flailing his arms wildly and fell in the aisle, hitting his head on the pew. I was certain he needed medical attention, but no one appeared to share my concern. Missy ignored his body blocking the aisle, her chanting increasing in tempo. Pastor seemed unaware that Mac had just suffered either a stroke or heart attack. Melissa never missed a beat, leading the choir in an effort to be heard over the tumult emanating from the pews. Mike Blunt glanced at Mac lying on the floor and shook his head slightly, disgusted by such a callous display of illness during the service, no doubt feeling that the decision to not make Mac an elder was justified. Dim Light looked confused, but his wife, Melina, danced her way to the center aisle before collapsing in a heap of flesh, apparently overcome by the same spiritual force that had struck Mac down.

My heart turned cold when I studied the faces filling the pews. The evangelicals—I knew all of them personally—were unhappy with the situation but they didn't care about Mac, only the display of raw emotions by the fundamentalists, who were having a wonderful time. After all, two people were lying on the floor, possibly dead, and there was more babbling and shouting than I'd ever heard in Trinity House. I was not going to sit there behind the organ and watch Mac die while these fools danced around his body in a pagan frenzy. I had my cellphone in my hand, ready to call for an ambulance, when Mac stumbled to his feet, assisted by Ben Franken, an older man who'd been sitting next to him.

Vanity Blunt looked as shocked as me, her phone in her hand. Our eyes met and our gazes turned to Mac, who was smiling and trying to sing, Missy not expressing the slightest concern.

Vanity's face was contorted in uncertainty as she reluctantly returned the cellphone to her bag.

It was too late to call 911.

MESSIAH

I don't know what happened when Lady and I made up and cleared the air and I don't care because no one has ever expressed such strong feelings for me. She really loves me. I mean, she really loves me. And I love her the same way now. Never mind what I said before, about not having an emotional relationship with her. I definitely do and I make sure she knows it. I mean, she was committed to becoming my wife, free and clear, with Jesus' blessing. I'm on cloud nine, what with our making love every day because we're working together on the garden. And she's telling me about how divorce isn't a mortal sin; there are no mortal sins for Protestants, only for the Catholics, who we all know are pagans. The only thing that matters is that we believe in Christ and his message of love— in our situation, I'm the only one who has to believe because she now openly admits being an agnostic. I don't care because she isn't badmouthing Evangelical Christianity anymore. I guess she listened to my opinion about our beliefs being closer than she thought.

Of course, we'll have to think about our feelings, talk every day, make love to be sure we aren't getting carried away with the passion, and wait a few months, seeking God's guidance before announcing our plan to become man and wife to Trinity House. I'm letting her take the lead because she's a really good planner. But I'm not worried because I love Lady, more than I could have imagined.

We get a lot done while planning the garden and making love in the guest room. By the time I go to Sunday service with

Missy, all I can think about is seeing Lady sitting so proudly behind the organ. I've forgotten about Melissa's youthful body and exuberance because, to be honest, Lady is just as sexy, has more stamina, and her enthusiasm is tempered by experience. She's better in bed.

Pastor delivers a thought-provoking sermon on staying tuned in so that we don't miss God's call when he reaches out to us. I agree with that and bring my hands together in rousing approval, throwing in several Amens to boot, because God has spoken to me through Lady's voice. You've got to be listening because Jesus doesn't shout, not like Missy and the other Fundamentalists, who apparently think He's deaf. Melissa has done a great job with the choir, just like she did with the band. They're playing one of my favorite hymns when I see a flash of light behind Pastor. I can't see the choir. Lady is engulfed in the effulgence. Then Pastor is gone, so I turn to Missy next to me but I can't see or hear her. I turn around and all I see is brilliant, white light everywhere, as if I'm in God's presence.

I turn back to Pastor, blinded by the radiance. I hold my hand up to cover my eyes. Then I hear a voice as gentle as a dove piercing the din.

Macbeth Lunatic.

I feel a joy greater than I've never known, even stronger than when I admitted that I was in love with Lady.

"Yes Lord," I say, gazing into the light, no longer afraid.

A figure appears where Pastor had been standing. It can only be Jesus because the young man is wearing the same robe as in the painting Missy had hung over the sofa in our living room. I wonder how the artist knew red was Jesus' favorite color. I guess that shoulder-length hair was popular back then, just like in the painting. The serenity of his expression is shattered when Jesus shakes his head.

I am disappointed in you, Macbeth. You have been seduced by the great harlot, who John spoke of in Revelations. If you are to redeem yourself and secure a place in my presence, you must disavow the whore and share my prophecy with your brothers and sisters of Trinity House.

I raise my hands in supplication. "Whatever you ask, Lord."

INQUIRY

Mac had collapsed in church and I had done nothing about it, even though he is the center of my life. I had failed again. That would be four strikes; it's possible that some of the earlier strikes were only foul balls, but this was definitely a strike out. I had failed Mac in his hour of need. It didn't matter that Vanity Blunt hadn't called an ambulance either. She had only had an affair with Mac whereas I was in love with him. Apparently, I had no more concern for the man I loved than a stray dog lying in the gutter. No wonder I had married Pastor.

I mentioned my concern to Pastor after the service. He dismissed Mac's unprecedented collapse as nothing; not yet ready to publicly proclaim my love for Mac, I turned to Missy for help. That was a waste of time.

Mac had become a Fundamentalist and she was ecstatic to have him join the fold of superstitious cretins. Apparently, he had been addressed by an angel during the church service and was to wait, praying constantly and listening for another message, one that would impact everyone at Trinity House. I can't remember how many times Missy said "Praise the Lord" during our conversation but it exceeded the number of digits on my hands and feet.

I expressed my concern to Vanity Blunt. Her response was noncommittal. "I told you about my past with Mac in private—"

"Don't give that a second thought," I interjected.

She sighed, smiled at me, and continued, "The short time I was with Mac, he showed no sign of the kind of emotional reaction we saw in church last Sunday. In my opinion, it must have been a medical issue, which is now undiagnosed because of Missy's controlling position. Those Fundamentalists are more of a threat to themselves than they are to the rest of us."

"Thanks for being honest, Vanity."

She looked at me closely and said, "Why are you so interested in the spiritual development of the church's landscaper, experiencing what was certainly interpreted as a typical charismatic episode by those people?"

I smiled condescendingly and replied, "As Pastor's wife, it's my job to keep tabs on the congregation, in this case so that he can do his job." I'm not an actor like Vanity, but I tried to convey the message that her past improprieties would never be part of my reports to Pastor. Apparently, she received my message.

"I appreciate your discretion."

The next day, having completed my investigation, I spoke to Mac about what had happened. His response was disheartening, to say the least.

PROPHET

I'm a new man after my spiritual awakening in church, a servant of the Lord who will not be distracted from His work. Jesus had warned me about that harlot—I assume he was referring to Lady because I was in love with her—who had been sent by Satan to seduce me, to distract me, an obstruction to completing the Lord's work. God only speaks to men when it is really important, so for Jesus to come to me now could only mean that something really important was about to happen. I'm no fool, so I ask Jesus, "What am I supposed to do. I don't want to break any laws, like shooting people or blowing things up—I'm not the Unabomber."

You must prove yourself worthy of being my prophet before you can learn what is to come.

"Isn't there something I can do in the meantime? Shouldn't I prepare the way?"

Jesus extends his index finger and touches my forehead. I wake up, but I'm no longer confined to my physical body. He has given me the power to see the world from His perspective, to soar, free of physical restraints, unhindered by limited, familiar perceptions. Only God could make that possible, so I take it as a sign that I have been chosen. He has also given me information only He could know, further proof of his identity, not that He needs to prove himself.

It is in such a divine state that I am approached by the harlot who had seduced me, to make me a tool of Satan.

"How are you feeling, Mac?"

I want to wrap my hands around her throat and choke the

evil that had consumed her, ridding the world of such an unspeakable abomination. Jesus saves her life, taking my spirit to a safe distance, several feet over my left shoulder. From my vantage point I'm able to control my desire to take the life of the evil woman confronting me.

"Why do you ask?" My voice is trembling with anger, and fear that she may use clever words to confuse me.

"You collapsed in church. Vanity and I were both about to call for an ambulance when you got to your feet. We're worried about you. We…I don't think it was a spiritual experience like Missy often experiences, it was unexpected, and we thought that…well, we—Vanity and me—you might have suffered from a stroke or something like that, from the way you suddenly collapsed…"

I'm not sure if I'm Macbeth Lunatic or a ghost because I'm looking at myself and Lady, and I can't tell what's real. Can I speak through the body I'm looking at, the Mac who Lady thinks she's talking to, never realizing that I'm watching from above?

"Jesus—" I begin.

Lady Church is a harlot and cannot be trusted. Do not even speak to her because she will deceive you, as she has done for ten years. You are facing an agent of Satan, so it is important that you do not mention me. It is not yet time for the battle of Armageddon. Do you understand?

"Yes," my avatar says.

"What the hell does that mean?" Lady asks.

"I will not speak to you again, Jezebel. You are the great harlot, the source of iniquity, the prostitute who brought me to the brink of destruction."

She understands my words, her eyes conveying surprise at having been outwitted. Instead of retreating, the harlot looks into the eyes of my avatar and says, "I did some reading about what might have happened to you and I'm scared to death, Mac. You probably had a stroke, a blood clot in your brain. The effects are unpredictable and possibly devastating. You need to go to the doctor for a thorough examination because it could kill you."

My avatar nods. She doesn't know I am watching her from a safe distance, trying to ignore her words, knowing she is deceitful and wants only to destroy me and prevent the completion of my duty. But I see the concern disfiguring her face, the wrinkled forehead, eyes open wide, lips downturned.

The harlot waves her arms and says, "Do you even know where you are?"

My avatar nods and shares my thoughts. "I'm going to move something…that fertilizer into a pile someplace…of course, next to the church."

The harlot's face breaks into sobs, tears running down her cheeks, but I am immune to her pretense. Blind to my resolve, she says, "I don't know who I'm talking to—it doesn't matter—I would like to talk to Macbeth Lunatic about our relationship. Can you at least do that, Mac?"

Jesus sends me back into my avatar because I have calmed down enough not to wrap my hands around the harlot's throat. Her name is Lady Church, and she thinks she's my wife because of our long, personal relationship. I like looking at her, a lot more than my real wife, who isn't as good-looking or as concerned about my health.

"It's okay, Lady. Don't worry about me. I know you don't believe in God or the Holy Spirit, and I'm not about to get in an argument with you about what happened to me. This is something outside your area of interest and thus none of your business."

Her hands are on her hips. "You are my only interest, Mac. I'll put my personal beliefs aside in order to get you to talk to me. I won't sit idly by knowing that you may have a medical problem that hasn't been diagnosed."

I forget Jesus' warning and smile at her. "Why don't you make some coffee while I get started unloading this fertilizer, and then we can talk, but only as long as you don't get judgmental."

She goes inside to do as I ask and, after a few minutes, returns to watch me, even helping a little, since she's wearing loose-fitting work clothes. I kid her about her new wardrobe and she says she got them just for me. Jesus isn't expressing an opinion, so I figure it's okay talking to Lady for now. I guess he's given me the strength to resist her clever and deceitful words. Of course, she doesn't seem insincere at the moment, pretending to be worried about me. She doesn't argue when I tell her about my vision, that I only received the first part of the message from God, to test my resolve. I can see from her twitching mouth that she wants to argue. When I finish, Lady reminds me of my words, that our viewpoints aren't that different after all, and that I can trust her. She's only thinking of me because she loves me as much as Jesus does, even if she isn't a deity. That's a pretty serious commitment and I'm not arguing because I feel safe with her. By the time I remove the last bag of 10-20-10 NPK fertilizer from the trailer and stack it on the pile, I'm comfortable being with Lady, almost as if she were my real wife.

"I hate to put you on the spot, Lady, but—"

Before I can finish my sentence, she says, "Don't you ever say that again, Mac. You cannot put me in an uncomfortable position because you are my only concern, and us being together eventually."

I nod and blurt, "Has Pastor said anything about the storage shed to you? We need a place to store all this, someplace out of the weather."

"Pastor told me that he didn't think it was a good idea for him to intervene between the elders and the…the hired help. He actually referred to you as if you were a contractor. I wanted to call him a hypocrite or worse, but I was afraid… I'm ready to declare my feelings for you openly and end this charade, but I know it's more difficult for you, what with Missy and her dependence…"

Lady has a habit of giving expansive responses to simple questions. Instead of getting a simple answer, I'm confronted with two very troublesome problems, neither of which I'm ready to deal with. Jesus is silent. "Well…" I begin, hoping she'll interrupt and propose a solution.

She's looking at me inquisitively, not as if she's expecting me to say something specific, but more like she doesn't know what words are going to come out of my mouth. I finally continue, "I don't like talking to Dim Light because he doesn't listen well and puts off any decision he has to make. He isn't going to want to spend the money to build a shed for what is going to be a substantial agricultural program—"

"Then just leave those bags of fertilizer piled up out here for everyone to see and smell. It won't be long before someone complains, especially with my gentle reminders, and then you'll get your shed." She's smiling proudly and I forget that we're standing outside where everyone can see us. I put my arms around her narrow waist and kiss her, as if we're in the guest room in the church. She doesn't resist. Struggling for air, I bury my head ever deeper into her, my lips touching her neck, eyes, ears, dipping into her shirt, until I catch myself.

I jump back, shocked at my forwardness. "I'm sorry. I don't know what came over me, I can't imagine—"

She's smiling as she interjects, "I guess you want to get on with our lives as much as I do. Let's not make our announcement through the rumor mill, however. We'll figure out a way to straighten everything out. There's no rush, not after ten years together."

I nod obediently.

"By the way, would you like to go inside and let me ravage you?" Her eyes are mocking me, reminding me of our last sexual encounter. I nod, certain that her confidence is based on a fluke, an anomaly.

I understand why she got loose-fitting jeans when she slips out of them as fast as greased lightning. But she isn't sexually satisfied as quickly as she removed her pants, and I am beaten again. I'm gasping for breath, Lady's torso draped across mine, her supple fingers caressing my face, when Jesus warns me that she is Pastor's wife and that he is an unwitting tool of Satan, along with the harlot, Melissa Tight.

Jesus has changed his mind about Lady, no longer calling her a harlot. That can only mean that he approves of our relationship.

PROSELYTE

After getting back together with Lady—with Jesus' approval—
I attended Tuesday evening Bible study with Missy. Jesus had
suggested that I had to discover the prophecy on my own, to
prove my worthiness. The speaker is Melina Light. She's
talking about Revelations, but I can't take my eyes off her
breasts, which I've admired for years, but now they were close
enough to almost grab. Jesus empowers me to leave my body,
so that I can prove that I'm worthy of receiving his message. I
watch as my avatar asks questions and gets Melina's attention.
Soon, she is speaking only to me, through my avatar, and I
understand her message.

QAnon is the key to understanding Revelations and the end
time, which is occurring before our eyes. The Rapture is only
a few years away, maybe months. Jesus joins me, sitting in a
chair in the row ahead of me and Missy. He turns around to
explain why I'm in attendance.

*Melina Light will be your first disciple. She will make you strong
because she is close to my heart.* He thumps his fist against his chest
for emphasis.

"How—"

*You do not have to speak with your voice to talk to me. I am Jesus.
You need only wish to converse, and I will be here.*

I nod and try to do as I'm told, *Should I speak openly of you to
her?*

Jesus shakes his head and says, "I have prepared her mind
and she will receive you with open arms but she is not ready
for the whole truth. She has been waiting for you. But do not

waste time. She is ready now but not in a week." Jesus turns around as Melina is explaining the relationship between the Catholic church and the Jewish conspiracy to rule the world. I want nothing more than to wrap my hands around her very large breasts, bursting from the low neckline of the tight dress she's wearing.

There are a few questions after she finishes speaking. I keep mine to myself, convinced she'll answer them in private. Her eyes are locked on mine as the small group leaves the room. Missy expresses her support for the QAnon theory, but she's cut off by Melina.

"Do you mind if I speak to Mac alone for a few minutes? The Lord has made me aware of the reason he was touched during the Sunday service."

Missy nods quickly and leaves us alone. Before I can respond or Jesus can express His opinion, her hand is rubbing me through my pants. "Go ahead Mac, take what you need, what will give you the strength, the power to keep your resolve in the difficult days ahead. I am here for you. All of me. Take me."

I take her large, firm breasts in my hands as she unbuckles my belt and gets my pants down, before turning away and lifting her short dress, presenting herself to me. She isn't wearing any underwear.

"The Lord told me that you would need support today, Brother Macbeth, so take what I have to offer, what He told me to give you."

She has a large, tight ass, so I give it to her, my hands massaging her breasts, which she's managed to expose, her waist encircled by her dress. I'm convinced they've been supplemented with silicon. I don't mind because I'd been wanting to get my hands on them for a while. She leans against the lectern and within a minute, she's moaning, her breath coming in gasps. There is no better proof of divine inspiration and encouragement for our act of obedience than that Jesus spoke to Melina and me independently and brought us together for the Bible study. Jesus appears to one side, nodding approvingly, waiting until I've consummated my contract with Melina, before expressing his satisfaction.

You have done well, Mac. Unlike Lady, Melina can be trusted. She will serve both of us well during the difficult times ahead, and you should turn to her as often as you need. Lady Church, on the other hand, will need to be tested before she earns your trust.

I'm breathing heavily when Melina stands up and verifies what Jesus told me. Wiping her thigh with a tissue, she says, "Oh my Lord, Mac, you are very close to God. We'll have to keep in close touch so that you don't get distracted and miss the next message. This is a critical period." She tosses the tissue in the trash, zips up her dress, straightens her hair, and leaves me standing there, tucking in my shirt, watching her go. I can't wait for more inspiration.

CONSPIRACY THEORY

Melina's Bible lesson on the end times had made an impression on me and Missy, so the next day we begin learning about the heroic efforts of President Trump to fight the unnamed cabal committed to the work of Satan. Armageddon is imminent and everyone has to get involved if Satan's army is to be stopped. We are horrified at the proven acts by politicians and celebrities, who should have already been thrown in jail. The president is trying to expose the conspiracy but his efforts have been thwarted by the Deep State. I have to learn about the Dark Web to learn the truth, yet another secret world I'd never known existed. Jesus shows me how to do it and leaves me to contemplate the truth without his intervention. He will speak to me when the end time approaches. I go on the Dark Web every day and learn the truth. Missy joins me in my home office and one day, aroused by the daunting task facing us, we share a sexual experience. It is unsatisfying and we are self-conscious afterward, but it doesn't change our common fear of what is coming.

Melina is my real inspiration during these difficult days, meeting me anytime, anywhere, every spiritual encounter different, doing whatever it takes to keep me focused on God's mission. One day, we're in a motel room on the highway and she ties everything together: QAnon, the Deep State, President Trump, the Cabal, are all predicted by the stars. Astrologists had predicted events thousands of years ago, even longer but no one had understood the message. Then she drops the bombshell.

"Pastor Church is an unwitting tool of Satan."

On this particular day, she's like the new Lady Church, making me beg for mercy before she climaxes, so I'm a little confused.

"How is that?"

She climbs out of the bed and begins to dress as she replies, "He opposes the Lord's people. Haven't you seen the expression on his face when we're joining with the Holy Spirit?"

"The Lord's people?" I stammer.

She prompts me to fasten her bra as she continues, "He calls us *Fundamentalists* as if that were a pejorative. Jesus has sent me a sign, that Pastor plans to force God's true people out of Trinity House." She faces me, determination on her face, and adds, "That is why God has sent you, Macbeth Lunatic, to save us, and why I am your servant—a very satisfied servant I might add."

I'm always surprised at Melina's insight and this is no exception. "You mean that Pastor is trying to turn Trinity House into a—"

"A superchurch. Yes, an evangelical congregation that doesn't adhere to the Word of God, but only whatever interpretation is convenient, so they can get rich and feel good about it. That's what he's doing. That's why he found that little tramp, Melissa Tight, to be the music director." She pauses and looks at me seriously as I help her slip her dress over her head.

"Stay away from her, Mac, she's the spawn of Satan."

Jesus has left me on my own, so I decide not to share my dalliance with Melissa. "She looks like a temptress to me."

"Damned right!"

Melina helps me get dressed before leaving the motel room, blowing me a kiss before getting into her Audi. I have a lot to think about and wish I could talk to Lady, but I have no business at the church. I really like my spiritual relationship with Melina, but she isn't Lady—the only woman I'm in love with. After all, Jesus hasn't denounced her, only warned me that she has to prove herself. I'm sure she will rise to any occasion.

Melina's dire prediction is proven correct at Wednesday prayer meeting. We're exchanging glances, her eyes telling me that she wants to comfort me, when Pastor denies that these are the end times. He lays out his argument, that not one of the signs described in the Book of Revelations or alluded to in the Gospel of John has appeared. His case is weak because it doesn't include any of the classified data I've discovered on the Dark Web. Melina and I exchange more looks, and I notice that half the congregation is skeptical of what Pastor is saying. Missy squeezes my hand during his sermon, reminding me of our recent love making. She's smiling at me the way Melina is, and then I notice Lady, sitting behind the organ, tranquil as Mona Lisa.

Jesus doesn't speak to me directly, but he empowers me to step out of my body and join Lady on the stage, to take a seat next to her on the organ bench. An unbeliever, she's unaware of my presence although she is watching my avatar. I reach out to touch her hand, resting on the keyboard. She suddenly looks at me, not seeing me, and smiles. I decide there and then that I will do the Lord's work, but I am going to stay with Lady through thick and thin.

Jesus' voice speaks in my mind. *You are becoming wise but remain vigilant because the end time approaches.*

JEZEBEL

Jesus doesn't contact me every day, so I remain focused with Melina's eager assistance. I'm having sex and making love more than ever in my life. I can't refuse Missy, who is my wife, so we're making love every night and it's no longer dissatisfying. I'm beginning to enjoy her soft body, especially the sense of freedom I feel, knowing I can fall asleep next to her and make love again in the morning. We've rediscovered our romantic relationship, thanks to Jesus and QAnon. And then there's Lady, who I have finally admitted to myself that I love more than Missy, even more than myself. It's not like I have to make love with Lady; I see her every day, look forward to our *chance* meetings as soon as I've finished making love with Missy. Missy is happy. Melina is happy. I'm very happy, but Lady is not, and that spoils the entire situation.

"I think it's time to make our feelings for each other public, Mac. I don't see any other way than declaring our relationship in church, asking for forgiveness, getting divorced from our spouses, and starting a new life together. I promise that I will be as good a wife to you as I've been to Pastor...that might not sound so good—"

"I know what you mean, but there's something I've got to do first," I interject.

We're not in bed, just in the garden, so she doesn't touch me the way I like, just leans towards me with a confused expression. "You can tell me anything, Mac, so let's hear it. What do you have to do?"

I hope Jesus doesn't take offense when I say, "Clearing up

some loose ends. Don't press me, Sweetheart…don't get in a hurry Lady because there's something I have to do, I have to save the church."

She's very happy about my misspeaking. "Okay Mac but don't get carried away. I'm still worried about you, after your apotheosis."

I know she doesn't believe I had a spiritual awakening and she's just being nice, which I appreciate. I nod and casually reply, "Just don't go anywhere."

Having committed myself to installing the new sound system in the church, I'm dealing with Melissa Tight on a daily basis. Her attitude has changed and now she wants me in the worst way. Maybe she and Pastor are arguing. I don't care because I'm having sex with three women and my plate is full.

"You missed the boat Melissa and now I'm not available, just like you weren't available for the last six months. Do you know what that was like for me?"

Instead of answering, she removes her blouse and bra, revealing her world-class breasts, drops her skirt and pushes her underwear down. I'm speechless, so she removes my clothes before pushing me on the bed.

"Fuck me, Mac, like you did before."

I forget Melina's warning about Melissa being a harlot. I do as I'm told and she's grimacing, moaning, clawing at my back, pushing me away, pulling me tighter, biting at me, until I'm released from her spell. It was good. There's something about Melissa that brings out the primordial man in me.

"Are you okay?"

Gasping for breath, she says, "Intercourse is somewhat painful for me, but my gynecologist says that it isn't harmful. It's just another way of experiencing sexual pleasure. I've been avoiding you because I didn't know that, and Pastor doesn't have vaginal intercourse with me—"

I can't help interrupting. "What…in the ass?"

She nods and says, "It's okay but not the same as getting fucked, the way you just did." She giggles and continues, "I think the pleasure was greater than the pain, and definitely better than getting it in the ass." She laughs out loud now.

I'm speechless as she climbs out of bed and gets dressed, never taking her eyes off me. She pushes the sheet back and examines me closely before saying, "I can see that you're ready for another round, but I'm not. It was excruciatingly pleasurable, an experience I can't face twice in one day."

I finally find my voice. "I'm not a toy you can take out and play with whenever the mood strikes you."

She scoffs. "Give me a break, Mac. That's all any woman is to you, but I don't hold it against you because that's all any of us are. We fulfill each other's sexual fantasies. You and I know this, which is why you're ready to go another round. I wish I could…"

I jump out of the bed, prepared to denounce her as a harlot, but she begins stroking me. Her youthful hand is as soft as calfskin, and I can't remember what I was going to say. The gentle contact continues as she nuzzles my neck and whispers sweet nothings until I have a sexual release. She licks my semen from her fingers, and says, "Do you feel better now?"

Her words remind me of our last encounter. I finally find my voice. "You're right about us fulfilling each other's fantasies, but I can't do this again. You are unbelievably sexy and an outstanding sex partner, but this is the last time."

"Really?" she asks half joking, her eyes daring me to take her so soon after ejaculating.

"You are Jezebel and part of Pastor's conspiracy. The Deep State. You're working for them and I can't be part of any of that…"

She laughs out loud, caresses my genitals, and says, "You will do whatever I say Mac because you are addicted to sex just like me. We need each other."

She kisses me passionately, arousing me again, before quickly stepping back, examining me approvingly and laughing. I feel like a sex tool. A walking, talking dildo. Jesus says nothing and I wish I could talk to Lady.

BETRAYAL

It was a very difficult time for me, after Mac's breakdown—I was certain it was a stroke. My feelings for him were unchanged; in fact, they were much stronger after his expression of support for rearranging our lives to be together. The coincidence of his medical emergency, our mutual avowal of love, and his having a secret mission hadn't escaped me. I was intrigued, but he wouldn't talk about it. I could get anything out of the old Mac, if I asked the right question. That was the thing with Macbeth Lunatic; he could keep a secret as long as no one asked him about it, but he folded like a house of cards when confronted. At least that's how it had always worked for me, probably because we were in love. That's a nice phrase, promising years of mutual support and happiness, but there's another side to love: People aren't perfect. We are all prone to making mistakes—my entire life—and repeating them, to the horror of those who love us, sometimes even destroying our lives. Mac had the potential to become a tragic Greek hero.

I couldn't stand being alone in the kitchen, making a loaf of sourdough bread for Pastor (he loves homemade bread), trapped in my gilded cage. I put the bread in the oven and stepped over to the church, hoping to find someone to talk to. People came and went all day in the main building, especially with the electrical work being done. Maybe I'd get a chance to talk to Melissa Tight, our music director.

Imagine my surprise when I found Mac coming out of the guest room, his appearance accompanied by a fragrance I couldn't quite place. He hadn't told me about working at the church today and he always let me know when he would be in the area, so that we could talk, and I would get him a snack or something to drink. It must have been an emergency.

"Oh my, god, Mac! You must have read my mind. I was so lonely, cooped up in the kitchen by myself, that I came over here hoping to find someone—anyone—to talk to. Can you believe that I was looking forward to speaking to Melissa Tight? She's a nice girl, but she's really focused on her music. Still, it would have been better than talking to myself. And now I find you here. Did you get an emergency call?" Out of breath, I stopped my tirade, giving Mac an opportunity to say something.

"You just missed her—Melissa, I mean. She called me with what probably seemed like an emergency to her, to check on the size and placement of the extra fuse box that will be required for the new sound system. Like you said, she's really into her music. I was between jobs, so I dropped by, no time to call you. Sorry about that."

He wasn't lying. But he wasn't telling the truth either. I didn't care because I wanted to speak to him about his secret mission. I kissed him quickly because we were inside, before blurting, "Tell me about your prophecy. Maybe I can help?"

I had confused him, so I elaborated, "Tell me what you have to accomplish before we can be together in public, as man and wife." I kissed him again, this time on the lips, making a point of inserting my tongue into his mouth.

He responded in kind, probably unaware of what my tongue had learned. I finished the kiss, leaned back, and shared my discovery. "Have you been drinking, Mac? Don't lie to me because you never did before. You know I'm on your side no matter what. I'm going to be your wife soon."

A sigh followed by a thoughtful nod made me think that he had unconsciously wanted to be found out. Boy, was I wrong; he started to respond, but then something happened and the face I had grown accustomed to, the man I'd fallen in love with, morphed into the embodiment of anger, twisted by primordial rage, a caricature of Mr. Hyde.

"I know you're working with Pastor, to push God's people out of the Promised Land and take it as your own. Melina has put the pieces together and made it clear to me that the reason for my spiritual enlightenment was to prevent this travesty against the true followers of Christ."

What he was saying made sense in a way, especially with the idea coming from Melina Light. She may have been a Latina bimbo, but she was pretty sharp, albeit superstitious to a fault. "I think I know what you're talking about but you need to explain it better."

I gasped when a flask appeared from his back pocket. He took a short drink and elaborated on his accusation. "Pastor and Melissa plan to transform Trinity House into a megachurch, leaving the Fundamentalists in the lurch. He's sold his soul to the devil."

"Is that it? That's your big conspiracy? My goodness, Mac, of course Pastor wants to make something of Trinity House. He's never made a secret of his plans, especially after he hired Melissa to expand his musical outreach program. I guess that such a plan would appear to Melina and some of the Fundamentalists as an attempt to undermine them—they are so politically motivated since Donald Trump was elected president—but they only feel threatened because they adopted such an extreme political platform that they can't get along with anyone."

"So, you admit it?"

"I don't admit any personal responsibility for Pastor's plans, although I think they are quite reasonable. I know him as well as I know you Mac, and I can vouch for his sincerity. Pastor wants to reach more people and bring them into the fold, and he's doing that in traditional ways, like—" I stopped because he wasn't looking at me.

He pulled his flask out and took another drink.

"Look at me, Mac, even if you're ashamed of taking that drink. Meet my eyes!"

He did as I ordered, meeting my gaze; meekly at first but then, something happened that caused him to shove the flask into his hip pocket, face me and practically shout, "You use such smooth words that I bet you could talk a raccoon out of its skin, but those are just words, spoken by Satan with you as his mouthpiece. These are the end times Lady and the battle being fought right now will be won or lost because of the efforts of God's chosen few. You don't know what's happening. You don't even believe in God! How can you judge me about things you don't admit exist? How can an atheist like you possibly understand the battle between Good and Evil?"

He stared at me, confident of his incontestable statement of fact.

Mac was not himself, so I didn't speak to him openly; instead, I acted contrite, a role he had apparently relegated me to for the moment. "I see your point, Mac, but I'm confused…"

His eyes were narrowed suspiciously as he responded to my unfinished thought. "About what?"

Pleased that he was interacting with me rather than ranting, I continued, "If these are the end times, why wouldn't God want to get as many people involved in His work as possible? I'm not sure how He would do that, but wouldn't Pastor's plan to expand the church's mission be a good idea?" I admit that I was playing the role of Pastor's apologist, but he really was trying to alleviate the burden of an uncertain life for those with a superstitious mindset.

"You're using clever words again, and you have no right to talk about God or his plan, as an atheist."

Mac was unreachable, so I changed my approach. I decided to challenge him. "By the way, when did you become a Fundamentalist? You've always expressed views perfectly in line with Pastor's and most of the congregation."

"My eyes have been opened to the truth. Not that you would understand the truth if it bit you. You sold your soul to the devil without even realizing it. God help you, Lady."

My next words slipped out. "If I'm such a hopeless sinner and tool of the devil, why are we in love?" I smiled at him adoringly, knowing we would eventually be together, but I grimaced inwardly at what his response might be.

I could imagine circuits within Mac's damaged cerebellum and prefrontal cortex shorting out, sparks flying in every direction, misdirecting other neurons, hormones so far out of chemical equilibrium that his brain was paralyzed; but he finally spoke.

"Jesus—the angel I mean—warned me about you. You have been found wanting because of your disbelief."

I laughed out loud, seeing no reason to do otherwise. "Is Jesus speaking to you right now?!" I taunted.

"I thought I could trust you."

I scoffed in response and said, "You can, Mac. I won't tell anyone about your spiritual experience. This is between you and me. But do you really think you are talking to Jesus Christ? Because that would take having a personal savior to a whole new level, which should be shared with the Christian world." I challenged him with my steady gaze.

He blinked.

"Jesus told me to say I was speaking to an angel."

I understood, or so I thought. "Jesus wants you and Melina Light to oppose Pastor and Melissa in implementing their plan for a megachurch that excludes Fundamentalists. Is that what you've been keeping a secret?"

Mac nodded.

I kissed him, glad to have settled that foolish point. Church politics had never interested me. But now the fragrance I'd noticed earlier, when Mac had appeared from the guest room, took physical form. That was the cologne worn by Melissa, a distinctive and expensive rose scent. I was too angry for words when I shared my discovery with Mac.

"What the fuck?!" I slapped him with all my might. He didn't flinch. Macho asshole.

I was shocked and frightened when he suddenly grasped my arms and slammed me against the wall. I hadn't fully comprehended his physical strength until that moment. Our eyes met, peering into each other's minds, and he released me. My feet reconnected with the floor.

"Did you have sex with Melissa Tight in the guest room just before we met in the hallway? Yes or no."

I was already frightened, doubting my own intelligence for falling in love with Macbeth Lunatic. The name alone should have been enough to dissuade me from forming an emotional relationship.

He raised his hand as if to hit me, then lowered it, choosing a verbal assault. "You have entered into an unholy alliance with Pastor and Melissa, to drive the Children of God out of the promised land."

I wasn't going to risk being physically assaulted again, so I stepped back, out of his reach, before saying, "I want to make sure that I understand what you are doing, Mac. You just now had sex with Melissa Tight, a woman you say is trying to isolate the Fundamentalists, so I have to wonder why?"

"I don't understand."

"Why did you have sex with a woman you believe to be a proponent of secular objectivism?"

"There you go again. Using big words."

I sighed, took a deep breath, and said, "Why did you fuck Melissa Tight when you believe she is your enemy?"

Mac's brain was short-circuiting. The answer produced by the spongy goo he thought of as Macbeth Lunatic was wrong in so many ways.

"Yes, I *fucked* Melissa Tight, and then she used her hand to give me another amazing experience. And I can tell you that she's a lot better piece of ass than you any day. Jesus never told me not to fuck her and so I gave it to her, but it's all part of His plan to resist her and Pastor's efforts to force God's people out of Trinity House. I won't let that happen, even if it means having sex with the enemy. And I'll do it again if I have to. I was chosen because of my talent…"

My voice was trembling when I asked, "What talent is that?"

He took another swig from his flask and looked at me contemptuously as he spat out, "I can get women into bed, just like I did with you. All you women are the same. Prostitutes who only need to hear the right words to spread your legs and open your mouths."

My chest exploded with his words, thrown at me with such malice and derision. I turned away from him, my ears ringing from his vile assault, and ran to the rectory. With the door closed behind me, safe within my gilded cage, I couldn't stop the sobs of pain and remorse.

HOLY SPIRIT

I'm not proud of the way I spoke to Lady. Melina had assured me that it was necessary to cut our ties with the enemies of Jesus. I don't feel like Lady is an enemy or even an adversary. I still feel the same about her. It isn't a permanent break-up, only a temporary separation until I finish whatever it is that Jesus wants me to do. That part is unclear and Melina hasn't shed any light on the topic either, but she sure keeps me focused. She's in my head, obviously the work of the Lord, because she isn't as good looking as Lady, or as easy to deal with. In fact, Melina is a little crazy. And it pays off in early March when tragedy strikes Trinity House, in the form of the China Flu, as President Trump refers to the latest assault on our American values. It's a sign of the end times when members of the congregation are struck down.

Apparently, I had been Vernon Huckster's best friend. All I did was cut his grass, do odd jobs around the mobile home he lived in, sometimes pick up groceries on my way to his place. He paid me for everything. I wasn't some kind of saint or anything. Anyway, he got the China flu and died suddenly, so his daughter asked me to deliver his eulogy. Not to downplay the tragedy of Vernon's death, but this is an opportunity to make up with Lady. I hadn't told her about Melina just like I hadn't mentioned having sex with Melissa. Jesus had warned me about trusting anyone too much or burning my bridges, which I took to especially apply to Lady— the bridge part I mean.

Needing some help from Lady, who studied writing in

college, I stop by the florist shop to get some red roses, her favorite flower. I also cut some firewood for her because it's still cold at night. She might like to sit in front of a fire and read a book. When she answers the door, she's a little formal but she brightens at the sight of the roses I'm holding.

"Why, Macbeth Lunatic, why in the world did you bring me roses?" She's warming up fast.

"I wanted to apologize for everything I said the other day, and especially for letting myself get seduced by Melissa Tight. I'd sworn to myself that I wasn't interested in any woman but you...I'm not very strong when it comes to women. Anyway, I'm really sorry about that...about causing you pain and all..."

She thanks me and asks me if I'd be willing to bring some wood inside because they'd run out. I go to get a few pieces while she puts the roses in a vase next to the front door, leaving the door open. It takes a couple of trips to fill the woodbin. She leaves the door open for the sake of decorum while she accepts my apology. Being kind of pressed for time, I head back out and, with her standing in the open door, explain that I have to write Vernon's eulogy, admitting that I hadn't known what a eulogy was until then.

She smiles the way she used to, before I spoke so mean to her, and says, "Would you like some help?"

I don't know why I went off like that against Lady, accusing her of being in league with the devil and all. She can't be working with Satan because she doesn't believe in Heaven or Hell or God or evil. The same way she can't fully understand my beliefs, I can't comprehend hers. We can only know things one way at a time. Anyway, I can kill two birds with one stone if Lady helps me with Vernon's eulogy, maybe a whole flock. For one thing, being agnostic, she doesn't support either the Evangelical or Fundamentalist groups within Trinity House. She just wants a peaceful place to spend time with her neighbors, without raised voices and such. I can't argue with that.

Because of her neutral viewpoint, Lady helps me insert some religious political speech into Vernon's eulogy. That's another bird. I have to learn to listen to every word that comes out of her mouth because, when I'd acted so ugly the other day, she had voiced what Jesus wanted me to do. At this point,

I know he wants me and Lady to be together because he let me learn about my purpose from her rather than telling me outright. The Lord is wiser than all of us.

We work in the church office, using the computer in a public place to avoid any improprieties. By the time we finish, I know what Jesus wants me to do. Lady and I have expressed my memories of Vernon in a moving eulogy, written a manifesto listing the complaints of the Fundamentalists, who feel marginalized by Pastor and his megachurch concept, and we've fallen in love all over. I've been telling her what a jerk I am so much while we're working that she goes to the organ and plays a song, singing in her soprano voice. I had never heard *Put Your Hand in the Hand*, but it's my favorite Christian rock song now. Another sign of Jesus' support for our being together.

She walks me to my truck, not touching me but her eyes telling me what I need to hear. She loves me as much as Jesus does. Pastor joins us and speaks to me directly. "I can't wait to hear your sendoff for Mr. Huckster. He was a good man. Trinity House will miss him."

I add, "We'll all miss him, even those who never knew his name."

Pastor smiles knowingly. "I hear the voice of Lady in those words Mac, and I can't tell you what an inspiration she's been to me through the years. She has a way of saying what's in our hearts, even when we are unaware of our own feelings."

"Yessir," I say. "Now I guess I better be getting home, to start trying to memorize these inspirational words. I don't want to confuse everybody at Vernon's funeral by stumbling because some of them are unfamiliar."

It took a real effort, with help from Missy, to finally memorize the speech, which is what Lady had said it was. Missy is convinced that Lady is a Fundamentalist. I don't try and explain why that isn't the case, for fear of revealing my intimate acquaintance with the woman I'm soon going to join in marital bliss. To make my life even more difficult, Missy is especially attentive, after reading the eulogy, and we make out on the couch before having really good sex. It reminds me of why I married her to begin with. I spend a romantic evening with my wife but somehow feel like I'm cheating on Lady.

Delivering Vernon's eulogy is the first time I've ever spoken in public and I'm nervous. I'm ready to recite the words Lady helped me write and Missy helped me memorize. I haven't needed inspiration from Melina because Missy has been doing a good job of keeping me focused on the task at hand. I've also avoided any sexual contact with Lady, who seems to understand my feelings more than anyone else; she'd shown me how I really felt about Vernon, about Jesus, myself, the world at large, my life, the list could go on—just by writing about a dead man I had thought was a stranger until she'd shown me otherwise. Lady is the center of my world and I adore her as if she's the Virgin Mary. Jesus corrects me—Lady is *like* Mary, while not being the same.

I'm wearing a black suit Missy helped me choose, standing behind the pulpit, looking at all the faces lined up on the pews, filling the nave with expectation. Pastor had kept his statement brief, knowing he would be the last to speak, at the grave, and introduced me as a man known to the entire congregation.

Thanks to Lady, I had memorized a eulogy-slash-speech that focused on the real reason most of the congregation had collected on a Saturday afternoon. They were expecting me to say something profound.

Lady is sitting at the organ because Melissa is going to perform a song she wrote especially for Vernon's funeral. So, I can't see Lady from where I'm standing behind the pulpit. I would look like an idiot, turning constantly to look at the organist, raising a lot of brows asking questions I didn't want to answer yet. Totally confused and as nervous as a long-tailed cat in a room full of rocking chairs, I recite the speech verbatim. Ten minutes are spent summarizing my personal interactions with Vernon Huckster. There are scattered Amens. It doesn't look like he knew too many people in the congregation. Staying with the speech I had memorized so laboriously, I end the eulogy with a well-crafted sentence, written by Lady, that naturally transitioned to the *speech* part of my eulogy.

"Vernon didn't die from pneumonia, a viral infection unleashed on an unsuspecting world by the godless authoritarian regime that rules China, or even old age. In fact, his death is a result of our limited comprehension of reality, trapped in these bodies of dust as we are. No, Vernon isn't dead. It was simply time for him to join Jesus at the throne."

There's a lot of applause and voiced support for that thought, so I risk a glance at lady, who is smiling supportively. I have to remind myself not to look at her again, especially considering what I'm about to say.

I'm having second thoughts about my next words, which seemed so appropriate when I practiced them with Missy. Now I'm not so sure. I can't believe Lady didn't talk me out of penning a tirade like this. But I know why she didn't try and stop me; she doesn't have an opinion about such things and wanted only to avoid setting me off again, like when she'd caught me in the church, smelling like Melissa. So, she'd helped me write a manifesto that would destroy the tranquility of Trinity House, a list of demands that it was impossible to satisfy, ending with an ultimatum and a threat to tear the church asunder. Most of the grievances I'm about to elaborate as the basis for the Fundamentalist demands are nothing more than complaints that had festered unspoken, becoming cancers in the current fractured political climate gripping America.

I don't have to continue. I've performed my duty to Vernon and his family. I can just give a prayer or announce a moment of silent prayer. After all, I'm standing behind the pulpit. I'm in charge. I'm not going to do it.

This is your Garden of Gethsemane. It was Jesus, reminding me of my responsibility. *Will you betray me as Judas did?*

I am filled with the Holy Ghost, empowered, all doubts cast aside. I call on the congregation to pray for President Trump and the people who are fighting alongside him to defeat the Deep State. I refer to QAnon, supporting my claim of the end times with Q's need to hide from the Deep State, a tool of Satan. I don't wait for the congregation, but immediately pray aloud for the soldiers on the front line in this final battle and ask for divine support so that I can do my part. There are a lot of Amens and Hallelujahs, mostly from the Fundamentalists.

I deliver the memorized words verbatim, following Missy's instructions on intonation, a word I learned from Lady. I finish and the church is silent, except for Melina Light. She's sobbing, her hands in the air in supplication to Jesus. I am overwhelmed by the Holy Spirit and blessed to leave my body, to witness events from an everchanging position, first from the choir box, then the first row, near the ceiling. Dizzy from the experience, Jesus delivers me back to my body, and I become aware of the words I'm speaking. They are not part of the speech I had memorized.

"The day of reckoning is at hand. The true followers of Jesus will be vindicated on Easter, when God will demonstrate His power and make known His wishes."

DISCIPLE

Melina Light insists that we have intercourse before discussing whatever is on our minds, like it's a religious ceremony rather than just fun. This has been her rule all along, so I follow it. She's waiting when I enter the motel room. She's naked and within minutes, I'm giving it to her, and she wants it hard, as if I'm forcing myself on her—for inspiration she says. When she regains her breath, she straddles me and explains the reason for our meeting.

"I was biting my tongue during the beautiful eulogy you gave for what's his name…and fighting the temptation to share what the Holy Spirit was revealing to me through your words. You are truly inspired by Jesus. And I've been chosen to be your disciple. I am so honored to have been selected as the first person to be given the opportunity to follow you. There will be many others."

"What about Dim?"

"Who?"

"Your husband. What's his opinion about my message, about you being my disciple?"

She thinks a moment before saying, "Dim knows that I'm spiritual. He's lost without my guidance and support. Don't worry about him."

I'm not feeling inspired, so I ask, "Is he okay with our having sex in a motel room? Does he even know?"

"Like I said, don't worry about Dim, which reminds me, what about Missy? I've noticed that you two are much closer than I've seen you in years. Is she sapping your strength?"

"What?"

Melina's surprisingly soft fingertips play with my nipples, sliding down to my navel, swirling there, before she answers, "Missy is a believer but also a liability, definitely not on purpose. She doesn't know her own spiritual strength, which is why the disconnect between her energy and yours is hurting you. You should stop having sex with her. Jesus chose me to be your spiritual support because our energy patterns are synchronous."

"What does that mean?"

"God works through the Holy Spirit to communicate with us and sometimes intervene in our lives, using the zero-point field. But energy has wavelengths and frequencies, just as God determined it should. We don't have a say in how He chose to make the world operate, but we do have the choice to recognize His system and fit our lives to it."

"And?"

She sighs in exasperation and adds, "Communicating with God through the Holy Spirit is dependent on the kinds of spiritual waves we receive and transmit. You and I are using the same kinds of waves at this moment, although it could change without notice. Which is why we must act soon, as you so eloquently expressed at Vern—whatever—in your speech."

Now I get it. "Thanks for explaining." It makes sense, the way Melina described it. It was like 120- and 240-volt electricity. That's why I don't want to install the sound system. I'm not very good with things I can't see and touch with my hands, but I could touch her firm breasts. I like the idea of having a disciple, especially one who inspires me through sexual fun.

PUSH BACK

I was proud of Mac's delivery of Vernon Huckster's eulogy, not so much about the manifesto I'd helped him write. I was caught off guard by his adlibbed prophecy. Helping him with the proclamation had been my way of expressing dissatisfaction with my life, a middle finger raised to tell Pastor what I thought of his megachurch concept, which had never been more than a dream. In a stroke of genius, Mac had added a divination to his speech, a statement guaranteed to fill the pews on Easter. He hadn't mentioned it before, so I assume it was inspired by Jesus at the last moment. I didn't press him on that subject because I knew Mac, even if I didn't fully understand exactly what neurological problem he was suffering from. If I had questioned his spiritual experience, he would have avoided me, depriving me of the opportunity to influence his behavior.

The congregation's response to the body of his manifesto was buried under concerns about his prophecy. These people, Fundamentalist and Evangelical, love their prophecies, the more outrageous the better, as long as they don't involve anything smelling of behavioral modification. Furthermore, prophecy and conspiracy were synonyms to every one of them. It was a brilliant move from my perspective, creating as it were a new source of entertainment.

Vanity Blunt, feeling close to me as one of the *in crowd*, was first to voice concern when she appeared at my door the next day. She looked ready for a shoot, her designer jeans topped by a turtleneck sweater and short jacket. I invited her in and made a pot of coffee, while she shared her thoughts about Mac's speech. She didn't know that I'd helped him write it and I saw no reason to enlighten her, not immediately.

"Can you believe such arrogance?"

"Which side are you on? I asked, challenging her discretely with my tone.

"The same as you, of course! He did it because of what happened to him, his stroke or whatever it was. Nevertheless, his supporters—"

The beep of the coffee machine interrupted her. I poured two cups and we went to the living room, pleasantly warmed by the firewood Mac had delivered. When we were settled on the sofa, I responded to her last statement.

"I didn't know the lawn keeper had a following. I was there when Mac Lunatic went on a rant about some kind of constitutional right to believe whatever…and other silly things, but no one shouted their support. I think he just got carried away. Like you said, he did have a *spiritual experience*."

Vanity posed with her coffee cup, before responding, "He isn't the lawn boy anymore. Brother Lunatic is a Messiah. Right here in Modoc, we have a man who has attained the status of a demigod."

I loved her choice of words. Vanity was a bright spot in my life in Modoc, not having lost the sense of enjoying life she'd felt before retiring to the middle of nowhere. I didn't want to let her think that I agreed with whatever she was thinking, however, so I made my perspective clear while not violating Mac's right to privacy, at least until we announced our relationship.

"It's quite a conundrum. Trinity House has remained intact for twenty years, despite the teleological split between those who call themselves Fundamentalists and—"

"What are you talking about?"

"The Fundamentalists are committed to interpreting the biblical narrative literally, probably because they don't like to think. The Evangelicals, on the other hand, are fairly reasonable people. These two groups have gotten along because Pastor made a point of finding their common beliefs and focusing on them. Brother Lunatic's manifesto blew all that away. I don't think the Fundamentalists are arrogant so much as simply tired of being in the minority." I paused and took the first step towards my emancipation.

"However, as an agnostic, I repudiate everything he said after the eulogy. I'm not taking sides, and I wash my hands of the entire situation, like Pontius Pilate." I rubbed my hands together to make my point.

Vanity laughed, spilling some coffee on the carpet. I waved her apology aside, so she replied, "I never suspected. You helped Mac write Vernon's eulogy, didn't you?"

I nodded, sipped my coffee, and answered, "I only helped him polish it, make it understandable, supply a larger vocabulary, all with Pastor's approval. That's the kind of leader he is. Pastor is a seeker of the truth and, although blinded by ideology and dogma, he is openminded and fair. I didn't choose the words Brother Lunatic used but only helped with oratory, but I had hoped he would have second thoughts and stop after the eulogy." I didn't want to say anymore yet.

Vanity's eyebrows lifted for a second at my apparent confession, but she didn't seem offended. In fact, her next words suggested that she liked the idea of speaking to a nonbeliever. "Mike doesn't know what to do. On one hand he is socially conservative and is aghast at Mac's open revolt against a smoothly operating church but, on the other hand, he's glad to see someone speaking out against Pastor."

This piqued my interest. "Please explain."

"It's just Mike. He resents authority, even if it's necessary and justified. After all, Pastor is obviously more qualified on spiritual matters than a lawyer, but the way Mike goes on, you'd think he was a minister himself."

"I've noticed that he opposes almost everything Pastor proposes in Church Board meetings. I'd assumed it was just how lawyers speak."

"That's true but with Mike it's also his personality. I wouldn't be surprised if he becomes a reluctant follower of our new Messiah just to get under Pastor's skin."

We laughed together and I wondered why I hadn't been closer to Vanity over the years. I was as prejudiced as anyone else and had thought of her as a blonde bimbo, which is funny coming from me—my hair was a lighter shade of blonde than hers. Most likely, we had simply aged and were less uptight about ourselves and more tolerant of others.

We started getting together several times a week after our meeting of the minds. Vanity had been right about the repercussions from Mac's speech. She must have let slip that I'd helped Mac write his manifesto—with Pastor's knowledge—because I began receiving calls and visits from both Fundamentalists and Evangelicals. Apparently, I was an expert on what Mac was trying to accomplish; thankfully, no one held me personally responsible although several of the women I spoke to wished that Mac hadn't written such an eloquent speech. I didn't apologize.

One thing everyone I spoke to had in common was a sense of pride in President Trump, and his leadership against the forces of Satan. The Fundamentalists tended to buy the whole QAnon conspiracy belief system in toto whereas most of the Evangelicals drew the line at child sex slavery, not because they didn't think Democrats were capable of such horrendous acts; such extreme evil would have been discovered through the heroic efforts of Fox News and Rush Limbaugh. I didn't see a political split within the congregation. Everyone had the same superstitious world view and believed the president was sent by God to save them from the evils of democracy. Okay, I admit that I'm one of those evil, baby-stealing, liberal Democrats. I kept that to myself, not even admitting it to Mac, although I think Pastor suspected.

Despite the nearly identical views of the two factions making up the congregation of Trinity House, this contentious group of emotionally dependent individualists found the one thing they could not agree on: The evangelicals refused to accept that Mac had been chosen by God as the Messiah, especially not for them. Pastor found himself portrayed as the antichrist in this bizarre, apocalyptic farce, which dismayed him after the years he'd spent nurturing his flock.

"Are you sure you didn't subconsciously slip some of your ideas into Mac's speech?" Pastor asked, sitting at the dinner table with a piece of chicken hovering in front of his mouth.

I shook my head and the morsel disappeared. "You know I don't think like that. I didn't know what QAnon was until I read Mac's inarticulate, incomprehensible notes for the eulogy. I was shocked at his wild statements about your being in league with Satan. Even his most ardent supporters think that was hyperbole, to make a point, a style of speech they've become accustomed to after three years of Donald Trump in the Whitehouse." I had never spoken against the President before, so this was another step towards my emancipation.

Pastor didn't respond to my jab at a man who, if not his hero, was certainly considered an ally. His brow was furrowed in thought as he ate most of his dinner in silence, finally speaking, when only a few rice grains remained, scattered among some peas waiting to be scooped up. "Have you talked to Brother Lunatic since the funeral?"

I hadn't, which worried me, but I was able to answer the way Pastor wanted to hear and not add bold-faced lying to my list of mortal sins. "No. He brought plenty of firewood his last delivery, and I've been busy with so many visitors this week that I haven't had a chance to even drop in on the church."

Pastor carefully cleaned up his plate and said, "Mac and I had a conversation about Revelations. Apparently, he learned a lot from your tutoring on creative writing because he has brought the whole QAnon nonsense home to Trinity House. His prophecy about the *True Believers* being vindicated wasn't just rhetoric designed to get people to church on an important day for all Christians. He now proposes that this is part of the initial assault by the Great Beast, to infiltrate God's army through the churches and weaken them, thus circumventing the eventual outcome predicted by Revelations. In other words, Mac thinks Satan is going to win, it's happening right now, and I've been fooled by the deception. God is going to strike down the unbelievers on Easter, leaving the chosen to carry on the battle."

Those weren't the ideas of the Macbeth Lunatic I was in love with, so Pastor must have been speaking to the Mac who was ready to hit me, the emotional man with no executive control over his thoughts or actions. I decided to push the envelope. "You're reaping what you've sown, Pastor. What did you expect, inciting these superstitious people to believe every word coming out of the lying mouth of Donald Trump? You should never have endorsed such an evil man, just because he played to your belief in the sanctity of an unborn child's life. You made a deal with the devil and now he's collecting."

Pastor's jaw dropped, revealing that last bit of his dinner on his tongue. He finally collected himself and responded. "You are of course correct, Lady, I just wish you had said something before. Perhaps I wouldn't have made such a one-sided deal. Maybe it wouldn't have mattered. Who knows? Still, your recent interest in Trinity House is commendable."

I smiled and shrugged but didn't answer.

For the first time in our marriage, Pastor looked at me as if I were his intellectual equal. "I've always known you didn't share my belief in the Christian precepts written in the Gospels. These matters are personal and it isn't possible to maintain a pretense of belief for years—"

"I wanted to accept your beliefs Pastor because I had none of my own. I really tried…"

He patted my outstretched hand and responded in a cold but not angry voice, "Of course. I never doubted your support for my work. Not for one moment. You're just not cut out to be a Christian, but you are a God-fearing woman, a loving wife and mother, a pillar of support through thick and thin, the person I was glad to have at my side, and now you're still here during yet another crisis."

I was dismayed. Pastor was as good as me at keeping things to himself but, unlike me, he knew when it was time to speak openly. I wasn't ready, not in the middle of what I saw as a crisis of leadership. Or stewardship. I avoided getting too close to my recent conversations with Mac in my response. "I never disparaged your beliefs. How could I, having none of my own? Over the years, I've come to see that we know so little about the universe that there's no reason to dismiss anyone's superstitious beliefs, unless they contradict observations we have made with our own eyes."

"Yet you use the word *superstition* to describe beliefs you don't accept. That is a biased perspective."

I'd had this discussion with Mac many times over the years and was prepared to summarize my viewpoint. "You are right Pastor, and this is where I part ways with superstitious belief systems. I accept that humans don't understand where we came from, what happens to us after death, how the universe came into existence. I accept that we may never know. That's okay with me. I don't have to have an easily summarized explanation of every unknown phenomenon to feel one with the universe. It's possible that your belief system is a parametrization of something we haven't discovered yet. That's why I don't ridicule or condemn it, or you, or any of the congregation, but I cannot accept such a primitive paradigm as truth."

Pastor lifted my hand, which he'd been holding, kissed it gently, and said, "I wish we'd had this conversation twenty years ago, not that it would have changed my mind about marrying you; rather, your insight would have been a positive influence on my approach to pastoring. I suppose you didn't speak openly because I was older, overconfident, and didn't ask for your opinion, and you are such a gentle person. I apologize for the way I've treated you, and I welcome your opinion about anything, from this day on."

I was flabbergasted, but I don't think my jaw dropped. I didn't think this was a good time for the bombshell, so I said, "I've never felt abused or anything like that, Pastor, but I do appreciate your openness now. I'm proud of what you've done with Trinity House and I support you fully in dealing with whatever nonsense Mac and his followers are spreading. Just tell me what you'd like me to do."

BEST FRIENDS

Pastor's admission of uncertainty, of needing my help in the crisis that was rapidly engulfing Trinity House, had been as much of a surprise as Mac's agreeing to make our relationship public. I was confused. Needing a distraction, I was thankful when Vanity invited me to visit Missy Lunatic, to purchase some of her private stock of organic vegetables, grown in a hothouse Mac had built for her.

I was becoming very fond of Vanity and enjoyed hearing her voice, speaking in nuanced tones as if preparing for a role. I had thought she was a poser, trying to impress everyone with her brief acting history, but I learned otherwise; Vanity was a natural and, if she hadn't married Mike Blunt, probably would have become a celebrity. She had given up a lot more than me for a life in Modoc, Oklahoma. When I asked her about this, I learned that we had more in common than either one of us could have imagined. It hadn't been the prospect of appearing topless in a movie that had ended her career; she would have been comfortable appearing nude because she was proud of her body. It had been her parents threatening to have nothing more to do with her. She hadn't been independent enough to ignore their threats; and the real reason she was in Modoc was that she hadn't wanted to deal with life. We hugged when she admitted to being as hopelessly dependent as me, sealing our friendship.

Missy led Vanity and me on a tour of the 5200 square-foot mansion Mac had built on their forty-acre farm. We were sharing incredulous looks, whispering to each other like schoolgirls, as Missy explained that Mac liked to build things. She hadn't asked him to build such a monstrosity but he'd done it anyway, and she hadn't complained because there had always been plenty of space for social events, like family reunions and birthday parties for their daughter, which had always been attended by the families of the children. By the time we passed through the house and followed a covered pathway to a steel building, Vanity and I were both wishing we'd married Mac. We were giggling as Missy led us into the hub of her internet business.

Accepting my role as the neutral spokeswoman for Trinity House, knowing we weren't really in Missy's beautiful business office to buy some squash, I got the conversation started. "I'm so envious of you, Missy. I could never have done this, build an internet business based on a couple of acres. You must be so proud of Mac, not to mention your own efforts."

Missy smiled proudly at Vanity and me as she replied, "Mac and I have worked hard and God has rewarded our efforts."

"Amen," Vanity voiced. I nodded affirmatively.

Vanity followed up her *Amen* with a question. "Has Mac gone to the doctor since his spiritual encounter, just in case he may have been stricken by something…something caused by such a powerful experience."

Missy showed us her perfect greenhouse tomatoes, squash, and zucchini, making us wait for her answer. "Mac and I agree that he is only a man and thus may suffer some side-effects from personal contact with the Holy Spirit. This experience will probably shorten his life but, if nonbelievers like doctors and nurses were to intervene, the effect would be devastating."

I couldn't think of a reply to such a foolish statement.

Vanity was not at a loss for words. "I see your point, Missy, but people do suffer from strokes and heart attacks. It would probably convince more people of the truth of Mac's prophesy if he had a clean bill of health—"

She shook her head vehemently before saying, "Faith is the key. Without faith we are lost. I know that's a difficult idea for some people to accept because we can so easily console ourselves with platitudes and placebos. Mac is serving the Lord and he accepts the personal risks that entails. After all, Jesus was crucified to atone for our sins. Mac isn't Jesus but he is trying to follow in the Lord's footsteps."

Even Vanity was speechless at such a meaningless statement, but she eventually found a response. "That is such a spiritual interpretation Missy, and I'll be praying for Mac to survive his possession by the Holy Spirit."

Despite her apparent sophistication, Missy didn't catch Vanity's jibe, or ignored it. We bought some organic tomatoes, squashes, and asparagus and paid with cash. When we were back in her Mercedes, Vanity challenged me. "I know you're in love with Macbeth Lunatic. It was obvious from the way you looked at Missy, unbridled envy setting your eyes on fire. Don't bother denying it. Oh my god! I can't believe I told you about my brief affair with him—but you didn't look at me the way you looked at Missy. How long have you been seeing Mac?"

It was my turn to surprise her. "Ten years, but you're right. Learning about your affair was part of what caused me to realize that Mac and I are in love. I was annoyed but not jealous, especially since it was several years ago."

Vanity laughed out loud before turning serious and asking, "Does he feel the same?"

"Yes, but he's a little difficult to deal with right now. As soon as he completes whatever he thinks he's doing, we're going to go public and get divorced from Pastor and Missy. Probably after Easter."

"I hope he lives that long. He's a walking time bomb, waiting to go off, and anything could be the trigger."

I nodded hopelessly. "I don't do anything to antagonize him after reading about blood pressure and strokes. Of course, it doesn't matter what I do after the fuse he lit under Trinity House. The congregation has split just like you predicted and he put himself right between the opposing forces. The only good news is that he seems to be oblivious of his position."

Vanity backed out of the driveway, shaking her head and grinning. "Ten years. I can't believe Mac cheated on someone as beautiful and sweet as you. I could understand having an affair when your marriage isn't doing so well; that's why I turned to him, and I'm sure that's why you two originally got together..." Her words trailed off.

I finished her sentence. "But we didn't break it off because we became best friends before we ever made love. It was more than a year before we even kissed. He feels more like my husband than Pastor and I know he feels the same way. We talk about it all the time."

"I'm just glad we weren't best friends back then. And I can assure you that I have no interest in Mac, haven't for years; Mike and I have gotten our act together and I'm not interested in anything as exciting as a romantic affair. At any rate, I hope you gave him an earful when you found out."

"Yes, but it didn't help. He's been seeing Melissa Tight, getting together in the guest room in the church—"

The car swerved onto the shoulder briefly. "That son of a bitch!" Vanity shouted. "I'll kill him for you, if you're too squeamish. It's obvious that Mac is using you to get what he wants, and maybe part of that is companionship, but that's too much, Lady, can't you see?"

"See what?"

The car remained in the lane while Vanity explained what I should have seen all along. I was repeating the error I'd made with Pastor, falling for the first man with a smooth tongue who came along. Someone to take care of me. I was simply changing horses, getting a newer model. I admit that it looked bad, but that wasn't the case. For one thing, Mac and I had a real relationship; I wasn't simply serving as his wife or mistress, a prostitute, but was the person he talked to about whatever was bothering him. He felt bad about his weakness for sexual liaisons. Besides, I loved him and that made everything different. I would forgive him no matter how many times he strayed because I loved him and there was nothing that I could do about that. I finished my weak defense of my pathetic dependence by expressing my confidence that Mac wouldn't go looking for sexual partners if he were with me, someone he loved.

"All those romantic novels you read in college went to your head," Vanity began in rebuttal. "It doesn't matter that Mac means well, if he treats you like…like a prostitute or worse, a girl he likes to talk to but doesn't take seriously. When push comes to shove, sex matters between two people who say they're in love, which makes faithfulness critical to a healthy relationship."

I wanted to point out that she was a bigger fool than me because she actually believed the nonsense that she'd just shared with me. Apparently, it was okay to have extramarital sex as long as you asked for forgiveness later. It was all swept under the rug with even less effort than the Catholics expended. At least they had to go to confession and tell the priest. These Protestants only had to admit their sins to Jesus to be absolved of responsibility for their actions. I was not the fool, because I wasn't pretending Mac was anything other than what I'd seen with my own eyes. I accepted the consequences of my actions and dealing with a philandering man was something I could accept within limits, like when I wasn't available to satisfy his basic instinct. That's the price of being in love. I kept those arguments to myself.

"I see your point but I'm in love with Mac, for better or worse."

Vanity patted my hand comfortingly and said, "I understand how you feel. I guess that's why I stayed with Mike after he had an affair, which probably triggered mine—revenge or something like that. I got over it and I'm glad we stayed together."

"So, did you tell him about your affair, to relish the sweet taste of revenge?"

She laughed. "God, no. I didn't feel the need to make him feel as badly as I'd felt. That would have been cruel and unusual punishment. I was satisfied knowing that two could play at that game."

I felt better at her honest answer. I was in a completely different situation than Vanity, however: for one thing, I had no desire to get even with Mac over his dalliances and, for another, I didn't share her false sense of monogamous fidelity, which was obviously inapplicable to a lot of people; but most of all, I couldn't go to an omniscient deity who already knew about my behavior, and confess all in absolute privacy. My hypocrisy wasn't that great. I might have been a hypocrite all my life but that was going to end after Easter.

Despite our different views on extramarital affairs and religion, it was nice to have a best friend, especially someone a few years older. I looked at her profile while she was watching traffic, admiring her patrician features. She looked like someone born into money even though she'd come from a middle-class family just like me, an only child like me, blessed with good looks like me, but also possessing a quiet poise that hadn't been bestowed on me. Then I had a thought, which prompted me to laugh.

Vanity looked at me, a pleasantly expectant smile on her features. "Let's hear it. What's so funny?"

"Our backgrounds are so alike that we could have grown up in the same house. Imagine a slightly altered past, one in which you and I were—"

"Sisters!" she exclaimed, weaving again but remaining on the asphalt. "That's exactly how I feel, Lady. You are the younger sister my parents refused to give me, despite my asking them repeatedly to give me a sister for Christmas."

I laughed again because she hadn't figured it out yet, so I rushed to say, "And, just like in a romantic comedy, I'm going to marry an ex-boyfriend of yours!"

We were still laughing, casting uncertain glances at each other to make sure it really was funny, when Vanity pulled into the rectory driveway. It was a genuinely humorous situation to both of us. Maybe it's a strange quirk of my personality, that I saw Mac as having brought Vanity and me together, yet another reason I would never leave him. For another thing, confessing everything to Vanity meant I didn't have to keep her at arm's length anymore. I could let my hair down around at least one person, something I hadn't been able to do in more than ten years. She didn't mind that I was an agnostic.

I had repressed so many feelings over the years that I felt like a teenager, talking so openly with Vanity. However, there remained a sin so abominable that it couldn't be shared, especially with an older sister who believed that life began at conception.

Would a priest accept confession from an agnostic?

GARDEN PARTY

I had gotten involved with Vanity's church garden to placate Pastor and be near Mac, but after seeing Missy Lunatic's productive and prosperous hothouse enterprise, I was determined to make ours the best church garden in the county. Pastor had insisted that I become more involved with the congregation. I could have told him that I detested him, his church, and his congregation, but I didn't feel that way anymore. I was biding my time until Easter, when Mac and I would drop the pretense of our previous lives. At any rate, the garden didn't require that I pretend to understand what deviant thoughts were in the heads of Pastor's flock. It now appeared that my poor planning was going to grow into an oak tree, throwing me into direct contact with Mac's other romantic or sexual liaisons, all with him behaving like some kind of prophet. I felt as if I were a contestant on a game show, *Macbeth Lunatic's Lovers*.

Mac was mine, as far as I was concerned, despite both of us being married but not to each other. I hadn't interfered with his family, his marriage to Missy, her continuous efforts to brainwash their daughter to be as superstitious and ignorant as she, his business decisions, or even his religious beliefs. Our connection was more spiritual than physical although we had sex regularly. In fact, a lack of sex at home was a factor in Mac and me getting together; Missy hadn't liked it anymore after they'd been married ten years, so Mac had been looking around, if you know what I mean. Unfortunately, I didn't see him often enough to keep him satisfied. That's probably why he hooked up with Vanity for a couple of weeks and had several one-night stands with Melissa Tight. He's a real hound dog if he isn't getting enough sex at home. I wanted nothing more than to take care of that for him.

Missy was the problem of course. I didn't particularly like her because she was married to Mac—that and her fundamentalist religious beliefs. It was simply impossible to carry on a conversation when every other sentence coming out of her mouth was, "Praise the Lord." Apparently, I was so jealous of her that anyone could see if they knew what to look for, like Vanity. Nevertheless, I knew about their relationship and accepted it for the moment. I had unconsciously accepted Easter, the day Mac's *prophesy* would come true, as the day of our openly declaring our love and starting a new life together.

Vanity Blunt was an entirely different issue. I had wanted to put rat poison in her coffee when she told me about her dalliance with Mac, but I loved her as a sister now. She hadn't known about his relationship with me at the time and had felt dutifully guilty afterward. However, the thought of that little slut, Melissa Tight, lying in the guest bed with Mac, moaning with ecstasy, made my blood boil. She didn't fool me with her good little Christian act; she was a sexual predator. Vanity had confirmed my impression of what she called the *hot twat from Topeka*. The uncertainty caused by my relationship with Mac, in the presence of so many sexually active women pretending to have devoted their lives to Jesus was wearing on me, causing me to express my dislike of Pastor and his sanctimonious behavior. I had spent decades perfecting my role as the preacher's wife, only to see my efforts undone by jealousy. I had another reason to hate myself.

Until recently, Mac and I had been on different pages in the same book; he'd been in the first heat of romance whereas I was several chapters ahead, where two people are totally into each other. To him, we had just been having sex and enjoying being together but weren't supposed to be jealous of each other whereas the chapter I was reading clearly stated that I would be crazy not to hang onto my man, even if he weren't my husband. Mac now paid lip service to being committed to a future with me. There was no way to know if he meant it, not in his present condition, but I was becoming more certain every day that Vanity's appraisal had been accurate. Mac would say anything to maintain our relationship—friends with benefits.

When the day to break ground for the garden arrived, I fed Pastor, made the bed, cleaned up the kitchen, and pretended to pray before going out to meet Mac, a pot of fresh-brewed coffee waiting. I wasn't surprised when he arrived fifteen minutes late. He'd been doing that a lot since his miraculous conversion from an intelligent and trustworthy man into a prophet. Don't get me started. I ran into the rectory to fill an insulated cup with his favorite, custom blend, which had taken three years to figure out. I knew how difficult that simple act was for him. He'd been slipping into a fugue, forgetting things, having sudden bouts of anger, staring into space, signs of his worsening condition. He wasn't recovering from his probable stroke and I was certain that Vanity was right; Mac was about to drop dead, as if struck down by Satan while doing God's work. It was difficult to swallow my shrieks of frustration.

I was trying to understand our relationship myself after my abortion. I knew there was a solution but couldn't figure it out. He acted as if I weren't standing there, twenty feet away, so I strode over and offered the cup. "How did you sleep last night?"

Mac sipped the coffee before saying, "I don't sleep too well these days, Lady. God's work is never done."

That was nonsense. "God wouldn't ask you to do more than you're able to do, Mac. I accept that you were touched by the Lord, but you've never experienced such a miraculous event before. You may be overreacting. Do you see what I mean?"

He nodded, sipped his perfect coffee again, and headed towards the tractor he was going to use to break ground on the church's garden. "Sometimes, I wish you were with me more Lady, to help me understand what Jesus—the angel I mean— is telling me. I get confused…"

I glanced around to make sure no one else had arrived, rushed forward, and grabbed his arm. "Mac…I will always be here for you. You can call me anytime…in fact, the next time you have a vision or something, text me. I'll try to help you sort out what God is telling you, what you don't understand so well—"

Our conversation was interrupted when Pastor came out of the rectory, wearing jeans, a heavy coat, and a frown. I was no longer contrite while performing menial tasks for him, which upset his authoritarian schedule. The vulnerability he'd revealed to me, his uncertainty about the future of Trinity House, had been forgotten, replaced by the same dogmatic resolve people like him always relied on in difficult times. Mac ignored Pastor because of the tension that had redefined their relationship after Mac's apocalyptic pronouncement. He was no longer deferential and respectful but instead surly and combative, as if they were competing to lead the congregation up the stairway to heaven. Despite being Pastor's wife and an agnostic, if not atheist, I supported Mac in this theological competition.

"It looks like you're ready to start the Lord's work."

Pastor's friendly overture, barely concealing the frustration he was feeling because of Mac's precipitous revelation, was met with a noncommittal, "Whatever," tossed over Mac's shoulder as he climbed into the driver's seat of the open tractor and started the diesel engine, ending the conversation. I knew Mac's face so well that the changes in his facade after his spiritual rebirth didn't confuse me. Mac wasn't angry with Pastor; he was struggling to understand his new conception of reality, the world he was now convinced was real, the world that was going to end soon. Mac was afraid. I had tried to dissuade him from this apocalyptic perspective, only to be rebuffed. Nevertheless, I knew that once he'd taken his seat on the tractor, Mac would focus on the furrows he was about to create. He had become so distracted by whatever prophecy (probably delusion) his vision had revealed that he couldn't concentrate anymore.

Pastor, on the other hand, was angry at Mac's apparent rejection of his peaceful overture. He scowled, sipped his coffee, and half-smiled at me, possibly an acknowledgement of the years I'd spent playing his devoted wife.

I noticed Mac's coffee sitting on the towbar of the tractor and rushed to retrieve it, handing it to him with a supportive smile, before rejoining Pastor. Mac put the tractor in gear.

Pastor confronted me and said, "What's going on?"

I wasn't sure how to interpret his question. Was he asking me why Mac started the tractor before everyone else had arrived, making it difficult to celebrate the event? Maybe cut a ribbon or something? Or had he noticed my quickness to get Mac his coffee? Uncertain and guilt-ridden, I chose the easy answer. "Mac's going to start breaking ground on the garden, Pastor. Time is money."

Pastor looked at me the way he always did. Throughout our twenty-year marriage he'd always treated my ambivalent responses as proof that I was an idiot who couldn't read his mind and say exactly what he wanted to hear.

"Vanity is going to videotape the groundbreaking...for the Trinity House website. Why isn't Mac waiting for her?"

Pastor knew as well as I that his query begged the question; Mac was a different man after his vision, inspired by an angel to save Trinity House from an undefined calamity, or perhaps a biblical disaster. I shrugged. The real issue was that I was in love with Mac. It wasn't fear that kept me quiet, but uncertainty about Mac's feelings in his present mental condition. One more thing to worry about.

Our meaningless and bifurcated conversation was interrupted when Vanity appeared, her smartphone already recording as Mac lowered the plow to penetrate the recently thawed soil. We hugged quickly, gave each other a peck on the cheek, and she pursued him, sprinting between vantage points in her designer hiking boots as the steel blades broke through the hard surface to reveal a sandy soil Mac hadn't thought worth the price of seeds to cultivate. He would return in a few weeks to plant squash, melons, tomatoes, onions, potatoes, and other vegetables, and apply lots of fertilizer. Vanity would probably document the planting; and I would be there for Mac, helping when I could, trying to reduce his personal burden. The old Mac, the man I'd fallen in love with, wouldn't have given such an enterprise a second thought, knocking it out with a grin, but the new Mac resented any activity not directly related to the message he'd received from an angel. Misery was written on his face.

I watched Vanity chase Mac's tractor around the muddy, weed-infested field. I had despised her as a has-been starlet, until she'd admitted having an affair with Mac; then I'd hated her for being intimate with someone I cared about; but when I'd learned that we were cast from the same mold, she had become the sister I'd never had and the person I held closest, after Mac. Yes, I watched her, smiling at her efforts to get the best shot, waving, laughing with her, enjoying the moment. It was like being with Mac, so I guess I loved her; in fact, I'd told her so on several occasions. Thankfully, she'd expressed the same feeling. We had laughed until we'd cried at our romantic situations. Despite being a highly respected member of the community, Mike resented Pastor for being an authority even if only on spiritual matters. Since Mac's close encounter with Jesus, he and Mike had become allies because of their common opposition to Pastor. Vanity and I weren't only sisters but cheerleaders for the same team! Finally accepting that I was in love with Mac, she had pledged her support for whatever I chose to do because we had become family.

I glanced down at the dress I was wearing, meant to get Mac's attention, then at Vanity's designer jeans. I looked like a floozie, an ignorant country girl. I was about to go inside and dress more appropriately but was confronted by Mike Blunt, a man described by his faithful wife as ponderous.

"This is so exciting, Mike, don't you agree?"

"An undertaking as substantial as a faith-based, vegetable garden the fruits of which will be shared with the community is not too different from the first crops planted at Plymouth by our ancestors who, though facing seemingly insurmountable obstacles, did not allow themselves to be discouraged and endeavored to persevere in their effort to claim an unspoiled land from the savages that occupied our pubescent nation."

I smiled in response to his insufferable grammar, refraining from expressing my progressive, liberal ideas about the genocidal and misogynist roots of the United States. "Well put, Mike. We're just like the Pilgrims, right here in Modoc. It's exciting to be part of something so special." I had become adept at biting my tongue when speaking to Pastor's flock, especially the *elders*.

"Vanity's action is consistent with her taking a not inconsequential interest in the garden," Mike said tautly. He was insufferable, didn't even speak legalese well, and a narcissist, but he wasn't stupid.

"She was the inspiration for the endeavor."

He nodded tautly.

I continued, "Mac is an expert with the plow and the hoe. His attention to detail has impressed me for years. I enjoy watching him work around the church and rectory. Vanity has probably noticed his…" I paused for effect before adding, "physical fortitude, born of spending his time working with the earth instead of sitting behind a desk. Plowing deep and harvesting the fruit of his labor." I added that last for my own benefit. I hadn't given Mac the opportunity to reap the harvest he had sown, and I hated myself for it.

Mike turned to me and said, as if deposing a witness for a misdemeanor, "Vanity's sudden interest in the garden is not inconsistent with a pattern of obfuscation, intended to hide something she doesn't want others to discern. Don't you agree?"

I was accustomed to Mike's manner of speaking, but he had never been as explicit in saying what was on his mind before. With his words, he had actually accused Vanity of hiding something. This was more than I had expected from a gardening event on a Saturday morning. I cleared my throat for effect and chose my words carefully before responding.

"Brother Lunatic is a handsome man. God blessed him with good looks and a strong body, but he was also blessed with an unassuming personality. The salt of the earth."

Mike looked at me as if I had just told a flagrant lie under oath, his lawyerly mind looking for a way to expose my false testimony. His eyes narrowed instinctively as he retorted, "Macbeth Lunatic was blessed with a libido the size of Kansas, Lady—no offense meant. He's a fox in the henhouse. Men like him keep the angels up nights."

I was surprised at his openness. He was right of course, but I had never imagined Mike Blunt speaking so frankly. He must have seen something in Vanity's recent behavior to make him take pause…something subtle related to admitting her past affair with Mac. I trusted Vanity more than Mike's intuition, with respect to her trying to steal Mac from me. She was simply enjoying doing something creative. I returned his questioning gaze with a penetrating look, one eyebrow lifted slightly as I replied, "Isn't it possible that your sudden awareness of Vanity's interest in Mac's work for Trinity House, and anything it might imply, could be related to his openness in sharing the vision given to him by an angel?"

Unperturbed, he half-smiled at me and said, "The evidence is not unambiguous, so we cannot rule out that possibility. However, as you may know, I support his claim to having communicated with an angel, subject to verification by events not yet evident."

"Yes, you did, Mike…" I stopped to think about my next words. He was anticipating what I might say. Whatever I think about Mike Blunt personally, he is one of the most astute members of the Trinity House board, so I gave him a crumb to chew on.

"Mac's sudden notoriety may remind you of when he first joined Trinity House." I paused only a second before adding, "He quickly set his sights on Trinity House after coming to Modoc, like a swashbuckler landing on the deck of a ship, sword in hand. Through his *pro bono* landscape work, he brought stability and reinvigorated the congregation, doing the Lord's work in his own way." Now, I raised both eyebrows to challenge his memory. Maybe he would remember events as Vanity had described them…or not.

Mike apparently remembered events the same as his wife. I almost laughed at the dour look that came over his face. Before he could respond, Melina Light arrived with her husband in tow. I really disliked Dim Light because of how he treated Mac. But it was Melina who got my attention. She was dressed inappropriately for February, more excited than usual, not bothering with greetings, rushing into the field, getting Mac's attention by jumping along next to the tractor, taking his offered hand, kissing it in front of her husband…and me.

Convinced that Melina was my newest adversary, I turned to Dim and expressed my disapproval. "Your wife is acting like a groupie, Dim. What's going on? Has her fascination with occultism led her to using psychedelic drugs to hear God's voice?"

Wearing his usual confused expression Dim replied, "Melina has a gift that most of us don't possess. The Lord speaks to her more clearly than to ordinary people like me…and you." He looked at me as if we were both losers in the spiritual world, which made me angrier than the possibility that Melina had seduced Mac.

I couldn't keep from saying, "Melina's spiritual beliefs are becoming more like those of the pagans who influenced the Catholic church—she was raised Catholic in Argentina, wasn't she? They worship false gods down there…"

Dim looked at me uncomprehendingly, so I answered my own question. "Sexual intercourse is fundamental to every pagan belief system in the world. It's based on the seasons Dim, which bring death and rebirth for the world, including humans. You know…have sex and the world will continue…it works."

He scoffed and said, "People don't think like that anymore. Melina has no romantic interest in Macbeth Lunatic. You shouldn't be so cynical, Lady. He's sharing a message given to him by an angel. Some people, like Melina, can sense his spiritual transformation. Don't judge others by your own limited view."

I looked at Melina, riding on the tractor with Mac, sitting on his lap, her ample breasts brushed by his arm around her narrow waist, her short skirt riding up her thighs. Mac had never taken me for a ride on his tractor. I could almost feel his anticipation pressing against me. Mac and Melina were going to have sex right there in front of us, plowing the field. And Dim would probably approve of their actions. I saw no reason to point out the obvious, so I turned to Mike Blunt for consolation. Vanity was still videotaping Mac and Melina having virtual sex on the tractor, Mac plowing the soil, Melina making sure he plowed her.

I cleared my throat to get Mike's attention and quietly said, "*Menage á trois.*"

"Huh?" he mumbled, as aware as I of Mac and Melina's sexually promiscuous behavior.

"I'm glad Missy isn't here to see this."

"What are you talking about, Lady? There's nothing going on with Mac and Melina…and certainly nothing with Vanity. I can't believe you would even suggest something so…"

I half-smiled and finished his sentence, "…human. Never mind, it was just a passing thought."

Mike started to answer but was interrupted when Missy Lunatic arrived, which strengthened my belief in a universal intelligence, if not a god. I hugged her, exchanged pleasantries, and with an outstretched arm, indicated Mac sitting on his tractor in the field, with Melina Light sitting on his lap, a look of sexual rapture on her face.

"Why is Melina Light sitting on Mac's lap? Is he showing her how to drive the tractor?"

I tossed a sarcastic smile at Mike Blunt. The forlorn look he returned repudiated his earlier dismissal of a possible romantic connection between Mac and other members of Trinity House. Mike knew as well as I what was happening. I was not going to respond to Missy's question, leaving him to explain the unexplainable. The subtle shake of my head was reinforced by a stolid look.

He chose to tell a white lie, too surprise to speak legalese. "Well…yeh, that's what it is. She got so excited at seeing a tractor—I guess she was never on a farm—well, she just ran over to the tractor…and he pulled her up, to keep from running over her…she was about to get run over…"

Dim added, "That's right. Melina's a city girl. Never been on a farm in her life, not even since moving to Modoc…" He looked no more confused than usual at supporting a story that contradicted his own eyes.

Missy is very gullible, so she accepted Mike's explanation. Having seen how Melina had joined Mac on the tractor as if it had been planned, I wasn't willing to go along with his fabricated story. Besides, I didn't like Missy because of her relationship with Mac, which aroused my connubial instincts towards him.

"She looks pretty comfortable if you ask me. And why is he holding her so closely? She isn't a toddler."

That got Missy's attention. She squinted at the couple sitting on the seat of Mac's tractor, facing away from us, Melina blocked by Mac's body, leaving what they were doing with their hands to the imagination. My mind had filled in the blanks and already written a novel. I was beside myself with jealousy when I added, "I wonder where his hands are…"

Pastor interrupted. "Let's not get carried away. The Lord is moving unheard through the congregation of Trinity House, and Mac has been visited by an angel, creating a sense of anticipation that has enervated everyone, especially those who are most sympathetic to the Holy Ghost…like Melina. We are only human and we get confused during such spiritual times and our actions can be misconstrued…"

I had never gotten used to Pastor's poor grammar. "Who do you think is overreacting—Melina or Mac?" The words slipped out of my mouth. I wanted to cover the offensive organ but didn't, hoping my verbal error wouldn't be noticed.

Dim chimed in, "Melina is very religious, as we all know. She speaks to angels almost every day…they've told her that Mac is a true prophet. She has to be near him to get the signals clear…"

I wanted to laugh in his face.

Missy said, "Okay. Now, I understand, Dim. Thanks for explaining."

She was an idiot, or else she didn't care what Mac did. I wondered if any of these people cared about anything. I was prepared to accept their apathy as another obstacle in my battle for Mac's soul, and then Melissa Tight appeared. She had come to the church to work on a piece of music she was writing for the band. She was dressed like me, in a spring dress with a hemline just above the knee.

"Why is Brother Lunatic fondling Mrs. Light on the tractor?"

The tractor was now plowing a furrow that faced us. Mac had apparently forgotten that we could see him…his right hand was massaging Melina Light's large breast. Vanity was videotaping them and, from her position in the middle of the field, she must have gotten a good view. She lowered her phone, before walking towards the rectory shaking her head. Mac released Melina's breast, but she didn't stop doing the mambo in his lap. Pastor responded to Melissa's query as Vanity stepped onto the concrete porch.

"Let's not get carried away. Research has shown that when we can't see clearly, like at a distance, we see what we expect to see, the image filled in from memory or else we make it up. He was simply repositioning his hand on the wheel."

Melissa's retort gave me pause. "I know what a hand on my breast feels like, Pastor, and his hand was checking for ripeness." She turned and stalked into the church, leaving everyone confused, except me and Pastor.

She was having an affair with my husband—Pastor Church—the leader of Trinity House, and she was expressing dissatisfaction with some aspect of their relationship. I was glad to have Pastor distracted so I smiled at him, patted his arm gently, and said, "I think Miss Tight imagines what it would be like to have a beau who could take such liberties. But in Mac's case it was an optical illusion."

Apparently, I had become an expert, because everyone accepted my judgement. Except Vanity.

"He was squeezing her breast like a ripe grapefruit—maybe a cantaloupe—I know because I was fondled many times during my acting career, and she wasn't complaining. I don't want to judge because there's a lot going on right now, what with Mac's vision, Covid, the race riots, and all that."

No one responded to her analysis.

I watched Mac and Melina on the tractor when they turned into the next row, where we couldn't see his hands. I knew how his limbs moved—his hands, arms, shoulders, neck, all of him—well enough to know where his hands were. Melina had come to the groundbreaking wearing a short skirt with no leggings, in February. I was willing to bet she hadn't bothered with underwear either. The others wandered off, leaving Dim and me to watch as Mac and Melina plowed several more rows. Dim finally drifted into the church. I kept watching Mac, who was definitely plowing Melina.

When Mac turned the tractor towards me on the last row, I saw his face. And a lot more. In the ecstasy of their public intercourse, Melina's short dress was lifted out of the way, an experience with which I was familiar. She hadn't recovered sufficiently to hide her expression of sexual bliss. I wasn't filled with righteous indignation, affronted, or even shocked. I was jealous and wished it had been me on the tractor with Mac. Melina was a walking-talking sex doll, complete with huge breasts and an excitable disposition. I didn't see their behavior as debauchery, adultery, abomination, or even sin.

She was my competition and I wanted Mac more than her. I had to eliminate Melina Light.

NINETY-FIVE THESES

To Lady and the others watching from the rectory porch, it must have looked like Melina and I were having sex on the tractor, and we would have been if it hadn't been for logistical problems. She hadn't worn underwear but I was fully clothed. I fondled her with both hands while she steered. She had what she called a spiritually powerful orgasm while trying to do the same for me, rubbing against my groin. Melina is twenty years older than Melissa and not even in the same class—sexually speaking—so all I got out of the experience was an uncomfortable erection. I guess our spiritual frequencies weren't aligned that day. It may have been my fault. Trying to enhance the experience, I was imagining Melissa sitting in my lap the whole time.

Speaking of spiritual matters, I haven't heard from Jesus since Vernon Huckster's funeral. He hasn't told me what to do next and I'm a little concerned. Melina isn't however, because she has daily communications with the Holy Spirit, even if they aren't as clear as mine. I'm supposed to expand on the prophecy I'd received during Vernon's funeral. By the way, his daughter thinks he would have been pleased with my eulogy. I've been rereading it every day and thinking about it, but it doesn't make sense to me, even though it was well written. There's nothing to add. Melina hasn't been much help, only suggesting that I talk to people face to face. That's what she's doing, so I've been talking to people, repeating what I'd already said and adding some more complaints Missy thought of.

But all of that begs the question of my impromptu

prophecy from the Lord, about Easter being a fateful day, possibly referring to His retribution on the unbelievers. I have to wait for Jesus to explain that better. For now, I'm doing as Melina suggested.

At Missy and Melina's urging, I make a list of what Lady humorously calls my *Ninety-Five Theses*. She has to explain her pun and I laugh too, but I don't think the Fundamentalists have as much to complain about as Martin Luther did back in 1517 AD. Also, I'm starting to wonder why Jesus chose me as His prophet when I'm not even a Fundamentalist; at least, I wasn't until I spoke so forcefully at the funeral, now they treat me as if I was a politician. The Evangelicals look at me as if I betrayed them. With all this going on, I'm pretty confused by the time I get up the nerve to speak to Pastor about it. He's very polite and respectful and things should end right there in the church office.

Pastor's holding the printout of my *Ninety-Five Theses* in his left hand, his reading glasses swinging like a pendulum in his right. He looks as confused as me when he finally says, "I have tried to militate in favor of most of these items and Trinity House already is…" He pauses to put on the glasses and skim the list, before finishing, "teaching Creationism in Sunday School. We can't add it as a subject in the Pre-K and kindergarten classes because those receive Federal funding. We would have to give up substantial financial aid, which we could do if our students were paying tuition. That day will come but it hasn't arrived yet, so we have to compromise with Uncle Sam."

The reading glasses are swinging again, expressing Pastor's impatience with my list of foolish demands. I have a copy too, so I go to the item that everyone felt was important, both Fundamentalists and Evangelicals. I point at the fine print and Pastor's glasses return to rest on the bridge of his nose.

"The items are sort of listed in order of importance. What about the fifth bullet?"

He squints and replies, "What exactly is *equal representation*?"

I'm not sure either but I don't want to admit it. I'm becoming angry at Pastor's condescending and insulting attitude. He's speaking to me as if I was…as if I were the lawn boy, just like Lady said. Trembling with anger, I answer his stupid question, voiced only to belittle me and my people.

"*Equal representation* means that Fundamentalists should have the same number of members on the Board as the Evangelicals." That gets his attention.

The glasses come to rest on the desk in front of Pastor, his eyes now focused on my face, maybe my nose rather than my eyes. "The Board is comprised of four members, with me as the chairman, the tie breaker. They were elected by the congregation last year. There was no election campaign because the congregation had determined, through transparent processes, that these were the people they wanted to represent them. A few names came to the surface and they were elected. So, what are you talking about?"

To be honest, I hadn't paid any attention to the whole Church Board campaign. I'd been too busy making a living. Thus, I don't have an answer.

The glasses are back in motion as Pastor's words fill the silence. "For another thing, the people of Trinity House are not divided into political parties. The differences between what you call Evangelicals and Fundamentalists in your list of grievances are smaller than the range of opinions within either one of these artificially labelled groups. Trinity House is not a country, a state, or a city; it is a family of 343 like-minded individuals who have chosen to worship God in the same way."

He slaps the list of grievances on the desk, sets the glasses on them as a paperweight, and looks into my eyes this time. I want to look away but I can't.

"What's really bothering you Mac? If you don't speak openly, we can't find a solution. Why did you suddenly become a self-appointed political leader in a nondenominational church? And ask yourself why we are having this conversation in the first place."

He's trying to ridicule me. No, he's actually making fun of my not having gone to college, as if that makes me stupid.

"Please precede, Mac, but I would add that you seem to have a deep-seeded resentment against authority, and you see the Board as being an authority that is dictating rules for you to live by. Is that even close to how you feel?"

"Why is Dim Light an elder?" I finally ask, my voice

trembling with barely concealed rage.

He's surprised by my question but recovers quickly. "So, that's it? I like the way you get to the point, Mac, even if not always immediately." The glasses come to rest again, this time next to the printed list.

"He was elected to be an elder. The process is written in Trinity House's founding document, our Constitution if you like. However, I think I see where this is going, so let's cut to the chase. You can correct me if I've assumed too much."

I nod, so he continues, "Dim Light has been given a responsibility for which he is obviously not qualified and is treating you like a hired hand. You can't help but question such an unjust situation and I don't blame you."

I find my voice. "Then why don't you correct it?"

"Because I am not a dictator, even if I do stand in a pulpit and speak authoritatively several times a week. My authority is limited to how our consensual doctrine will be presented to the church and the community. Brother Light was elected by Trinity House to become an elder and, in a separate election, chosen by the congregation to be on the Board and given responsibility for building and grounds maintenance."

I'm struggling to control my outrage against such injustice. My fists clench tightly as I say, "Can't you override his decisions?"

The glasses were in the hand again, Pastor's head shaking. "Only the Board can do that. I don't have the authority." The glasses come to rest, dangling from his right hand, as he adds, "If you'd taken an interest in Trinity House before having a close encounter with the Holy Spirit, you could have become an elder and not be answering to Dim Light."

That doesn't sound right to me. Lady told me about the conversations she'd witnessed, not to mention those that had occurred out of her hearing.

"You're a smooth talker, Pastor, I'll give you that, but I'm not buying what you're selling, nor are the Fundamentalists, a group you pretend doesn't exist. You're running an old boy's club here in Trinity House, which is why someone like Dim Light ended up on the board to represent the Fundamentalists. I see you as clear as day now and the others will too, after I tell them what I know—"

He starts to interrupt but I don't give him a chance. "You wrote the bylaws and made sure you would always have the dominant voice, just like any two-bit dictator in a third-world country. You are a liar and a despot." Not waiting for a response, I march out of the church office, my blood boiling, certain of what Jesus had wanted me to figure out on my own.

The next day, having coffee in the church, I tell Lady about my conversation with Pastor. She chastises me for getting angry when he was only trying to find a solution. Then, when I'm agreeing with her, she changes course and tells me that it wouldn't have mattered what I did because of the systemic prejudice of Trinity House, set in its bylaws. When I ask her why she's so interested in what we Christians are doing, she laughs and plays a song she had just learned. Her voice is like an angel's as she accompanies herself on the organ, giving me a private recital of an old Christian pop song called *Burning Bridges*. I had certainly burned several bridges recently, especially those that led to Pastor.

A couple days later, Lady is waiting with a cup of coffee for me when I come to the church to meet Dim. She doesn't lift an eyebrow when I fortify the coffee with rum.

The soil is too sandy for farming, which is why Trinity House had purchased ten acres so cheaply. It wasn't all going to be part of our community outreach program, however, so only one semi arrives loaded with fertilizer. Manure wouldn't be enough on this poor soil, not if we were going to be feeding the hungry with nutritious vegetables. The delivery driver asks where I want twenty pallets of fertilizer placed, which reminds me of a conversation I'd had with Dim Light.

I say, "We've got a semi arriving, loaded with fertilizer for the garden. This is a good time to construct a sturdy—"

Dim's head is shaking as he says, "Just get it out of sight. I don't want to see bags of fertilizer lying around during the Easter holiday."

The storm cellar under the church is big enough to hold several hundred people in a pinch, like during a tornado. It's well-lit and empty, except for some banquet tables and chairs and decorations and such. For whatever reason, there's a ramp leading to the basement. Maybe it's one of those federal rules Pastor mentioned, requiring wheelchair access to get financial assistance for the preschool. There actually was one little girl in a wheelchair attending the preschool, her tuition paid by a federal program. I'm wondering why such a sturdy basement, suitable as a storm cellar and equipped with a wheelchair ramp, didn't have emergency lighting as required by the building code. The thought of a couple hundred people jammed in the basement, with no power and thus no lights is scary. I sure don't carry a flashlight with me when I go to church.

At any rate, Jesus solves the dilemma of having the church grounds unencumbered by bags of fertilizer and needing a convenient place to store this important resource. In his words, I should "Render unto Caesar that which is Caesar's," so I move thousands of pounds of fertilizer into the basement. The thought of ignoring Dim's instructions and doing things differently, possibly calling the Oklahoma Agricultural Safety Commission, never enters my mind. Such action would violate my oath of allegiance to Trinity House and Jesus hadn't told me to go against the elders. My actions are implicitly approved by the Board because several members drop by and watch me store an explosive material under the church. I place the last pallet in the basement and wave to Pastor and Dim, before loading my tractor on the trailer.

Dim Light joins me as I'm preparing to leave. "Good job, Mac. I'm glad to see that unsightly mess cleaned up." He's grinning, pleased as punch.

I've been talking to Lady every day, but not having sex. She's mostly a spiritual counselor who uses a lot of metaphors. I think of one to share with her when we're left alone just before I leave.

"We reap what we sow, and I think Trinity House is planting a formidable garden. I can't wait to see the harvest."

She laughs nervously.

PROSTITUTE

Pastor tried to work with Mac, despite being called a liar to his face. When I'd told Mac about the systemic prejudice within Trinity House, I hadn't meant that the Fundamentalists were being repressed socially, only that the majority of the congregation had less-radical views about the relationship between the Bible and the modern world. Fortunately, Pastor was a good man whose heart was in the right place, so he turned the other cheek. From Pastor's description of their last encounter, Mac had probably suffered additional brain damage during their argument. Vanity was dismayed when I told her about it, insisting that we had to override Mac and Missy and get him to a doctor. Unfortunately, there was nothing we could do but watch and try to be there the next time it happened, hopefully to call an ambulance while he was unconscious or obviously impaired. Without interference from Missy. At any rate, his mental condition settled down over the next couple of days, his anger subsided, he admitted that Jesus hadn't recently spoken to him, and he was still committed to our emancipation.

Not wanting to contribute to his next brain attack, I didn't mention the tractor episode to Mac, but Vanity had a lot to say about it. She showed me some video that wasn't going to be part of her promotional package for the garden project. Melina's short skirt was out of the way and several of Mac's fingers were buried in her, stroking hard, while his other hand was squeezing her ample breast as if he were milking a cow. Vanity's video caught the moment for posterity, the sublime expression on Melina's face, the look of surprise on Mac's when he saw Vanity recording the moment.

"I think it's safe to say that Mac is doing the mambo with Melina," Vanity said dryly when the clip had finished.

"I know what you're thinking—"

She held up her hand. "No, you don't. I'm not going to lecture you about what a wolf he is, or how easily he succumbs to every tramp who spreads her legs for him. That's not what I'm thinking."

"Then…what?"

Vanity sighed and began, "I wasn't completely open with you Lady, about Mike's sexual dalliances. It wasn't only one time and it wasn't in the past. It's continuing, even today, as we speak, he's…" Her eyes filled with tears.

I rushed to her, blurting, "Is he having an affair with Melina…Melissa?"

"Probably, but that's not what I'm talking about. Mike is just like Mac, a wolf in sheep's clothing." Her red, swollen eyes looked into mine as she continued, "I thought Mike had learned his lesson after my discovering his infidelity and calling him out, but…it's my fault for not flaunting my affair with Mac in his face. I kept it to myself, thinking I would spare him the shame of knowing that his wife had deliberately hurt him. I was wrong."

"What…has something happened?" I stammered.

Her head, framed by a coiffure of neatly trimmed blond hair, wobbled hopelessly. "This all happened last year, but I'm certain that nothing has changed. Mike went to a regional meeting of the American Bar Association in Milwaukee. He'd invited me to join him, which I declined because I'd gotten used to staying in Modoc while raising the children. Anyway, I changed my mind and flew up to join him. I know he drinks when he goes to these conferences, so I was expecting to find him out with some other lawyers, carousing. I got a key to his room when I proved I was his wife, and I wasn't acting when I told them about expecting to have a pleasant weekend."

The images of Mac and Melina on the tractor were flashing before my fear-clouded eyes as I exclaimed, "Don't say it! Please, don't tell me what you saw!"

Vanity gently pulled my hands away from my eyes and said, "It was worse. I entered what I expected to be an empty hotel room and found Mike in the act. And the woman he was fucking was as gorgeous as Melissa Tight. I stood there silently as they consummated their relationship. Then, she noticed me standing at the door with a suitcase."

"Oh my god! What did you do?"

"She was fumbling around, trying to get Mike's attention, when I announced my presence by asking if she was a prostitute. It so happened that she was, so I turned away while she got dressed and left the room, thanking me on her way out."

I understood why Vanity had shared such a personally traumatic story with me. Mike needed to have a sexual experience more often than she had been willing to share it with him. Some men would have accepted the status quo but men like Mike and Mac didn't understand the unimportance of sex as a regular activity once children had been raised successfully. Their hormones raged as if they were teenagers. Vanity, Melissa, and Melina had simply been servicing Mac's undiminished hormonal demands. But where did I fit into the equation?

Before I could point out the similarity of my position to the prostitute's, Vanity shook her head and interjected, "You are not the prostitute Lady, but instead the victim like I was. However, the situation is complicated by Missy's presence. She is definitely not a prostitute, but a sincere and devoted wife who will be hurt, but that doesn't make you the prostitute. My situation with Mike is much simpler...do you see what I mean?"

My thoughts were swirling, my stomach suddenly overturning, the world floating into a void as I shouted what I had always known. "I am a prostitute! I'm nothing more than a harlot, a slut who satisfies men's pleasure for a price. That woman Mike fucked was at least honest."

I laughed loudly and continued, "I should have become a professional. I'll bet I'm as appealing as her, right?" I glanced at Vanity but she wasn't going to answer my rhetorical question.

I continued, "And we don't want to forget that I do

windows!" I was on my feet now, out of control. "I'll fuck anyone who offers to take care of me. Hell, I'll even have children for them, taking the risk of dying in childbirth or being abandoned with my offspring. I don't care what happens to me as long as I don't have to think about the consequences of my decisions. Fuck me! Just fuck me! Just do it! Just fuck…"

I collapsed on the sofa, sobbing, a thunderstorm of tears drenching my blouse.

Vanity's hands were caressing my face in an attempt to console me. "No, no, no, no, no, sweetheart, that's not what you are. You fell in love with Pastor, even if you don't love him anymore. That's all real. It's so real. It's nothing like a woman who takes money to lie on her back and let a man pretend to be making love with her. No, no, no, don't ever think that way. I don't ever want to hear you talk like that again." She comforted me until my tears subsided and I was able to speak.

"I know you mean well, Vanity, but my position really is no different than that of the prostitute Mike hired in Milwaukee. It might be different for you. I don't know what you think, down deep, and I'm not going to speculate. I sold my soul to the Devil when I married a man like Pastor. We have nothing in common, except our belief in fantasy, his illusion being religious and mine more existential—where will my next meal come from?"

Vanity and I kissed, caressing each other's cheeks and arms for several minutes, until she said, "You are not a prostitute, no matter how you frame it. You are a middle-age woman who is correcting errors she made in her youth. Is that an acceptable interpretation for you?"

I nodded. I scoffed. Then I said, "I probably would have committed suicide if I hadn't met you. My situation is untenable."

"Honey, don't do anything without talking to me first. I'll always be here for you. Your situation has a simple solution, one Mac has confirmed even after his spiritual awakening. You are going to be with the man you love after Easter."

"What about Missy, and Pastor? What happens to them?"

"Divorce is common among Christians, just like with everybody else, even Moslems. Jesus isn't as authoritarian a leader as some would have us believe. Breaking up a marriage is never easy, but it can be done well, as so many divorced Christians can attest. I'll send you a link to a good web site." She took my hand in hers and added, "Based on what I've seen, I think you are making the right decision. As a bonus, you won't feel like a prostitute after you and Mac are together. That's something to be excited about."

My response was delayed until I found my voice. "You saved my life."

We hugged for a long time.

NEGOTIATIONS

Seeing Lady sitting beneath a picture of Jesus calms my nerves, even though she's a devout agnostic. I can't help saying, "You are a lot like our Savior."

She looks over her shoulder and replies, "I suppose you're referring to my reason for being here, Brother Lunatic, because I don't look anything like the depiction of Jesus in that painting." She makes her point with the flick of a wrist, an index finger emphasizing her rebuttal. I'm struggling not to speak my mind.

Pastor interjects, "I think he was referring to your well-deserved reputation as an openminded member of the congregation Lady, a talent that has come to our attention of late. Perhaps you can shed some light on the complaints Mac has recently shared with the congregation. Any ideas?"

Lady had refused to talk to me about what I should say or, more importantly, what she would say during this meeting with Pastor. She doesn't like being dragged into a sectarian argument—a phrase she'd made me look up on the internet. I don't have anything new to say, but at least her presence will keep me from getting so angry this time.

She clears her throat, avoiding looking at me, and partly answers Pastor's question. "Mac is antiauthoritarian, which isn't surprising with a nondenominational congregation like Trinity House. He resents you Pastor, as well as the Board, and anyone in a position to make rules he's expected to follow." She looks at me like I'm someone she's never seen before and adds, "Anyone could claim to have had a personal experience with the Holy Spirit, which is why the Catholic Church goes through a complicated procedure before declaring someone a saint. Mac is basically making such a claim, without proof or even circumstantial evidence."

Pastor looks at me as if he's my father and says, "Well, Mac, would you like to refute Lady's comment?"

I sure do, like that she thinks I'm crazy. She doesn't believe me and all that business about our beliefs not being that different…wait a minute, that was my suggestion and all she did was not argue. Besides, she isn't a Christian at all, so what do I care what she thinks, but maybe this is a test to see if I really love her and she's waiting for my response. Damnit! She should have been an actress, the way she's looking at me so casually, as if we hadn't made love that morning. I have to say something but without help from Lady. I'd spoken to Missy about my meeting with Pastor and she hadn't been any help at all, telling me to let the Lord speak through me. It ain't that easy.

"Well, I guess that's true, about my not liking to be told what to do. But I figure we're all like that, like she said, about Trinity House not being a regular church." I try not to smile sarcastically at her, but a little bit slips in. "But I take offense at her calling me a liar. Why would I pretend to have an…have an angel appear and talk to me in a vision? That's the most ridiculous thing I've ever heard. There's absolutely no reason for me to make up something like that." I frown at Lady, who surprises me by responding.

"I did not accuse you of being a liar, Brother Lunatic. I only said that you have not offered any proof of your close encounter with the Holy Spirit, any evidence that would satisfy the Catholic Church, and they've been doing this kind of thing for quite a while."

While I'm thinking of something to say, Pastor adds, "It would be helpful, if not conclusive, and most certainly convincing, if you could give proof of your physical and mental health. When was your last physical exam?"

"When I got out of the Army. I'm in perfect condition."

Lady scoffs and I frown at her again.

Pastor says, "That was more than twenty years ago. You could have developed any number of neurological diseases in the meantime. I'll tell you what I'll do, Mac, if you get a physical and are judged as healthy as you think you are, I will support your claim of speaking with the Lord because I'm convinced that your *prophecy* is about bringing the members of Trinity House into closer communion with each other and the Lord. Fraud is not an issue, but there are problems of the brain that can cause delusions. I don't think that's the case with a healthy young man like yourself, but it's my duty to make certain. It's kind of like the Catholic Church's verifying sainthood." He nods at Lady, who's smiling triumphantly.

His proposal isn't so bad. I just get a physical, blood pressure checked, height and weight measured, a tongue depressor, a stethoscope against my chest...then I remember some of the other tests the Army docs did when I'd had my entrance exam. They'd asked me about blurry vision, sleeping habits, whether I heard voices, mood swings, stuff like that. Doctors are pretty smart and I don't think I can fool them, but then a compromise occurs to me.

"I would be happy to oblige you, Pastor, but I think we're all supposed to see the Lord's sign together with no interference of any kind. I'll go get that medical exam, to prove that there's nothing wrong with me, but not until after Easter. That's just two months from now. If I break the chain of events, the people of Trinity House won't receive the message meant for them. The angel was clear about that."

Pastor's head is shaking when Lady says, "That is an unreasonable request, unless you agree to a few conditions."

"Like what?"

"Until the good people of Trinity House have been assured that you are not a raving lunatic, a colloquial name for someone suffering—"

"Wait a minute, that's my name. What are you saying?"

Lady holds her hand up to calm me and it works like it usually does, then she continues, "That is a coincidence, but at any rate, the congregation needs assurances that you are not raving madly, before they can accept your vision. You must refrain from any more accusations against Pastor or the Board and limit your oratory to spiritual matters."

"Why?" I ask.

Pastor continues, "Because otherwise you have a grace period to make one-sided claims against the people who were chosen by the congregation as their representatives. This is not a political campaign and there is no place in Christian dialogue for unfounded accusations against our spiritual leaders."

Lady's smug smile tells me that I should agree to the conditions.

"I know something about the law," I say without thinking. I don't know anything about the law, maybe a few phrases picked up in TV shows. "That's a gag order, to keep me from speaking the Word of God."

Pastor responds, "That's right, Mac, because we have granted you a sixty-day injunction before requiring proof that you aren't suffering from an undiagnosed medical condition. We all wait and see without altering the situation. Does this seem reasonable to you?"

"What's in it for me?" I ask, grimacing when I glance at Lady, who is shaking her head slightly. Too bad I hadn't kept my eyes on her.

Pastor sits up straight and says, "I think you're confused, Mac, probably because of what you think you have witnessed. You are an honorable man, so I'll give you the benefit of the doubt, but I am certain that you are suffering from delusions brought on by a stroke. I can't force you to take care of your health, but I can speak out against false prophets, no matter why they arise. I am convinced that you are a false prophet, while still being a good man. Which of these men am I speaking to now? In other words, can I trust you to keep a bargain?"

I risk a quick glance at Lady, whose head's slight motion is telling me to agree, so I say, "I won't say anything else about you or Satan, or the Board being deceived into working for the antichrist, or how the Fundamentalists are being preyed on by the Evangelicals. Is that good enough?"

Lady suddenly speaks. "I have serious doubts about your ability to fulfill promises, Brother Lunatic."

WAKEUP CALL

Lady's parting words at my meeting with Pastor sting. She thinks I'm a double-crosser, that I'll go back on my word at the first opportunity. That is so far off that I wonder why I had agreed to divorce Missy and spend the rest of my life with her, a woman who obviously doesn't know me at all. Jesus had been silent on the matter, so I confront Lady while I'm getting ready to spray herbicide on the field.

"I don't understand why you would say in front of Pastor that I'm unreliable. Can you explain that?"

She laughs out loud. "Are you fucking kidding?"

In the ten years we've been together, she'd never used that word. "When did you become a barroom tramp?"

She slaps me. I don't do like the last time. Instead, I pretend like it hurt even though it only stung a little. I would probably have to get used to being slapped. Missy had never even acted as if she was going to do that. Lady was a whole different woman. "Why did you do that?" I ask.

"Jesus, Mac. You just called me a tramp." She caresses my cheek and continues, "I already feel like a whore, having sex with two men...I'm sorry. It's not your fault."

But it is *my* fault and I finally realize it. Something that had been bothering me for months if not years, a sore that had become infected, suddenly broke open like a blister. If I hadn't seduced Lady, she would be satisfied being married to Pastor even if it wasn't her idea of love. I'm nothing more than a homewrecker, a man who looks for vulnerable women, taking advantage of them, discarding them the way I had Vanity

Blunt. I'd met my match in Melissa Tight and she'd turned the tables on me. My mind is in turmoil, torn between two realities, what I'd thought I was and what Melissa had shown me I really am.

I have an idea. "Slap me again."

Lady looks at me as if I've lost my mind. "Do it, unless it hurts your hand."

Her face tightens and, without warning, she hits me again. She's still angry, so I encourage her to keep slapping my face. The stinging of my cheek is only a tiny fraction of the permanent pain and suffering I've inflicted on her, destroying her self-esteem and breaking up her marriage. After she's slapped me a dozen times, we're both crying and she wraps her outstretched palm around my neck, matching the movement with the other hand. I'm crying into her neck, unable to stop the flow, not thinking about what it means for a man to cry like that. Suddenly aware of our exposure, in the field next to my truck, I flinch. She doesn't let me get away.

"In two months, we will make our feelings for each other public. The world won't end if someone sees us like this today."

She knows why I wanted her to punish me. I feel no desire to hurt her any more than I already have because she isn't to blame. She has done nothing wrong. I wrap my arms around her slender waist and explain my position.

"You and I were always meant to be together. I became a womanizing jackass because I didn't meet you in junior high. If I had, there's no telling what we would have accomplished together. I kept screwing up until I stumbled into you, and I did it again, messing your life up. But this is the real thing and I'll do whatever you ask, Lady. If you want me to walk out on Missy, I'll do it. Today. Jesus has brought us together in a way we could never have done alone."

She clears her throat before explaining herself. "You had a problem with fulfilling obligations Mac even before your *close encounter*. I can't afford to trust you, not because of any personal embarrassment but because you've been a manipulative, womanizing asshole all your life."

She looks to me for verification, which I give by a nod.

"I just don't know what to expect from you, Mac. I can't live the next twenty years of our lives wondering if you're fucking the neighbor—I'm going to use that word because that's exactly what it is, unconstrained animal lust. I'm putting up with your behavior in our current situation, but it will be totally unacceptable when we are together. I will not tolerate your fucking another woman, not as long as I can satisfy your sexual needs. And I don't want to hear about your need for different experiences because I'm more than happy to inject some excitement into our lives. Pastor has been lying on top of me, pumping until he had a premature ejaculation, for twenty years, and you aren't that different. You both treat me like a prostitute."

This is difficult. Lady says I can't be trusted and with the same breath tells me I have to stop seeing other women after we're together. I can't wrap my head around that. It's like a really nasty job—spreading manure or cleaning up a horse barn—that you don't think about until the day arrives that you've got to do it. Two months sounds like a long time, but when Lady starts telling me what I've got to do to be with her, it feels like I'm already up to my waist in manure.

"Say what?" I stammer.

"You heard me just fine. You and I are going to walk down the street proudly, knowing we are in love and no one is going to come between us."

Her look is saying that this is why she called me unreliable in front of Pastor. She's challenging me to accept her ultimatum or end a relationship that took ten years to grow into what we have. Missy had never done that. But now that Lady is talking about—I'm not sure what she's talking about, so I ask for clarification.

"You're talking as if we're gonna stand up in church and say we're in love, then we'll divorce Missy and Pastor, and just keep living here in Modoc. I've got a company to run, a livelihood, even if there's nothing keeping you here. I don't know what will happen if I just throw in the towel."

"That's a good summary, Mac. We'll obviously stop attending Trinity House. There are several other churches in Modoc that will serve as well. This is Oklahoma after all. And yes, we can announce our decision in church if you want to be public. However, I was thinking of informing our spouses and moving out of our homes, suing for divorce, and beginning our new life. All quietly. Of course, Trinity House will have to find a new landscaping and building maintenance company."

She's smiling and it all sounds so easy, the way she says it, like going to the grocery store, not spreading a huge pile of manure. Trying to get in the mood and demonstrate my sincerity I say, "I guess I better break up with all my girlfriends, then."

She laughs and teases, "Don't dump them all at once or you may have another stroke." Her reference to what she thinks happened to me, rather than accepting that I was touched by the Holy Spirit, is a reminder that she's an agnostic. I'm okay with that because I've been talking about philosophy with her and she's coming around to accepting that believing in God isn't as crazy as it sounds.

Lady follows me around as I spray chemicals to stop weeds from taking over the fresh soil, what with warm weather just around the corner. She talks about a lot of stuff, not just the *big day* as she calls it. And she shares several things she's noticed, like that I've been supplying fuel for the equipment I've been using to take care of the church grounds.

I'm finishing up by myself when Lady goes to prepare Pastor's dinner. I can't help laughing out loud at the image of her life that she shared with me: scullery maid, cook, housekeeper, and whore for Pastor, all for the measly price of her room and board. Distracted, I don't notice the approach of Dim Light, no doubt checking up on me, to make sure I'm doing a good job. Even though he has no idea what I'm doing.

"Did we get it all covered, Mac?" I want to punch him in the mouth, hopefully knocking out some of those yellow teeth filling the gap between his thin lips.

Remembering what Lady had said about my fuel costs, I ask him about reimbursement and point to several five-gallon gas cans in the trailer. "I spent more than two-hundred dollars on fuel, gas and diesel last month, between keeping the parking lot clear and planting the garden. It isn't the cost so much as the time I'm spending filling these cans and refueling equipment. I could install a tank for cost that would—"

Dim's eyes flew open in mock surprise. "Don't you have

fuel tanks in your other trucks? I've seen them. What's the problem?"

I really want to punch him, my fists are even clinched, but I calmly answer, "My service trucks are unavailable right now because this is our busiest season, with spring planting approaching. You've seen me using one here in the summer, when my equipment isn't fully utilized. The lawn equipment doesn't use as much fuel as the tractor. This is a problem, Dim, and it should be dealt with. It's a foreseeable cost of planting a large vegetable garden."

Dim's thin lips turn down in a frown while his small, beady eyes examine the cans stacked against the back of the church. His tiny brain makes a decision and he speaks. "We can't have all these cans of gas and diesel laying around like this. Why can't you take them with you?"

"It must have escaped your attention that I don't drive the same vehicle every day. I can't carry twenty gallons of fuel around with me everywhere I go. That's four of these five-gallon cans. Look, Dim, we need someplace to store twenty gallons of diesel. That's the bottom line."

I stifle a laugh, thinking about how Lady had described Dim, and add, "Maybe I should put them with the fertilizer in the basement?"

Instead of laughing at my joke and letting the cans remain where they are, he says, "Good idea. You shouldn't have had to ask my permission about such a simple issue. Don't bother me with details in the future."

The voice of Jesus suddenly sounds in my ears. "Don't worry about tomorrow, for tomorrow will bring its own worries. Today's trouble is enough for today." I understand his message.

"You got it, Dim. Whatever you need, just let me know."

I'm not going to argue anymore because, for one thing, Lady and I will be severing our ties to Trinity House on Easter.

ADVOCATE

There are no words to express the anticipation I felt after Mac explicitly committed to ending our inconvenient, if not unfortunate, marriages. My accusation of perfidy at the meeting with Pastor, when I'd acted as Mac's interpreter, had been intended to elicit the response I got from him the next day. I crossed my fingers that he would immediately begin the painful (for him) process of ending his multiple extramarital affairs. Thankfully, I didn't have to spend my days contemplating the outcome because Vanity had problems of her own that she wanted to share. I was glad to hear about everything because we had no secrets from each other, except for my personal secret which no one would ever learn about.

"I can't believe what's happening, Lady. Mike is taking sides with Mac, as if this were a civil rights issue. Mike couldn't care less about the Fundamentalists, he calls them fools almost every day, but he's become their strongest supporter on the Board, all because Pastor responded forcefully to Mac's most recent challenge to his authority."

I had to share my news. "I don't mean to change the subject, but Mac has committed to our public betrothal. I'm excited but scared at the same time because…well, Mac is Mac. I could find myself standing in church and saying I love you, only to have him disavow ever having met me." I was crying at this point, and Vanity was quick to respond.

Suddenly sitting next to me, her arms around my shoulders, her kisses soft on my face, she said, "Mac loves you more than he can say and, for the first time in *his* life, he means every word he says to you. I can see it in his eyes. He isn't looking at Melissa the same way, and he's become noncommittal toward Melina Light, who sees herself as his disciple. She's both hard and easy to deal with, both her and Melissa Tight. I've met women like them before. They find a weakness in a man and take advantage of it, getting into the minds of their victims, but Mac knows he's been compromised. Knowing that, he'll find the strength to rid himself of their pathological attention."

We became entangled, kissing each other compassionately, our tears expressing a shared sense of uncertainty, whispering nothings to each other. I was immersed in her spiritual presence, wanting to remain there forever, floating in clouds tinted by the sun setting outside the window. We had become one person. I was too weak to extricate myself from whatever I was experiencing, so I luxuriated in the sublime sensation of sharing life with someone besides Mac.

Vanity scoffed and stammered, "Speaking of brainwashing...I feel like you're in my brain. I'm light headed..."

I breathed deeply before responding. "I feel the same, probably even more because I'm younger than you. I'm as helpless as a kitten, Vanity. I just want to be with you. As a friend, although I can understand how women who feel the way we do could let it get..." My words trailed off, replaced by a timid question.

"Do you think it would be okay if we kissed, on the lips. I want to kiss you so badly—"

"No," she replied, her voice dripping with disappointment. "That's how it begins. I had a lesbian relationship before I met Mike, with an older actress who mentored me and who I loved, I felt the same way about her that I do about you right now. She kissed me and I fell in love with her. It lasted several months, until she dumped me for another woman. It was wonderful but it ruined our relationship in the end, and I don't want something like that to happen with you. I love you too much." Then she kissed my cheek.

She added, "Genuine affection is just as pleasant without the risk of ruining what has grown between us. Let's not spoil it."

I nodded contritely and, unable to keep the excitement out of my voice, said, "I'm so excited right now. Whew! My god, Vanity, I may faint… Even Mac doesn't get me this excited."

She kissed my cheek again and replied, "I feel exactly the same way. Let's talk about Mike. That'll calm us both down." We laughed and she added, "The next time you get together with Mac, remember the feeling we shared today and—who knows—maybe Pastor will be in the mood tonight?"

If what I was feeling could be put in a box and pulled out at a convenient time, I would welcome Pastor's advances, but that wasn't possible. Feelings, especially the hormonally driven ones Vanity's caresses had arroused in me, had a shelf life of a few minutes. Still, I could try it with Mac. I would see him the next day and, to be honest, I relished the sensation of making love with him more than Vanity's touch. Maybe I could merge the two experiences.

Vanity and I calmed down while she told me about Mike. He had found his calling as a lawyer. He had an alpha male personality, which training in the adversarial legal system prevalent in the United States had amplified. I laughed when she shared examples of how he behaved towards her at home. It was as if she were telling a joke as the story unfolded, how Mike had unknowingly taken Mac on as a client because of Pastor's opposition to his message, which Mike thought was false advertising. Supporting his unacknowledged client with every bone in his body, Mike had accused Vanity of colluding with Pastor when she'd asked if there was a legal way to get Mac to a doctor for a checkup. I almost fell off the sofa laughing when Vanity paraphrased Mike's response to the whole QAnon conspiracy aspect of Mac's prophecy.

"That the constitutional right of Mac and his knucklehead supporters to believe all this QAnon bullshit is undisputed isn't the issue, instead we have to focus on the repercussions of the Fundamentalist claims being not given the consideration due any such beliefs, for what is a man if not his beliefs? The court cannot but support such a claim for justice, liberty, and freedom of…"

She was laughing so hard she didn't finish summarizing Mike's support for Mac and the Fundamentalists. When I expressed disbelief that a lawyer would fall into the *False*

Dilemma Fallacy, her head froze, facing me, her piercing blue eyes penetrating my soul. "Haven't you been listening? Mike has been trained by an accredited law school to reduce every situation to a black-and-white representation. This is exactly what I expected from him, an opportunity to showboat his lawyerly way of speaking, confusing things even more. Mike can't handle more than two controlling factors in any situation, whether it's visiting his parents or going to a high-school play, a basketball game, even church for Christ's sake! There always has to be two sides. We can't just get along. His entire life, and mine since I married him, has been lived on a chess board, switching sides with every client, event, whim. It has become far more than just his job, it's a way of thinking and living, one that is driving me crazy."

It was my turn to comfort my best friend. I did my best, struggling to find words to convey unfamiliar feelings. "I don't know which one of us is in the worst position, but I can say with certainty that my situation is about to change whereas yours will continue. Therefore, I think we should stop worrying about Mac and me and instead focus on you and Mike."

"Am I that bad?"

I tried to put myself in Mike's shoes, if you can imagine that, but it worked and I found a response. "You and Mike are not about to begin a new life, so we should talk about how to keep your marriage together. I know Mike—not as well as you but from a different perspective—and I don't think he's an asshole. He's exactly like you said but it's kind of fun to talk to him, like talking to someone who speaks a different English dialect."

Vanity laughed unconvincingly, her hold on my hand tightening. "I'm at a loss, so what do you suggest?"

I tried to recall the psychology classes I'd taken in college, which had been supplemented by internet searches, but then I realized that I couldn't give Vanity advice. I should just ask questions. It was easy to understand why anyone, except Fundamentalists like Missy, would resent Mac's recent conversion to the most radical view possible. What wasn't so obvious was why any of this mattered to Mike Blunt, dedicated Evangelical, trained lawyer, well-respected within the community of Modoc, elder and member of the Board of Trinity House. I needed more information, so I took Vanity's hands in mine, looking into her worried eyes.

"Can you recall any interactions Mike and Mac may have had outside of the church?"

"What do you mean?"

"Have they ever had business dealings? Has Mac ever come to your house? Did he ever set foot in it for professional reasons?"

She thought a moment and began, "About five years ago, Mike wanted to install an air compressor in the garage, something that could be used to run air tools; he's restoring a 1957 Ford Thunderbird because that was the year he was born." She shrugged—I chuckled—and she continued, "Mike is not an electrician, so he blew several fuses and melted some wires in our house after his attempt at home electrical work. There was even a small fire, which he put out with a fire extinguisher. I had recently had an affair with Mac, so I suggested him as a reliable general home repairman. Mike called Mac and the repair work was done, along with upgrades to the wiring. Despite Mac's professional behavior, Mike resents him—he drops hints about Mac being a greedy Jew, things like that—because Mac didn't give him a discount on the cost, charging his regular rate, but what sealed their relationship was that Mike was embarrassed about what had happened. In his mind, he owes a debt to Mac, a debt he has to repay at some future date. That must be why he's supporting a man who has obviously suffered a stroke, against the man who created the spiritual sanctuary of Trinity House."

It made sense. The old Mac. The predictable Mike. There is nothing new under the sun.

"They're going to eventually have a fist fight because your affair with Mac is going to come out."

Vanity was horrified. "They wouldn't do that…"

"Yes they would Vanity, because that's the way boys are—neither one of them acts like an adult."

She laughed, her head bobbing up and down.

THE FOUR HORSEMEN

Pastor's sermons are always good, so I'm looking forward to hearing about the Four Horsemen of the Apocalypse. I'm pretty sure I'm riding one of those horses, from Pastor's point of view, when Missy and I take our seats on the fourth row. I'm beginning to understand Melina's insistence on having sex all the time after seeing the change in Missy since I'd been touched by the Holy Spirit. We'd made love just before coming to church. And she's glowing now, as if Jesus had spoken to her just as clearly as he had to me. I sit down feeling as if Missy and I are a happily married couple. We're not arguing about anything, we're learning about the Deep State together, she's touching me constantly, and we're having sex every day, sometimes several times a day. I think we're glowing together, and everyone can see how happy we are, especially Lady, sitting at the organ and watching us.

Imagining myself sitting on a stallion like one of the horsemen Missy told me about, I take a quick look at the Evangelical side of the nave, where Mike Blunt is sitting with his wife, Vanity, who I'd had an affair with a few years ago—until I realized that she couldn't get a teenager excited. She is beautiful, a sight for sore eyes, but not capable of satisfying a man for more than a few weeks. A cold fish. I smile politely at several Evangelical women I've had brief affairs with, their eyes telling me that they want me to take them to one of the side rooms and give it to them. My attention is brought back to the pulpit by Missy's gentle nudge against my side. If I were to stand up, she'd accompany me to a side room for another dose of all those chemicals they say are released during sex. She wants to do it, I can tell from her hopeful smile, expressing her wish to satisfy my every desire. I risk a peck on her forehead and get a grateful smile in return. There'll be plenty of time for that later.

Pastor takes his place behind the pulpit, the look of enlightenment on his face saying that he's about to share the Word of God with us. Melissa leads the choir in a popular Christian rock song and we take our seats, waiting to see what God has revealed to Pastor. I can feel the anticipation, amplified by Missy next to me breathing heavily. I give her a look that promises fulfillment of her sexual desires after church and she squeezes my arm.

Why hadn't she been so receptive to my advances during the last ten years of our marriage?

I would never have fallen in love with Lady. I had already fallen in love with Missy and would have been happy with her. After all, just look at the life we created together—a daughter in college, successful landscaping and organic gardening enterprises. With Missy sitting next to me, I can't remember why I ever let Lady seduce me.

Pastor's voice brings me back to the here and now.

"A casual reading of chapter six of the book of Revelations might suggest that the End Times will occur rapidly, as quickly as it takes to read the words, but that isn't the case. It is an illusion born of our insufficient concept of time; a limitation God does not have. For example, the Book of Genesis refers to the creation of Heaven and Earth in six days, but why would God be limited to the calendar? He could have created the universe with a word. He chose to refer to seven days for His work because of our physical nature, to set upon us a regularity that reminds us of His power. With that thought in mind, let us examine events when the Lamb of God removes the seals from the Book. When the first seal is opened, a horseman appears on a white steed, carrying a bow and wearing a crown. He has come to conquer the earth. The consensus among most scholars is that Conquest has been unleashed, although there is some disagreement about when this event occurred. Most argue that this would have been a prediction of the first-half of the twentieth century, representing the rise of Fascism in the persons of Hitler, Hirohito, and Mussolini, following so soon after the horrors of World War One. Some argue, however, that this is a reference to the sudden appearance of Islam because of its rapid spread throughout so much of the world, subjugating one-quarter of the world's population with minimal death in wars. These scholars have a point, as long as we assume that God meant for us to interpret the order of the horsemen's appearance literally."

There are a lot of "Amens" coming from the Fundamentalist pews before Pastor continues, "The reason I accept their interpretation, at least for now, is because it's consistent with the other horsemen and what their appearances signify. But before we go on, put yourself in the place of a Christian living in Egypt or any of the lands of the Middle East when the Muslim hordes appeared. They may well have thought those were the End Times, but Christ didn't return and here we are, more than a thousand years later, and He still hasn't returned. Remember that as we continue."

Shouts of support sound throughout the church at Pastor's gentle reminder to pay attention. He's really good at presenting the Word of God clearly, so that even people who never read the Bible can understand. I haven't opened it in a few months and only know about the four horsemen because Missy explained on the way to church. She reads the Bible every day. I risk a look at Lady. She's looking at me and Missy, and she isn't smiling.

Unaware of my exchange of looks with Lady, Pastor continues, "When the Lamb of God removed the second seal, a rider on a red horse appeared, wielding a sword with which to throw the world into confrontation. This horseman brings war, arguably the wars of the twentieth century. I would remind you that the End Times will not be recorded in a Netflix series, an event we can binge watch before being taken in the Rapture to join the Lamb of God at the throne. Every man woman and child will suffer before the end, and that hasn't happened yet." He looks around the suddenly silent, chastised congregation and picks up where he left off. "Upon the third seal being removed by Jesus, a rider on a black horse appears, holding a scale in his hand, giving orders of what a man should pay for a loaf of bread. This has been interpreted by the majority of scholars to refer to drought and famine of a worldwide scale. This interpretation is traditional because it suggests that a global famine will occur and since no such catastrophe has happened, it is assumed that the third horseman hasn't yet shown his face. One fact of human psychology is our willingness, even eagerness, to avoid facing unpleasant facts, which will certainly be the case when the fourth horseman appears. I'll get to him in a minute."

He pauses and sips from his water glass as a hushed murmur flows through the pews. Finally, his face revealing the anguish he's about to share, he continues.

"The third rider is not unleashed with a charge to cause pain or suffering, and Revelations says nothing about starvation. Instead, the appearance of the rider of the black horse is accompanied by specific instructions on the prices and availability of food. This horseman has been amongst us for more than a century, having appeared soon after the horsemen with the sword, who rides with War. This rider brings wage and price controls, socialism, communism, and government control over what you and I can buy and how much we will pay. Satan's true objective is revealed not in frontal attacks, but by insidious, innocuous challenges to what God has shown us to be His Word. For all intents and purposes, the price you pay for a loaf of bread is determined by the government, by Satan himself, who has taken the reins of power and released the third horseman!"

Half the congregation is on their feet, including me and Missy. There are some folks dancing around, and Melina looks like she's about to faint. Missy squeezes my hand. Lady is playing a few bars from *Onward Christian Soldiers* on the organ with Melissa keeping time on the tambourine, as pleased as punch. Lady doesn't look very happy. I'm just glad I wasn't riding any of those horses, leaving me to wonder what comes next. Maybe Lady knows.

When everyone has settled down, Pastor doesn't miss a beat in picking up where he left off.

He begins in a quiet voice, forcing me to listen carefully, "When the Lamb of God removes the fourth seal from the Book of God, a rider on a pale green horse appears. His name is Death and he is followed by Satan, who does not ride a horse because he is the fallen angel, his powers surpassed only by God's. Satan and Death join the other horsemen, who are still acting unhindered in the world. However, Death, his hand guided by Satan himself, is given direct control over one-quarter of the Earth, to wreak devastation using war, famine, pestilence, and natural disaster."

The church is silent, every ear waiting for Pastor's next words. His gaze sweeps the benches, finally landing on me.

"Some scholars are still waiting for the third horseman to appear, looking for widespread famine and starvation. Improvements in feeding the developing world have lulled them into a false sense of security, all while the rider of the black horse has been telling us what to do for more than a century. Revelations does not reveal how much *time* should pass between the appearance of the four horsemen, or how long they will run amok…"

Missy and I lean forward with everyone else to hear Pastor's interpretation. He briefly scans the straining faces before focusing on me.

"The appearance of Death, accompanied by Satan himself, cannot be identified by the pain they will inflict on Mankind globally, but instead on the curious limitation of their powers, which was meant as a sign for those who read with an open heart."

More shouts of support and anticipation.

"One fourth of the Earth could mean land mass, nations, people, ethnicities, the list goes on. Keeping in mind the warning about considering time only from a human perspective, we must look at the totality of pain and suffering these two monsters will bring down on us. What possible division of the Earth is suffering from violence, hunger, disease, and natural disasters?"

I'm thinking hard and so is Missy. We're looking at each other, silently wording our guesses. The entire congregation is doing the same. We're all looking around, confusion spreading like the plague. Then it hits me. I whisper to Missy, who nods and squeezes my hand.

"The raw data are unavailable to analyze these four causes of misery and death, but that shouldn't keep us from completing God's work. Let us begin with disease. It doesn't matter if Covid 19 is a naturally occurring virus, a hoax, a bioweapon created by the Chinese, or a population-control tool used by the Deep State. This phenomenon has been linked to substantial numbers of deaths in one-quarter of the nations on earth." There's an indrawn breath by the congregation, except for me and Missy. She squeezes my arm again.

Pastor continues, "We are living in the End Times and thus must remain vigilant. Satan is already loose in the world and this means that no one hearing my voice can escape what is to come. Those who've already joined Jesus at the throne will be watching us, to see how we perform under duress; and I can promise you that there are dark days ahead, which will require all of us to be at full strength. Our prayers for each other have defended us against Satan and Death, but I'm concerned about the recent demise of Vernon Huckster, one of our own, taken by this Covid 19 pestilence unleashed by Satan. If we let down our guard, Satan will take us one by one, and Jesus will not be pleased at the premature appearance of souls who let themselves be killed by Satan so easily. Revelations is clear, that we will probably die as martyrs before the Rapture occurs because Satan knows where we are, through the very institutions we have constructed, his work made easier by the use of digital computers, social security numbers, driver licenses, our smart phones. Being deceived by any one of the ways Satan has devised to fool us will be tantamount to failure and God will not be happy."

Someone shouts, "What can we do Pastor, if Satan is assaulting us from every side?"

Pastor nods deliberately and, giving his words serious thought, responds, "We must follow the best advice available to us to resist the disease Satan has unleashed. Follow the CDC guidelines and live, so that we will be available to resist Death and Satan when they unleash unimaginable horrors on the Earth."

Someone behind me shouts, accusing Pastor of being in league with the Devil, so I turn around. It's Melina. She breaks into Spanish to continue her diatribe, and I'm on my feet, joining her, calling Pastor a dupe, a fool tricked by Death into supporting Satan's false narrative about how the government, which he has already admitted is infiltrated by Satan through intervention in a free economy, is going to help us resist Satan and Death. Others join me. It becomes pandemonium. Some people are dancing, overcome by the Holy Spirit. Melina has fainted, slumped in her pew, Dim making sure she doesn't fall to the floor. The spirit of God lets go of me and I retake my seat, Missy at my side, nodding supportively.

Lady is shaking her head, frowning. I choose to look into Missy's supportive eyes, wanting me as much as I want her.

Pastor waits until everyone else has followed my lead before addressing our concerns. "Satan is adept at deceiving humans but his power is not unlimited. He cannot put blinders over the eyes of every man on Earth, to make us see a different reality than what actually exists. It is God who is the ruler of the world and not his servant Satan, a fact we should keep in mind in the days, months, years of tribulation that lie ahead."

His steely eyes slowly examine the faces filling the pews before coming to rest on me. "Someone who has no experience in dealing with Satan beyond their own daily struggle to stay in touch with our Savior can be deceived by the serpent, whereas I have spent my life preparing for this moment, opening my heart to God's message, learning to recognize the hand of Satan, revealed by the insincerity and unpreparedness of his messengers. These well-meaning but unfortunate souls should not be shunned but brought back into the fold."

Lady starts playing, accompanied by Melissa and her band. Everyone stands and the celebration begins. Melina has recovered from her experience with the Holy Spirit, speaking in tongues, dancing, joined by several others, while the Evangelicals try not to stare. Melissa's band performs several popular songs, accompanied by shouted hallelujahs and a lot of Amens. Missy, apparently thinking about Pastor's sermon, limits her response to dancing in front of our pew. I notice Lady frowning at me, despite the spiritual ecstasy flowing through the congregation.

When Missy and I get home, I can finally satisfy her sexual desire, contained for too long during the service. She pretends like she doesn't want it because that's a game we play. But she wants it. She wants it so bad. Her cries of anguish, from having to wait so long to be satisfied, tell me how much she wants it.

I give it to her again and again, until she's whimpering, overcome by sexual euphoria. I'm thinking that maybe Melina would like to restore my spiritual harmony, so maybe I should text her, but then I recall that she's probably doing the same thing as me. She is married after all. I give it to a submissive but eager Missy again, using a lot of lotion to avoid either one of us getting chaffed.

I can't wait for Pastor's Sunday evening sermon.

SPLIT DECISION

Pastor had discussed his sermon with me, asking for my opinion, listening to my comments. He hadn't done that before, so maybe he was starting to think of me as more than his live-in maid and sex worker. His sermon was very good and his response to the Fundamentalist objections raised by Mac was the epitome of good leadership.

On the short walk back to the rectory, I expressed some doubts about how well his message had been received. He agreed with my summary and held the door for me to enter our living room. The door closed behind him and I turned to tell him about the lunch I'd already prepared, knowing how busy Sundays were for him. Instead of his usual summary of the service, how he'd performed, the response of the congregation, he approached me and pulled me close, his lips pressing against mine arduously. I didn't fight him but thought of Vanity's advice. I imagined her hands unzipping my dress, lowering it to the floor, gently cupping my breasts, removing my bra and probing between my legs. I closed my eyes and indulged myself in the fantasy, imagining Vanity making love to me and, when that was no longer possible, her image was replaced by Mac's. I was pleasantly surprised to discover that she was right. The experience was pleasant. I mean, to be honest, Pastor is a good-looking, well-endowed man, and he'd always been gentle with me.

One good thing about having sex with Pastor, a man I had never loved, was that we didn't lay in bed and cuddle afterward the way Mac and I do. Don't misunderstand me, it wasn't that bad, Pastor always held me afterward and told me he loved me and made other meaningless statements, but we always got dressed almost immediately, unless it was nighttime. Then, we stayed in bed but kept our distance—for a good night's sleep, he'd always said. And he was right. I suppose that physical intimacy is a luxury that only the young can afford.

Pastor was so accustomed to our sexual relationship that he didn't act as if we'd just had the most intimate encounter known to humanity when we sat down to lunch. He wasn't touching me, although I instinctively touched his arm several times, an act he acknowledged with a nod and a smile before we ate the chicken casserole I'd heated in the oven after our sexual encounter.

Without my asking, he explained that the Sunday evening sermon was going to come from the Gospels, the topic being forgiveness. He would focus on the words of Jesus. First accusing, then making amends, Pastor was a general in the war against Satan, the never-ending struggle to get all these confused people to behave themselves in the face of uncertainty.

The Trinity House Board met after lunch and I performed my duties as the secretary. I was too busy taking notes in shorthand, a skill I'd learned in high school and college, to pay attention but when I transcribed them for the record there was plenty of time to reflect on what was said, which I'm going to summarize.

The Board consisted of Pastor as chairman, the tiebreaker vote. Mike Blunt and Dim Light represented the two factions of Trinity House on the board, their divisive viewpoints reinforced by less-vocal but more contemplative members. Mary Jenkins was an Evangelical who had always supported Mike. She had a perfect voting record. She was a typical Oklahoman, however, and was opposed to any kind of change, a perspective shared by Dim's fellow Fundamentalist on the Board. Edith Tagortan saw any change as an indication that the End Times had arrived. I had listened to her end-of-days warnings for twenty years, expressed every time there was an election. Mary had no patience for the protests by the Fundamentalists about unfair practices, especially when Mac and his supporters insulted Pastor. Dim, a Fundamentalist because of his marriage to Melina, pointed out that they felt marginalized. Mary repeated what Pastor had said when confronted by Mac, about the lack of civic responsibility among the Fundamentalists. Mike Blunt was the wild card because of his uncertain allegiance.

Mike said something incomprehensible, which I interpreted for the others as a proposal to change the Trinity House bylaws, to make it easier for everyone to participate and thus feel less marginalized. Feeling betrayed, Mary strongly opposed Mike's suggestion, but the motion was approved without Pastor's tie-breaking vote. Eligibility to become an elder and a member of the Board would no longer require a college education. I had the impression that no one on the board was aware that this had been an unspoken barrier to the Fundamentalists, who were overwhelmingly from the working class. Mary wasn't happy, but she was polite and accepted the outcome.

I was impressed that Mac had actually done something constructive, moving people, changing society, making a difference. And to think that he'd done this while suffering from a stroke, or worse. I was tempted to consider the hand of God, until I remembered that Mac was probably going to die because of all this...this bullshit!

The evening service, attended by a slightly smaller group of believers than in the morning, was a letdown after Pastor's stirring denunciation of Mac as a tool of Satan. But his message of reconciliation, supported by what the Board had decided, was well received. Mac refrained from interrupting, shouting accusations and unfounded rumors. Everyone behaved.

Missy looked miserable, afraid, terrified. It wasn't hard to figure out what was going on because of my own experience with Mac's sexuality since his *spiritual experience*. He had become abusive, demanding, even violent. Missy was certainly taking the brunt of it, being sexually abused, even raped, by a man who was no longer in control of his actions. I tried to make eye contact with the unfortunate woman but she never looked my way. Missy wasn't very inquisitive in general and apparently her thoughts were turned inward, towards problems beyond the horizon that defined the world for the rest of us. I could relate to her situation. I couldn't speak publicly about her suffering because my intimate relationship with Mac was a sin in the eyes of Christians, and it wasn't yet time to come out of the closet. Her suffering would have to continue a while longer.

I wanted to confront Mac and drag him, kicking and screaming, to a hospital so that the truth would be known. I didn't do that because I was afraid of something I couldn't identify—maybe of losing what I had because, despite how I felt about my life, I was an upscale prostitute rather than a street whore, which was probably how Mac was treating Missy. On the other hand, she was a successful businesswoman whereas I was…I was nothing more than a—Missy was as capable as me to deal with Mac, who I was certain wasn't dangerous to anyone but himself.

THE PRESIDENT SAYS...

I'm not convinced by what Pastor tells me about changing the bylaws so that anyone can be on the Board, even if it was verified by Lady. It's all kind of confusing and there's one thing I've learned over the years: If something can't be said in simple English, it's a coverup for someone's secret agenda. I don't need a college education to recognize what's going on. My suspicions are confirmed when I talk to several members of the congregation.

For example, I'm talking to Ralph Newcomb one day—he's a Fundamentalist—and I tell him that he can be on the Trinity House church board if he wins an election. He doesn't know what I'm talking about, so I ask if he's going to run for office. He's still laughing when his front door closes in my face. Then I talk to Mary Jenkins, a member of the church board, when I'm doing some work at her house. She doesn't mince words.

"Did being married to Missy finally turn your brain to mush?" She says. "I'm not going to talk about imaginary political parties within the congregation. Despite your recent conversion to extremist ideology—I wouldn't be surprised to see you wearing a turban come Sunday morning—most people in Trinity House know you're spouting nonsense, except for the lunatic fringe. Some notions are just pure bull and everyone with a lick of sense knows it."

I take offense at what she said about Missy. "It's not right to speak that way about Missy. She's a God-fearing woman and a good wife, and an astute farmer and businesswoman."

The words barely die in the cold air, before Mary Jenkins retorts, "Lord almighty. Missy never got past the first chapter of Genesis. I know because she was one of my students in Sunday school. She's a sweet girl but gullible as they come. Not somebody you want to talk seriously to, unless the topic of conversation is the price of asparagus in December."

It's obvious that Mary Jenkins has a closed mind, so I don't talk to her anymore, but fix her leaking roof, cut her grass, and fertilize her garden.

As I'm finishing up, she comes out to pay me and says, "The only reason that imbecile Dim Light is on the Board is that half the congregation was too lazy or stupid to pick up a pencil when they came to church and mark a ballot, or write in the name of someone they liked. For the record, I wrote in your name Macbeth Lunatic because you should be on the Board, not because of your beliefs but because you're involved in day-to-day matters and you're a hard worker. But go see a doctor. I think there's something wrong with you."

With that parting shot, the door closes, leaving me holding a check, wondering if maybe I should get a physical. I've never been to the doctor in my life and I'm as healthy as a horse. Obviously, seeing a doctor doesn't make you healthy.

I can't forget what Mary Jenkins said about Missy. Nobody ever talked that way to me before about my wife. I guess when you get older, you don't much care what people think, so you say whatever crosses your mind. Of course, I'd been speaking out loud recently without thinking about my words, trusting Jesus to guide my speech, and it was working. Everybody was listening to me. Pastor was calling me names. I was persecuted, just like Jesus. No. There's nothing wrong with me; and Mary Jenkins and all the Evangelicals are in for a rude awakening come Easter.

A few days later, I talk to Dr. Halpern, the doctor who had taken care of Missy when she was pregnant with our daughter. Neither Missy nor I had seen him professionally since then because we were healthy. But I sometimes go to his house to do repairs; maybe I should explain. I take care of Trinity House's congregation's landscape and handyman work personally, despite having ten men working for my business, doing home and garden maintenance. Dr. Halpern had been asking me when I was going to get a checkup for twenty years. He had been straight out of medical school when Trinity was born, so he's not old or anything, not much older than me in fact.

I want an opinion about the China flu from a doctor I trust, and Dr. Halpern is the closest thing. It's Saturday afternoon and he's having a martini, while I'm replacing an attic exhaust fan and doing some other minor work. I finish up and join him on the deck just as he empties his glass. He uses those martini glasses you see in movies. I'm not sure how to broach the topic, so I'm shifting my weight from foot to foot. He sets his glass down, looks at me and shows why he's a medical doctor and I'm the landscape technician.

"Would you join me, Mac? I like to sit on the deck and have a martini on a chilly day because it reminds me how much colder it is in Chicago. That's where I grew up."

I nod and he stands up, handing me a check for the work I've done, then leads me into the garage, where he has a kitchenette, including a full-size refrigerator. He makes our drinks and explains the reason for his invitation.

"You've been a very busy man Mac, what with operating a thriving business, maintaining the church's grounds, raising a daughter, being involved with almost every charitable activity in Modoc, and…" He pauses and turns to offer me a proper martini, not some gin dumped over ice, and leads me back to the patio as he continues.

"Despite being a devout, thoroughly invested, contributing member of the Modoc and Trinity House communities, you've maintained a secret life…" He pauses and sits, encouraging me to take a seat before offering a toast.

I'm not sure where he's going but I touch my glass to his and take a drink, choking when he continues, "An alternate life in which you have had a string of romantic affairs with women both within and without the Trinity House congregation." He stops, obviously waiting for me to say something.

I take another drink, to replace the one I spit up, and say, "I'm sorry about that. You caught me off guard. I guess that was your purpose…but why?"

Dr. Halpern sips his martini and says, "I took a few classes in psychiatry when I was a medical student, but it wasn't my forte. Nevertheless, I've been practicing medicine in Modoc for twenty-two years and I've dealt with about half the population professionally, even you and Missy, when Trinity was born. Despite not seeing you in the office, I've had ongoing interactions with you and Missy on a regular basis through Trinity House."

I take advantage of his pause to say, "Why are you telling me this now? Isn't there some kind of doctor-patient privilege? You can't talk about what you suspect and that's all it is, unsubstantiated speculation."

His response is even more composed than Pastor's. "Observing your interactions with Lady, Vanity, Melissa, Melina, Missy, and a half-dozen other women from the congregation, with whom your liaisons were more ephemeral, has become a hobby of mine. I neither condemn nor condone your personal behavior Mac, but I wanted to take this opportunity to speak to you about your health." He takes another drink from his glass and adds, "I would like to hear about your recent encounter with the Holy Spirit. I wasn't in church that day and I missed it."

"Why?" I ask, finishing my drink.

We have another martini and I admit that I was contacted by Jesus in person. I don't see a problem because he's a doctor and can't repeat what I'm saying because of the Hippocratic oath. I tell him everything Jesus has told me as we sip our martinis in the cool afternoon, the sun dipping towards the horizon. I feel as if I'm speaking to Jesus himself, sharing my feelings of desperation, accompanied by an equally strong sense of purpose. Dr. Halpern listens and keeps our glasses full until I run out of things to say. But there's one last thing on my mind.

"I've been told that I had a stroke by Lady and Vanity. Pastor believes it too but he's being cagey. I've talked about this with Missy and we agree that I may suffer collateral brain damage from being so close to the Holy Spirit. I accept my situation because it's no different from being crucified, thrown to the lions, or…"

Dr. Halpern finishes my incomplete thought. "Or ostracized, pushed to the periphery of society because your beliefs are not in agreement with the majority. Nevertheless,

Mac, we have to remember that we are human beings. Jesus would not want you to die in order to share his message. It was Paul who spoke of the need to die as martyrs to prove our faith. Whoever wrote Revelations—probably not the apostle John—was someone like you, a man who received a message from an unknown source and struggled with the question of his own sanity. I can't say whether or not you are hearing the words of Jesus or Satan. They would sound the same to our ears, but not to our hearts."

"What should I do?"

Dr. Halpern sipped his martini, looked at the sun approaching the horizon, and said, "My medical opinion is that you should go to Oklahoma City for tests that can't be done in Modoc. I don't give advice about personal decisions. I told you that your case is a hobby. You have never been my patient, Mac. Still, I'm certain that you won't follow my medical advice because you value being the Lord's messenger above your own life." He shrugged.

Okay. I get it. He's been watching me for years. But he isn't going to speak out. He wants me to live, despite being Jesus' messenger. *Why does he care about me?*

"There's time for one more round," Dr. Halpern says, picking up our empty glasses as his wife appears in the French doors leading into the remodeled house. I'm fascinated, watching her take the glasses from his hand. She's as attractive as Lady or Vanity, but she's never accepted my overtures… never even responded. I hadn't made the connection until this moment. Dr. Halpern's wife is one of the women I'd tried to seduce several times over the years. Her rejections had been edged with humor, but always firm, never hinting anything more than what her words conveyed.

"I apologize…" I begin.

Alyssa Halpern hands me a chilled glass and says, "Save your apologies for Missy, who will be publicly shamed when you divorce her."

I had been transported to a world occupied by people like Lady. Alyssa joins us on the patio with a martini and I learn that they've been studying me together because she's a nurse at the county hospital in Washita. But they don't make me feel like I'm in a scientific study, it's more like they're my neighbors and have noticed my activities. They'd kept their observations to themselves until my sudden change in behavior, speaking to me only about my health. I'm really enjoying talking to them, hearing about myself from medical professionals, but they're not willing to give me advice other than what Dr. Halpern has already said. I notice that they're being careful about keeping their distance from each other and me.

"Why are you all tiptoeing around as if we all had rabies or something?"

Alyssa answers, "The Covid virus spreads rapidly and kills the most vulnerable, like the elderly and people with breathing problems. Jim and I wear masks all day and, to be honest, it's rather difficult to have a martini while wearing a N-95 mask. We're outside and there's less chance of passing it to you. Obviously, we're both at a high risk because of our work."

I'm not thinking when I say, "The president says it's a hoax. Don't you think he knows what he's talking about? After all, he has information from the whole medical community." I feel foolish right away, speaking to a doctor and a nurse like that.

Dr. Halpern responds, "Pastor pretty much said it all in his Sunday morning sermon. It doesn't matter where Covid came from. It's real and we have to deal with it. I think President Trump meant that he believes it came from an unnatural source, like a bioweapon lab, or a biology experiment gone awry. He's not a good orator."

I look at Alyssa, who's nodding as she says, "But that's not very interesting Mac, not nearly as much as what's happening in Trinity House because of your—I'm not sure if it's a revelation or a prophesy, referring to Easter Sunday as it does. I don't imagine you've had any further communications from the Holy Spirit or you would have shared them, but what do you think is going to happen?"

She's not trying to argue with me, to show how much smarter than me she is—like Lady—so I answer honestly.

"Because of me being chosen as His messenger, I don't think it's about the end of the world, the Second Coming or anything like that. I think I'm a lesser prophet, although I'm not a prophet…I'm really confused."

Dr. Halpern is nodding as if he understands. "In that case, considering what has already happened, not to mention your outreach program—talking to people like you've started doing—it looks like you're sharing a message of reconciliation and harmony."

Alyssa quickly adds, "I agree. Deep social hostility cannot be dealt with until it is brought into the open. That is exactly what you've done, Mac. The systemic inequalities of Trinity House have been laid bare and can now be addressed."

I realize that smart people like Dr. Halpern and Alyssa don't take sides just because they disagree with somebody on a particular issue. Inspired, I say, "That makes sense. Personally, I can't wait to hear Pastor's Easter sermon. He'll probably have the whole congregation singing and dancing together by the time he's finished. I'm sure my doom-and-gloom interpretation was overstated…"

Dr. Halpern's head was shaking imperceptibly as he replied, "Alyssa and I are flying out to the West Coast, to spend Easter with her family in Los Angeles, but we'll be following events at Trinity House on social media."

UNINSURED

My conversation with Dr. Halpern and Alyssa had been inspirational, so I tell Lady all about it the next day. Her response is not what I'd expected.

"Convenient, isn't it, that the Halperns will be out of town, the county, even Oklahoma, when the shit hits the fan." She challenges me with her unrelenting gaze.

"What are you saying?"

"I know the Halperns Mac, after living in Modoc so long. They are good people, despite believing in the Second Coming of Christ. However, they don't have my sense of ethics or morality. I've spoken to them, especially to Alyssa; and they appear to be rational—after all, they're both health care professionals—but they actually believe all that mumbo jumbo Pastor spreads like manure every time he stands behind that goddamn pulpit."

I'm confused, having expected Lady to agree with Dr. Halpern's suggestion. "I don't understand why you speak so poorly of them after how well they treated me."

Lady faces me and says, "I told you to go to the doctor immediately after your revelation, and I've repeated my request every time I see you. You ignored my pleas, a fact the Halperns would have figured out. You are nothing more than a hobby— the exact words Jim Halpern used—to him and Alyssa. You're a lot more than a hobby to me, Mac."

Standing behind the rectory with Lady, the unseasonably warm February day reminding me of the planting ahead, a task she would share with me, I suddenly reach out and pull her to me, wrapping my arms around her waist. She responds in kind, her arms encircling my neck, her lips caressing me, tickling. I don't care who sees us. I want to be with Lady. I'm breathing heavily when she says what we both know to be true.

"I love you, Mac. I'm going to take care of you. To be honest, I hope someone sees us right now so that we can be finished with this nonsense. Pretending that we aren't in love is against the laws of nature and God. But, do you know what else I figured out?"

Her kisses have made me deaf, so I just shake my head.

"I think your revelation will be nothing more than proclaiming our love. Is that okay with you, or would that be a disappointment?"

I slump into her surprisingly strong arms, her slight frame preventing me from collapsing in a heap at her feet on the damp earth. I feel good. Lady's going to take care of me, but I don't want to lie down on the dirt even though Jesus says it's only for a moment. Lady is calling someone instead of taking care of me like she promised. She's so far away. Jesus tells me that it's okay to take a nap because I've been working hard, so I smile at Lady and go to sleep.

I wake up from my nap to find Lady and Missy arguing.

"You had no right to call an ambulance. This is none of your business."

"What was I supposed to do Missy, throw cold water in his face?! Mac passed out in front of me and was unresponsive, so *of course* I called an ambulance. My God, have you become a Seventh Day Adventist?"

I'm woozy and not yet able to speak, so I listen. Jesus doesn't have an opinion.

"You've never had any respect for us Fundamentalists, treating us like second-class citizens, using big words to make your ideas sound more like the word of God than ours but, let me tell you! You will never follow in Jesus' footsteps until you can become a child. It's right there in the Book of Matthew."

"I didn't come here to debate your superstitious beliefs, Missy. Mac is very ill. If you'd been there, if you'd seen his eyes roll into his head, dropping in his tracks, then you might have a clue about what it's like to see someone you…to see someone struck down in an instant."

Lady pushes past Missy and approaches me. I can see her and hear her voice, but that's all. I can't speak or even lift a finger.

"I'm sorry that you had to hear our argument." She takes my hand and continues, "I love...I mean that Jesus doesn't mean to harm you, as his prophet, so everything is going to be okay. This is only a test." Her eyes are filled with tears, which overflow onto her cheeks, surreptitiously wiped by casual swipes of her hands, as if she's hastily wiping her nose or getting something out of her eye.

Missy steps up close to Lady, righteousness hanging over her head like a halo, and says, "Sister Church is right about that, but she probably broke your vow with the Holy Spirit when she called an ambulance. I wish I'd been there, so that well-meaning but confused unbelievers wouldn't have risked everything you've accomplished."

I want to thank both of them for coming to the hospital but I can't say a word. I'm trying to smile when Lady leans over me, smiles lovingly, and says, "How do you feel, Brother Lunatic?"

I want to laugh at her attempt to disguise our relationship, seeing her struggle to keep from caressing my face, a tactile sensation that would probably bring me out of my stupor. I settle for a weak scoff.

Lady's head dips towards me, wanting to reward my effort with a kiss.

"What did you do to him?!" Missy exclaims. "He's choking. You shouldn't be here. In fact, why are you here?!"

Lady turns to Missy and says, "He passed out while doing landscape work at the church, Missy. That was less than an hour ago. Have you already forgotten that simple fact?"

Missy is starting to suspect Lady's reason for remaining in my room, which she makes clear when she says, "You have done your duty Sister Church and you can leave now. I am here to take care of my husband, so please leave us now."

Lady nods politely, releases my hand, and steps back from my bed, leaving me with the feeling that I'm in a lifeboat drifting away from a sinking ship, with no supplies and no one to save me. She leaves the room, throwing me a look that warms my heart and assures my recovery.

When Lady is gone, Missy caresses my cheek and says, "I used to think that Lady was a good Christian, but I don't feel that way anymore. She brought you to the hospital, despite our agreeing that Jesus doesn't want interference in His communication channel with you. Anyway, I'll get you out of this den of Satan tomorrow, so you can continue the Lord's work."

I want to tell her that I love Lady and want a divorce. Failing that, I must have gotten her attention, because she leans close and says, "Don't worry, Mac, I'll take you home tomorrow and Jesus will take care of the hospital bill. This place is nothing more than a bunch of money-grubbing Sadducees looking for a profit. I'll take care of you."

My expression of fear at being in Missy's care is lost in translation.

MENAGE A TROIS

I know I'm on a wild ride when Missy takes me home in a wheelchair. I can get up to go the toilet, but I can't take a shower, so I use the tub for a couple of days. Despite my condition, I've got to see Lady, so I call her and talk her into visiting me while Missy is in Oklahoma City on business. Anticipating Lady's touch, her caresses, her kisses, even her voice, rejuvenates me.

"Why did you want to see me, Mac?"

I'm as surprised as her when I stand up from the wheelchair confidently, and step to her, wrapping my suddenly strong arms around her waist.

"I wanted to tell Missy about us, but I couldn't speak…until now." I revel in Lady's presence, her odor, feelings I can't define. Her uncertainty motivates me to remove her dress, her underclothes. She does the same for me. We fall into the king-size bed Missy and I share. I'm in the act of penetration when Lady stops me.

"Have you been raping Missy?"

I'm totally lost. "What…?"

"She hates you, Mac. I've been watching her as I always do. Her face reveals a fear of punishment, fear of what will happen no matter her action. You have been abusing Missy."

"What are you—"

"I'm talking about sexual abuse, forcing yourself on her, causing her physical pain and mental anguish. She is miserable. I've noticed changes in your behavior myself."

"Like what?" I begin.

"You've been raping Missy, haven't you? Yes or no. I don't

care which answer you give, but I don't want to hear excuses. You better think about this Mac, if you have any hope of spending the rest of your life with me."

She looks at my softening penis, her eyebrows raised.

Missy is my wife. She's supposed to submit to me, which she has always done. But that isn't what Lady's talking about. I remember how Missy begged me to stop penetrating her, several times during the previous week, before I went to the hospital. I'd taken her cries of pain as pleasure. She probably wishes I were dead.

"Yes."

"That ends right now. She'll let you know if she wants to have sex with you and we'll deal with that problem at a later date. Okay?"

I nod.

Lady kisses me, begins to rub me and I respond. Being with her is like confessing my sins. I'm myself again by the time we climax together.

Draped across my chest, she's laughing at me when she says, "Who's your best girl?"

"You are, and always will be."

"Are you going to divorce Missy?"

"Whenever you say."

"Am I going to be the second Mrs. Lunatic, the only woman who will share your life and your bed, the woman who will be at your side on your deathbed, still in love with you?"

I roll over, pinning her under me. I brush my lips against her cheeks, her neck, kiss her nipples.

She giggles. "You haven't answered my question."

"I hope so," I say. "But you never know what tomorrow may bring. If you and Vanity are right, my next brush with Jesus could be the end. It's possible that the messenger is expendable. I hope not because I really want to be your husband, not just your boyfriend."

Her face turns serious, but not really serious, if you know what I mean. "Stop raping Missy, Mac. Leave her alone. I mean it. You should apologize. Do you understand?"

I nod meekly. Chastised. She wriggles to get more comfortable and continues, "And you're running out of time to dump all your other girls. Do you need help?"

"What?" I mumble, not fully understanding her words.

"Should I confront Melina and Melissa and tell them to get out of my way? I'm ready to announce our betrothal right now and dealing with those two sexual predators would be the easiest thing in the world for me to do."

"Let me try first. I don't want to cause them unnecessary emotional pain—"

She suddenly pushes me off her, rolling me onto my back. Lady is stronger than she looks. Her finger is wagging in front of my eyes. I'm trying to understand what she's saying.

"Listen to me, Macbeth Lunatic. I am going public with our relationship. I don't give a damn about Missy, Melina, or Melissa, or what impact our betrothal will have on them." Her finger comes to rest between my eyes and she continues, "If you want to have a say in this, you'd better act quickly because it's less than two weeks until Easter. Got it?"

"Yes, ma'am, I understand. I have to end my sexual relationships with everyone but you and I don't have much time. Just in case I forget, could you remind me every time I see you?"

She grins and kisses me, the lips of an angel. She collapses against me. I'm on cloud nine.

The next day, Lady suggests that I should break up with Melina first because it won't be easy. She's not just a sexual predator but also older than me, and probably enjoying my attention more than Melissa. I know what she means because, like I said, Melina's best characteristics are her huge breasts and sexual prowess. Recalling how much fun it was to have sex with her, I'm slow to respond, so Lady offers to break it off for me. I laugh when she describes how much she would enjoy slapping Melina's face. We're both laughing when she slaps my cheeks gently, mixed with loving kisses. She's made her point, so I promise to get right on it.

A couple of days later, I get my chance when Dim meets me at the church while I'm working on the sound system. I don't know why I had insisted on having a licensed electrician do the work because it isn't any harder than installing an entertainment system in a house. I'm running wire from an existing outlet to where the sound system controls are going to be installed, when I hear Melina's voice.

"Here he is! Oh, Mac, come and give me a hug!"

I turn towards her voice, my promise to Lady forgotten, anticipating a pleasant interruption of my work. My smile and my excitement evaporate when I see Dim standing in the doorway. He looks more confused than usual. He may be angry, maybe only upset.

Melina throws herself at me, pushing me backwards. I don't know what she's thinking, with Dim standing there. His presence gives me enough time to remember my vow to Lady. This is a good time to come clean, to admit my sexual relationship with Melina and end it. I'm imagining Lady standing next to me. Wanting to avoid her unsympathetic words, I come up with a more charitable approach.

"I'm so glad you came by. Both of you. Your timing couldn't have been better."

Dim collects his thoughts a moment and says, "Why's that, Mac?"

"For one thing, you can see the progress I'm making on the sound system. We can talk about that later." I stop, uncertain if I should mention Lady or not because she had omitted telling me how to break up with Melina. I decide to wait until Easter, like we had planned.

"There's something else we need to talk about, Dim—you and Melina and me."

Dim looks confrontational, when he replies, "What's that, Mac? What's going on between you and Melina that apparently involves me? I mean…why would I care if my wife is carrying on with another man?" He's angry and I don't blame him, imagining Pastor raping Lady night after night. Me raping Missy night after night.

Not sure of what's going on, other than my feelings for Lady, I say, "Melina and I formed a bond that transcended sexual desire. We have had intercourse many times and her intimate support is the only reason I remained focused on the Lord's work. But that time has passed."

Before Melina can respond, Dim says, "So, like, it's over? You've been having sex with Melina for…how long has this been going on?"

Melina interjects, "Jesus revealed Mac's need for spiritual support to me, after his encounter with the Holy Spirit. We didn't share our spiritual relationship with the congregation because there are many nonbelievers within Trinity House."

That's all true.

Dim asks, "Is it over now?"

I can fulfill my promise to Lady by ending my sexual relationship with Melina Light right now. I'm about to answer his question when Melina interjects, "How can we answer a question like that, Dim? Mac and I are tied together by the Holy Spirit."

I remember Lady's opinion about Melina, that she was a sexual predator. I'm conflicted, but Melina looks different, no longer an enthusiastic lover promoting my message; she has become a temptress, sent by Satan to distract me from the Lord's work. I'm torn between these two women.

Dim looks at me for confirmation.

I want to say how God has led me to Lady, but I'm going to remain silent on that question. "Melina's support has been unimaginably important to keep me focused, but I can stand alone now. Jesus has given me the strength."

Dim seems to understand. "God works in mysterious ways to do what has to be done." He's nodding, struggling to accept what he's hearing.

Melina says, "Let's not be too quick to judge. Mac and I have a special relationship through Christ—"

I'm thinking about Lady's slim, physically fit, body draped across me when I interject, "It's over, Melina. We've been acting as servants of the Lord, but now we have a different purpose. We have to prepare for Easter."

Melina appears to be devastated, an act that proves Lady right. She was taking advantage of our spiritual relationship for physical pleasure.

Dim says, "So, that's it? It's over?"

Melina interjects, "I trust Mac's word, as the voice of Christ. His relationship to our Savior is deeper than I can fathom and I must accede to his authority."

She has moved on, no longer wanting to have sex with me. I'm not surprised to hear her pronounce, "Trinity House should celebrate the confirmation of Mac's message from the Holy Spirit with style. This will be a day to remember for generations. We should have a fireworks display. This is a very popular tradition in Argentina and throughout Latin America."

Dim isn't thinking clearly, overwhelmed as he is by the end of Melina's sexual liaison with me. I support her suggestion. Fireworks are an American tradition so why not? What better reason to have a pyrotechnic display than celebrating the reincarnation of Jesus? It's a compelling argument, one which convinces Dim Light.

"Good idea, Melina. I'll speak to the Board about it."

I can't wait to tell Lady. We're going to make Easter about more than brightly painted eggs and going to church.

One down, two to go.

ALTERCATION

I don't think it's over with Dim. He just didn't want to have it out with me while Melina was standing there. That's fine by me because I suddenly can't stand the sight of her fat ass, face painted like an Indian, dressed like a whore. I don't ever want to see her again, but I sure want to see Dim. If he even looks at me sideways, I'm gonna let him have it. Jesus even told me it's okay to share my feelings, and men like Dim don't hear what you're saying to them unless there's some physical force behind your words. That sonofabitch has been working against me ever since he joined Trinity House, five years after me. The church hadn't needed an elder to take care of the facilities but, if they had, it should have been me. Oh yeh, I know what he and Pastor have been up to. Lady hadn't wanted to tell me the whole truth, to spare my feelings, but I can read between the lines. I'm never going to be an elder, all because of that prick, Dim Light, and the fact that Trinity House isn't much more than a frat house.

Come to think of it, I'm fed up with Baby Boomers. That's what it is. The real bottom line is that those old farts have screwed up the world and don't want to let younger people like me clean up the mess they made. I laugh out loud at the thought of geezers like Dim and Pastor, not to mention Mike Blunt, seeing themselves as wise, defending the world against the unwashed multitudes. My laughter grows and grows, until I can't see when I pull in behind the church.

I'm laughing so hard that I start crying, what seemed so funny a minute ago now reminding me of the glass ceiling that keeps me seated in the fourth row at church, never joining the elders on the front row during the Christmas special. The humor and misery pass and I'm left feeling empty, wondering why I've got 500 pounds of fireworks in the back of my truck, to celebrate Easter while a bunch of Baby Boomers look on condescendingly: *Good job, Mac, that's a good boy, they're going to be so pretty, aren't you excited? Do a good job and we'll even let you keep doing our dirty work, for free.*

I've got to get away from their voices, hounding me. I throw the door open and lurch out of the cab, falling to my knees, covering my ears with my hands.

"Stop talking to me!" I shout. "Shut the hell up!" Now they're laughing at me, deafening me. I'm on my feet, stumbling to the side of the truck, screaming to cover the sound of their laughter.

It stops and I'm left gasping for air in silence. The blessed quiet of late winter in central Oklahoma.

My solitude is broken when Dim's blue Lexus pulls in behind me. My fists instinctively clinch into tight balls. He approaches me with his characteristic confused yet arrogant smile. If he says one word, I'm going to wipe that smirk off his face.

"Hey Mac, I thought I'd come by to make sure we get those fireworks stored inside. It's supposed to rain tonight, not cold enough to snow."

My fists relax. Not now. "Gonna give me a hand are you, Dim?"

He heads down the wheelchair ramp to the basement, tossing over his shoulder, "I'll stick to management and leave the physical labor to you young folks."

I follow him, pushing a hand truck carrying several boxes of fireworks. Dim opens the door and says, "What's that odor?" He's sniffing like a bloodhound.

"Diesel."

We're storing fuel for the tractor in the basement, because of the cold weather and unsightliness of fuel cans behind the church. He flips the light switch and the basement is dimly lit by a few 60-watt bulbs serving as placeholders until proper illumination could be installed. That had never happened. There's no emergency lighting either, a fact I'd mentioned on more than one occasion. I don't feel like bringing it up today. The response had always been that it was a storage basement, not a storm shelter, that nobody was ever going to have to seek refuge while they were at church. It had never happened, not even once, in twenty years.

I put the stack of fireworks against the wall and partly remember something relevant. "We can get one of those plastic storage sheds. I could put it up away from the church and the rectory. That would fix the problem. With the fuel storage I mean."

His mouth grimaces slightly, his head shaking. "Nah. It'll air out by the time you get everything moved in. No one comes down here anyway, so we'll take care of it later." With that, he inspects the basement while I stack cartons of explosives next to fertilizer and diesel fuel in an enclosed space.

I finish and start out the door, wanting to get home, wishing I were going home to be with Lady. While I'm closing the tailgate on my truck, I look towards the rectory. She's standing there, watching me from the porch but not moving to join me, probably because of Dim's presence. One more reason I don't like that S.O.B., he's keeping me from talking to my best girl, soon to be my wife.

Dim appears, waves to Lady, and confronts me. "Why did you put fertilizer, diesel fuel, and fireworks in the basement together? That's a dangerous combination."

I admit that since I was touched by the Holy Spirit, I have forgotten a lot, what with all that spiritual thoughts passing through my brain, which was never that great to begin with. But I do remember why the basement is filled with flammable and combustible material. I also recall that I complained about it and was overridden. I even recollect accepting the situation because Jesus had told me to not worry about it. I share my memories with Dim.

"I never did any such thing."

I blink uncomprehendingly. "You just had me put 500 pounds of fireworks in the basement after taking a look yourself and noting the strong odor of diesel. I'm experiencing side effects after a brush with the Holy Spirit, yet even I can remember what happened less than an hour ago."

His face assumes that Baby Boomer air of age-based

wisdom. "There's no point in arguing with an idiot like you. It'll be fine, just don't put any more cans of diesel inside. We'll get to the rest later."

This is the last straw. "Are you referring to me as an idiot because I'm not an *elder*, an old man who should be sitting on the porch in a rocking chair? We're sick and tired of you old men and your rigged elections."

Dim's mouth tightens as if he doesn't know what to say. I help him. "We're on to you. Maybe that's the revelation Jesus is going to reveal on Easter. Maybe there's going to be a popular uprising against the tyrannical rule of old men over everyone else."

That gets Dim going. "I've been very patient, what with you and Melina carrying on in the name of the Lord, but don't push it, Boy."

Talk about pushing, *Boy* is a big red button on my chest, so I let Dim have it with both barrels. "If you hadn't been an old man, Melina would never have contemplated serving as my personal sex worker. Of course, it was great having sex with her, sometimes two and three times a day, because it kept me focused. Her tits alone are enough to keep a man focused. And she was so aggressive that I have to wonder if she's getting enough satisfaction at home."

Dim suddenly looks shaken, his gaze dipping briefly, before he retorts, "I can't believe she talked about our private—"

I cut him off. "She never said a word, but you just proved my wild and crazy speculation. Now, you tell me, which one of us is an idiot?"

Dim advances, enraged jealousy twisting his features. I understand and I should have already had my fists up, ready to land the first blow because I'm pretty mad myself. I move towards him and challenge him. "Go ahead, *elderly* man, try and hit me, maybe you can get your fists up, better than your—"

His lunge catches me off guard. He's heavier and taller than me, and we fall to the ground, flailing but not really trying to hurt each other. I don't really want to hit him and it's obvious he feels the same, so we slap and push each other as I get out from under him, knocking him on the grass. I'm on my feet first, but I'm not holding my fists up in preparation for battle. Instead, I offer my hand and he accepts it.

We're standing there, feeling like fools, and he says, "I'm sorry, Mac, I don't know what came over me."

"I do," I say. "You love your wife and I had an affair with her. Even if it was part of the Lord's plan, that's gotta hurt. I wasn't very Christian in goading you, when you were already hurting from all that…"

Dim nods. "I started it. You're not an idiot. I was just blaming you for my mistake…we'll take care of that later."

Lady suddenly appears, her lovely face the picture of relief. "I guess you boys worked it out?"

Dim and I nod like schoolboys chastised by their teacher. She manages to brush against me, sending a bolt of lightning up my spine. I can see from her eyes that she's proud of me.

THE THERAPIST

I was appalled to see Dim and Mac rolling around on the ground like school boys, but relieved that their altercation hadn't come to blows. A good deal of the emotional stress between them had been released during their brief physical encounter. The next day, I spoke to Dim about it, certain that Mac had kept my name out of the entire affair. I got an earful because he was as talkative as Missy.

It turned out that he suffered from erectile disfunction and the pills hadn't worked. They don't work for everyone. His initial, subdued response to learning that Melina was Mac's *spiritual* advisor was because he'd reluctantly consented to her having extramarital sexual affairs to satisfy her needs, which she had spoken of openly before their marriage. It was his fault, or rather his body's fault. I felt sorry for him. I shared something I'd learned during my years of being married to Pastor, who liked to have regular sex with his wife.

"If the pills don't work, it might be psychological. You and Melina have been married five years, which is a good time to reevaluate your original expectations—what you both wanted from the marriage. I can't think of a better opportunity than this to discuss your relationship with Melina openly. Take stock of the situation."

I didn't need to hear about Dim and Melina's three previous marriages each. I pretended to care about what he was saying and was beginning to understand why Mac was an alcoholic by the time Dim said, "So, do you think Melina and I can get past this?"

I don't know why Dim thought I could solve his personal problems, especially when they were the result of recurring deep-seated psychological issues. He wasn't the only one. The congregation of Trinity House suffered from every psychosis I'd learned about in undergraduate psychology classes. I guess they acknowledged my disinterest in their superstitious beliefs, perceiving me as an objective observer of the mess they had made of their lives. Or maybe they sensed what a bad job I'd done with my own. We were kindred spirits.

"Melina shouldn't have sexual carte blanche. That's not going to work."

He looked confused.

"There should be limits on her sexual behavior, which she needs to understand. Maybe you're already doing that. How would I know?"

He scoffed uncomfortably and struggled to think of something to say. "Not unless you call letting her do whatever she likes setting limits. How can I get her attention? How can I get past this problem? It's destroying our marriage."

I had to unpack his multiple questions. I hate it when people do that. I responded to his ambiguous queries in reverse order. "Have you had erectile dysfunction before, Dim?"

It turned out that he'd suffered from a lack of interest in his sexual partners after about five years during his previous marriages. I was glad to share my amateur psychological opinion with him.

"You have two choices, Dim."

He was listening attentively, eager to choose a door, possibly one leading to a satisfying life with Melina or, just as likely, another divorce.

"I should have said that you have three choices, because you can always ignore the problem and let God solve it for you."

He shook his head. Apparently, he loved Melina.

"Okay. You should talk to Brother Lunatic about how he sees women, what about them gets his attention, why he was attracted to Melina, who is ten-years older than him and not a beauty queen, even though she is attractive. What I mean is that he found her very appealing, despite her not being a centerfold model…"

"So, I should find a way to lust after her?"

"I don't know, Dim. Ask Brother Lunatic. You guys should be able to talk about it, after your meeting of the minds yesterday."

He smiled sheepishly and asked, "What's the second approach?"

I didn't have one, hoping he would go for door number one, so I spoke openly. "Talk to her about it. Feel free to get angry, express your feelings about what happened, but also be understanding. Listen to her and acknowledge that she felt Jesus wanted her to serve as Mac's spiritual consultant."

His head was shaking as I spoke, which didn't surprise me.

"You're right, Lady. Mac and I understand each other a lot better now, and I think we can talk about his relationship with Melina. It's worth it because I really want it to work this time."

I assumed that he meant he wanted his marriage to work. I just wanted him out of my house. He suddenly seemed eager to leave, so we had a meeting of the minds. I walked him out and gave him an encouraging word as he drove away. It was unseasonably warm, so I stood outside for a few minutes, looking at the stars, trying to remember the names of the constellations, thinking about Mac…and Easter. My reverie was interrupted when Mac's pickup pulled into the rectory driveway. He never came by at night, even when Pastor was out of town. It just didn't look right.

He went to the back of his truck, lowered the tailgate, and brought a bundle of firewood, purchased in a store. He'd always brought me wood he'd cut himself. Something was going on.

"It's supposed to be cold…yeh, real cold, soon. What, with Pastor out of town, I didn't want you to be without a fire."

I hadn't realized just how much he loved me until that moment. I wiped a happy tear from my eye and said, "Thank you Mac but, as adorable as your pretense at worrying about me being cold on such a warm evening is, tell me the real reason you came by."

"I wanted to see your face, hear your voice…I need some advice from you, Sweetheart—" His words came to a stop, leaving me gasping for breath.

I dared to respond, "What is it, Honey?"

It was done. We had addressed each other using the sacred words used only by couples who were devoted to each other.

Mac grinned at me and made me question my doubts about the existence of God, or at least some cosmic entity that cared about the lives of individual people. He asked me what he should do to put things right with Melina and Dim. He felt guilty about what his close spiritual relationship with her might have done to their marriage. I held back tears of joy, knowing that, despite several strokes, Mac was still the man I'd fallen in love with.

"Dim needs your help, Mac. He's suffering from a kind of erectile dysfunction that can't be corrected with pills. He isn't excited about Melina any more. He's waiting for your call. You should tell him how you convinced yourself that she was a woman you couldn't resist as a sexual partner. I might add that, when you've done that, you should explain your approach to me so that—"

"I don't know if I can do that Lady because you're the love of my life. I didn't have to convince myself to fall in love with you. It wasn't lust but real love. I mean that and you know it."

Mac has a way with words.

"Have a couple of drinks, then tell him what it was that made you want to…what made Melina irresistible as a sexual partner. Obviously, you're not infatuated with her, but you couldn't keep your hands off her in public, the day you two plowed the garden together. Just tell Dim about your state of mind during that encounter. He witnessed it, so he'll be able to relate. It will mean the world to him and probably save his marriage. You owe him that. But don't mention me. Figure out a way to do it without my name coming up, at least not personally."

He understood. I wasn't involved in his ménage a trois with Dim and Melina. I reminded him that being in love with him was like Dim's being in love with Melina. I wanted him to do the right thing. I knew he was coming around when he insisted on giving me a passionate kiss next to his truck, like a couple of high school sweethearts. I slept well that night.

My job as Pastor's wife had become full time. Having gotten Dim and Mac on the same page, I had the pleasure of another personal conversation with Missy Lunatic the next day.

It didn't take long for her to cut to the chase. "You wouldn't believe it, Lady. Mac was so profoundly impacted by his encounter with Jesus that he…he insisted on doing things…having intimate relations all the time…"

I imagined myself leaning back in a leather armchair (I was sitting at the kitchen table), contemplating her words. Since she didn't seem prepared to finish her thought, I spoke up. "That must have been very upsetting. I believe you told me that you and Mac were brother and sister in Christ?"

She nodded.

"I don't know how to say this Missy and please don't misunderstand but—let me think—there are two issues. First, is sexual intercourse painful for you?"

Her head was shaking forcefully as she said, "Not unless it's two or three times a night, which has been happening lately. But I started using a lotion I found at the drug store."

That was more than I wanted to know. "That's good news. My next question is more sensitive, but I don't want you to take it the wrong way. Do you sometimes think about women in—"

"I'm gay, or whatever they call it," she blurted. "I know that's a sin but I can't help it. For example, I would like to make love to you right now, you're so beautiful and understanding. Nothing like Mac or any man I've ever met."

It took a minute for me to respond. She waited patiently, her eyes undressing me the way Mac's did every time I saw him. Finally, I said, "You should speak openly about your true feelings and Jesus will forgive you. To be honest, I don't think being homosexual is a sin because it isn't a willful act. You didn't decide to be attracted to women. It's just who you are."

She perked up. "You mean, it's okay to want to be with a woman rather than a man?"

I nodded. "That is the view of many churches. God hasn't spoken authoritatively on the topic, to my knowledge."

Suddenly worried, she said, "What about Mac? It's my duty as his wife to serve him. It's in the Bible. How can I refuse his desires?"

I was enjoying my conversation with Missy, not because she spoke like a teenager despite being my age, but because—well, you know, she was out of the way. One less broken heart.

I used my extensive knowledge of the Bible, especially the New Testament, to allay her concerns. "Jesus never spoke about lesbian relationships, only the need to love each other, without mentioning gender. He wanted us to be brothers and sisters in His name, leaving us to work out the details."

Missy taught the pre-K Sunday school. I watched her face as she struggled to remember the lessons she had recited to a generation of young children. Finally, after a thorough search of her memory, she said, "You're right, Lady. Jesus only wants us to love one another."

I couldn't help asking, "Is there someone you're sweet on?"

She nodded shyly. "Melissa is such a nice girl—"

Her confession of a lesbian infatuation with the music director was interrupted when I choked on the coffee I was drinking. I made a mess, spewing caffeine-infused fluid everywhere, even spraying Missy. She actually had to wipe my sputum out of her eyes before saying, "I reckon you have a different opinion?"

There was no reason to keep what I knew about Melissa Tight to myself. I fought to maintain whatever judicial demeanor I had accidentally acquired when I said, "I don't know if Melissa shares your personal feelings but, from what I've heard, she is a person of strong character."

"You mean she might be bisexual. She's probably had an affair with Mac, the way he carries on. There's no telling how many women he's taken advantage of."

I wanted to kiss her, but she might have misunderstood, so I limited my response to, "I've heard stories…"

"Oh my god! And he's forcing himself on me? I'll have no more of that, even if it is okay most of the time. What do I have to do Lady, to live my life the way I want to?"

That was an easy question but I felt ethically constrained to speak as if I weren't in love with her husband. "Divorce is an option for you, Missy. Trinity House isn't the Catholic Church, and it has no rules. That's why we all joined. However, you should consider marriage counseling first."

Her mind was made up. "It's time to face the truth. I love Mac but we are incompatible. We both love Trinity and each other but not like a married couple, not anymore. We aren't fighting. It should be no problem to work it out. We can even both be members of Trinity House. Mac will understand."

I couldn't help asking, "Would you like to meet Melissa Tight? I can arrange an introduction."

Missy's head looked like it would come lose from her neck. I took her cranial gyrations as agreement. That would be fun.

After learning about Missy Lunatic's natural desires, imagine how surprised I was when, the next day, Vanity wanted to take our relationship in a similar direction. Vanity and I had been talking every day and getting together several times a week. She was my older sister. But I couldn't imagine a lesbian affair with an older sister, if I'd had one. I was the one who had been initially overcome by the closeness of our relationship. Vanity had straightened me out, sharing her experience of how a lesbian relationship had ruined a friendship.

I was conflicted when I faced Vanity Blunt in the rectory's living room.

"I know I said it was a mistake, but I was talking about the past. It didn't work out because neither of us had other options but now you're going to be with Mac and I'm trying to keep it together with Mike…"

That was it. Vanity and Mike were having marital difficulties, maybe he'd had another affair. I changed the subject, trying to turn down the heat I felt from her proximity.

"We both know how strong our feelings are for each other but that's not what's bothering you, Vanity. Tell me the truth."

Instead of telling me the truth, she slid against me, and took liberties only Mac had been allowed. I gasped for breath when her finger penetrated me and gently stroked my clitoris. Her free hand unbuttoned my blouse, her tongue caressing mine. I loved Vanity and it was easy to let her continue, another finger joining the first, taking me to places even Mac hadn't discovered. I didn't resist her but laid back and enjoyed what I'd known from our first kiss would be the most pleasurable experience of my life. Her lips caressed my cheeks, my nose, my eyes. I let her take me far beyond any sexual experience I'd ever had and I was begging her to stop but not pushing her hand away. It was the most incredible experience of my life.

"How was it?"

I was still gasping for breath when I mumbled, "Oh my god, Vanity. Is that what it was like with your mentor?"

She nodded. "After you give me an experience like yours, I'll tell you what's on my mind."

Still feeling the high, I did as she'd instructed, duplicating the movements of her fingers, my hands on her breasts the same as hers had been on mine, my tongue in her mouth penetrating her, making her an object of my sexual curiosity. She was crying out, ineffectually pushing against my hand, moaning, speaking as if I'd given her a truth serum. My lips were wrapped tightly around her left nipple, sucking as if I were a hungry infant, when she spoke the truth.

"I'm a lesbian!"

After my conversation with Missy, I wasn't impressed, so I kept up the pressure until her cries of ecstasy had lessened. I spoke honestly when I said, "You gave me the most incredible sexual experience of my life. I hope it was as good for you."

It felt good, our breasts pressed together, our nipples touching. I pushed Vanity over on the sofa, so that I was laying on top her, and kissed her passionately. My original feelings for her had been justified. I loved her in a way I would never love anyone else.

"Did we just ruin our relationship?" she asked.

I shook my head, remembering my conversation with Missy. "No. I think it's stronger than ever because I'm…well, I'm not lesbian, although I'll probably never have a more satisfying sexual experience in my life than we just shared. I wouldn't mind doing this again in the future because even Mac doesn't make me feel so—no one can replace you Vanity, at least not with respect to my total emotional commitment."

"Was it that good?"

"Oh my god! I love you and I always will, even if I love Mac a little more, probably because he has a penis that he can shove in me and scratch an itch I have in my vagina."

Vanity laughed out loud, became quiet, and asked, "What should I do? I confronted Mike about his affairs and he told me to remember my place."

We were both still feeling the effects of our shared experience, kissing and touching, so it was difficult to think. I kissed Vanity's finger, covered with pap from my vagina, thought about what I was going to say, remembered how close Easter was, and made a decision I was certain I would not regret. A change of heart as it were.

"You should get together with Missy Lunatic. It turns out that she's in the same situation as you. She wanted to do what we just did but she doesn't have your charm or looks." I made a point of kissing Vanity passionately, probing her mouth with my tongue with those words. She melted like butter, her hands wrapping around my waist.

"She is kind of cute." She kissed me quickly, took a deep breath, and said, "I guess I have to live with Mike and his traditional approach to sex, but...are you sure about Missy?"

"She hit on me. I pointed her towards Melissa just to get out of the situation, but you and she are a perfect fit."

Vanity sat up, showcasing her large, firm breasts, and said, "What about you? Was this a one-night stand?"

Another multiple question. This was an easy one. "I love you Vanity and I always will. I also love Mac. We're a family."

"What does that mean?"

I couldn't help laughing. "No matter how much I enjoy sharing sexual experiences with you Vanity, you *cannot* fuck me, and I love the way Mac executes that simple, primordial act. I like to get fucked, an erect penis in my vagina—only Mac's from now on. It doesn't matter that the sensual pleasure we just shared was out of this world."

Vanity laughed, her hand covering her mouth. "I know what you mean. Maybe I'm not lesbian, but only bisexual..."

DEVIL'S ADVOCATE

In my wildest imagination, I wouldn't have thought I would find myself defending the superstitious fundamentalists, but that is exactly the situation I was in when Pastor shared his worst fears with me. I detested everything these people held sacred. I didn't care if they were fundamentalists or evangelicals. They were all superstitious fools.

"I may have been naive in founding a nondenominational church in Modoc. It has all gone so well for twenty years, I was starting to think that the members of Trinity House had risen above doctrinal arguments, but maybe I was allowing my personal dream to cloud my eyes. Maybe it was a fool's pursuit."

I was accustomed to these conversations and I had always spoken openly without revealing my agnostic views. But that cat was out of the bag, so Pastor understood my meaning when I responded.

"I'm not going to insult you by asking a rhetorical question. However, there was nothing foolhardy or irrational about creating Trinity House, a nondenominational church in a small city like Modoc. You filled a spiritual need for a couple hundred families. You've done very well by them, and you shouldn't be looking backwards, not during this crisis."

Pastor helped himself to a second serving of chicken cacciatore and some green beans. "So, you agree that this is a crisis?"

I never have seconds, so my plate was empty, leaving me to soliloquize while Pastor partook of the healthy meal I had prepared. "Every human society, as well as all the great apes, is in a perpetual state of crisis—flux if you like. Focusing on humans, it comes as no surprise to me that our superstitious beliefs are as tumultuous as everything else we do. Specifically, I remember canvassing the city, speaking to people about what you wanted to create here, being rebuffed, sometimes having encouraging conversations. It wasn't obvious that Trinity House was going to succeed, but you wouldn't let go, which is why I married you." I smiled and risked batting an eye.

Pastor nodded and I continued, "You founded a community of nonconformists—I'm talking about both evangelicals and fundamentalists—who had a shared vision of communicating with their god. You have done an outstanding job keeping these disparate groups in harmony, like a musical conductor—Leonard Bernstein for example. The symphony continued until the piano's C-Major string broke...a black swan appeared."

He swallowed a mouthful of chicken and said, "What do you think is going on with Macbeth Lunatic?"

I was happy to speak openly about Mac, at least with respect to his revelatory experience. "He has had a series of strokes. I can't believe he's still alive. His followers have simply found a new revelation to grasp futilely, to avoid dealing with life, an act clearly beyond their capacity. I wish this had never happened Pastor, but it has been dumped in your lap."

He wiped his mouth and said, "I guess it's easy for you, not being a Christian, to dismiss his spiritual experience."

"Think whatever you like, Pastor. I don't care. If you are conflicted about the question of whether or not Macbeth Lunatic actually had a close encounter with the Holy Spirit, then you should give him the benefit of the doubt. For myself, it's cut and dried. He's suffering from delusions. He had a stroke and will probably be dead before the garden he's planting will produce its first sprout."

It was easy to hold back my tears because I hated Pastor and his beliefs at that moment.

I sat woodenly as he got a half-full bottle of wine and filled our glasses. He sat down and said, "I agree with your assessment, but I can't be sure if this is God's will or not. What to us is a stroke is nothing more than collateral damage to God.

After all, by fulfilling his obligation to God, especially if it leads to his death, Mac will have become a martyr—sort of."

I sipped from my glass and replied, "You are talking like a superstitious fool, Pastor, looking for convenient excuses to explain the death of a congregant. Just like when you initially refused to admit that Vernon Huckster died of the Covid virus. On the other hand, you may simply be taking advantageous of the superstitious beliefs of others to lead a comfortable life." I glared at him and took another sip of wine.

"I can't believe how I misunderstood you, Lady—"

I cut him off. "We were young and saw each other through rose-colored glasses. That is all water under the bridge. We are talking about this black swan event, Macbeth Lunatic speaking for the Holy Spirit. I understand your necessarily cautious approach, but I say he's full of shit."

Pastor started to speak, thought better and sipped from his wineglass, so I did the same.

"The only reason you're facing this situation is that the Fundamentalists are more gullible than the Evangelicals. They are so desperate for some excitement in their lives that they'll believe anything, even all that QAnon nonsense. Macbeth Lunatic has gotten their attention. He's their latest fad. My god, Pastor! In his current mental condition, QAnon is the voice of God! Has this fact escaped your attention?"

I had stood up, wine glass in hand, during my rant. I retook my seat.

Pastor sipped his wine and said, "I see your point, but it isn't that easy. I can't stand behind the pulpit and tell people they are stupid. I can't even tell them they are mistaken, or confused. I can't tell them anything they don't want to hear. You know this, Lady. I can only nudge them towards being better Christians—you do agree with that objective, don't you?"

I nodded.

"It is a fundamental tenet of my faith that God will speak to anyone at any time, if that is His will. I hear what you're saying, that this gap between the physical world and the beliefs people—including me—hold closest to their hearts, can never be bridged. I think I agree with you but we have to try. That is what we've spent the last twenty years doing, showing people a way to live in the world while acknowledging the world to come, even if the details of the afterlife are uncertain."

I was tired of hearing the same story over and over. I didn't understand how he could be so rational, recognizing the inconsistencies of Christian dogma, and yet accepting them as the truth. "The afterlife is uncertain, Pastor, the entire superstitious enterprise is an invention by primitive people, promulgated by men who wanted to be in charge. Well, look where it got us…" I dropped it, knowing I was spitting into the wind.

He thought about my words a few minutes before responding. "Are you suggesting that I should speak against Brother Lunatic despite the support he has within the congregation?"

"Why not? Maybe his supporters need to recognize the need for their spiritual leader to be an ordained minister and not the lawn keeper—stand up for the truth. Call him out publicly. The worst that could happen is the loss of a few members of the church, but I can assure you that Macbeth and Missy Lunatic wouldn't be among them." I had said too much. My heart was racing, wanting to get it out in the open, end this charade. My concern was unwarranted.

"Why is that?" he asked.

"I've spoken to both of them since his *spiritual* experience. It isn't about saving face to Mac and Missy. They see his mission as simply a task God has given him, which he has to complete against all opposition. He is not trying to start his own church. Your speaking out would be seen as no more than the act of a man misled by Satan, not something worth quitting Trinity House. They would try to wait you out, but there's a deadline on Mac's prophesy."

"Short attention span," Pastor calmly replied.

I nodded. "That doesn't work because these people will have made up their minds before Easter."

"How many families do you think would leave Trinity House if I denounced Mac and insisted he seek medical attention?"

It was always about money, but it wasn't Pastor's fault because he had a church to run. He wasn't a greedy man. "When Mac and Missy didn't leave, the only ones who'd emigrate would be the stubborn ones, a couple of families who aren't very good Christians to begin with."

Pastor scoffed. "I'm not sure but that it wouldn't be a good idea to have more agnostics within the church. Your view isn't clouded by misinterpretation of the Bible or wishful thinking about the afterlife."

It was my turn to laugh. "Being married to you for twenty years, meeting a lot of other ministers, I think there's an agnostic standing behind thousands of pulpits across America. You just can't admit it, not even to me, because of the risk of ruining your credibility. But you don't need to worry Pastor because I've never spoken to anyone about our conversations. They are our family secret. You mean well and you *are* helping people, using the only approach that works with those you've chosen to lift out of the depths of wanton ignorance. Keep up the good work." I waved my nearly empty glass as a toast.

He studied me a minute before saying, "You know, there are some within the congregation who feel that I've been leaning too far towards the Fundamentalist viewpoint, that I've become like President Trump, kowtowing to extremists to keep their support for political reasons. I didn't know I was a politician. That's how crazy it's become, when a minister is accused of playing a political game…"

I had only one answer. There was always only one answer. Money. "Where does Trinity House get the majority of its funding?"

"You know the answer."

"Then you know what to do."

FALSE PROPHET

It's been hard to keep my hands off of Melina, despite my revulsion at her appearance now that I'm committed to Lady. I don't want anything to do with her (Melina that is), especially after coming to terms with Dim. I still think he's a dumbass but he isn't an asshole, like Mike Blunt. I'll get to that later. The only reason Melina hasn't gotten into my pants is that Dim and I talk all the time. He had never used his finger to stimulate her sexually. Having passed that hurdle, he reported successful intercourse when he thought of her as a pair of large, firm breasts attached to a very tight vagina. Apparently, his erectile dysfunction was in his mind. Melina is coming on to me so hard that I'm practically begging Dim to get her off my back.

"She's used to you, Mac," he says.

I'm not having any of that, so I lay down the law. "Either you satisfy your wife sexually, or I am going to tell her a lie, that I find her fat, ugly, revolting, and anything else I can think of to hurt her feelings. I'm sorry Dim, but I can't carry the burden of Melina's sexual needs anymore. I'm a married man."

"Okay. But I'm having trouble with the idea of ignoring her and then sexually assaulting her. I don't know when to switch…when I should suddenly show her who's the boss. Do you see what I mean?"

I explain how he has to use his nose, to smell when she's ready. He finds this idea incomprehensible, but he tries it, and reports success. At Lady's suggestion Dim and I are friends on Facebook, so I get regular updates on his progress. From my end, I notice a subtle change in Melina's behavior. She's still touching, kissing, calling me her spiritual soul mate, but she stops texting me that she wants to hook up at our usual motel. Dim's so excited at hearing this that he says something he probably hadn't meant to say.

"Pastor and Mike Blunt are so wrong about you, Mac. You are not a false prophet. That is just so wrong…"

Lady has shown me how to learn from others' social mistakes, so I immediately change the topic, "I don't know Dim, after all, that garden is a pretty big project. I'm not sure if I can keep up with it. I'm a lot busier than I thought I'd be when I agreed to plant and tend it."

He's forgotten his own words. "Uh, yeh…okay, but will you be able to at least take care of it this year, get us through the harvest?"

"No problem. The work will be done, even if I have to pay someone else to do it. I have a deal with Trinity House, and I never welch on a promise."

Thanks to Dim's warning, I'm prepared for Pastor's sermon the week before Easter. The sermon is directed at me, accusing me of being a false prophet, but I've done some research with Missy's help. Only God knows the truth. Pastor is not God, nor has he ever claimed to be a prophet like me, so he doesn't have a leg to stand on as he quotes Jesus, warning about false prophets in verse after verse. I'm enjoying his sermon, secure in the knowledge that I speak for the Lord. In fact, I don't know why Pastor is responding so defensively, acting as if I want to become the leader of Trinity House. To his credit, he finishes his sermon on a positive note.

"The Gospels warn of false prophets, pretending to share news of Jesus' return. We are vigilant against such pretenders. There is another kind of false prophesy, which doesn't speak of the End Time, but only of ambiguous miracles and wonders. Jesus left it to us to discern such falsehoods in the words we hear on a daily basis. They are not of themselves evil, but they can lead to evil acts by souls that are not following our Saviors' path."

Jesus wants me to stand up and call Pastor a hypocritical tool of the devil. I don't because Lady's expression is telling me to be respectful of Pastor as Trinity House's spiritual leader. Reminding me of our deal. I want to tell her that she's wrong, about Pastor deserving respect just because he's standing behind the pulpit because he went to college. Him and his college boys club. If you ask me, all those college men have so much nonsense in their heads that they can't hear the voice of God, even when He's shouting in their ears. Jesus is shouting in my ears after the music begins. Missy is more excited than she had been lately, Melina is dancing down the center aisle with her hands in the air, joined by several other women and even some men, Lady is hiding behind the organ, ignoring me. I'm feeling the Holy Spirit joining me, taking me outside my body, where I watch from the vantage point of one of God's chosen.

I'm joined in the vastness of the nave by Jesus, looking down on the congregation, his arm around my shoulder. "Are you ready to face Satan as I did and spend forty days in the wilderness?"

I nod, feeling one with my Savior, floating above the people I had been commanded to save. "What should I do, my Lord?"

Jesus kisses my cheek and says, "You must stand up in my name and tell the people of Trinity House that I would have them share the resurrection of my physical body in the sanctity of their homes, in prayer and thanksgiving, in communion with their families. They should not meet together in one place, not on this Easter. I will be disappointed if they fail me in this matter, and they will risk everlasting damnation."

I nod weakly. "How am I to do that, Jesus?"

"It will be a virtual Easter, shared using computers and cell phones."

"Why?"

His eyes are hazel. They look into my soul as he says, "Few within Trinity House are ready to join me at this time. Those who heed my words, coming from your mouth, will have time to study my teachings before they are called to stand before me. It is not yet the End Times, despite what many believe. You must convince Trinity House to be patient and wait for the time that no one knows. I'll share a secret with you, Mac, if you'd like to hear it."

"Of course, Jesus, what is it. I will tell no one."

"Even I don't know when the end will come. There isn't much purpose to the end of the world if anyone except my

Father knew the date. Do you understand?"

I get it. Perfect sense. Jesus is like God's conscious mind, but he doesn't know what's really going on. Even the Holy Spirit doesn't know that. Only God knows everything. I nod affirmatively and say, "Of course, Jesus. I will do as you say. I won't be kept from my mission because of any resistance, not even from Pastor—"

Jesus scoffs and interjects, "He is a Pharisee, who has not heeded my voice. They are all deaf to my words Mac, except you. Thus, it is your duty to save them from eternal damnation by doing as I ask."

I dare to look into His eyes, lit by the glory of God, an effulgence surrounding His brow, expanding to engulf His body, then Jesus is gone, leaving me with my promise to do His work. I will not be deterred from what must be done. I am a servant of the Lord. I will not be kept from my work, even if it means I must die from the side-effects of being His loyal servant. I return to my body. I'm standing next to Missy, who's doing as good a job of ignoring me as Lady. After spending time in the rafters with Jesus, I'm not sure if I'm really present in the world, maybe I'm not here at all, only a reflection from wherever I am. I can see that the people sitting around me, standing and singing, dancing, speaking in tongues, are all looking at me, examining me for imperfections of the spirit, finding me wanting. They believe the nonsense Pastor has spoken from his pulpit, disregarding the wishes of our Savior. Jesus was right. I am the only one who can hear his voice.

When the service ends, I share my thoughts with Pastor and Lady, who are standing together at the door like they always do. I'm smiling grimly, knowing how my words will be received.

"That was an excellent sermon, Pastor." I'm working hard to keep from saying what I want to say. Lady is looking at me as if she doesn't know me. Missy is standing next to me. I glance at her, an uncertain smile suggesting that she probably supports me, so I continue, "Jesus doesn't use a calendar but He is aware of time. This morning didn't seem like the best time to share what I've been shown, so I'll wait until this evening. I guess we'll both be working on our messages this afternoon…"

Lady's eyes open wide in surprise. Missy takes my arm, reminding Lady that she's my wife. I squeeze her hand and, aroused, desperately wanting and needing Lady, suddenly lusting after Missy, I don't hear Pastor's response to my statement as I lead my wife out of the church, disappointed that I was not going to be sexually gratified. I shoot Lady a longing gaze, which she returns with triumphant disdain. I want to be with her so bad it hurts, but Missy's supportive hand on my arm reminds me to keep up the charade for another week.

COMING OUT

"I'm proud of the way you stood up to Pastor," Missy says, sitting next to me in my truck. "I can't wait to hear your latest revelation. Maybe you can tell me about it during lunch?"

I'm not thinking about food. I struggle to drive my truck home after church. I'm so aroused that I seriously consider pulling over and taking Missy right there in my full-size pickup. She's talking about Pastor's sermon and what it means for the congregation, how willing they'll be to hear my prophesy, which I'm going to share during the evening service. I don't hear her words, sneaking looks at her, imagining what it's going to be like when I get her home, in our bed, and satisfy my natural sexual desires. Lust for my wife.

I follow her into the kitchen, dropping my coat on the floor, my mind on one thing. Oblivious to whatever she's thinking, assuming her thoughts are the same as mine, I catch up with her in front of the refrigerator, wrap my arms around her waist, pull her close, begin unbuttoning her blouse.

"What are you doing, Mac?" She pulls away and faces me. I'm speechless.

"I don't do that anymore," she states flatly.

"Don't do what?" I venture.

"I know that you've probably gotten used to…well, you've been taking liberties lately and I let you get away with it. Either way, that's over. I'm not going to be your sex slave anymore. You can go to the bedroom and masturbate."

This is my wife talking, not Lady or Vanity or Melina or Melissa, or any one of the other women I've had sex with.

Missy is my default lover. She can't just refuse me. It's in the Bible. "You're my wife, Missy, and you must submit to me. Making love is the most basic form of submission. You can't refuse…"

She closes the oven door, turns to me and says, "I do not wish to have sexual intercourse with you, Mac. That is my right, to not do something like that with…"

I'm lost. We've been having *sexual intercourse* for twenty years, with a couple of dry spells, but we'd been on a roll recently. It doesn't make sense. "I don't understand, Missy. We made love this morning and you were howling like a banshee, wanting more, begging me to finish it. What's going on?"

Her eyes roll, before looking left then right, not meeting mine. She mumbles something. I mumble something. We're not communicating, until her gyrating eyes finally meet mine.

"I love you, Mac, but not…not the way you think. I don't find you romantically attractive, and I only married you because I was stupid and ignorant and lazy and you were a good prospect as a husband. And you've done a great job. I'm not refusing to have sex with you because I think you don't deserve it—what am I saying? What I mean is that we had a good thing going, until the Holy Spirit touched you, and you suddenly needed to make love all the time. Of course, once your penis is inside me, I like it just like any other woman…but I don't feel satisfied afterwards. Do you know what I mean?"

The answer is no. I approach her, arms extended, repulsed by her open palm across my cheek. "No!" she says forcefully.

"You're my wife!"

"I am telling you that I do not want to have sexual intercourse with you. If you force yourself on me, you will be committing a felony. That is an Oklahoma law. I know that I've gone along with your recent sexual advances, but I'm not doing it anymore."

I'm frustrated. "Who have you been talking to? Where did you get these crazy ideas?"

"They're not crazy. What's crazy is letting you manhandle me when I don't want anything to do with you, at least not in the bedroom. I think that…no, in fact I don't like having sex with you because I'm…because I'm—"

"Because you're what? Going through menopause? Has it become painful for you? You should have told me before. Now I feel like a jerk, making love with you, causing you pain, I'm sorry—"

Her head is shaking as she interrupts me. "I'm gay, lesbian, and I'm not attracted to you. I don't know if I ever was. It just seemed like the thing to do, getting married and all. I haven't changed. I've always felt this way and after talking to Lady—"

"Lady!" My head is about to explode. So, this is Lady's idea of helping me break up with the other women in my life. "It's none of her business what we do—what you think about being married and all. I can't believe you…"

Actually, I can believe it, because Lady is very persuasive when she wants to be. We talked about it a few times. I even called her manipulative, a label she didn't much care for.

"It doesn't matter if I talked to Lady Church or not Mac, what matters is that my feelings for you are like, well, like for a brother or something. Why do you think it's been ten years since we made love?"

I'm not thinking so well, so I say too much. "I didn't notice—" I wince but she doesn't get angry.

"I know you've been carrying on with women all over town. I was glad you were distracted—and no, I haven't done the same. I was ashamed of the way I felt, until I spoke to Lady Church. She's really smart, especially about the Gospels. Did you know that Jesus never said a word about being gay or lesbian, it was Paul who spoke so strongly against…anyone who didn't fit his idea of walking in Jesus' footsteps? He never even met Jesus. In fact, his vision, his encounter with the Holy Spirit, wasn't much different than yours…"

My mind's racing, remembering all the times I'd gotten together with women, how Missy had never once asked me where I'd been. I must have been a blind fool, thinking she hadn't noticed. She hadn't cared if I was having affairs, and mow she doesn't suspect Lady's agenda for encouraging her to come out of the closet. Not that she would care if she did know.

I pretend to be disappointed. "Damn, Missy, I wish you'd said something earlier. We could have talked about it, maybe gotten you into therapy or—"

Her hands are on her hips as she interrupts firmly. "I don't need therapy, Mac. There's nothing wrong with me. In fact, I feel as if a burden has been lifted from my shoulders. I should have had therapy when I pretended to be someone I'm not, but it's not your fault. I should have recognized it myself and gotten help before I even met you. Don't get me wrong, though. I don't feel that our life has been a waste of time, not at all. I'm just going to make some corrections now, knowing Jesus would approve."

Missy is out of the way just like that. That's how smooth Lady is. I can't help but wonder how much influence she had on Pastor's sermon about false prophets. She's cutting strings, unraveling the spider web that my life has become, freeing me to be with her. That's a nice thought.

I have to prepare for the evening service, so I get a legal pad from my home office and start jotting down ideas, struggling to recall what Jesus said during the morning service. Missy helps while the meatloaf bakes. She's really good at staying focused on the important points, which is why she's such a good businesswoman. While we're eating lunch and talking about my message, I find myself smiling at her, touching her like a close friend rather than a lover, and I realize that we had become very good friends. She is my wife although not for much longer. Quoting Lady, Missy points out that Jesus never expressed any strong feelings about personal issues. I nod supportively.

Damn, Lady is good.

SOCIAL DISTANCING

I was intrigued by Mac's proclamation to share his prophecy at the evening service. I didn't know what he was going to say, but I was certain that he'd had another vision (read schizotypal episode) during the morning service. Mac is not a lunatic, despite his surname. Even under the influence of the Holy Spirit, he wasn't going to propose that we all hold hands and dance around the church naked. Knowing how his mind worked, how he listened and learned, unlike most people; and aware of the developing split within the congregation, I was certain he would share a message of unification and renewal.

Vanity dropped by after lunch, while Pastor was working furiously to write a sermon that would refute whatever Mac was writing just as ferociously. I was glad for the interruption in my Sunday afternoon.

"I can't wait to tell you about the evening service," I said conspiratorially.

We kissed, our tongues sharing feelings we couldn't reveal with Pastor in the other room. "I can't wait," she gasped when the kiss finally ended. Before I could speak, she shared her theory of Mac's big announcement; he was going to call Pastor a fraud and call for the Fundamentalists to form a new church. I reminded her of Mac's deal with Pastor and pointed out that she was projecting from her life with Mike. When we'd finished discussing her personal situation, I proposed that Mac was going to say something mundane.

"Like what?" Vanity asked.

"Mac is not a warrior like Mike. He isn't looking for a fight. He's going to say something simple but obvious, like…like saying that he doesn't know why God reached out to him, maybe just to get our attention."

"That's it?! You are Mac's common-law wife and all you can think of is that he's going to announce that we should all get along? I'm disappointed, Lady. I expected more from you."

I knew she was kidding, so I risked slipping a hand under her blouse, grasping her firm breast, squeezing it. "Are these real? You're over fifty and your breasts are like those of a teenager."

She let me fondle her a moment, and then placed her hand over mine, pressing my hand against her ample bosom. "These are what God gave me. Squeeze them, kiss them, tickle them, lick and suck them, fondle them to your heart's desire because they are very sensitive."

I wanted to continue our conversation in the spare bedroom, where I could oblige her without interruption, when Pastor emerged from his study for a glass of water. Distracted, he barely acknowledged Vanity's presence before returning to his work. I took my guest to the other room and made a point of doing everything she had asked. I was lying naked next to her on the bed, breathing heavily from the best orgasm of my life, when I finally got back to the original topic.

"I know it sounds simplistic, but Mac isn't by nature a troublemaker. After his stroke or whatever it was, he's hallucinating but not having thoughts that come from nowhere. Even Jesus—Mac doesn't share all of his personal communications and I have to read between the lines—talks like Mac, who has never called Pastor incompetent. Mac respects Pastor. He is simply angry about how people get elected to the Board, especially Dim Light, so I think he might call for a snap election."

Vanity began to get dressed, thinking about my words. Finally, helping me with the zipper on my dress, she said, "The way you described his altercation with Dim, I think he's moved beyond complaining. He's ready for action."

While we were fixing our makeup in the guest bath, I reminded her that I'd been with Mac more than ten years. I knew him a little better than her. We laughed together when I pointed out that she'd only been with him for a couple of weeks. We kept our hands to ourselves for the rest of her visit, finally saying goodbye with a quick hug on the front porch.

Feeling melancholy, I got my jacket, told Pastor I was taking a walk, and braved the chilly March weather. Following a familiar path, my feet took me to Kansas Street, where oak and maple trees stood naked in their winter outfits, pubescent buds promising the return of spring. As with so many people, spring is my favorite season, but this was going to be an Easter to remember. A new life. I strolled along the cracked and broken sidewalk and imagined the earth's tectonic plate moving beneath me, carrying me toward the setting sun and an unknown future. One thing was certain, however; there was going to be a volcanic eruption on this chunk of rock, if not on Easter Sunday, then soon. I knew there was a very real possibility that I would be left standing at the altar, that Mac would back out or, worse, have a fatal stroke. The sidewalk took me past Trinity House, the landscaping waiting for spring, the gravel parking lot looking less manicured than usual, several deep ruts revealing underlying mud. I looked up at the steeple, where Pastor had insisted on installing a speaker to emulate the bells of Notre Dame in Paris. I passed between the houses lining Kansas Street, built in the forties and fifties for returning soldiers, simple places to live without pretense. The driveways had been filled with boats, travel trailers, motorhomes, and people—until the Great Recession. Now, they were filled with ten-year-old cars and trucks, garbage, and the dreams of a generation of Americans. My path took me to Tenth Street and a row of even more decrepit homes, some with boarded windows, abandoned cars occupying their driveways. These houses backed onto Trinity House's property. Only one was occupied, the rusty car that graced its driveway belying the existence of people within; sometimes backed in, once with the trunk open, bags of god-knows-what visible to me as I hurried by. I'd never seen the occupant, who I assumed was unemployed and probably a wino or drug addict. They probably weren't even paying rent. The police had become tolerant of squatters recently, as long as they didn't cause trouble.

The car was in the driveway. One of the inhabitants was approaching the sidewalk—actually two because the young, Hispanic woman was pushing a baby stroller. She was wearing a mask over her mouth and nose. To be honest, I don't know why I assumed she was Mexican because most of her face was covered. As it turned out, I was right. She started towards me and froze, her eyes desperate, pleading, as if I were going to deport her on the spot. I smiled weakly.

"Hello. I'm Lady Church. My husband is pastor of Trinity House, over on Kansas Street." I waved in the direction of the church and smiled.

"Why aren't you wearing a mask? Didn't you hear about the CDC guidelines? You probably have Covid and are exposing me and my baby to it. What kind of person would do that?" She whirled the carriage around and headed in the same direction as me.

I didn't move. I knew about the virus—Pastor had even referred to it in his sermon and Vernon Huckster had died from it. Some people called it Covid-19, but President Trump called it the China Flu, the Kung Flu, and the more-reasonable Wuhan Virus. It wasn't a big problem in China anymore, so why should I worry about it, especially in Modoc, Oklahoma? I slowly followed the young woman's path, wondering why she was so afraid. She had practically fled from me, as if saving her baby from the Black Death. And her English had been as good as mine, spoken with a slight accent, so she wasn't an undocumented Mexican. The sound of my footsteps on the aged cement stopped.

"Why am I having this conversation?" I asked myself.

Unable to answer my own rhetorical question, I continued my circumnavigation of the block that Trinity House mostly owned, before turning onto Illinois Street. I had a difficult chat with myself as I sauntered along the broken sidewalk, until I came to the playground the congregation had built on a piece of Church property, donated to the city of Modoc. I recalled Mac building the fort, installing the slide, putting up the fence surrounding the playground. The young woman was there, as if waiting to confront me again. She was swinging her little girl on a swing set I had watched Mac install. The baby, the young mother, the swing set, Mac—the abortion.

I stumbled to the bench Mac had built, fell on it, sobbing, overcome by grief at the child I had given up. I had murdered Mac's baby! I couldn't stop myself. I cried and cried, wiping my nose on my coat sleeve.

"Are you okay, ma'am?"

I looked up, to see brown eyes filled with concern, for me—a murderer, a homewrecker, an adulteress, a godless, hedonistic whore. "I'm sorry…oh god! I'm so sorry for what I've done…please forgive me." I struggled to stand but fell back on the bench, guided by this young woman's strong hands.

"I don't think you feel this bad about not wearing a mask, Mrs. Church. My name's Esther. I work at the county health clinic on Oklahoma Street…"

I couldn't stop myself. "I killed my baby. I could have been here, in this park with a baby, like you, but I murdered him…her…I'm so sorry for what I've done…"

Esther's arm encircled my shoulders, her gentle voice telling me that I hadn't murdered a child, only stopped an embryo from becoming a person who might have lived a miserable life. I wasn't a murderer. She understood because she'd had to make the same decision several years earlier. Her little girl was growing up in a nurturing environment, playing in the park, doing normal things instead of struggling to survive.

"I feel so bad," I mumbled.

"So did I, before I got counseling to help me get over that guilt. I'm willing to bet you didn't go back for that, right?"

I shook my head, looked into her compassionate eyes, and confessed everything. "I got pregnant from a man I've been in love with for ten years, and I wanted nothing more than to carry his child and break the web of lies that defined both our lives. I didn't tell him but acted on my own…"

Esther's eyes were soft, caring, as she invited me to share my life with her. "Do you have children, Mrs. Church?"

I told her about Seth and Joseph, how much I had enjoyed being with them when they were babies. I fell to sobbing again when I recalled that I wouldn't have that opportunity again because of my selfish act. She held me, comforted me, helped me accept what I'd done and move on, not denying the guilt I felt and would feel for the rest of my life. No one at Trinity House had ever felt so close to me as Esther at that moment, a stranger, a woman who'd wanted to avoid me as much as I'd been afraid of her, until we'd been brought together by coincidence. She offered me a paper mask from the familiar-looking bag stored on the stroller. I put it on and we shared playtime with her daughter, whose name was Margarita. We parted ways in front of the playground, her going left to return to the modest house she could afford on what the county paid her. My path led to the right, to face the tectonic plates that were about to either split apart and form an ocean basin or collide to create a new continent.

I was still wearing the mask Esther had given me when I was met by Pastor in the living room.

ALONE IN THE DARK

I don't know what to expect during the Sunday evening service but I'm going to be watching Lady for her reaction. I hadn't heard from Jesus since the morning service. Missy is really supportive about what I'm going to say but she doesn't want to make love to bulwark my confidence, now that we're no longer having sex. Aware of her feminine aura, I'm very excited, which reminds me of Melissa Tight. This is practice for the ultimate test. I take a couple of minutes to weigh Lady and Melissa in the balance of pleasure. Despite the fact that Melissa is the most beautiful and sexiest woman I've ever met in my life, not to mention her enthusiasm before, during, and after sex, Lady wins because I love her. Lady had probably never been as exciting as Melissa, but I enjoyed seeing her naked, getting dressed. She was more than ten years older than Melissa, so that was saying a lot. Confident of my decision, I can understand Missy's newfound freedom as an emancipated woman. I don't care because my mind is on Lady, and Melissa. Despite my decision, I'm worried about that. Melissa is the irresistible force. Lady is the immovable object. I'm the guy who has to solve that problem, which is entirely of my own construction. Meanwhile, Missy is prancing around on cloud nine, oblivious of my discomfort, cavorting as if just released from prison, touching me, giving me an occasional quick peck on the forehead, driving me out of my mind with lust.

Lust. I have to remember that. That is the key to dealing with Melissa. Goddamn! I want her. Oh, Sweet Jesus, I want her. Oh, Jesus, I want her…so bad it's all I can think about. I remember Lady's promise of releasing fire and brimstone on me if I cheat on her again. Not trusting me. She let it slide with Melina, but Melissa Tight isn't a spiritual advisor. She's just a really hot young woman who I am addicted to. My balled fists are pressed against my forehead in turmoil, expressing the conflict of my love for Lady, who Jesus approves of—he said so—and Melissa, who Jesus does not approve of. But Melissa is so…no man can resist her without divine intervention.

My agony is interrupted by Missy, whose cheerful demeanor makes me realize that I'm in hell. The woman I've been living with for more than twenty years declares that she is a lesbian, so naturally I'm suddenly attracted to her. Every time she comes near me, her odor drives me to the edge of insanity. The only thing that would draw my attention away from Missy would be Melissa standing naked in my living room. That's how bad it has become when Missy explains.

"I get it now, Mac. Jesus is telling you that President Trump is not omniscient and the Covid virus is real. I wouldn't have believed it if it hadn't come from Jesus' mouth. Just because he's leading the fight against the Deep State doesn't mean that President Trump has all the answers. After all, he's never had a vision like you, directly from an angel sent by the Holy Spirit."

I shake my head in confusion, so she continues.

"You're going to stand up and tell everyone what the angel has shared with you. Trinity House must follow the CDC guidelines, including not meeting in groups as large as the congregation, and celebrate Easter with social distancing."

I make her repeat it so that I can write it down. I don't know how to use the computer as well as her. Out of frustration, she pushes me out of my chair and types as I ramble. Missy is pleased with the result, her chest bursting with pride, as she shows me the result on the computer screen. I'm so excited that I reach for her, but she pushes my hands away, before standing and giving me a peck on the cheek. I don't know what to think.

Things are changing too fast, especially today, after my encounter with Jesus during the morning service. Those are always so exhausting. Missy sees my distress and leads me to the bed room, helping me lay down, comforting me, assuring me that everything is going to be okay. This is God's will.

Just before I fall asleep, I think, "Is this the Missy I married? Maybe this Missy was always there, afraid to speak out. I've ruined her life. Made her do things she found disgusting, like having sex with me. So, why is she so nice to me now?"

She bends over me, kisses my forehead gently, and leaves me in semidarkness, promising to wake me up in time to prepare for the evening service. I want to thank her for being so kind, but the words don't come out of my mouth. My lips are sealed. I lift a hand to wave, but nothing happens. Her image fades as my eyes close against my will, leaving me in an unnatural darkness, not even a faint glow penetrating my eyelids.

Am I dead?

MUSICAL INTERLUDE

I was still wearing the mask Esther had given me when I took my place behind the organ for the Sunday evening service. Her terrified reaction to being close to someone who might be carrying a deadly virus had made an impression on me. I googled Covid-19 when I got home and discovered that she wasn't paranoid. She was simply following the advice of doctors all over the country. Masks appeared to work, not to protect the wearer but people around them. Maybe I had Covid-19 and didn't know it? Apparently, it took days to feel sick and meanwhile you're spreading the virus. I also read about the Spanish flu epidemic in 1918. I was going to wear a mask anytime I was within six feet of someone else, and always during church services.

From some of the looks I got, you'd have thought I'd shown up in a bikini, but the people gawking at me couldn't see the disgusted grimace I'd swallowed for twenty years. It was kind of fun.

Something was wrong with Mac. I saw it the moment he entered the church, leaning on Missy, left eye drooping, his mouth a caricature of his usually confident smile. He'd had another stroke, worse than before. I wanted to leap from the organ bench, take him by the hand, and lead him out of Trinity House, out of the clutches of people who were trying to kill him, and to a hospital. I was willing to spend the rest of my life with him, even if he were a vegetable, but I didn't want to sit by and watch his life destroyed by these superstitious fools.

My fingers pounded the organ keys. I couldn't have stopped them if I'd wanted to. Every eye turned to me, pounding out, *Onward Christian Soldiers* on the organ. Thanks to the sound system Mac had installed, the notes reverberated throughout the church. Melissa Tight looked at me quizzically but approved of my spontaneous action, nodding her head slightly. I wanted to drag her to the piano, take her bewitching young face in my hands and shove it into the piano, tearing the skin from her cheeks with the piano wires, the hammers beating her lovely visage into a bleeding pulp. A sacrifice to the gods of music. I saw a look pass between Pastor and Melissa that verified what I'd suspected, but their relationship was more complex than her affair with Mac. I would have to figure that out later. I finished the song before the pews had filled. It was a full house by the time Melissa and the band completed their musical rejoinder.

Missy led Mac to their seat on the fourth row, glowing as if they'd just had sex, an unlikely event after our recent conversation. She was taking care of him, irony if I ever saw it; she was killing Mac, believing his suffering and even death was the price of being their deity's spokesperson, a god so powerful that contact with it permanently damaged mortals, yet too weak to prevent such side effects. Mac was nothing more than a sacrifice to a pagan god, so that these assholes could get along for another year. I didn't like the idea of Mac being a sacrifice to Missy and Pastor's god. Not one bit.

I was fuming, ready to run to the center of the nave and shout the truth. I didn't because I would have closure soon. Choosing Easter as the day of our announcement had been my idea and it would be unfair to blindside him two weeks early. I wanted to see Mac, so I remained at the organ when I would have normally taken a seat on the first pew. Feeling like a revolutionary, I was going to play whenever I wanted during the service, my tuneful assertions based on Mac's visage. I would play whatever music felt right but not finish it—like the musical interludes in a film.

I kept one eye on Mac while Pastor gave a watered-down sermon, common for Sunday evening service. He'd spent more time than usual on this one, however. I wanted to laugh when I realized he was thinking the same as Vanity, who gave me a triumphant look from her seat on the first row. I risked a single low note during a pause in his sermon. She got my point and smiled uncertainly in response. I wished she were sitting next to me, helping with my experiment in musicology. Melissa was smiling approvingly, encouraging me to keep it up, ready to join in. She was excited, feet bouncing in high heels, long fingers flicking as if massaging the organ keys with me. I was horrified, to think that I was sharing a creative moment with that little hussy, who'd seduced Mac...and probably Pastor. She'd insinuated herself into every aspect of my life, and now she dared to share this emotional moment with me.

Missy waved discretely to me, probably acknowledgement for my help in straightening out her marriage. Melissa looked as if she were trying to think of a way to join my random interludes.

I let go with a bar, ending with a ¼ beat, C-flat note, giving a dissonant tone to what Pastor had just said. I had no idea if I'd played over him or not and I didn't care. To my dismay, Melissa's band followed my intro with several bars, building on what I'd done out of frustration. The thought occurred to me that she was simply having fun, enjoying herself, but I saw her smile as a contortion of her full lips, twisted into a condescending smirk. "I can take whatever you have," her smile was saying.

Missy finally got Mac to look at me, making me wonder if she suspected what was going on. *Had he confessed?* This was getting too complicated. Mac smiled or rather half smiled; the left side of his mouth was as unresponsive as his left eye. At least he could raise his left arm, his hand partly curled in what I assumed was a thumbs up. Maybe they were just enjoying my musical play. I hit a couple of notes to acknowledge Mac and Missy. Melissa responded. We had become a Vaudeville act.

Pastor went off script, probably in response to the musical interruptions, and revealed his underlying concern about his authority being challenged. Whether by Mac, or Missy and me, was unclear from his ambiguous statements. He spoke of himself in the third person, couching his fears as those of all spiritual leaders. My interludes began to track fluctuations in his voice pitch, as if refuting his baseless concerns. Melissa and her band skillfully followed me. We had become part of a multimedia presentation promulgating ignorance, superstition, magical thinking, and mask wearing. Snippets of familiar songs—a few bars from both classic and contemporary Christian Rock songs—sprang from the organ to be augmented by Melissa's band. I was having fun. Mac was smiling. Everyone was happy except Pastor, who was trying to get back on message. The congregation was enjoying the show, so he didn't publicly express his annoyance at Melissa's and my musical misbehavior. He eventually returned to his notes and finished what had probably been the most eclectic sermon of his career.

"Keeping all these things in mind, we must remain united and vigilant in our fight against the forces of evil, which hide behind false prophesies disguised as the Word of God."

I launched into a Christian Pop song, interrupting whatever Melissa had planned; but she didn't miss a beat, joining me in what I must admit was a very stirring rendition of *Praise You in This Storm*. Melina Light led a group of experienced glossolalists in their interpretation of the song's words, translated into gibberish. My eyes were on Mac as Melissa and her band took over, back in familiar territory. When I glanced at her, she smiled at me, signaling that she wanted to talk about my idea later. I wanted to hate her, but she really was a nice young woman, who happened to have ongoing sexual liaisons with the two men in my life. Maybe her involvement would soften the blow when I declared my true feelings; Pastor would have someone to turn to for comfort after I left him—I was going to file for divorce the day after Easter. My mood picked up when I realized that her being in love with Pastor got her out of my way. Melissa would probably become my friend the way Vanity had. I tickled the keyboard a little when I thought of having a threesome with the two of them. She responded by shifting to a different key, the lead singer catching the change and not missing a beat. I liked Melissa. What a difference sharing something besides men can make in a relationship.

Pastor had regained his composure by the time the post-sermon exhibition had finished. He invited Mac to come to the pulpit and share his recent message from the Holy Spirit.

Mac stood up without assistance from Missy. His left eye was open and his mouth was uniformly resolute to accept Pastor's challenge. But he walked with a limp, favoring his left leg as he made his way unassisted to the dais, where he walked uncertainly to the pulpit. Mac had never stood in Pastor's place before and anxiety clouded his face.

I had no idea what to expect, so I added some flare as he approached the podium, my brief musical notes followed by the band's melodic comment. Melissa was beaming.

I couldn't see Mac's face from my seat at the piano. But if I took my regular seat on the first row, I wouldn't be able to add my musical comments. Torn between two objectives, I looked towards Melissa, my eyes hopefully expressing my desire without appearing too eager. Maybe she would assume I was leaving her in charge of the new musical program. Bless her heart if she didn't understand and motion with a nod for me to take my usual seat. Pastor was seated behind Mac on the dais. I casually got up, every eye in the church on me, my mouth and nose covered by a pastel-blue mask. I wanted to laugh when Melissa's band played a light march while I strolled proudly, as if walking the runway in a fashion show, and took my place on the first pew.

Not being an experienced public speaker, Mac couldn't help staring at me. Everyone else was looking at me too. He thanked Pastor for giving him an opportunity to speak to the congregation and revealed the real reason he was watching me so closely. We hadn't spoken about what he was going to say.

He was obviously flustered by my presence, or my appearance, perched on the front row.

"I'm not sure how to begin... I have a prepared statement, worked on it a couple of hours today, just making sure I didn't get confused with what the Holy Spirit communicated to me during the service this morning, but seeing Lady—I mean Sister Church—sitting at the organ, making certain we all saw her clearly, I know that God does indeed work in mysterious ways. I haven't spoken to Sister Church about what I'm here to say—just wanted to make that clear."

I had no idea what he was getting at, and neither did anyone else. The church was as silent as a cemetery.

Finally, Mac continued, "Never mind all that, I'll just read what I wrote with a few added words...here goes." His head turned downward as he unfolded a piece of paper removed from the pocket of his sport coat.

"The Holy Spirit has spoken to me directly and I've

experienced one or two visions, not like watching TV or anything. I wasn't smart enough to understand right away, so He had to repeat the message—that's probably why I've been feeling a little poorly lately. Anyway, I finally got it through my thick skull during this morning's service."

He gently knocked on the side of his head, making me grimace anxiously beneath my mask, to a wave of uneasy laughter and a few Amens.

"Trinity House is in danger. I mean physical danger, destruction like a biblical plague or flood. I don't know if this catastrophe is going to happen only to Trinity House, Modoc, or maybe include Oklahoma, America, even the world…"

A groundswell of murmurs flowed through the church accompanied by indrawn breaths. I was holding my breath because something told me Mac wasn't finished.

His head was nodding understandingly as his words continued, "I know. It sounds hopeless, but the Lord gave me a path to assure the safety of Trinity House—the congregation I mean—and it's a fairly simple solution. It's also why I'm so surprised to see Sister Church wearing a face mask. You see, here's what it is…" He turned back to his notes and continued reading.

"Easter Sunday should be spent in our homes, with our families, rather than celebrating Christ's resurrection together as we usually do—"

His words were drowned out in the ensuing uproar. I nodded towards Melissa, trying to get her attention with my eyes and head motions. Finally, I held my hand up and pointed towards Mac. She understood my signal and the band gently brought the emotional energy in the church back to a reasonable level, so that Mac could continue reading.

"I looked into what kinds of catastrophes could happen, that would threaten the people of Trinity House. Here's a short list. Oh…I'm starting with local disasters and ending with global catastrophes, like a meteorite, like the one that killed—may have killed the dinosaurs. That's a debatable point. Okay. First, Trinity House could get hit by a tornado with no warning, after all they touchdown somewhere. It could be here. Even more unpredictable, an airplane could fall out of the sky and crash into the church. It has happened. There could be a lightning strike that sets the church on fire in the middle of pouring rain and maybe even a tornado. I found plenty of examples of that terrifying experience on the internet. It's also possible that the catastrophe would be played out slowly, which is why Sister Church's appearance got my attention just now. I wouldn't be surprised if the Holy Spirit spoke to her, albeit less openly than to me, causing her to show us one way of preventing disaster—"

Bedlam ensued. Mac never got to mention a world-ending doomsday event like an extreme solar flare, searing the earth and pretty much wiping out civilization, if not life. I learned about that later.

Now familiar with crowd control, Melissa got the unruly congregation to settle down with a perfectly chosen Christian song about the love God feels for man. She would be a very good preacher's wife someday, maybe Pastor's? I gave her a thumb's up and she waved back. Mac's expression was what I would expect from a man who'd had several strokes within a month; he smiled at no one in particular, except when his eyes met mine. He waited patiently for the clamor to subside.

"There's no reason to be upset. I looked into what we can do to make the best of the situation. For example, we can use our computers to talk to each other at the same time, using a video app like Zoom, or Skype, or several others. I'll be glad to make one of them work for everyone. It's not like Easter is cancelled, it's just going to be different. We'll still be celebrating Easter together and it'll be a new experience."

His words fell on deaf ears. Melina was in the aisle, dancing and speaking in tongues, joined by others. But now there was a translation of her gibberish. I was very glad my mouth was covered by a mask when Tabitha Ramirez declared that Mac had misunderstood the words of the Holy Spirit. I laughed out loud. The music drowned my expression of incredulity. I kept my eyes on Mac, meeting his uncertain and anxious gaze, conveying my support. When Melissa had restored order, Mac finished his prepared words.

"I know that what I'm saying goes against our tradition but remember that Jesus spoke out against what was accepted practice in his day. The Sadducees and Pharisees weren't evil men, but a new age had dawned." He smiled, his facial expression almost normal, and finished with, "It could be that I'm wrong, but I've received several messages, not a one-time bulletin. Maybe I'll get an update from the Lord before Easter, maybe clarification on what to expect but, at any rate, I'm going to heed the warning."

I heard minds closing, mental doors slamming, shutting out Mac's message, not wanting to think, not even if it would save their miserable lives. He made one last plea, "Remember Sodom and Gomorrah, how Lot pleaded to save the people after being visited by the angels. Don't be like those people, be like Christ's disciples instead and accept that the Lord has spoken to you, even if he didn't show his face during our evening service. We have to trust Him."

No one was listening. He thanked Pastor again and, accompanied by a perceptively chosen song played by the band, strode back to his seat, three rows behind me. My eyes were beaming my support but he never looked at me. When the service was finished, I joined Pastor to bid the congregants a good evening, still wearing my mask. There were comments, mostly negative, which I replied to respectfully while expressing my support for Mac's prophecy, especially since I'd been led by the Holy Spirit to share his message. I'd never witnessed, much less been the target of, such hostility in my life. More than half the congregation wouldn't even meet my eyes, peering at them over the mask. Those who did look at me shook their heads imperceptibly, conveying their disapproval in a more civilized way. I was flabbergasted.

When Mac and Missy faced Pastor and me, she said, "I don't know, Lady. After what I heard—the Lord's words channeled by the more spiritual among us—maybe Mac misunderstood the angel's message. He's not as spiritual as some others. Jesus would want us to celebrate his resurrection as a community. He'll protect us."

I wanted to slap her face, or maybe punch her, even though I'm not violent by nature; not having the aggressive nature to knock some sense into her head, I should have confronted her. I expressed my understanding of her confusion, support for her decision, and reminded myself that Easter was only a couple of weeks away. Of course, I had a dilemma of my own; I believed in Mac and if he didn't want me to attend Easter service, I wouldn't; but then how could I declare my true feelings? How could I divorce Pastor?

I tried to communicate my confusion with my eyes when I faced Mac. I'm not sure if he understood because his left eye was drooping again and his expression was...dazed and confused, so I was explicit.

"I was surprised—to say the least—to learn that one of the possible catastrophes that could befall Trinity House was a plague. I think it was the hand of the Lord that led me to meet a neighbor, a young woman with a baby who treated me as if I were the angel of death, shunning me, until I..." My voice broke and it took a moment to regain my composure.

"We became friends and I learned that I have to think of others, not just myself. I think you understand what I'm saying, Brother Lunatic, considering the personal suffering you alluded to..." I paused, remembering where I was and raised my voice. "These people are not believers, or they would have accepted your prophecy. For myself, I will not be attending Easter service." I had done it. If Mac said, "No Easter service," we wouldn't be celebrating Easter with the congregation. It didn't matter.

Eyebrows were raised, especially Mac's. That was the moment when he knew beyond a shadow of a doubt how much I loved him. His confidence returned, assured of my commitment to our future life together. He nodded. "You won't be sorry Sister Church. The Lord doesn't fool around when it comes to serious issues like this. Jesus' message— delivered by an angel—warned of total destruction, not a couple of broken bones. For myself, I can celebrate His resurrection at home even if by myself." He looked at Missy uncomfortably.

I saw uncertainty in Missy's hazel eyes but couldn't have cared less. She was no longer an adversary, or even an obstacle.

I finally said, "I guess we'll be watching Easter service together...sort of, using the live feed that will be available after the upgrades to the audiovisual system. I'll be glad to stand up in church and admit being misled by a self-proclaimed prophet, if it comes to that, because you aren't a false prophet, Brother Lunatic, but only a good man trying to save his brothers and sisters in Christ."

The silence was eerie, broken by Pastor's confident voice. "I truly believe that the Holy Spirit spoke to you, Brother Lunatic, but Lady's wearing a mask this evening isn't proof. I respect your beliefs and I thank you for speaking openly. Nevertheless, the people of Trinity House are not convinced by your speech, despite your elocution."

Mac glanced at me and my mask and confidently retorted, "You know, Brother Church, you have nothing to lose by being cautious when it comes to the safety of the congregation. Sometimes a leader has to lead rather than just push their way to the head of the crowd. They might get angry, a few might even leave, but your reputation as a fair and openminded spiritual leader would be increased. Please reconsider your position. We have two weeks."

I grinned behind my mask at the thought that Mac, the handyman, had just given Pastor a dressing down. I laughed a little at the thought that I, an agnostic, was a more devout believer in divine revelations than even Pastor.

Vanity had been standing to the side during this exchange, quietly listening along with Mike, but now she expressed an opinion. Her words were directed at me, "Don't you think this is going a little far?"

"No, Sister Blunt, Brother Lunatic hasn't gone far enough, or his efforts would have been more convincing."

"Why the mask?" she asked sarcastically.

My grin was hidden behind a few layers of paper. "Wearing a mask is one of several recommended protocols that should be enforced during the Covid-19 pandemic. The mask is to protect you from me, in case I've contracted the virus. It's even possible that the calamity Mac has prophesied may be this deadly disease. There could be a new strain that strikes first in Modoc, like the aircraft disaster he mentioned. Someone has to be the first victims of every catastrophe, whether natural or manmade."

I knew what she was thinking. We wouldn't be sharing outrageous sexual experiences anymore, not until I removed the mask from my face. Her eyes dimmed with disappointment, a feeling I tried to return, my mask concealing my joy at being free of her dominating sexuality. I loved her like an older sister, not an older sexual partner, and I was totally satisfied with Mac. Whatever Vanity and I shared was like eating too much chocolate.

Mike Blunt added, "There is some merit in what Brother Lunatic said, if we accept the parol evidence of Sister Church's appearing with a mask covering her face, an unexpected outcome unless he was in-fact speaking on behalf of the Holy Spirit, irregardless of which we should not lose sight of precedent, which cautions against premature judgement of the outcome of affirmed events."

I ventured, "Will you be joining Brother Lunatic and me on Zoom, then?" I was smiling sarcastically behind my mask.

He pretended to be thinking—Vanity's eyes rolling in the background—before answering, "We'll have to go with the preponderance of the evidence, which I haven't had time to examine completely at this time, but there is precedent to consider when faced with novel situations not having a sufficient, unambiguous, case history, such as we are now faced with."

My hidden smile was condescending when I said, "Whatever."

Vanity struggled to swallow a laugh. I wanted to hug her but I had barricaded myself behind my newest defensive device—social distancing.

Melissa Tight was the last person to leave, taking my hand in both hers and sharing her feelings about the evening's activities. "That was wonderful, Sister Church. It must have been a spur-of-the-moment idea, well I loved it, of course we'll have to work on the details. I think we caught Pastor off balance there, once or twice." She was looking at Pastor.

Pastor. That's what she'd said. Melissa was so excited that she'd forgotten to keep up appearances, referring to her lover by his first name in a public forum. And he didn't catch it. Just as well because I didn't care, but it was good to have confirmation. I turned to Pastor and said, "I'm sorry about that, but I got carried away. I don't know what came over me. Maybe it was the anticipation of what Brother Lunatic was going to say."

I turned back to Melissa and continued, "I was so relieved that he didn't prophesy a revolution or something."

Her lovely head, topped by wavy, light-brown hair tied in a tight bun nodded vigorously. "I think a virtual service would be a lot of fun myself. Something tells me that this Covid virus is going to eventually arrive in Modoc and we shouldn't expect special favors from the Lord. After all, the rest of the world is suffering a lot more than us."

I liked her more and more. "I meant what I said. I'm going to be celebrating Easter from the rectory because I don't think Brother Lunatic is a false prophet—a confused one, certainly a surprising choice, maybe even in error. Nevertheless, he's not predicting the end of the world—"

Melissa and I had inadvertently become a team during the service. She interrupted me to say, "He had that on his list but it wasn't at the top." We grinned at each other, then her expression became serious. "I don't know what to do. I'm counting on Pastor—Brother Church—to help me decide." Another slip-up, this time corrected, and then a look tossed at Pastor that said it all. Oh yes, these two were doing the same thing as Mac and me.

They were so familiar that Pastor hadn't noticed her slip either before sharing his view. "I'm going to be praying about this, seeking inspiration, but I'm sure the Lord will either confirm or refute Brother Lunatic's prophesy and we'll get this settled. Still, it would be a good idea to put together a sketch of a virtual service. Maybe you two can work on the musical side, which is very important, and I'll throw in my two-cents worth, just in case."

I knew what that meant—just in case. I was laughing behind my mask.

STRIKE OUT

Lady wasn't kidding. She's serious about our getting together after Easter. Missy is like a bullhorn in my ear on the subject, without knowing about me and Lady. She'd openly and proudly announced that she was a homosexual, actually a lesbian, a word I had to look up on the internet. So, I'm dealing with one woman who can't wait to get rid of me and another who can't wait to get her hands on me. It's a good bargain from my point of view, but there's a problem and her name is Melissa Tight.

"I had a musical epiphany during the evening service, which set tones reverberating through my mind and body. I'm still ringing. I can't wait to share that experience with you, Mac." Melissa's dress slides over her shapely shoulders with her final words, falling past her hips, collecting around her perfectly formed feet, which step out of the high heels that had hidden their perfection. Melissa has perfect feet. I've tasted her toes and they are exquisite. In fact, everything about Melissa is perfect. *The girl next door on steroids* is how Lady had described her.

"Well…" I begin, Lady's threats of hell and damnation echoing through my mind. Melissa wants to share an emotional moment with me, which can only mean that my wildest fantasies are about to be realized. All I have to do is nod. She'll do the rest. Take me to the seventh level of heaven. My head is nodding but something makes me add, "Oh, god, Melissa! I want to share your musical experience so bad it hurts but…well, I'm a married man and I don't want to…"

She ignores my words and drops her underwear around her feet, stepping towards me, finding my throbbing member in less than a heartbeat. Oh my god! I can't think with her warm hand deep in my pants, her fingers manipulating me, her other hand dropping my pants and my boxers. She has me in her grip. I'm gasping for breath as she presses against me.

"I need to feel a cock inside me, Pastor's fingers aren't enough, he just won't fuck me, so I want to fuck you right now."

I'm under her spell. I'm thinking that maybe this could be the last tango in Paris. For old times' sake. After all, she's all over me, in a way Lady couldn't have done even when she was Melissa's age.

"Make my day perfect, Mac, by filling me with your essence, the spirit of God!" She pushes me onto the bed, straddling me and impaling herself on my pulsating phallus.

I wince from the pleasure of penetrating her, imagining the pleasure she's about to give me. As she begins to move against me, causing us to moan in unison I remember making love with Lady. I stop moaning. It feels as good with the woman I love, the woman who, come Easter, is going to be my wife— unless I climax with Melissa. I'm pretty sure that Lady will forgive me for being seduced so easily. But fire and brimstone will rain down on me if I let it go all the way. My decision is made when I recall Lady's support for me in this very turbulent time. She loves me. No one has ever loved me.

I arch my back and heave Melissa onto the bed next to me. I'm half-dressed by the time she responds. "What the hell is going on, Mac?"

I didn't have to lie to keep Lady's name out of it. "I'm married. Missy and I have smoothed out some problems in our marriage, we're all set now. I'm sorry about how this makes you feel, but…well, my marriage comes first. She knows about our past relationship, but I can't do that again. I just can't hurt her again. I'm sorry…"

I'm half-dressed when Melissa explodes from the bed, slamming me against the wall, her furious countenance still beautiful. She has an adorable face, even when enraged. I pull her soft, musician's hands from around my throat, push her resisting body to the bed, toss her down, and elaborate. "I'm married and I've worked things out with Missy, so I can't carry on anymore Melissa, even with someone as sensual as you. I have no regrets about our relationship but it can't go on."

She sits up, pouting, making me want to take her in my arms and make…have sex with her. She's that exciting. When she sees that her childish display isn't working, she gets serious.

"I'll tell Missy and everybody about our affair."

I'm tying my bootlaces as I say, "Missy knows about our affair Melissa and she's forgiven me, but she wouldn't forgive me if I let you take advantage of my weakness for sexual pleasures—"

"You want to finish it?"

I nod. "I have to. You're a beautiful woman Melissa and blessed with a sensuality that most of us never experience. You are also very intelligent and gifted. I can't tell you how to deal with that combination of…talents, but one thing I am sure of is that you will not find satisfaction having affairs with married men. I know what it's like…the sense of adventure that comes from finding a new sexual partner—"

She leaps from the bed, still naked, her firm breasts in my face. "How many women have you had an affair with?"

My hands are reaching for her, my arousal undiminished as I respond, "That's none of your business."

She brushes against me, no longer wanting to choke me, and shows me her best pose, sculpted breasts silhouetted against the white walls in the stark light. My hands move towards her. She suddenly faces me and I know she's waiting, probably about to explode from unfilled expectations. At least, that's how I feel, having leaked seminal fluid in my underwear. Again.

"Take me, Mac, and do whatever you like. I'm your slave for a few hours." She's desperate and thus difficult to resist. I have to get away.

Fully dressed, I face her for a last time, resisting the impulse to take her as my sex slave for an hour or more, and say, "You are a good person, Melissa. Don't lose sight of that."

With those parting words, I walk out on the best piece of ass of my life, the repercussions of my decision echoing throughout the church as if emanating from Lady's organ.

"No one dumps me, Mac! I don't care about your stupid

relationship with that lesbian you call your wife! You can't do this to me, no one can do this… I'm going to make you pay!"

She's in the hallway, stark naked, her fists clenched in frustration and rage when I look over my shoulder and voice words I'm sure I'm going to regret. "I've already paid too high a price for the few moments of pleasure we shared. You are a Jezebel, sent by Satan to destroy men's lives."

I know I've gone too far when her shoe hits me in the back of the head, stunning me. She must have played baseball in college as a pitcher, because she'd put that one in the strike zone. I pick up the pace and get out of the church through a side door, half expecting her to appear naked with a butcher knife in her hand. I notice Lady standing on the rectory porch, a cup of coffee in her hand. I don't stop to visit but get in my truck as fast as possible.

I'm pretty sure she's smiling with satisfaction.

CLEANING UP

I noticed Melissa's car parked in front of the church on my afternoon walk around the block. She came by frequently to use the musical equipment and the computer; and lately she'd been working with Mac on the upgraded sound system. I knew what else they'd been doing. By the time I got back, disappointed at not having met Esther, Mac's truck was parked at the back of the church. I made a pot of coffee and took up my station on the front porch. I'd see with my own eyes if he was going to end his affair with Melissa. It didn't take long. He was practically running when he exploded from the side door, looking over his shoulder, rubbing the back of his head. There was no time to wave, much less come over to speak to me, because he apparently had someplace to be in a hurry. I expected to see Melissa appear behind him, but she apparently thought better than to chase her lover out of the church, probably naked, maybe with a knife in her hand?

He'd done it. Something made me want to investigate for myself, to see her face, how she'd taken it. I refilled my cup and sauntered over to the church, inventing an excuse before I opened the door Mac had just exited.

Melissa was fully dressed, as gorgeous as usual in a modest print dress and high heels, the epitome of a church choir director—I mean, musicologist. I didn't have to use my excuse because she was happy to see me.

"I'm so glad you dropped by, Lady. This is a great time for us to work on a Zoom church service." She was beaming, as if she hadn't just chased Mac out of the building, apparently fearing for his life. I would remember that and not do anything to upset her. She was almost fifteen years younger than me and I'd heard her mention playing softball in college, going to the gym several times a week.

"That's a great idea," I said.

We worked on creating a completely virtual service. She was so professional, pleasant, and intelligent that I found myself enthralled. I even made coffee in the church kitchen and we spent the afternoon working on her plan. After a couple of hours, I was convinced that she was fundamentally a good person who suffered from the same problem as Mac. The thought of taking advantage of her undoubtedly agitated emotional state and seducing her crossed my mind, but I already had a homosexual relationship with Vanity that I didn't understand. I behaved myself but we nevertheless grew close during those few hours. Apparently, we'd done more than create an outline for a virtual service, which I insisted she present to Pastor herself. We had become friends. I had become her confidante so I got my proof of what had transpired in the church from a participant.

We were in the office, sipping coffee, our outline of a virtual service displayed on the computer screen, when Melissa tested the waters.

"I need to speak to someone, Lady, and I don't know who to turn to during such an emotional experience as… I'm an only child so I don't have a brother or sister, and I move too much and my…my problem has kept me from making friends…"

I encouraged her to speak freely, promising that I would respect her privacy and help her find a solution if I could, above all assuring her that she was not alone.

She nodded, looked at me, the ceiling, the floor, the computer screen, the floor again, her green irises finally meeting my blue ones. Her gaze dropped again, focusing on the floor. Her right hand went to her brow, rubbing it as if she had a headache, her head making small motions, as if she were debating something with herself. Finally, the left hand joined the right, now rubbing her forehead vigorously. The frenzied activity ceased, she looked up at me, her expression determined.

"I have to talk to someone."

I nodded. "I'm here for you, Melissa, just like I am for everyone in the congregation."

She nodded again, now determined. "I am addicted to sex. I've spoken to psychologists and therapists. Nothing works. I've learned to accept it as a negative personality trait; actually, it's a disorder—hypersexual disorder. There's no cure. It's why I keep moving on. I always get involved with men in the churches where I'm hired as a musicologist. And it always ends the same. I go too far and have to move on, to greener pastures, where I can find unsuspecting men. I prey on them. Sure, they let me seduce them but if I'd left them alone, they would never have ruined their lives. I can't tell you how many broken marriages litter my path, and I'm only thirty-one!"

I didn't know what to make of Melissa's confession. Was she truly stumbling through life, unable to control her sexual desires? That isn't so difficult to believe, considering the mess Mac had made of his life. However, she could have been a sociopath and was manipulating me, but for what purpose? I didn't care if she knew about Mac and me. I had nothing to lose and thus couldn't be manipulated, so I decided to play along. Better to let a sociopath—another personality disorder—think they're fooling me than to leave a suffering young woman to her own devices.

"Has something happened?" I asked, remembering my success as a therapist with the other women of Trinity House.

Her eyes dart around the room, her head bobbing up and down, until she finally says, "I've been having an affair with Macbeth Lunatic. I think he's like me…"

This girl was perceptive. "I've heard rumors about his inappropriate behavior," I reply.

Her head bobs some more and she says, "Like when Melina Light was riding him for all he was worth when they plowed the garden. I'm pretty sure he's been plowing her regularly…" Thin fingers flew to her full lips. "I shouldn't have said that. I'm sorry."

I was in therapist mode. "There's no reason to apologize for what everyone who was there could see with their own eyes. Feel free to speak openly, Melissa."

She nodded feebly, and I continued, "What matters is

whether you felt any jealousy when you saw Melina behaving inappropriately with Brother Lunatic."

Without hesitation her head shook. "No, but that's the problem. I've never cared about any man, not even one of the men I've seduced, whose lives I sometimes ruined. I could have dealt with it but today—"

Overcome with curiosity, I interrupted, "What happened today? Weren't you working here in the church?"

"I was, until Mac showed up. I was so excited about the Sunday evening service, your musical interludes, and how the idea could become a part of the service, that I seduced…" Her words trailed off. She took a deep breath and continued, "I thought I had seduced him, but he actually threw me off him…he didn't want to break a promise to his wife Missy, who I'm certain is lesbian."

My heart was soaring, my voice straining to sound disinterested when I asked, "What happened?"

Tears appeared in her eyes for the first time as she said, "I freaked out, realizing it was time to move on…"

"What did Mac do, to make you freak out? Or perhaps after you freaked out?"

"Both. He got dressed and was leaving, saying nice things to me, about our relationship, about me as a person, but I wouldn't let it go. I wouldn't let him go. I threatened to expose him, our relationship, but he'd already made peace with Missy, even if she is gay. I had nothing to threaten him with. I screamed and threw my shoe, he called me a Jezebel, and I knew it was time to move on…" Tears were flowing down her cheeks now.

I risked holding her, knowing I had nothing to lose if she was a sociopath. I don't think anyone can tell real emotional behavior from a perfect copy, but it didn't matter to me, not in the church office, because the only threat Melissa posed to me was if she decided to stalk Mac. Even a sociopath wouldn't try to kill someone they'd simply had an affair with. He hadn't even embarrassed her in public.

I had an idea, devious from the outset, and certainly evil. Perhaps I was the sociopath? Certain of her relationship with Pastor, I wanted to test the waters of her repentance.

"That's all water under the bridge, Melissa. But I have to ask, have you had affairs with any other married men?"

Her head bobbed but her words failed to prove that she wasn't a sociopath. "I've had a lot of brief affairs, sometimes one-night stands, with dozens of men in Modoc, a few of them from Trinity House."

"Really?"

"Can I trust you?"

My head bobbed. "Of course."

"Mac was the first. Being like me, he was easy, and it was fun so it lasted a while—until today. Mike Blunt was easy pickings also because he thinks he's a macho man, but he wasn't very satisfying…" The manicured fingernails, painted red, flew to her mouth.

"I may have said too much."

"Say whatever you need to Melissa because what matters is that you reconcile your actions with your belief in the Lord."

"Well, Dim Light and I had a one-night stand. That's too bad because he is well endowed…there I go again."

This was a lot of fun, but it was time to cut to the chase. "I think I see your problem, Melissa. You are not Jezebel as Mac suggested. He was freaked out just like you and spoke without thinking. Why do you think you haven't fallen in love with someone? A beautiful woman like you must have had plenty of eligible men talking to you, asking you out on dates—hitting on you."

She hadn't mentioned Pastor, so she was keeping secrets.

"The therapists and psychiatrists agree that I'm avoiding becoming intimate—sexually and emotionally dependent, trusting someone else. It doesn't make sense to me. I was an only child and my parents were very nice. I wasn't abused or anything. My father was perfect, telling me stories at bedtime, giving me a kiss. My mom was annoying like all my friends' mothers. My parents think I'm perfectly normal."

"You didn't answer my question."

"Yes. Men hit on me all the time. That's how I connected with Mike Blunt and Dim Light. Their status within the community gave them dibs on me, in their minds—mine too, to be honest. I'm just so used to men wanting me that I never thought about who they were. Men are objects to me, rather than potential spouses, husbands. I judge them using a different set of criteria than if I were looking for someone to create a life with."

I nodded understandingly. "Maybe you don't want to be married. That's fine, but you might want to… What am I saying? Do you like married men more than single men, as lovers I mean?"

"Definitely. That's why I told you about the psychiatrists' diagnoses. What can I do? I felt so ashamed when Mac called me a Jezebel. I don't want to be a homewrecker!"

Melissa's angst seemed genuine, but she still hadn't mentioned Pastor. Deception was second nature to people like her and Mac. It had taken years to figure him out. I didn't see Melissa and Mac's behavior as being any more antisocial than joining a superstitious group like the congregation of Trinity House.

"You didn't seduce those men, Melissa. They were looking for sexual gratification and you were ready and willing to fulfill their desires as well as your own. I would suggest that you think about your real objective in having sexual liaisons. If your innermost desire is met by what you're doing, then don't change your behavior. However, you seem to be conflicted, so you have to ask yourself what you really want from life and do whatever it takes to accomplish it. You may already be on track to where you want to be. Did you ever think of that?"

She thought for a while. I sipped my coffee. Finally, she said, "I'm miserable, so I don't think I've found my place."

Like Mac, I suddenly had a message from the Universe. I laughed. Melissa's beautiful eyes, perfectly highlighted, turned to me, begging for an answer.

"Academia."

"What?"

"You are a brilliant musician, Melissa. You are wasting your time traipsing from church to church to avoid being accused of sexual deviancy. Go back to graduate school, bust your ass, fuck every man who's looking for action, get a doctorate, and become a part of the most liberal community in America. In the world. Learn a new language, find out who you are. And you don't even have to give up your evangelical beliefs."

Her almond eyes opened wide, revealing shades I'd never

imagined, effervescent in the fluorescent lighting. "Are you serious?"

I convinced her that she wasn't Jezebel, that she wasn't destined to being a musical gypsy, moving from church to church. Nevertheless, I was convinced that Melissa Tight was borderline sociopathic by the time I returned to the rectory to prepare dinner for Pastor. All of her concerns, shared with words and expressed in her eyes, were allayed; but we parted ways without her once mentioning Pastor, the man I wanted her to be in love with. I guess that was wishful thinking.

The next day, when Pastor had ensconced himself in his study, Melina Light appeared at the front door. I invited her in and she wasted no time removing her winter coat, to reveal sprayed-on jeans and a flowered blouse draped over her voluptuous figure.

I couldn't wait to hear what this cougar had to say. She was ten-years older than Mac and, judging from her full hips, about the same weight. I really couldn't see how she had seduced him. The only explanation was that he was like Melissa, suffering from hypersexuality disorder. Watching Melina fidgeting, her entire body quivering as if she were about to burst out speaking in tongues, convinced me that she was a good candidate for that medical diagnosis.

I didn't like Melina, not because of her religious beliefs, which were unfathomable, but because she rubbed me the wrong way. Several parishioners had publicly called her behavior outlandish over the years and left the church when it continued—as if Pastor could control his unruly congregation. I was convinced that Melina suffered from borderline personality disorder. She flourished in a society that accepted her ridiculous, vaudevillian behavior as normal. I had spent too many years bending over backwards to keep people like her happy, working with Pastor to limit the damage they did to an otherwise smoothly functioning community.

"Oh, Sister Church, I just love what you've done with the rectory." Her dark eyes, obscured with mascara and eyeshadow, swept over the simple furnishings filling my living room, as if she remembered my home from a previous life. She'd never set foot in my house in the five years she and Dim had been members of Trinity House.

"Would you like some coffee? Or do you prefer tea?"

She was a coffee drinker, preferably strong coffee mixed with thick cream and lots of sugar. She settled for my drip coffee diluted with soy milk and filled with sugar. We sat in faded blue armchairs, stained in different shades from raising two boys. I wondered why she'd come by to see me. She didn't seem interested in Pastor, not asking if he were home or what he was doing; he was in his study, putting it to good use.

"I needed to talk to you, Sister Church. It's about Brother Lunatic's misinterpretation of the prophecy he was given."

I sipped my black coffee, a habit I'd picked up from Mac. My mind was looking for an angle, a way to get Melina to go off script and tell me something she hadn't wanted to say when she'd decided to enter my lair. (I admit that I'm getting a little metaphorical, but my thinking had taken a turn to the left after my encounter with Melissa.)

"Did you drop by to explain your inappropriate sexual behavior during the garden ceremony?"

Her eyes shot open. Then they narrowed. "Of course not. There was nothing inappropriate between Mac and me that morning." She was so lost in her personal fantasy that she felt no need to explain her behavior to herself or anyone else. I felt differently.

"Several people, including your husband and I, witnessed what happened that day. As Pastor's wife, unpleasant tasks occasionally fall in my lap, so I'm asking again, were you having a sexual experience with Brother Lunatic on the tractor?"

"Of course not."

"Did he at any time touch your breasts or your genitalia?"

"Touch?"

"You know what I'm talking about, Melina. Did Brother Lunatic fondle, squeeze, rub, massage, hold, manipulate, or caress you where your husband usually does? Vanity Blunt videotaped the entire event and we have good footage."

She confessed everything. She was Mac's high priestess and spiritual connection to the Holy Spirit, his mistress who knew the pagan gods' wishes, channeling their energy in the metaphysical realm so that Mac could receive their message. I was surprised, to say the least, at her claims of mystical power, considering that her only talents seemed to be selling houses to sex-starved men and throwing emotional fits in public. There was no purpose in debating any of her claimed powers, but I wanted to know something.

"Why did you come to see me today?"

She looked as if she were about to start speaking in tongues before she finally answered my question. "You are very spiritual, Sister Church. I should have recognized—"

I didn't want to hear it. Maybe the world does work the way Melina imagines it. How would I know? But one thing I can see with my own eyes is when someone is hiding information and covering their subterfuge with superstitious nonsense.

"Knock it off, Melina. This isn't the time or place for that nonsense. I'm neither a customer nor a fellow con artist. Since you've had a change of heart, probably because you realized I'm not a blonde floozy you could bamboozle with bullshit, you don't want to say why you're here. Let me help you. You want to spend Easter like always, right here in Trinity House, so that you can dance around inappropriately, flirt with the married men, and pretend that you're spiritual. What you are is a walking, talking, fucking library of behavioral and spiritual disorders. You thought you could get me to convince Pastor that Macbeth Lunatic is mistaken, as if I am in a position to alter what Pastor feels in his heart, communicated from the Lord. You are not only an embarrassment to the church, but to women, to Latin Americans, to all people everywhere. You are crude, lude, stupid, ignorant, egotistical, arrogant…frankly, you should leave Trinity House and find a pagan, fertility cult to join."

She hadn't heard a word I'd said.

"In some respects, I am closer to the Lord than Mac, even if he is the Chosen One. You heard the message in the service last—"

I was on my feet. I went to the door and opened it. "Get out of my house. You are a pagan, if not a devil worshipper. You can be sure that I will inform my husband of your views. Furthermore, I will denounce you as a follower of the antichrist in church if you don't leave Trinity House immediately."

She didn't budge. I was furious and rage gives one strength, so I dragged her from the armchair, pushed her out the door, throwing her tacky, leather jacket after her.

"And don't you ever show your face on my doorstep again!"

I slammed the door, almost hoping she would reappear.

I didn't go to the gym like Melissa. The rectory had a well-equipped exercise room. I used it to release frustration, and I was a very frustrated middle-aged woman, going through a very difficult menopause.

When Melina failed to reappear, I took out my frustration on dumbbells, rubber bands, a barbell, a treadmill, and even a punching bag. I was soaked in sweat but calm, when Pastor appeared for lunch. He noted my condition, nodded, and shared my feelings.

"It can be difficult at times. I don't fault you for what you said to Melina Light. It needed to be said and your response was restrained."

"I'll take a shower and get lunch." Despite not being in love, Pastor and I were very comfortable with each other.

SUMMARY JUDGEMENT

Missy insists we talk to Lady about our marriage. That's a pretty funny idea, getting relationship advice from the woman I've been having an affair with for ten years, the woman I'm about to overturn my life to be with. It's awkward for me but not for Missy, and Lady shows what a fine woman she is, advising Missy and me not to let this ruin a healthy relationship, one based on more than sexual orientation. She reminds us of everything we have in common and how we shouldn't do anything that would leave us resenting each other. In a way, it's a useful thing to do, the three of us getting together, because when Missy and I leave, I feel a lot better about the whole business. Missy seems as happy as I've ever seen her. We'll see if she feels the same after Easter.

It's the Sunday before Easter and I don't know what to expect from Pastor. Lady had nothing to report all week. Missy and I take our seat on the fourth row, behind Mike and Vanity Blunt, and I realize that I've been looking at the back of his head for ten years; it had been balding for a while and then he'd started shaving it. He's one of Pastors' good old boys. I've never liked him. I treated him respectfully, however, especially after he'd intervened in the Board's deliberation and voted to treat the Lord's prophecy seriously. I sit down and scoff, remembering Lady's remark about Mike having been trained to speak gibberish, like Melina Light's speaking in tongues.

"What is it, Mac?"

I turn to Missy, who is much more attractive as a lesbian, and conspiratorially whisper, "Mike Blunt is a lot like Melina

Light, but he went to college to learn how to speak in tongues."

She laughs and slaps my arm affectionately. I can't help thinking that she's a really sweet woman, now that she was freed of an obligation I'd never intentionally—that's not fair or even true; she'd always been the same sweet person who's sitting next to me, but she'd never been as carefree as she is today.

I'm feeling pretty good, but not just because Missy and I are getting along so well. The thoughts that have been driving me crazy all week are suddenly still when I enter the church. They stop at the front door. I'd been getting fragments of another message from Jesus, but He didn't use words, just putting thoughts in my head. They aren't really thoughts, actually, but more like feelings or premonitions. For example, I know that all these people are going to come to church on Easter, despite His warning, and they are all going to die. All week I've been either crying over the imminent tragedy or laughing at their stupidity, letting pride destroy them. Missy had tried to reassure me but it didn't help because I know she is going to follow them all to their deaths. Lady is the only one who can console me. She doesn't have to promise that she will be staying home because I already know that she's going to heed my warning.

I'd pointed out that she's a hypocrite, an agnostic following the words of a self-proclaimed prophet. Her response had been an assurance that she would follow my advice even if I'd claimed no greater authority than my own intuition. We'd make our public announcement even if I'd gotten the date wrong; otherwise, it wouldn't be necessary. Her tone hadn't brooked any disagreement.

Lady's sitting at the organ wearing a mask. It's gray cloth, but Melissa's is bright yellow. The whole band is wearing masks, even the choir. I look around and notice that more than half the congregation is wearing masks—the Evangelicals. I've always sat with the Fundamentalists because of Missy, even though our beliefs aren't quite the same. It doesn't matter because we're all serving the same master. Still, seeing Lady wearing a mask makes me feel naked, breathing god-knows-what into the air. She'd explained it to me and I'd checked it out myself. I'd even bought some paper masks at the drug store. Missy had showed me a web site that repudiated all that nonsense about wearing masks, so I'd left them in the glovebox of my truck. Now I wish I'd put one in my pocket.

Lady and Melissa repeat their dueling banjos theme and it adds a lot to the service. The band is socially distanced on the stage, the vocalists removing their masks only while performing. The same thing works for the congregation, the Evangelicals at least. They're making the best of a difficult situation. The Fundamentalists are snickering and carrying on as usual. I can see that Pastor is disturbed by what he sees. He shares his concerns in his sermon.

"The Lord hasn't spoken clearly on the subject of Brother Lunatic's prophecy. He has left it to me to decide what is best for the people of Trinity House, which is what I will explain this morning."

Mike Blunt leans towards Vanity and I overhear him say, "He's talking like a judge, which can only mean that he's going to pass summary judgement against the plaintiff. He denies the existence of a question of fact. No jury trial." His head is shaking as he adds, "Pastor is not justified in the instant case to not follow the ecumenical common law tradition, established by centuries of practice, of *stare decisis.*"

I don't hear Vanity's response because Lady and Melissa play a brief interlude while Pastor sips from his water. I only catch the end of Mike's statement. "...speak up for him, as his legal counsel."

He nods thoughtfully as Pastor continues justifying passing summary judgement on me, whatever that is. It doesn't sound good. Lady and Melissa's music soundbites convey the meaning of Pastor's lengthy, scripture-filled, justification for his decision. By the time the sermon ends, I have an idea what Mike was talking about, and what he's going to do.

After the service, Missy and I are speaking to Dim and Melina on the front porch of the church when Mike joins us, wearing a serious expression. He faces Dim and says, "There's going to be a board meeting at two o'clock. I hope we can count on your support?"

Dim nods naively. "Sure, I'll be there."

"Good," Mike says and then addresses me. "I think we can win your case on appeal. Do you have a minute?"

APPEAL

"There is a not insubstantial question concerning the facts of Mac's announcement, irregardless of the subject of his statements which are legally within your area of expertise, but having affirmed that you have been denied *certiorari* by the highest authority, we must follow precedent and have a jury trial." Mike stopped, expecting a challenge.

Having made a point of learning how to translate his muddled legalese, I understood what he was saying. He had a valid point. Mac had become his client after the morning service.

Mary Jenkins wasn't a lawyer but she was a medical doctor who had a practice in Modoc and drove to Oklahoma City several times a week, to teach classes and do rounds at Mercy Hospital. She was my age, but with graying black hair and a few extra pounds, which didn't affect her impatience with Modoc's paternalistic society.

"Knock off the mumbo jumbo, Mike. Even when said in English, it's plain that Mac's claims shouldn't be dismissed out of hand. Not unless Pastor has received some guidance from the Lord, which he obviously has not. However, I don't think we need to go so far as forming a committee or, worse, having an election. The Board can dispense with this claim in a fair and just manner."

Mike didn't think he was speaking gibberish. That was how they'd taught him to think in law school and his mind had been a sponge. "A *per curiam* decision would not be inconsistent with Oklahoma appeals jurisprudence. Mac has affirmed the truth of his statements, and Pastor's request for certification was denied, which impliedly serves as an affirmative statement in support of the truthfulness of Mac's claim. Mac has agreed to a bench decision, so I would move to weigh the facts of this case *en banc*."

Edith Tagortan was the youngest member of the Board at thirty-seven. Her philosophy was a mirror image of Missy Lunatic's, including her dependence on conspiracy theory news sources. She hadn't understood a word that had been said, so she turned her doleful eyes on me and asked, "Could you read the record back, Sister Church?"

Translating Mike's obscure language for Edith had become so common that no one, not even Mike, looked at me when I responded. "The Lord hasn't spoken to Pastor about Mac's prophecy, that we should celebrate Easter at home in a virtual service, so we have only his word to go on. He could be mistaken, but everyone agrees that he's an honest man and no deception is intended. So, it has been suggested that the board should decide whether or not to treat his warning seriously. Brother Blunt has suggested that you all should talk about it now."

No one corrected me, so the discussion began. I took notes. During the ensuing hour, Pastor's overriding concerns, the reason he had decided to rule against Mac, became obvious. He was concerned about how it would look if half the church attended Easter service while the other half watched from their homes. This could be the last straw in a congregation that had become increasingly divided. He pointed out the glaring divide between the two factions during the morning service, made apparent with the wearing of face masks, like a red scarf, or beret. Dim took issue with that. He had no intention of leaving Trinity House and neither did Melina. They understood that there were some doctrinal differences, and even social ones like wearing a mask for a fake disease, but it wasn't as if they felt persecuted or anything. His words were echoed by Edith, who added that it would be best to let everybody be themselves, so that they could really trust one another.

Mike admitted that he had no intention of wearing a mask, that Jesus would take care of him because of his strong faith. I had to translate that for Edith, who was surprised to hear that he agreed with her. I was surprised myself, when I was called on to describe the virtual service Melissa and I had put together, with Pastor's approval. I demonstrated the software on the computer, and the Board watched Melissa and the band practicing, their music streaming in real time to the conference room.

The four elected board members decided unanimously that Trinity House was strong enough to spend Easter in a hybrid celebration. Pastor was left to cast the last vote, required for a *per curiam* decision.

"I'd like to thank Brother Blunt for bringing this matter to my attention. Without clear guidance from the Lord, I reacted viscerally to the uncertainty of the times we are living in. I was mistaken. Irregardless, this is not the time to be afraid but instead to face an uncertain future with confidence, knowing that we are servants of God."

REVERSAL

After talking to Mike Blunt, I'm pretty excited because he's a lawyer and a member of the Board. Mike explains our case— he actually calls it that—but it takes a couple of repetitions before I understand what he's saying. Pastor doesn't have the authority to decide something that affects the whole congregation. That can only be determined by a vote of the congregation, or by the Board.

When I get home, I share what he's told me with Missy, who's looking very sexy and coming on to me. She's sitting next to me, touching me, leaning against me, all over me. I figure she wants a little bit of what I'd been giving her recently, despite being a lesbian.

I'm hearing indistinct sounds, voices maybe, murmuring, but their thoughts are clear. I take her firm, small breast in my hand and force my lips against hers, my tongue pressing into her warm mouth. She bites me.

"Jesus! What did you do that for?" I can't believe she bit me the same way Melissa had. What's going on?

Her finger is slowly waving in front of my eyes. "Remember what Sister Church said? We have to learn to see each other through a new set of lenses, which means you don't see me as a pin cushion anymore. I'm not your sexual partner Mac but only your wife. I love you very much and always will, but I do not enjoy being manhandled by you. I never have."

I'm struggling to remain in my body because I know that if I become a bystander, Satan will use my body to hurt Missy and that's something I don't want to happen. I leap to my feet, stumbling, tripping over the coffee table, staggering into the wall, falling to the floor. She's on me in a second, her arm around my shoulder, the lips that moments before had rejected me as unfit now caressing my cheeks. She helps me to my feet, back to the chair, where I collapse, unable to move. Welcoming the darkness, I am in Jesus' hands.

"Wake up, Mac, look who's come to visit." It was Missy's voice and I'm disappointed because I was dreaming of being with Lady in a house that I'd built for her, on a lake with oak trees, horses, cattle, and…

"The Board decided *en banc* to reverse Pastor's premature decision. This is not an admission of an error of judgement on his part, far from such an interpretation the instant decision is reflective of the previously unfulfilled and unrecognized wishes of the congregation."

"Huh?" I mumble, trying to sit up.

Missy interjects, "The church board has overruled Pastor, and we should expect an apology at the evening service—"

Mike corrects her premature statement. "As satisfying as such an outcome would be it would do more than grant the plaintiff a legal remedy, requiring further adjudication because of the punitive nature of such a remedy. An equitable remedy based on *Promissory Estoppel* is not available."

"Huh?" Missy and I say together.

Instead of rolling his eyes like a normal person, Mike bends over and speaks slowly. "Pastor is not going to apologize, but he is willing to announce a new plan for the Covid-19 virus, including a virtual Easter service that will be streamed from the church and shared among the congregants who plan to follow your advice, Brother Lunatic. I suggest you accept this offer because it's the best you're going to get."

I don't understand. I sit up and exclaim, "It isn't about the China flu, we don't know what's going to happen. Only God knows and He's leaving it to us to listen to His words and act accordingly, to save ourselves."

Mike's eyes remain fixed on me. "I understand, but this is the deal. I had to fight hard to get it, so don't let me down. Remember, the reason you were contacted by an angel and given a message to share with Trinity House was to save their lives, and that objective will be accomplished if they remain in their homes on Easter Sunday, which is now a viable option."

"I see your point. Okay. I guess I'm supposed to…well, I guess I'm going to follow Sister Church's example and wear a mask."

Mike nods.

"What's your plan, Mike? Do you plan to join me on line for Easter?"

He smiles, rubs his clean-shaven chin, then his shaved head, and says, "The jury's still out."

Missy says, "God doesn't need a jury Brother Blunt and, come Easter, He'll take action whether we like it or not."

I thank Mike for his efforts but I can't do much more, so Missy sees him out, before rejoining me on the sofa.

I can't get up, so she feeds me as if I were an infant, hugging me between spoonfuls, the touch of her lips now comforting against my face. Her love for me is apparent, treating me so well after what I'd just attempted to do. Tears come to my eyes but I can't speak so I gaze at her. Tears are flowing down her cheeks, their paths redirected by her head's erratic movement. That's how we spend the afternoon.

I'm almost as good as new when it's time to get ready for the evening service. I'm moving around, walking without assistance, but changing clothes isn't a good idea, so I wait while Missy takes a shower. She appears in a tight dress she'd never worn except on our anniversary. Words slip from my mouth.

"Oh my Lord, Missy. If I were a lesbian, I'd be all over you."

She sits next to me, giving me a quick peck, and says, "That's just about the sweetest thing you've ever said to me, Mac. I know how difficult this is for you and you're doing really well, we just have to keep it up, to get past those moments when you…when your—"

I finish her sentence. "When my hypersexual personality shows its ugly head. I'm sorry about earlier…"

DRY RUN

Mac's condition was getting worse. At first he refused to tell me what had happened after the morning service but I made him confess to having spent the afternoon conscious but unable to move, after collapsing on the living room floor. My shrieks of terror were probably heard all the way to Oklahoma City. Despite hearing murmuring, seeing vague shapes out of the corner of his eyes, voices telling him to do things he would never do on his own, he refused to go to the hospital. I had to be satisfied with his promise that he would do whatever I said after Easter. He was so desperate for sexual relief, even admitting that he had considered turning to Melina Light, that I spent a few hours with him in the church guest room, despite my fears that sexual activity might initiate another stroke. That was Monday.

Melissa dropped by on Tuesday to test the virtual service app she had written (with no help from me). She'd studied computer programming in college in addition to music. Vanity had agreed to be our test subject. Melissa and I were going to move around the church, singing, talking, trying to simulate the different acoustic and audio signals while Vanity gave us feedback on the virtual experience from her living room. Melissa was upbeat as she began the experiment, turning the system on and taking Pastor's place behind the pulpit. I was at the organ. Vanity's image was displayed on the 55-inch LED monitor above Melissa's head, where it could be seen from anywhere in the nave. I couldn't see her until we finished the first test. I felt a sense of pride when I heard Vanity's voice, knowing that Mac had installed the new multimedia system without expert help.

"I can see the two of you in little windows on my screen. You're both so beautiful that it's like I'm watching a professional—"

Melissa interjected, "That's the idea, Sister Blunt. If the virtual experience isn't professional, no one will want to share it. This isn't about Easter Sunday, but the future of Trinity House as an online worship center."

Melissa remained at the pulpit, reading from the Bible, while I moved around, playing her electric piano, tapping the drums, singing from the choir box, all while she kept reading from the book of Matthew and typing on her notepad computer. She was making notes and adjustments to the system at the same time. Smart girl. Vanity heard every sound and reported the experience as like being in church. Melissa was beaming with justifiable pride when I went into the nave to simulate the congregation.

"What do I do now?" I asked.

Vanity was laughing as she suggested, "Jump around and speak in tongues like Melina Light."

Melissa laughed, tapped on her iPad, and music poured from the speakers throughout the nave, a recording of last Sunday's evening service. When Trinity House was brought to life, she shouted, "I want to check the bandwidth, so you should move around while speaking. I couldn't hear Vanity's response as I strolled around, expressing my opinion about the exercise, shouting when prompted by Melissa, jumping occasionally. I think a middle finger escaped from my fist once or twice. Vanity refused to summarize her experience virtually, making Melissa and me wait ten minutes while she drove to the church. I made a pot of coffee while we waited. She burst into the kitchen wearing tight jeans and a short jacket, opened to reveal an even tighter top that revealed enough cleavage to get my attention, causing me to forget myself and hug her affectionately.

Melissa was unimpressed. "Thank you so much for helping, Sister Blunt—"

"We don't need to use formal names. Call me Vanity, Melissa—if I may be so bold?"

Melissa nodded emphatically. With the ground rules understood, Vanity attempted to seduce Melissa, who wasn't only not buying, she had no idea what was being offered. This girl was as solidly heterosexual as Mac. However, she wasn't oblivious of what was happening; her response was simply different than what Vanity and I would have expected.

"I'm envious of you two, happily married, grown children a testament to your success as Christians, and such close friends, despite…" Her words trailed off.

I understood Melissa's dilemma because I had the same doubts about my life, despite the *testament* of having two sons. She had skeletons in her closet that she wanted to show someone, but she wasn't Catholic either. No official confessor. We were both stuck with our demons. Now I had another secret to keep from Vanity, not seeing any good reason to bring up Mike's affair with Melissa. It was easy to not make a decision, so I didn't respond.

Misunderstanding Melissa's veiled reference to what some call a ticking *biological clock*, Vanity self-consciously defended our relationship. "Lady and I are close friends, nothing more. Perhaps you should make more women friends Melissa, then you wouldn't feel so lonely."

"I know what you mean." Melissa's expectant gaze was met by uncertainty on my part, but she continued anyway. "Lady has been an inspiration to me and…"

"Spit it out," Vanity said to fill the silence, her tone surprisingly abrupt.

"I've spoken to several universities and…well, I'm overwhelmed that I've been invited to study music at the Julliard School in New York. I feel so bad—"

"About what?" I blurted.

"I've invested so much effort in Trinity House, working with Pastor on his dream, and I feel—"

Vanity took Melissa's statement in a different direction when she asked, "Did you have an affair with my husband?"

That settled that question.

Melissa's lovely head bobbed, loose strands of velvety brown hair floating. "Yes, ma'am, I did but it was six months ago. I know it was a sin, but I…but I didn't want to—"

I interjected, "We talked about this Vanity, so you

shouldn't be surprised. Melissa suffers from the same affliction as Mac, you know. She wasn't trying to ruin your marriage or anything like that."

Vanity ignored me. "How long did it last?"

Melissa shrugged before saying, "A month or something like that."

"Who broke it off?"

Melissa didn't want to answer, so her mouth twisted into a shape that made speech impossible.

"Why did you break up with Mike?"

Her full lips finally resumed their normal shape, quivered slightly, and said, "I'd rather not say."

"This is not the time for social niceties, Miss Tight." Vanity's lips reflected Melissa's surname.

Her eyes looked around the nave, finally finding a reply in the air over the pulpit. "I'm a lot younger than him. It was fun but we weren't compatible. I'm sorry for what I did. I'm going to graduate school, so I won't be around anymore…to tempt him again. I hate to abandon the dream Pastor and I shared, but it wasn't going to work out, not with me being who I am. I'm taking Lady's advice."

She wouldn't admit her affair with Pastor, even after declaring her intent to leave Modoc for greener pastures.

Vanity interrupted my thoughts. "I'm not trying to run you off, Melissa. I'd simply like to have some idea of my husband's extramarital affairs and what they mean to him. For example, did he ever tell you that he loved you?"

Melissa's brown hair shook from side to side.

"Do you mind if I ask who else you've had an affair with?"

Full lips frowned, then blurted, "I'm sorry, Lady, but I thought I was in love with Pastor, probably because we had the same dream, an unrealizable dream as it turned out."

"Let's get more comfortable."

They followed me into Pastor's business office and we sat down in armchairs, our coffee cups arranged on the oak coffee table. Vanity was looking at me with a sly smile, her eyes challenging me to join the party, to dump more guilt on poor little Melissa's lovely head. I didn't see any reason to do that because I'd grown fond of her. That was water under the bridge, even if she didn't know that she'd tried to steal two men from me. I returned Vanity's smile with a slight shake of my head, before addressing Melissa.

"I suspected that he was having an affair, but why did you feel obliged to answer Vanity's impertinent question?"

"You must think me a homewrecker and overall bad person, and I probably am, but I feel guilty about it. For example, I avoided being with Mac for months after Pastor and I started…"

Vanity finished the sentence. "Sleeping together? Are you a one-man woman, or do you sleep around?" That was harsh but well deserved.

Melissa had apparently given some thought to my suggestion that she cloister herself in a university and stop pretending to be a virgin. She didn't bat an eye when she replied, "It depends. Of course, I don't tell the men I'm seeing about each other because every relationship is special to me, even if it doesn't sound like it."

I realized that my reaction had been rather ambivalent. However, Melissa hadn't seemed surprised, probably because Pastor had explained our marital situation to her. Still, I felt that I had to say something. I tried to sound affronted when I said, "Well…I'm shocked! I can't believe you had the gall to just up and tell me that you seduced my husband, the spiritual leader of Trinity House. Why, I ought to slap—"

Vanity laughed out loud. Melissa giggled. I fought not to grin but failed. We all laughed together and went to the kitchen to refill our cups. As we retook our seats, Melissa, now comfortable with Vanity and me, said, "Pastor told me about your beliefs and how that affects your marriage Lady, but still, why aren't you more upset? Is your…I mean, uh… Are you having an affair?"

I was starting to get tired of Vanity laughing at me and I let her know with a scowl. She scowled back and we both smiled. I loved her too much to get angry with her. I could have kept my mouth shut and pretended to be a saint, with no physical or emotional needs but I didn't think it mattered. If Melissa shouted it in church, the result would be the same. I nodded as Vanity grinned, so I turned to her and said, "If I come clean, so do you—"

That wiped the grin off her face, but not for long. "Sure, we can trust Melissa. She's one of us."

Melissa looked confused.

I cleared my throat and just said it. "Macbeth Lunatic and I have been having an affair for almost ten years. We are deeply in love. We're both going to divorce our spouses and get married to spend whatever time we have left together."

Melissa's jaw dropped and she turned red as a beet. She had to set her cup down to keep from spilling coffee on her tan skirt. Her expression was textbook embarrassment. Her jaw began working, her mouth trying to emit sounds, then syllables, finally a sentence fragment. "What I did…"

Grinning from ear to ear, Vanity rephrased Melissa's thought. "You stole Lady's husband and her boyfriend, the man she actually loves. It's almost like you were sent to destroy her life."

I gave Melissa a break. "She's just kidding. It does look like that but the reality is that I'm glad you've been distracting Pastor. And despite his infatuation with you, Mac broke it off when I threatened to make his life a living hell. I wouldn't have left him of course, but I had to make such a Draconian threat to get his attention."

Instead of apologizing to me again, Melissa turned to Vanity, a smile tickling the corners of her mouth. "Knowing Mac, I'm willing to bet that you had an affair with him too, although not as lasting as Lady's. Am I right?"

Vanity nodded. "It lasted a month. I felt guilty about it because I love Mike and he loves me—just like Mac and Lady—even if he can be easily seduced by an attractive and seductive woman." She held her hand up to stop Melissa from voicing another round of apologies. "You weren't the first, but I think you're probably the most attractive, even more beautiful than the prostitute I caught him in bed with."

Melissa blushed again.

Having cleared up who was in love with whom, Melissa told Vanity and me about the day Mac broke up with her. Vanity laughed so hard that coffee came out of her nose and she got hiccups so bad that Melissa had to pound her back. Vanity and I dissuaded Melissa from apologizing to any of the men she'd had an affair with and encouraged her to keep up her relationship with Pastor, secure in the knowledge that I had no complaints. She agreed to our stipulations and assured us that, although she was very fond of Pastor and supported his dream, she would be leaving Trinity House the week after Easter, to spend a few months visiting her parents before moving to New York City.

BUTTERFLIES

I've been avoiding Melissa after what happened when we broke up but, a few days later, she asks me to come by the church on Wednesday morning if I get the chance. She wants to make sure the wiring diagram is consistent with the work I'd done. Documentation. She's happy about the performance of the sound system. I reluctantly agree, afraid she's going to meet me with a knife or a gun, her high heel shoe having failed to kill me. When I arrive, she's friendly but professional, her only acknowledgement of our affair expressed by two words.

"It's over."

She isn't trying to undress me or doing a striptease for my private enjoyment. We spend a couple of hours together because I'm the only one who knows where all the wires go, thanks to Dim and the Board not wanting to pay a professional electrician to do the job. I'm finding her new behavior very exciting, kind of like resetting the clock, starting over. I'm about to make my move when Lady shows up, a cup of coffee in her hand.

"How's it going?"

I don't know what to say, expecting the two of them to get into some kind of cat fight, but instead Melissa explains how the circuits are in agreement with the wiring diagram, which she holds up as proof of our platonic, professional collaboration. She goes on to explain how any competent electrician or audio engineer would be able to upgrade the system in a couple of years. I'm flabbergasted when Lady kisses my cheek, with Melissa standing there smiling supportively, before the two of them go outside to discuss the garden.

I'm closing up the electrical panels but my attention is focused on the voices that suddenly reappear. I don't like what they're saying. Lady and Melissa have made a pact with Pastor, an agent of Satan, to undo what I've accomplished. I've done everything Jesus asked of me and, with the help of other believers, the people of Trinity House will survive the cataclysm. But now they are undermining my work and I can see it in their eyes. Women who should be mortal enemies are smiling, giggling like schoolgirls, because they are plotting against me. They are going to ruin everything. Stupid goddamn women! I need to silence them, even if it means doing them harm. What are a couple of lives compared to hundreds? These thoughts are not mine, but those of angels, Jesus is silent himself. I refuse to injure either Melissa or Lady, but the voices insist that there is no other option. I fall to the floor, kneeling, and press my head against the wall, breathing hard and telling the voices to get out of my head.

Lady appears, rushes to me and drops to her knees, her soft hands pulling my head away from the wall, caressing my cheeks. I slide into her arms, mumbling.

"What is it, Mac? What are you trying to tell me? Do you want to go to the hospital?"

I shake my head. "Too late…don't do it…stop doing it, just stop and…and don't do it…"

"Don't do what, Mac? What are you talking about? You have to tell me more so we can prevent what's going to happen. Please tell me what I shouldn't do!"

Her tender hands enclosing my head restore my equilibrium. I can stand. Lady gets to her feet alongside me, her arm around my waist.

"I don't know what I was talking about, but it's so important that I'm freaked out."

She leads me to the office and helps me sit down in an armchair. "Let's think about it." She gets me a glass of water and hovers over me as I sip, sharing her thoughts.

"Thanks to Mike's intervention, the congregation of Trinity House has a virtual option for the upcoming Easter celebration and, thanks to your personal commitment, it actually works. Vanity worked with Melissa and me to verify that the home experience is as good as it could be for someone not physically present—"

I interrupt her. "That's not the problem. No one should be in the building on Easter. Not the congregation. Not the band. Not Pastor. No one. But your plan is to share the experience."

She kisses my cheek and says, "That's the best we can do, Mac. If no one comes to church on Easter, they will still be able to listen to Pastor's message, hear the electric piano I'll be playing in the rectory, Melissa and the band from their houses, and share the service."

"Okay. But don't do the other thing…"

"Right, let's get back to the original problem. You're obviously concerned that Melissa's virtual Easter will be undone by some precipitous act, which I assume will occur during the Wednesday prayer service, which is tonight. What might I do to endanger the congregation?"

It's gone. My mind is a blank. I shake my head and say, "I don't remember, but your actions are going to lead to the death of everyone if you don't choose another path. I'm sorry to say something like that to you. I'm sure I got it wrong. Jesus didn't tell me this himself…maybe it's a test?"

Her face is twisted in fear. "My god, Mac, what am I to do? And I imagine that your warning applies to Pastor, Vanity, Melissa, Melina, Dim, and god only knows how many others. There's no way to avoid the calamity you've foreseen, whatever it is."

I smile at her and say, "No matter what happens, Jesus told me that we're going be together for a long time, maybe forty years."

She smiles, coughs, and rubs her throat. "I think I'm catching a cold."

CATALYST

There was a festive mood in the air, reinforced by Melissa and I performing our dueling musician's routine. She had a band, including a saxophone, so they were a lot louder, but I always played a few bars before they responded. We had fun, and so did the congregation as they filtered into the church. Melissa was a gifted musicologist, who had spent almost ten years of her life trying to atone for her *original sin* by creating inspirational musical entertainment. I was proud of her for deciding to continue her musical education, taking a step into the unknown as it were, a life where her eccentric behavior wouldn't leave her feeling guilty. Maybe only less guilty.

I couldn't help thinking about Mac's warning, that I was going to personally contribute to the tragedy. Why was he so sure? I certainly gave no credence to his claims of speaking to Jesus, a fact he'd overlooked when sharing his prophecy with Trinity House. That was a good idea because the congregation would be envious if Mac claimed to have spoken directly to their *Savior*. I'd done some checking and found a lot of anecdotal stories in the mainstream news of premonitions of disaster, told by people who'd gotten off a plane at the last moment, for example. I got goosebumps thinking about it. I didn't think it was Covid 19, however, which reminded me to remove a throat lozenge from the bag lying next to me on the piano bench. I felt a slight fever. The flu vaccine was working as well as in previous years.

Pastor typically focused on Bible lessons during the Wednesday evening service and the week before Easter was no exception. He roamed through the Epistles of Paul, demonstrating the continuity of worship that Paul had encouraged throughout the early Christian church. He hadn't told me that he was going to explicitly support the concept of a virtual service, although it had been obvious that this was what the Board desired. He hadn't always been willing to align his spiritual message with church politics.

Mike Blunt had grown on me over the years because he was the only member of the congregation, besides myself, who understood Pastor's sermons and Bible lessons. He'd been following along on a digital Bible he'd installed on his phone, making notes and creating bookmarks, planning to review it later. After all, he was a lawyer. I knew that he would have a knowledgeable comment to make after the service. He was like that. After Melina Light and the other spiritual dancers and glossolalists finished playing musical chairs and speaking gibberish, it was time for the testimonials. Usually, people thanked God for giving them enough money to pay their rent (often from the church coffers), talking to a sibling or parent on the phone, getting a promotion or a raise, being inspired to become a better person, and so on. The tone was different on this particular evening, more confessional and harmonious. More than one Fundamentalist crossed the center aisle to apologize for hard feelings they'd harbored against an Evangelical and it went both ways. I watched in awe as the congregation shifted, a mass migration occurring before my eyes. Amidst all this movement, I was dumbfounded when Mike let Vanity lead him across the neutral territory to face Dim Light, who stood up to face him. They said a few words and hugged like I'd seen them do years before, as if they were members of the same congregation and shared a common spiritual belief, rather than reluctant collaborators.

When the dust had settled, the congregation looked like it had five years earlier. There were no Fundamentalist and Evangelical sides, no enclaves of devout versus casual believers, and even the loners who usually occupied the last few rows had been mixed into the mass.

The evening held another surprise for me, and I had an ominous feeling that this one wouldn't be so pleasant. Pastor announced the departure of Melissa Tight to continue her musical studies in New York City. Several thoughts crossed my mind at that moment, so I looked towards Mac in desperation. He was applauding along with everyone else. I glanced at Melissa, who met my gaze.

She was going to do it, make a clean break, tell everything. I could see it in her eyes. She was wearing a mask so I couldn't see her mouth, but her eyes were smiling, more relaxed than I'd ever seen them, not a care in the world, calm acceptance of the future. The eyes of a suicide bomber.

I shook my head imperceptibly. Her eyes flashed certainty as they moved up and down, confirming my worst fear. Mac was right. It was my doing. I had encouraged Melissa, thinking I was helping a confused young woman straighten out her life. I had meddled in the life of someone I didn't know and Trinity House was going to pay for my mistake. This was the wildcard Mac had foreseen, probably subconsciously recognizing that so much camaraderie between his girlfriends would have unforeseen consequences.

Melissa's eyes were proud as she passed me to give her farewell speech. I dared to shake my head emphatically. She went to the podium and initiated what had freaked Mac out. He was wearing a mask like half the congregation, but his head was nodding and he was applauding as she stepped behind the pulpit.

Vanity's eyes weren't smiling. Her head was shaking, her eyes on Melissa rather than me. She pulled down her mask and mouthed a resounding, "No!" It didn't matter. The dice had been tossed. More like the fuse had been lit.

Melissa explained how much she hated to leave but she couldn't pass up the opportunity to attend a musical college where she would learn how to spread the message of Trinity House throughout the world. It was an uplifting and humble speech. She could have stopped there. She could have shut up, packed up her car after the service, and driven to California to visit her parents or maybe drive to New York. But no, she had to clear the air, something she'd never done in her checkered past of leaving churches before her shenanigans came to light. This was all on me, and maybe Vanity.

I interrupted her musically but the band didn't play their part, probably because she'd instructed them to ignore me. She turned and faced me, her eyes comforting, telling me not to worry about it. I was way past worrying, not for myself but for the congregation. For the first time in twenty years, I was concerned about each and every one of them. I should have foreseen this and spoken to Melissa about it. She would have understood. Maybe I should have stood up and gone to her, taken her aside and whispered in her ear what was going to happen. She would have listened to me. After all, she trusted me enough to change her life and return to college.

I tried to stand but my legs wouldn't move, so I watched from behind my pastel-blue mask as the fate of the people I'd come to know over the past twenty years was decided by a young woman. A stranger in their midst. Tears welled up in my eyes and trickled down my mask with her next words.

"I'm beginning a new life. Like the Israelites wandering in the desert for forty years, I've been trying to discover who I am. Like them, the answer was right in front of me. I am who I am and nothing is going to change that. I know because I've tried everything to overcome my inner self, to walk in Jesus' footsteps…"

Vanity was shaking her head, silently voicing, "Stop talking," even miming zipping her lips shut. You could have heard a pin drop it the recently reorganized church.

On cloud nine, Melissa continued, "I am a sinner. Jesus will forgive me, but I can't let it go because that's the approach I've used in the past. Running from the truth doesn't make it go away. It only makes the ocean of sins threatening to drown me deeper. I know that many of you will not want to speak to me again, and rightly so, after I finish what I have to say. Nevertheless, like Brother Lunatic, I must speak the truth no matter how unpleasant it may be." Melissa paused, ignoring Vanity's frantic gesticulation, sipped from Pastor's half-empty glass, and proceeded to name all the men with whom she'd had an affair. My jaw dropped in surprise, even though I knew about the two men in my life. It took several minutes for her to finish her list, which included Mike Blunt, Dim Light, Macbeth Lunatic, and of course Pastor Church.

THE LAST STRAW

After my cordial meeting with Melissa and Lady earlier, I'm really surprised at Melissa's goodbye speech, which she gives with her mask pulled down. I never suspected that she was having sexual relations with so many other guys. I lose track because of her digressions, summarizing every affair in personal terms, but Missy's keeping count. Melissa had slept with fourteen men in Trinity House over the past year. No wonder she was indifferent about having sex with me. I was just another dude. Hell, this girl should have gone professional. I finally look at Lady. Her eyes are frustrated, her anguish reinforced by her head's motion, wobbling hopelessly. I get it. This is what I'd been warned about by the voices—maybe angels but definitely not Jesus. I don't know what she wants me to do. If I stand up and call Melissa a liar, I'm bearing false witness and besides, I don't think anyone is going to believe me, just like in that whole *Me Too* movement. No one is looking at me, not with Pastor's name on her list, so it's going to be okay. I must have been overreacting when I'd spoken to Lady earlier.

Lady is hitting some discordant notes on the organ, until Melissa turns to her and smiles confidently. Then, it dawns on me. But it's too late. The fuse has been lit and it's a short one. This is a really big firecracker. A stick of dynamite.

I hear one of Melina's fellow spiritualists speaking in tongues behind me. Everyone turns to the source of the disturbance, which spreads rapidly through the pews after the healing that had occurred earlier. We're all looking around, unfamiliar with the new social order. Our attention is quickly focused on Melina when she leaps from her seat next to Vanity and proclaims herself my spiritual advisor. Missy looks at me as if I'm an idiot while Melina describes our relationship in detail. Missy gives me a look that says, "You made your bed, pal, now sleep in it."

As if that isn't bad enough, a couple of other women share the sexual experiences they had with me. I'm looking as bad as Melissa by the time they finish. Missy gives me a head count. I had affairs with ten women over a decade. I'm not as big a sinner as Melissa. She has me beat by a mile.

My attention turns back to Lady. Tears are flowing down her cheeks and I know what's coming. After what has already occurred, I don't see how it matters. I had thought that she would do something to undo the carefully planned virtual Easter service, but I was wrong. Melina's confession of our numerous trysts had focused everyone's attention on me, even though I'd had a rather benign sex life compared to Melissa. I'm deceiving myself, a fact made painfully clear when Lady stands up from behind the piano and joins Melissa at the pulpit. Everything is clear now. Seeing Lady standing next to Melissa, two beautiful women who were a part of my life, I realize that the blame doesn't lie with Lady or Melissa. The voices suddenly return, whispering suspicions about the two women, warning me to keep quiet and exact retribution later. I cover my ears to shut out their incessant agitation, only antagonizing them to shout louder. The only way I can drown out their incoherent, indecipherable, and meaningless voices is to speak louder than them.

With my hands over my ears, I stand up and shout, "I am in love with Lady and we are going to be together no matter what!"

Apparently trying to calm the mood, the band fills the deafening silence with the gentle notes of Mozart's Piano Concerto Number 21, the electric piano accompanied by the guitar and drums standing in for a full orchestra.

The voices have stopped, so I lower my hands. Now everyone is looking at me, but I'm not standing there anymore. I'm hovering over the congregation. A spectator. The music is very soothing to me but it doesn't have much effect on the scene below me. Everyone is talking at once, Melina is speaking in tongues again, another woman is giving her interpretation and it isn't very complimentary of me. I'm probably possessed by Satan to have done so much, me and my fellow libidinous sinner, Melissa. Never mind all those people who voluntarily had affairs with us—two people were an easier target than two dozen men and women. Melissa doesn't seem to mind, standing behind the pulpit holding Lady's hand, trying to get the congregation to quiet down. Lady has something to add.

"Macbeth Lunatic and I have been in love for almost ten years. I should have divorced Pastor as soon as I realized how I felt about Mac, but I denied my feelings because of a misguided sense of obligation. That was my real moral failure, not to be honest to myself or Pastor. I'm not ashamed of what I did because it was inevitable that Mac and I were going to end up together. There is something I am ashamed of however…"

I feel the same way, especially considering that I'd remained married to a woman who detested my touch because she was a lesbian. If only Lady and I had recognized our feelings back then—what am I saying? It would have been the same result, standing in front of the congregation, or worse slinking off in the dark. Neither one of us would have done that. What's occurring right now was as inevitable as Lady and me falling in love. I hear myself supporting her, apologizing for being so stupid.

Lady smiles sadly at me and continues, "I am prolife but I don't see a woman exercising her reproductive rights as evil, or abortion as murder. Every woman must choose for herself. I had to choose…a few months ago, I learned that I was pregnant. I wanted to have the child because it was going to be the product of my love for Mac, our child."

She never told me about it. I watch as my body looks at her with amazement.

"I didn't tell him. I tried to several times, but he was dismissive and I got angry, so I did it on my own. I don't regret having an abortion because there was a good chance it would have suffered from a serious birth defect. What I regret is not telling Mac because…well, I feel like he's my real husband, not Pastor."

The looks directed at me have gone from disgust to revulsion. Now, I'm not only a wanton degenerate, but also a bad husband to a woman who isn't my wife—who is apparently blameless in all this. The church is filled with sighs of disgust, gasps of disbelief, moans of sympathy or maybe empathy, all directed at Lady. Another victim of marital abuse.

"I'm sorry," I hear myself say. "What you did was your decision to make, and it's perfectly fine by me. I would have agreed with you—"

Missy interrupts me, "That's not the point, Mac. You weren't there emotionally when she needed you, just like you weren't when I needed you… I mean in the past. You have not had the love of Jesus in your heart until recently. Just look what you put Sister Church through?"

I hear myself say, "I would have acted differently if I'd known you were lesbian! That's the kind of personal decision that should be shared with your *husband*."

"I'm sorry, Mac, I didn't know myself as well back then."

"None of us knew as much about ourselves last month as we do now," my other self says.

I can see from my lofty perch in the rafters that my worst fear has been realized. By focusing the congregation's attention on my feet of clay instead of my dire warning, Melissa and Lady have doomed all these people. I return to my body and begin to weep for them, too weak to give them a last warning, then I'm taken into Jesus' arms.

CLEARING THE AIR

Missy didn't argue when I called 911 after Mac's collapse during the Wednesday Bible service. Looking back, his timing couldn't have been better. We were like the bride and groom leaving the wedding reception to showers of rice and thrown kisses, except we didn't get in a limousine. Missy and I followed the ambulance in Mac's pickup. He was still unconscious when we arrived at the hospital and settled in for a long night. It was after midnight when a nurse informed us that he was stabilized but needed surgery that would require his transfer to a better-equipped hospital in Oklahoma City.

"Is he conscious?" I asked.

"Can we see him?" was Missy's query.

Mac shared a room with an elderly man. He was awake but several tubes and electrical wires prevented me from holding him. From what I could tell, Missy felt the same way. We stood there awkwardly, wringing our hands, waiting to hear him say something intelligible.

He smiled at us and quipped, "Which one of you is in charge?"

We kissed his cheeks from opposite sides of his bed before I said, "I guess you are, since you're conscious."

Missy was nodding, less confident than the last time Mac had ridden in an ambulance to this hospital, possibly staying in this very room, maybe even lying in the same bed.

Mac looked at Missy and said, "I really don't think the Lord meant to kill me. That part was a misunderstanding. Do you mind if Lady looks after me, after everything that happened…you know?"

She sighed with relief. "That's a good idea. Lady really loves you, Mac."

"I know, but I know you love me too, Missy. I feel the same way…I mean, damn, we have a daughter and a lot of memories, not to mention a life together. This doesn't mean whatever—"

"I know. Lady and I talked about it. Don't worry about any of that."

He looked at me, grimaced, and said, "Like you said, I'm not dead, so I plan to relax here a day or so and then get out for Easter, to celebrate the resurrection of Jesus from the comfort of my living room." His gaze shifted to Missy. "Will you be observing the event remotely with me?"

"I don't know Mac, not because of anything that happened today, but it's just hard to believe that Jesus would let something terrible happen to Trinity House. I think your prophecy was meant to warn us about Covid 19."

Mac nodded his reluctant acceptance of her decision and his gaze turned to me.

I spoke through my cloth mask. "I'll be sharing the experience with you from my living room because I don't feel very well. I think I'm getting a cold and I don't want to make anyone else sick." I coughed as if to make my point.

Mac and Missy exchanged worried looks.

He was getting sleepy, so Missy and I left him in good hands for the night. I asked about a Covid test and was informed that the hospital had several test kits available. Missy waited while I spoke to a nurse, then had my nose penetrated in a very unpleasant manner by an apologetic nurse, who told me that they would contact me within forty-eight hours with the test result.

I was shivering by the time I walked through the front door of the rectory, to find Pastor waiting. Too exhausted to talk, fighting for every breath, I rushed past him and fell on my face in the bed, still wearing my jacket. I was asleep before my head hit the pillow.

I awoke with Pastor next to me, sleeping silently as was his fashion. I listened to his steady breathing and compared it to my own unsteady, arrhythmic gasps, each one feeling like my last breath. This wasn't the flu. Pastor had undressed me and gotten my sleeping shirt over my head without my awareness. I emptied a glass of water sitting on my nightstand. The early morning light leaking past the edges of the blinds, moving across the ceiling and walls, framed what became a motion picture of my remembered life. There was Tommy Gallagher fondling my pubescent breast in junior high, Alan Martin sneaking a feel between my thighs at the movies, Robert Talisa's tongue in my mouth after the junior prom. I watched the scenes play out, reliving the horror of each and every event. I wasn't a lesbian like Missy, I had simply been waiting for Macbeth Lunatic to enter my life.

The movie ended suddenly when Pastor turned to me and asked, "How are you feeling?"

"I think I have Covid. I got a test while I was at the hospital. I should quarantine until I hear from them." I picked up a mask from my nightstand and slipped its ear loops into place. "I'm serious, Pastor. I'm highly contagious. Oh god, I hope I haven't already infected you…"

He climbed out of the bed, saying, "The most important thing is your comfort and health. What do you need right now?"

Pastor's response was exactly what one would expect from someone like him in a relationship like ours. He took care of me. I got worse and he watched over me while he worked on his sermons, not leaving me alone for more than an hour at a time. My fever had worsened but not enough to go to the hospital. It was the perfect opportunity to discuss his promiscuous past whenever I was coherent.

I remember him saying, "I'm sorry about what happened with Melissa. I can't make any excuses, but I don't love her, not even the way I feel about you."

"Shut up, Pastor. She's beautiful and you wanted to be with her. I understand. Have you had other dalliances?" I fell asleep and had to wait for an answer.

He later confessed to as many extramarital affairs as Mac during the same time interval, a fact I let slide because I didn't care. The next time I was able to have a conversation, it was on a different topic.

"I know it's Friday, and Sunday is Easter so…well, have

you let your personal feeling get in the way of…at least making an effort to encourage people to heed Mac's warning?"

The answer was yes, but he didn't know how to express his feelings spontaneously. Not having hours to spend tweaking his grammar, like for a sermon, he punted. "There has been a lot of backlash against Mac and thus skepticism about the message he was sharing—"

I didn't care anymore. I knew what was going to happen just as surely as Mac, without knowing the exact form the catastrophe would take, so I cut Pastor off. "Then you will have their lives on your head in the hereafter you believe in. I imagine that your last thought, before you enter oblivion, will be, "Why didn't I heed the word of God as presented through a sinner like Macbeth Lunatic?"

My serious (probably feverish) demeanor got his attention. He didn't acquiesce but instead doubled down. "We are all born sinners, not false prophets."

I laughed weakly and fell asleep.

The next time I was fully conscious was Friday evening. I awoke to find Mac sitting next to my bed holding a tray, a bowl of canned cream-of-chicken soup and a cup of yogurt presented for my dinner. My appetite had returned and I devoured his offering, wiping the bowls with my fingers. He apologized for everything, including being who he was. I shushed him because he was the man I'd fallen in love with, a man who appeared shallow at a casual glance, as deep as an ocean when examined closely.

"I love you, Mac. I can say that now. I love Macbeth Lunatic!"

He tried to match my enthusiasm when he avowed his own feelings, but he wasn't speaking with the passion a 103-degree fever engenders. I weakly resisted his kisses and caresses, before surrendering to the darkness.

ASSAULT AND BATTERY

A couple of days in the hospital and I'm feeling as good as new. At Lady's insistence, I make arrangements for an operation to clean up the mess inside my head the week after Easter. If she feels well enough, she's going to join Missy on the trip to Oklahoma City. They've become good friends. In fact, the only woman I'd had an affair with who hasn't become friends with Lady is Melina Light. I laugh so hard when she tells me about their last meeting that she's worried I'm going to have another stroke.

I figure that Lady and I are no longer welcome among the congregation. Whatever happens on Easter, I won't be returning to Trinity House, not even to work on the garden. It's getting close to planting time, but they can find someone else to do their landscaping and farming for free. That reminds me of all that fertilizer stored in the basement. I'd meant to at least get the diesel fuel out of such an enclosed space, even if Dim didn't like it sitting out in the open. It's dangerous. Remembering the fireworks stored in the basement for the Easter potluck celebration doesn't concern me because I had gone over the pyrotechnics display with several responsible members of the congregation. They didn't need me. None of that matters though because my sense of imminent catastrophe is as strong as ever.

I check myself out of the hospital Friday afternoon and stop by to see Lady, not knowing what kind of reception to expect. Pastor is surprisingly cordial, even letting me help with her dinner. We have a nice talk until she falls asleep.

Saturday morning, I'm not feeling as recovered as I'd thought when I was lying in a hospital bed. Moving around is a little tiring, so I'm sitting on the couch, not doing much. Watching TV makes my head hurt, so I'm just hanging out, eyes closed, listening to the joyful sounds Missy is making as she moves from room to room, doing her weekly cleaning. She's singing hymns and popular Christian rock songs, and her voice soothes my seething thoughts. *What is going to happen? Is there anything more I can do to prevent it?*

I'm thinking that the Lord couldn't have found a worse messenger to share his warning when the doorbell rings. Before I can get up, Missy appears and tells me to stay put. She goes into the foyer and returns with the last person I expected to see in my house. Missy is all smiles—even the appearance of a man she thinks of as a Pharisee standing at her door doesn't affect her upbeat mood.

"Look who dropped by, Mac! It's Brother Blunt in the flesh. What an honor to have a member of the *Board* visit us on a Saturday morning." Still ebullient, she turns to Mike and asks, "Would you like a cup of coffee?"

To say that there was no love lost between Missy and Mike would be an understatement. She's been giving me an earful ever since I got home. Mike is a hypocrite whereas I am simply a sinner. Apparently, one is worse than the other. The key was an event I'd missed in the Wednesday service; Mike had stood up and called Melissa a liar in church, which everyone knew was not the truth. She was just too convincing, having shared that Mike was a lot nicer than his blustering act suggested. Missy loved retelling that story. This latest episode only proved what she'd always known: Mike was a weak, unethical, immoral man, who gave conservative Christians a bad name. She despised him and all lawyers.

Mike's shaved head is red as he spits out, "Were you to offer me a glass of water, I would decline not caring to be seen as condoning the familial situation you have chosen to espouse, homosexuality and hypersexuality two faces of the same evil, sharing a conjugal bed and violating several state and municipal statutes and ordinances."

Missy's eyebrows raise in false confusion and she replies, "Would you prefer tea?"

Her innocent rejoinder distracts Mike from the purpose of his unannounced visit. He faces her and says through clenched teeth, "Nothing, thank you."

Missy shrugs and goes back to her routine.

I smile and say, "I appreciate your support for me and the message I've been sharing. You should be proud of what you did, getting the Board to allow a virtual church service for people who can't attend in person. I plan to use it on Easter. How about you?"

Mike looks at me as if I'd spoken Chinese. There's something else on his mind.

Not knowing the reason for his surprise visit, I continue, "I guess you didn't come by to coordinate a virtual Easter with Lady and me, so you must be confused about the timing…Melissa leaving the church, making her surprise announcement, which was as much of a shock to me as it must have been to you and Vanity—"

"You are responsible for all of this." His arms wave around my living room.

I scoff, and calmly reply, "I was on Melissa's list just like you Mike, but I guess Vanity didn't take it as well as Missy…or Lady."

"If you do not rescind your contract with Trinity House immediately, I will initiate legal action against you…you and the abomination you call your wife."

No one comes into my home and calls me and Missy names, especially not a hypocrite like Mike Blunt. But I'm too tired to jump up and punch him in the mouth. I settle for saying, "What's come over you? You can't talk that way, not in my house, not about my wife. And I thought I was crazy during my spiritual experience. But you've lost your mind!"

Mike takes several steps towards me, his fists clenched, before he says, "My wife doesn't want anything to do with me and it's your fault, you piece of white-trash shit!"

This is more than I'm prepared to deal with. I don't think I can even get up. "Calm down, Mike, why do you think your affair with Melissa is my fault?"

I understood what Lady had been saying for years when Mike retorted, "No one would have known if you hadn't gotten into Melissa's head, it was just an affair to her but not for you...but no, not you...you had to make her fall in love with you, and look where that led, are you happy?!"

"Melissa isn't in love with me. Lady is. Melissa was pretty clear when she said that she liked me because I didn't overanalyze things. I guess I'm a simple man and that appealed to her, at least for a while."

"I'll get an injunction against you, that's what I'll do, to keep your ass out of Trinity House and keep you away from Vanity, who seems to be infatuated with you, you goddamn piece of shit!"

"I've been in court a couple of times Mike and no judge in either Modoc or Oklahoma County would issue such a ridiculous order. In fact, they would probably censure you for making a frivolous claim."

He steps forward, towering over me, his finger in my face. "Who's the lawyer? A white-trash lawn boy like you—or me?"

I'm tired of his insults, issued in my own living room. He's so close to me that I can't stand up without pushing him out of the way, but he's not a little boy. Mike's strong, even if he is over sixty. He's treating me as if I were a ninety-pound weakling, taking advantage of my temporary weakness to feel like more of a man than he is. I'm not going to put up with it, so I stand up, joining my forearms and pushing them into his abdomen. Hard. He stumbles backwards, tripping, falling into the coffee table, before sliding to the floor. Now, I'm on my feet and he's on the floor. I'm not able to fight so I just stand there, wobbling over him.

The room is spinning and the voices have returned, and I listen to them this time. Standing over Mike, barely remaining on my feet, I foolishly antagonize him. "You came to my house because you suspect the truth. You can't satisfy a woman in the bedroom, not even your wife, and that's why Melissa dumped you, pretending that you're a nice guy rather than a wimp. Maybe you have erectile dysfunction, or maybe you're just a limp-dick jerk. That's probably what led Vanity to hit on me— she is pretty old after all—until I gave in. She does have a great body for an old woman, and she knows how to use it. I made her howl with pleasure and she came back for more, until I got tired of her. You weren't man enough to satisfy your own wife, so I'm pretty sure you didn't satisfy Melissa Tight. I satisfied both of them."

Mike clambers to his feet with no interference from me. I never see the fist that clobbers my left eye, knocking me back on the sofa, dizzy and unable to defend myself. Mike advances and towers over me again.

"I should kill you right now. I could do it with my bare fists, you motherfucker! I boxed in college and it would be easy to finish you. Why the hell not…" His fist is raised, ready to strike the blow that will end my miserable life. I wait for the darkness that precedes eternal life…probably in hell.

Instead, I hear a revolver being cocked.

"Step back and get out of my house, Brother Blunt, or the next thing your eyes will see are the pearly gates. As a lawyer, you know I could pull the trigger right now and charges wouldn't even be filed against me. I do not like you, never have, and now I know why. You are a bully who beats up on weaker people. Get out of my house!"

The fists that were about to end my life unclench, Mike's arms raised nonthreateningly. His attention is on the 44 magnum Missy is holding steadily, aimed at his chest.

"I'm sorry—"

"Shut up and get out." The pistol is unwavering as Missy's brown eyes tell Mike that she is ready to pull the trigger.

She follows him out the door, the revolver held in front of her like a cop. I hear her say, "If you ever set foot on my property again, I'll finish what you started, Brother Blunt."

I hear his car leave. I don't feel any worse except for my left eye, which is throbbing. Missy sets the heavy revolver on the coffee table and hugs me, kind of rocking like you'd do with a child. I appreciate it. I tell her that I don't need to go to the hospital. I'm okay. She calls the police department and reports assault and battery against me, giving Mike's name, address, and vehicle license plate number.

LOCK UP

The test results were positive. I was to remain isolated for two weeks, except for being cared for by Pastor. Still, we were to practice basic safety measures like me wearing a mask and him keeping his distance. I was to have no visitors, so naturally everyone wanted to talk to me. I hadn't almost died so the thinking was: How bad can it be? It didn't kill a sinner like Lady Church. To me, my acute but not life-threatening illness meant that God was going to smite Trinity House in some other manner—one of those catastrophes Mac had mentioned in church. I was glad to have Covid because I had an excuse not to be sitting at the organ on judgement day. Don't misunderstand me, however; I don't believe in the god of the Christians but I do accept the existence of the unknown. I was convinced that Mac's warning was legitimate, or at least plausible, given the situation and all. Even if nothing happened, it wouldn't change my faith in him. He wouldn't have spoken up unless he'd felt a desperate fear of annihilation of Trinity House, an irrational fear I interpreted as an indication that he knew something, whether subconsciously or communicated through some kind of sixth sense. You couldn't have paid me to go to church on Easter, even if I weren't sick as a dog from Covid.

I learned about the events of Saturday morning when Missy dropped by. I wore a mask and insisted she keep her distance. There was nothing wrong with my hearing, however, and she gave me an earful.

"Mike Blunt assaulted Mac, threatened to beat him to

death, so I had to run him off with Mac's 44 magnum."

I made her tell me everything, covering my mouth in terror as she described the murderous look on Mike's face when he stood over a weak and immobile Mac, his raised fist ready to strike the deadly blow. Missy obviously was a woman of action. I held back a grin as she explained what she did after running the Pharisee out of her house.

"I called the police and told them everything. They sent an ambulance for Mac and we took him back to the hospital again. His eye was swollen shut and he didn't know who I was. I made sure that detective understood that Mike had been about to kill Mac, boasting about boxing in college. I made sure they took me seriously."

I ventured, "Don't expect much help from the law. After all, Mike knows the judge in Modoc and the district attorney. They probably aren't even looking for him. Maybe they'll ask him what happened sometime next week. That's how it works in Oklahoma County—Oklahoma in general."

"I recorded their conversation without Mike knowing it. The whole thing about Mac having an affair with Vanity is known to the police. They were talking about motive and real threats because apparently the police know about Mike's violent temper, a personality quirk he doesn't display in church."

I listened in amazement as she summarized what she'd learned from the police detective who'd interviewed her. Mike had threatened several police officers and even the district attorney with violence, which hadn't been ignored by Judge Franklin. Mike had been censured and was on a kind of probation. The police really were looking for him. The detective didn't think he would be getting out of jail on his own recognizance. Our visit ended with a blown kiss, despite her wanting to hug me. I didn't want to make anyone else sick.

I related Missy's story to Pastor when he brought my lunch. He didn't express surprise at what had transpired because he'd seen Mike's violent side several times, but always kept under control. Pastor had spoken to Mike about his temper and ascertained that he was extremely jealous of Vanity, a beautiful and gracefully aging actress. He verified everything I'd heard from Missy. I only hoped the police found Mike before he returned to kill Mac. As bad as I felt, I would have rushed to protect Mac myself, but Missy had already demonstrated that she was more than capable of defending her home and her husband—now my spouse, for all intents and purposes—from unwelcome intruders.

Pastor left me alone and I immediately fell asleep. A dream in which Missy was defending Mac and me from Godzilla was interrupted by a familiar voice.

"How are you doing, little sister?"

Vanity's usual joyful expression at seeing me was absent. He lips were tight, eyes puffy from crying, smooth brow furrowed with uncertainty.

I spoke first. "I heard what happened. Missy told me. I'm sure that Mike was just angry, he loves you so much, Mac probably said something that set him off, you know how he is, always speaking—"

Vanity cut me off. "Mike is dangerous. I've denied it for too long, probably because I love him. Until now, I thought he only threatened men who hit on me or even looked at me inappropriately. It made me feel desirable. I was wanted and loved. Mike loves me. He went too far with Mac. I didn't come by to make excuses. I just hope this won't affect our—"

"Of course not. That's a silly question. Come over here and sit next to me so that we can hold hands."

She sat down on the bed and our fingers intertwined tightly. We shared a breath that expressed our love for each other before she said, "Mike was arrested in our living room. They actually put handcuffs on him before leading him away, pushing his head into the police cruiser. I should have foreseen this after so many years. He has punched men in the face for speaking to me in public, threatening to kill complete strangers on several occasions. This would have been just another case of a man protecting his woman's honor if not for Missy getting the best of him…"

"You don't have to say anything else," I interjected.

She shook her head, squeezed my hand, scoffed, and continued, "I spoke to Mike in jail and he's more upset about being outgunned by a woman than being in jail. He doesn't see himself as a violent man. What am I supposed to do about that?" Her voice broke into a stream of tears.

I sprayed disinfectant on my hands and hers, rubbed them together until she smiled, and then answered her question. "You are not Mike's guardian, even though you may feel like it sometimes. And you are not the reason for his violent temper. Do you want to hear the rest of the story?"

She nodded uncertainly.

"Missy told me that when she spoke to the police about what Mike had done, she was informed that he'd threatened police officers and was on probation, being watched by the court. His assault on Mac wasn't personal but only another example of his…well, his violent temper."

Her eyes opened wide then narrowed, her head shaking slowly in self-deprecation. "I should have known. I fooled myself for all those years. Thinking he was defending my honor. Mike has a violent personality. Not so much a short temper as a raging response to anything he sees as challenging his core beliefs, including his feelings for me. I have become a goddess to him, if you can believe that?!"

"You are very beautiful, Vanity. Mike must have felt that he'd reached for the stars and actually grasped one of them. Like the Greek heroes, he's been fighting to defend the honor of the goddess who accepted him, a mere mortal, into her bed."

"I was just one more thing he was fighting to defend. I should have told him about Mac myself. It would have been difficult but at least I would have had some influence on him, deflected the blame from Mac to myself, or at least accepted some of it. But this is no longer about Mike putting me on a pedestal and imagining himself defending my honor, or even fighting for what he believes. He's not going to walk away this time."

"What do you mean?"

Her grip tightened. "It makes sense now, that Judge Franklin didn't grant him bail, not at any price. He called it a cooling off period. Mike is going to spend Easter weekend in lockup."

I understood Vanity's anguish but I had no sympathy for a bully. "It might do him good, spending Easter in jail because he beat up and threatened to kill a man he knew to be suffering from a neurological condition. Judge Franklin's probably right.

Maybe Mike needs some time to think."

My feeble effort to prevent Vanity from getting too close and kissing my cheek failed.

DENIAL

I'd like to go and visit Lady but Missy won't let me because I'm kind of seeing double after my fight with Mike Blunt, which wasn't really a fight as much as his punching me, giving me a black eye. It feels like Christmas Eve or maybe New Year's Eve, waiting for the big day. Easter. It looks like the virtual congregation will just be me and Lady.

Missy makes sure I'm okay and goes to the grocery store for a few things because it'll be closed on Easter. I take the opportunity to have a couple of shots of gin from a bottle I keep in the garage. I'm getting around okay but my balance is off. But watching TV makes my head hurt, so I'm listening to the radio when the doorbell rings.

My first thought is that Mike came back to finish the job, but I've been assured that he's spending Easter weekend in jail. I don't think anyone else wants to kill me, so I get up and answer it. I'm more than a little surprised to find Melina and Dim Light standing on the porch. He looks uncertain and uncomfortable but she's wearing a determined and self-righteous expression. I invite them in and offer them some coffee or whatever. They decline a drink but join me in the living room.

I get the conversation going. "I wish you'd been here earlier, Dim. I know how strong you are from personal experience and I could have used your help." I laugh nervously.

Apparently, word hadn't gotten to them because his eyes open wide. "What happened?"

"Mike Blunt dropped by to threaten me with legal

retribution if I didn't leave Trinity House and I…well, I informed him that Vanity—"

Melina's expression had softened a little at hearing what had happened but her eyes are on fire when she interjects, "You had an affair with Vanity Blunt. Then you boasted to her husband when he was vulnerable. What a cruel thing to do. You deserved what you—"

It's my turn to interrupt. "Hold on there, Melina, he was calling Missy horrible, ugly names, standing over me, threatening me, in my own house. I was too weak to get up and punch him so I made him aware that he was living in a glass house. I haven't met any saints lately."

That shuts her up, on that subject at least.

Dim and I have been getting along pretty well, so I'm feeling some positive vibes. After all, he didn't try to kill me when he found out about my affair with Melina. We just pushed each other around a little without the necessity of firearms for self-defense or calling the police. I relate how Missy ran Mike off and had him arrested.

Melina is flabbergasted. "He won't be able to join us for Easter service. To be with his wife on such an important day. I can't believe they didn't let him out. It's not like he would run away or anything…"

Dim responds for me. "The judge probably thought Mike would do something without thinking first, like, you know, finishing what he'd started. I know Mike pretty well and he gets hotheaded about some things, especially Vanity. She's practically the Virgin Mary in his eyes. He would have been devastated at learning that she's only human like the rest of us."

I let it go, not adding that Vanity had told me that Mike didn't satisfy her sexually. He'd probably felt his manhood threatened. But that's not why Dim and Melina have dropped by the evening before Easter.

Melina's determined expression has returned, as if she's afraid that if she stops thinking about something, she'll forget and make a terrible mistake. I figure I've gotten the ball rolling so it's time for her to speak up. Dim's facade is back to normal, waiting for his excitable wife to take the lead.

"I don't know where to start," she begins.

I shrug, refusing to take responsibility for whatever she's about to say.

"Well, it's like…you know, it's like…" She clears her throat and spits out, "Lady was rude to me and you weren't honest about our relationship, about being a servant of God. I think you were using me for sexual gratification."

She looks offended and Dim is nodding as if her pretense makes sense to him.

I'm not as smart as Lady or Pastor or even Mike Blunt, but I know when someone is making excuses and avoiding saying something outright. "What are you getting at?" I ask.

"Lady threw me out of her house when all I wanted to do was make sure that Pastor looked at both sides of the issue and didn't make a hasty decision. As spiritual as Pastor is, he has not accepted the reality of our faith within the larger scheme of the universe. Why, he doesn't even accept that angels walk among us, when the proof is everywhere…"

I don't know what she's talking about. It's like talking to Mike Blunt, but at least he refers to real things even if in legalese. I had ignored Melina's rambling about astrology, demons, angels, secret messages written in heavenly code in the clouds, stuff like that, because I'd just wanted to have sex with her. She'd had nothing to do with the Holy Spirit contacting me, but her avid sexuality had been inspirational. I'll give her that much credit. According to Lady, Melina had been transforming my message, using a combination of sex and hyper-religiosity to inject an element of paganism into my warning about disaster, taking advantage of the opportunity to spread her extreme, hybrid beliefs. Lady had called Melina a virus that infected a congregation and, if left unchecked, consumed it voraciously, leaving a withered corpse when she moved on to greener pastures. I can't help chuckling at the image of Lady manhandling Melina, who is several inches shorter but with a twenty-pound weight advantage.

Melina takes umbrage. "What is it, Mac? Are you taking sides with Pastor?" Enlightenment brightens her features and she adds, "Of course not, it's Lady who you're taking sides with, the woman who treated me as if we aren't sisters in Christ. Do you agree with her un-Christian behavior?"

I scoff and reply, "Yes, but there are extenuating circumstances. Lady is not a Christian and she certainly doesn't see herself as your *sister in Christ*, as you put it. You are offensive to her, not just because we had an affair—she's very jealous of the women I've carried-on with—but because you've been blending pagan beliefs with Christianity. Trinity House is not the temple of Zeus. You don't belong here, you've never fit in, and Lady's always known it because she isn't influenced by religious beliefs. I am a Christian, as is Missy and most of the congregation, but you are not, but you aren't agnostic like Lady. You are a pagan, Melina. Lady has nothing against your beliefs, but she told me that you are also a con-artist—a flimflam woman I think she said. I agree with her, that you don't belong in Trinity House. You can find the right church…somewhere."

I let myself run off like that because I'm pretty sure why she's sitting in my living room. Like Lady said, Melina preferred to use subterfuge to get things done, even when it made no difference. It was a personal choice.

Dim mumbles, "I don't blame Mike for punching you in the eye."

I let it go.

Melina's response is more relevant. "You have confirmed what my horoscope has predicted. You are not a prophet. You are nothing more than a miscreant who takes advantage of vulnerable women for sexual pleasure, with no regard for the consequences of your actions."

Jesus is laughing—not so loudly that Melina and Dim can hear—and suggesting how I should respond. He may be the Son of God, but I'm not going to follow his advice in this case. For one thing, I'm not sure I can even get up from the sofa, much less toss Dim and Melina around like rag dolls while kicking them in their behinds.

I settle for saying what I feel is as close to the truth as I can get. "That may be so. I apologize for taking advantage of you, but I want to emphasize that I am only the Lord's servant. I know I'm morally weak. I don't know why I was chosen, being like that. Still, I did not seduce you, Melina, but instead you stalked me until my resolve failed. I think we should call it a draw. Despite all that, you were an inspiration to me when I felt foolish about speaking up…"

I scoff, getting a dour look from Dim and scorn from Melina, before holding my hand up in protest and explaining myself. "If everything Lady said about you is true, then we were the perfect odd couple to deliver God's message to Trinity House. Do you see what I mean?"

Dim's head is bobbing. "It's a story straight out of the Bible. God doesn't spread His word through the Pharisees, but through people like John the Baptist, and of course Jesus. It makes sense when you put it that way, Mac." He looks relieved at having found a solution.

Melina isn't buying it. Her mind is made up and only one thought is available for her consideration. She just hasn't spoken it yet and I'm starting to get impatient because I want to go to bed. I can't believe how much I sound like Lady when I finally say what's on Melina's mind, the reason for her sudden visit. "You came here to tell me that you've decided to ignore God's warning. All because Lady offended you and threw you out of her house. You are letting your emotions and pride get in the way of saving lives. You are willing to let those members of the congregation who look up to you die or be seriously injured, all because you're mad at me. Maybe you're a little jealous—like Lady. I am pleading with you to put the safety of the people we've come to know as family ahead of your pride. Don't let them down."

Her face is chiseled stone for almost a minute. Dim's mouth is twisting in agony. Finally, she stands up, a few sharp edges dropping away from the sculpted facade. "I can see now that I misunderstood the signs, that you are not the messiah. You are not spiritual or sick, but evil, and I was tricked because of my misreading your horoscope. May God have mercy on your soul, Brother Lunatic."

She turns away and heads towards the door with Dim following like a puppy dog.

GIRLFRIEND

I felt better on Easter morning, the fever tolerable and the headache diminished. I was still tired and my entire body ached, so I soaked a long time in the tub, leaving Pastor to fend for himself in the kitchen. He did fine, even bringing me some fruit and a bagel, before busying himself with last-minute preparations for the second-most-important Christian holy day. I had barely gotten out of the tub when he led Vanity into the bedroom. He knew how close we were and hadn't thought anything about letting her interrupt my bath.

Before I could stop her or even put on my mask, she was on me, pushing my bathrobe open, her hands on my breasts and buttocks, caressing gently, her lips eating me alive while avoiding my mouth—her idea of social distancing. I was too weak to resist, falling on the bed while she ravaged me, leaving me panting from ecstasy rather than Covid. She was licking her fingers when she finally spoke.

"I wasn't allowed to visit Mike but Judge Franklin's order permitted a five-minute phone call this morning. Apparently, the county wakes their prisoners up early for breakfast."

I slid my hand under her short dress, tickling her inner thigh. "How's he doing?"

Women and men are alike when it comes to our genitalia, even if they have different shapes. The merest suggestion that you are going to rub a man's penis will cause him to spill secrets or swear his allegiance to you forever. It is the same with women. When my fingers gently stroked her labia, pressing against them, promising penetration and ecstasy, Vanity's response was no different than Mac's or Pastor's.

"He has a private cell…" She began, stopping to sigh as my finger reached her clitoris, catching her breath before continuing, "No one has threatened him with sodomy, but he's very angry. I think Judge Franklin was right to keep him in jail because all he talked about was how Mac had raped me, and even you…" She paused to catch her breath as my finger began to massage her the way she had shown me, giving me an opportunity to redirect the conversation.

"Are you going to spend Easter service with me? I hope so because I'm feeling well enough to celebrate. Please stay with me. I have an extra robe you can borrow." I paused for effect before adding, "I personally wonder if we can reenact Christ's resurrection, perhaps even attaining the ecstasy of his ascension."

Vanity was moaning, mumbling, "Yes, oh god, yes yes yes yes, oh my god, oh my god yes!" Her beautiful face was a study in pleasure, eyes wide, her gaze meeting mine, her mouth open in surprise. A gasp and she added, "Oh my, Lady. Ohhhh…my goodness…" Her words trailed off into an incoherent string of vowels with an occasional consonant.

She had managed to get her dress off and now we lay naked next to each other on the bed, our fingers sharing our feelings without words. I had put a mask over my mouth and nose, which she left intact as she kissed my exposed flesh.

"Well?" I began. "Are you going to spend Easter with me and reenact Christ's ascension to heaven?"

Her lips released my left nipple. Conflict raged across her exquisite features as she leaned over me and said, "That is my idea of how to celebrate Easter, Lady, but Mike insists that I have to represent him in church. I don't know what to do. I really love Mike, just like you love Mac; with all their faults, we are in love with these idiots. What can I do?" Her head collapsed onto my breasts.

I encouraged her to face me—sort of, with the mask covering my nose and mouth—before I said, "Don't you understand? Mac's prophesy isn't about something personally embarrassing—god knows we already had that experience— but life and death. You know I'm not a superstitious person and I'm not just saying this because I believe in Jesus or whatever, but I trust Mac."

She laid her head next to mine, her mouth tickling my ear as she whispered. "Being in love with Mike means that I'll do whatever he says, so long as it doesn't pose an immediate threat to my safety. I have to attend the Easter service Lady, even though I want to celebrate in your arms."

I held her close, enclosing her with my thighs and arms, pressing our bodies together, forming one person, the entity I was terrified of losing. But my love for Vanity wasn't enough to make me forget why we were having this unpleasant conversation, disguised by a sensual pleasure I couldn't share with anyone else. I tried to make her understand the gravity of the situation using my body and my words, but she was as stubborn as me.

"I have to, Lady, as much as I want to be with you. Mike told me to go to church. He doesn't give me orders very often, so I do what he says. I don't know what to think."

I was reminded of Shakespeare, how his characters always made bad decisions based on tradition and emotions. I believed in Mac's prophecy so strongly that I got carried away.

I pushed Vanity away, struggling to sit up, finally facing her. "This isn't about some silly, inconsequential argument over dogma. Mac is worried—worried as hell—not because Jesus spoke to him but because he knows something everyone has overlooked, a detail that only his mind would have noticed. Mac knows Trinity House better than anyone, even Pastor, and he's scared to death."

"I know what you're saying, but I feel like..." I took advantage of her uncertainty.

"Jesus, Vanity, the worst that could happen if you don't do as Mike demands is that he'll be mad at you, until he wants to have sex. Stay here with me and let's share the experience of Christ's resurrection together." I couldn't believe the words coming out of my mouth.

Vanity kissed my forehead and said, "I know what you're saying but I have to do this. It's the opposite of what you think—"

I interrupted her. "If there is even the slimmest chance that Mac's warning is real, we have to take every measure available to save our loved ones."

"I don't want to argue about it, especially not with you, but I will be attending the Easter service at Trinity House. Please don't make this harder than it already is."

That was exactly my purpose, to coerce, cajole, threaten, whatever it took to keep Vanity from going to church. My greatest fear was that I would lose my adopted older sister and spiritual support. I wasn't going to back down, especially after speaking to Mac that morning. His resolve was as strong as ever. I even appealed to her superstitious side, reminding her of several biblical stories supporting Mac's claim to having been visited by an angel. Rather than convincing her of the possibility that his prophecy was true, I learned that she didn't believe in miracles, visions, or even angels. We hadn't talked much about the details of her and Mike's beliefs, but it turned out that they were more like Presbyterians than Evangelicals. They had joined Trinity House because Mike didn't like the formality of mainline Protestantism. They had stayed because Pastor was undemanding.

I childishly interfered as Vanity got dressed, first taking her pantyhose, then threatening to throw her dress in the still-wet tub. Unperturbed, she went to my closet and began examining my dresses. She scoffed when I threatened to never see her again, knowing I loved her too much to end our relationship. I threatened to tell Mike about our lesbian affair, to which she replied that he wouldn't care because I didn't have a penis. He was only jealous of men because all women were slightly homosexual in his view. After putting on her original clothes, she dressed me too, while I pouted and continued to beg her not to go to church. I promised her a sensual experience beyond her wildest imagination, which intrigued her but failed to change her mind.

Wearing loose-fitting jeans and a sweatshirt Vanity had pulled out of my dresser, I blocked the front door with my body. Pastor had already gone to the church.

"I appreciate your concern for my safety, but we aren't teenagers, even if one of us is acting like one. You know I can push you out of my way in your weakened state, so don't make me slap you around." She caressed my cheek and neck before continuing, "I put up with your wearing a mask while we made love because you think you have a deadly disease, but I won't hesitate to gently move you out of my way. Okay?"

She didn't understand that I wasn't acting. Maybe it was childish to try and stop her, but I'd hoped she would see how serious I was. I had failed. I pulled the mask off and made a last, desperate plea. "If you walk across the parking lot to the church, Covid will be the least of your worries." I stepped towards her, taking her head in my hands, gazing into eyes as blue as mine. "Let me kiss you one last time."

I pressed my lips against hers, my gentle peck turning into a passionate kiss that lasted more than a minute. Her arms had slid around my waist before I released her, tears flowing from my eyes.

It almost worked.

"I thought you were…I had no idea you felt that way…" Doubt crossed her face, her lips quivering, an uncertain hand to her mouth, but her head shook slightly. "I shouldn't go…staying with you is the best thing to do, but what about…?"

I saw something in her eyes I hadn't seen before, her expression, her nervous movement. Vanity didn't share my feelings, my sense of family, of being adoptive sisters. She was just having sex, like Mac with his girlfriends, she didn't love me the way I loved her. I was nothing more than a girlfriend. Suddenly overcome with shame for having been such a fool, I stepped back and opened the door, knowing I would never see her again. She rubbed my arm as she left, promising to come by right after church.

I closed the door and leaned against it as the world dimmed. I slipped to the floor and sobbed. Everything in my life was false; my marriage, my friends, being a minister's wife; all of it was a pretense, a life I slipped into every morning like a dress and hung in the closet at bedtime. But there was one thing that wasn't false: I loved Macbeth Lunatic with all my heart and I believed in him.

EASTER

I really want to go and see Lady, what with her being actually sick instead of just seeing double like me. I try but I can't get the key in the truck's ignition. I'm stuck at home. My vision had improved overnight but not enough to drive, so I go back inside and log into the virtual Easter service. Lady and I are the only members of the congregation participating. The software is pretty cool because it lets us talk to each other without interrupting the service. There's nothing happening in church yet except people arriving and taking their old seats, from before Melissa's confession. Before I'd screwed that up because of my insatiable desires—hypersexuality is what Lady and Melissa called it. I click on Lady's tiny picture. With my vision such a mess, I wouldn't recognize her photo if anyone else was taking part.

She fills my computer screen. Her eyes are bloodshot and puffy. She's been crying. I wonder if it's me again, so I ask, "What did I do this time, to make you cry? I'm sorry, really I am."

She smiles, her head shaking. "Vanity came by and…well, I realized that you're all I have. You're my entire world, Mac, does that scare you?"

I shake my head. "After this week, I think we're pretty much on our own, you and me, although we'll always have Missy and Pastor, our kids…" I realize that I may be wrong about that if Jesus has been open with me, about what's going to happen.

"Our children," she mutters. "Yes. They won't be in

church, so we'll always have them…"

"So, you really believe me?"

She nods. "Even if nothing happens, I won't think twice about it. We all make mistakes and getting spiritual messages like you did is a process fraught with difficulty. Either way I'll be standing right next to you, no matter what happens, through thick and thin."

I can see the interior of the church through several cameras, from different angles, all without losing sight of Lady. It's almost like being there, with her sitting next to me instead of Missy. Melissa is at the organ, playing Lady's role in the musical interludes that had become so popular. She looks very happy and excited. I don't understand why because, even if everybody thinks I'm a bad person after what happened in church, they surely are aware of the seriousness of the situation. I share my confusion with Lady, whose response is enlightening.

"You were just entertainment, Mac, like Melina and her followers. People believed you—that's part of the show—but no one took you seriously except me, and that's only because I know you so well. You weren't putting on an act, but I'm the only one who recognized it. I couldn't even convince Vanity— you know how close we are—to celebrate virtually, even with Mike in jail. The big show during Wednesday bible study was all the excuse they needed to treat you as another sideshow on the circus fairway."

A month ago, I would have dismissed Lady's comment as cynicism from an agnostic. Now, I see her point because I just can't believe that all these people think I'm a false prophet just because I suffer from the same affliction as their precious choir director. They hadn't turned on her, no siree bob, not gorgeous little Melissa, misunderstood and taken advantage of by all those men she'd seduced. Including me. That's all water under the bridge.

"What do you think is going to happen?" I venture.

Pastor gets up to give the convocation as Lady replies, "You know the answer, Mac. That's why you had a vision after your first stroke. Something's bothering you, something very dangerous and potentially deadly, something ticking away like a time bomb within Trinity House, waiting for the timer to run out, and I don't think it's Covid."

My phone dings but I can't read the screen. Lady tells me to hold it up to the camera on my computer so she can read it for me.

"It's from Missy. She says that she misses having you sitting next to her and she's starting to have second thoughts about her decision. She wants to rejoin you at home but she feels like she can't leave now. It's too late."

"Tell her to leave right now!" I shout, standing up in my study.

Lady sends a text to Missy that explains why she's responding instead of me. After a minute she says, "She's sorry for bothering us. She's better now. It was just a panic attack."

I can't believe this is happening. Lady patiently listens to my ranting and turns my unintelligible words into a couple of texts to Missy. She's shaking her head sadly when the exchange ends.

The service is getting into full swing by now, the festivities projected to my computer from the cameras in the church. It's a little confusing because of my vision but Lady explains what's going on. Pastor isn't following last Easter's program, instead he's eliciting testimonials from the congregation about how their lives have changed during the year. Lady relates a text from Vanity, that she wishes she'd accepted Lady's offer to celebrate the Ascension together because it's so boring. When I ask what they'd had planned, she just says that it wouldn't have been as much fun as spending Easter with me. I've become a lot more aware of alternative ways of living since learning that Missy is a lesbian, so I don't let it go.

"What does that mean?"

"What?"

"You didn't have to read her text to me, so this is something you want to get off your chest, so let's hear it, Lady. How were you and Vanity Blunt going to celebrate Easter?"

She rolls her eyes, which I know means that she wants to talk about it. "You have to understand that I was trying to keep her from going to church today, so I got a little carried away…"

I get it but I also know that where there's smoke, there's fire. "Okay, you got a little carried away, but from what starting point?"

Her head shakes quickly, her eyes rolling wildly, hands

flailing. Finally, she says, "Vanity and I have a lesbian relationship, which I'm not ashamed of. She's my older sister—"

"Women don't have homosexual affairs with their older sisters."

She looks me in the eyes and says, "She seduced me. I thought she felt the same as me, that we were sisters, but I was just her lover. I'm just as stupid as you Mac, even though that's not what happened between you and me…"

"I know. But I'm kind of particular about where my best girl's affection is directed. If you have another lesbian relationship, I'll make you wish you had attended Easter service. Do you understand?"

She grins at me and nods. "No problem Mac, but I'm more than your best girl now. I'm your woman and you are my man…do *you* understand what that means?"

I nod confidently. "Got it." I can control my hypersexual problem with Lady's help because I love her.

Lady and I are grinning at each other, reaching towards our computer screens, wanting to hold hands, as the service continues. I feel like a teenager. Pastor delivers a stirring sermon on resurrection and starting over, building a new life from what we think is a network of failed relationships, making the point that life is a series of failures that we must accept before we can rebuild. Lady and I are laughing all through his sermon. It feels good to hear such an inspirational message from Pastor because I know he's sincere, with none of the hype of a televangelist. Lady and I are both crying by the end and saying how much we love each other. I mean it and I know she does. We've been through a lot together.

A few members of Trinity House's congregation are wandering around, healing some of the divisions that had reappeared after Wednesday bible study. It feels so good to laugh with Lady, to share this special day with someone I love, with my woman. I laugh out loud and when she asks me what's so funny, I tell her and we share the joke.

"I should take the car and come to see you," she says. "This is stupid, not being together when the entire world knows about our relationship. I want to be with you right now, Mac!"

I feel the same, but neither one of us is in any condition to drive a car. "Let's enjoy the anticipation of knowing we'll be together soon. As soon as I can see straight, I'll come to you, and I don't know if I'll ever be able to let go of you after that…" I feel a little embarrassed about such a mushy statement but Lady seems to like it.

"Okay, but let's stay on the line. I have a sense of dread about this, as if one of your unlikely scenarios is about to happen—"

I scoff and interject, "Like an airplane falling on the church?"

"Exactly."

She's serious. I start to respond, but I'm interrupted by the howling of a siren, as if it were the apocalypse. It isn't Armageddon, only a tornado sighted a few miles from Modoc, heading our way.

SHELTER

After my disappointing revelation about Vanity, sharing the Easter service with Mac was a breath of fresh air. I felt better admitting that I'd been seduced into a relationship with Vanity that I had been uncomfortable with, despite the physical and emotional pleasure it brought. Now, I could do like she'd done and quote Mac's orders. I was to have no more lesbian affairs because he was just as interested in my emotional attachments as my physical acts. I was covered with goosebumps when I accepted his terms. He was my man. I was his woman. I liked the sound of those simple pronouncements. They were so final, as if nothing more were to be said on the topic.

I had heard the tornado siren many times over the years but this was different, possibly because of Mac's prophecy. It didn't matter because a tornado on the ground and heading for Modoc was not an abstract idea. It could cause devastation and possibly kill people.

I was about to ask Mac if there was anything we should do when I got a text from Vanity. The service had been interrupted at the sound of the siren and everyone was going to the approved storm cellar beneath Trinity House.

"Mac! I just got a message from Vanity. The congregation is going into the storm cellar. Is that safe?"

"Hell no!" came his response. "That's the last place they should go. It's filled with combustible…"

We both realized that his prophecy was about to come true. I frantically texted Vanity to leave the church and get into the ditch behind it and get as many people as she could to follow her. Her response was confusing so I called her.

"Get out of the church and into a low point, like the ditch, Vanity. Take the lead. Wave your arms and take everyone you can outside, away from the church!"

"We're going to the storm cellar. Pastor is leading us. It's bomb-proof. Just take care of yourself." She hung up, leaving me wondering what to do.

Before I could speak, Mac put it all together, sharing his vision, which had required the intercession of angels to be communicated to a superstitious group like the congregation of Trinity House. All of that had been undone by recent events.

"The storm cellar is a deathtrap."

"This is a great time to point that out, Mac!" The words slipped out. I knew that his *vision* had been the only way he could communicate after his stroke. I was trying to imagine how the world appeared to him, holding back my tears.

His head was shaking, tears filling his eyes, as he responded. "I can't see straight, much less text people. You have to text Pastor or Dim, tell them to get out of the basement."

I did my best, sending texts to every digital address I had for Trinity House, but I got no acknowledgements. I shrugged helplessly.

"Well?"

"No one responded. I'm not surprised. They're all…"

Mac finished my sentence. "They're all about to meet their maker. Text Pastor and Vanity not to use any kind of open flame if the lights go out. There's no emergency lighting system in the basement."

I did as he requested but got no response.

Mac was suddenly waving at me, pushing his phone in front of his camera, expecting a response, a translation. I read the text from Missy and summarized it. "Missy realizes that you were right all along. She smells diesel fuel and fertilizer and she's worried. In case she never sees you again, she wants you to know that she loves you—"

The power went out just then and I lost my computer connection to Mac, but I continued getting updates from Missy. It was pitch black in the storm cellar. People were using their phones as flashlights. The howling wind was reaching a crescendo, a freight train bearing down on me in the rectory. Pastor called and I had to hang up on Missy.

AFTERMATH

Despite my blurry, double vision, I have to get to Lady when the power goes out. That can only mean that the tornado is a threat and not a near miss. It's raining really hard and I'm having trouble staying on the road for the ten-minute drive to the church. Except the church is gone along with most of the rectory. It looks like the twister took out the entire church but I know better because I don't see a path of destruction, utility poles scattered like matchsticks, cars tossed down the street. There's plenty of damage to the cars in the church parking lot, however, and Pastor's Ford is upside down in the rectory's living room. I leap from my truck, blinded by the rain, and rush towards the devastated house.

"Lady! Lady! Where are you?!"

I toss bricks and wood aside, struggling to get to the central bathroom where she would have taken shelter. I'm blinded by tears, terrified of what I might find under the rubble.

"Mac…" comes a weak voice from beneath a pile of bricks, ceiling joists, and roofing, plywood and tiles twisted into an impenetrable barrier.

"I'm here, Sweetheart, just lay still while I get you out!"

There's no response, so I start tearing at the wreckage. I'm joined by firefighters and policemen and together we finally uncover Lady, bleeding badly, her arm twisted, one leg askew. She's unconscious when the paramedics finally get to her and gently lay her on a gurney. She's bad off. I can see it in the eyes of the man and woman who carry her to the waiting ambulance, which leaves with its tires spinning in the wet grass.

I'm right behind them for the fifteen-minute ride to the hospital, driving just as fast as they are because I don't want to lose sight of their taillights in the rain and darkness.

I can't see her because she's in surgery for several hours. I take a seat in the waiting room and call my daughter, Trinity, to inform her of what happened, that I'm sure Missy survived the accident. I know that's a lie and realize that Trinity is no longer *our* daughter because Missy is gone. I break down for a minute and Trinity helps me get it together. I don't tell her what I think happened. There'll be plenty of time for that later. I convince her that I'm fine and she shouldn't rush to Modoc because there will be nothing to do for several days, promising to call the second I hear good news. There won't be any good news forthcoming.

A doctor finally appears as the sun is setting and tells me that Lady's injuries are extensive but not complicated. They can take care of her in Modoc. She'll recover and be as good as new but not wake up for at least twelve hours. I should go home and get some rest. I thank the doctor profusely and suggest he should do the same.

My eyes are a little better after spending ten hours in the hospital, so I'm able to find *my* house. Imagining Missy moving around, making the now-empty structure a home, insisting that I have to eat, so I heat some leftovers and take a seat at the kitchen table. My hands are shaking, so I retrieve my stashed bottle of gin and pour myself a small glass. I sip it and remember Lady's warning me that alcohol is very bad for stroke victims. I have the spirits of two women haunting me, one making me eat and the other not letting me drink. I finish the glass with my dinner because if I haven't died already, one glass of gin isn't going to be the last straw. But I don't refill it.

The next day, I'm there when Lady wakes up. She's confused, not knowing that it's been more than twenty-four hours. The hospital doesn't know that she has Covid, so I'm able to hold her hand when I tell her what happened. She won't let me hug her because she's concerned for my health. We cry together over the tragic deaths of so many people we knew and loved. I tell her that she can spend a few decades with me since her house was destroyed. She accepts my offer.

I'm about to leave when she says, "There's one more, very important thing, Mac. Will you do this for me?"

"What is it?"

"First you have to promise to do it," is her reply.

I'd do anything for her so I nod, wondering what I just got myself into.

"You go to Oklahoma City as scheduled, but you don't drive. You either take a bus or pay someone to drive you there because I don't want to hear about you having a car accident."

"Sure but…what about you? I can't leave you here like this…" I waved my arms around the room.

"I don't think I'm going anywhere for a few days. We'll talk all the time, sharing our stories of hospital life, and then we'll finally be together. Okay?"

I go to Oklahoma City without Missy or Lady at my side. I take the bus because I don't want to be with anyone I know after what happened, even though I have a lot of friends in Modoc who don't know I'm a member of Trinity House. It's just like the doctors said it would be. They hook up electrodes to my head, measure my brain activity, then they knock me out. Just like Lady, I wake up but, instead of having my legs and arms in casts, I've got bandages around my head. My vital signs are stable and my brain is working better, although not as good as new. I can go home after a week, with several follow-up visits over the next few months, and I have to do physical therapy.

I'm at our new home, the house I built for Missy, waiting when Lady arrives in an ambulance, because I'm not physically able to take care of her, with her right leg and one arm in casts. My brain may be repaired, but I get dizzy easily and I'm as weak as a kitten. There'll be a nurse coming by to check on us— some kind of package deal our insurance companies worked out. What matters is that we are together. For what it's worth, Missy's ghost won't be haunting us because she'd given her blessing to our relationship before her tragic death.

But the Federal Bureau of Investigation is another matter entirely. Before Lady and I can even get comfortable, guess who's knocking on the front door.

EPILOGUE

Norman Gunner had been with the FBI for twenty years, but this was the strangest case he'd ever investigated. A modern, brick and steel church had been destroyed in what appeared to be a planned terrorist bombing, the blast zone damaging homes within a two-hundred-yard radius. He'd arrived with his partner, Moxxi Friedland, expecting to find a homegrown terrorist—Timothy McVeigh with a grudge to settle.

Macbeth Lunatic and his longtime mistress, Lady Church, were anything but terrorists. Agents Gunner and Friedland had spent several days interviewing the couple, who were officially *persons of interest* rather than suspects. Despite suffering several strokes, Lunatic had kept meticulous records of everything he'd done with respect to his unpaid building maintenance duties. Emails describing multiple unsafe and illegal practices had been confirmed by the FBI. Neither agent had ever heard of a cover-up that included so many details; they could have written their report exonerating Mac and Lady after the first round of interviews. However, the FBI was fascinated by what had transpired, certain that this field experience would serve the agency well in the future. That was the reason for the extensive interviews with Macbeth Lunatic and Lady Church, two star-crossed lovers whose fate hadn't ended as tragically as Romeo and Juliet's, despite the odds being against them.

The case was so complex and intriguing that inexperienced field agents were brought in to conduct interviews with the willing interviewees.

Studies were initiated to compare the initial reports to those collected later, leading to even more insight into the evaluation of witness interviews. Social scientists got involved, interviewing the subjects—now affectionately known as Mac and Lady—about their state of mind during the months leading up to the events of April twelfth. No longer persons of interest, Mac and Lady became celebrities within the criminology and psychological communities. The surgeons who had repaired the damage to his cerebellum wrote several scientific articles.

The investigation was wrapping up when Agent Gunner returned to the large, rural home where Mac and Lady were recuperating. Mac's driver's license had been reinstated and he was doing well, but not quite ready to get back to the vigorous lifestyle that had been taken from him when he'd been struck down in the prime of life. Lady was hobbling around, anxious to get her casts off, thanking Agent Gunner for being so kind and understanding. Apparently, she didn't realize that she could have thrown him out at any moment. That was why he'd grown so fond of Mac and Lady. They had nothing to hide, despite the circumstantial evidence incriminating them.

Agent Gunner sipped from the cup of excellent coffee Lady had insisted on making, despite hobbling on a crutch, and shared the good news.

"You two have been great. Thanks to your cooperation, law enforcement has a better understanding of how to discern coincidences from conspiracies using behavioral data. Aside from all that, I just want to say that I've really enjoyed meeting you guys, talking to you, well…well, it has reaffirmed my faith in America."

Mac replied, "I know what you mean, Norman, because I expected to be hauled off in handcuffs and chains. I know it looks pretty bad, and some of my friends have been telling me that I was the next *scape goat*." He waved his arms in the air and added, "I guess we can be friends, even if you are trying to stop violence and I'm…I don't think that was a good sentence."

Familiar with Mac's cognitive lapses, Agent Gunner replied, "That's right, Mac. The FBI is all about investigation, whether a crime has been committed—"

He didn't finish his sentence because Mike Blunt had aimed Vanity's Mercedes at Mac's living room as accurately as an

ICBM. The heavy sedan burst through the brick facade as if it were cardboard, tossing furniture and decorations everywhere, striking Agent Gunner on the head and rendering him unconscious. It didn't matter because he was immediately struck by the bumper of Mike's car and thrown into the interior masonry wall Missy had insisted on for tornado protection. Agent Gunner died immediately, but Mac wasn't sitting in the vehicle's trajectory. He jumped up and was able to narrowly escape the brunt of the impact, which drove the heavy car through the living room and partially penetrated the brick wall defending the game room.

Before Mac could regain his senses, Mike Blunt burst from the luxury car, a large pistol in his hand pointed at Mac's chest.

"I would have killed you the last time we met, but your dike slut wife got in the way. I'd like to beat you to death with my bare hands but…well, that's how it goes you goddamn—"

Desperate, Mac interjects, "Why are you so mad at me? I had an affair with Vanity a couple of years ago. So what? Lady tried to prevent her from attending Easter service, and then get out of the basement. I don't understand why you hate me, Mike?"

"Because you ruined my life, you piece of shit! Did you think a restraining order was going to save your miserable life? You raped Vanity and then you killed her! I should have spotted you from the beginning but you're a slimy motherfucker, you got past me, you fuck!"

Mac replied nervously, "Wait a minute, Mike. Lady and I did everything we could to save Vanity. She died because you told her that she had an obligation to represent you in church. That puts her death squarely on your shoulders, if you want to use such a simple metaphor…"

Mike Blunt shook his head but didn't answer.

It hadn't taken long for Agent Lynn McFadden, one of the junior agents who'd been interviewing Mac and Lady, to respond when the Mercedes sedan tore across the lawn and burst through the front wall of Mac's home. She arrived at the scene to see Agent Gunner's body mangled between the car's bumper and the brick wall, in time to hear Mike Blunt's threatening words. It was too late to negotiate. She didn't hesitate before pulling the trigger on her nine-millimeter Glock semiautomatic pistol, aiming to kill rather than incapacitate. Michael Blunt was dead before his body hit the floor.

Other Works by Timothy R. Keen

Black Dawn. An action-packed story about the first hybrid artificial intelligence/superhuman android and the people who want to control it.

Class of 1974. A collection of short stories about people who graduated high school the same year and shared a common feeling of disillusionment throughout their lives.

Aida. A story of what might be happening right now with respect to the creation of artificial intelligence, and how it might respond to the world it finds itself in.

A Change of Pace. An eccentric author moves to West Hollywood to write his memoir and discovers that life doesn't end at sixty-five.

Night Shift. A young family deals with their private demons as they uncover a plot to destroy the World Trade Center.

The *Unveiled* Series:

Awakening of the Gods. This first entry in the series reveals that Homo sapiens are not alone on Earth.

Servants of the Gods. In this prequel, set forty-seven-thousand years in the past, Homo sapiens become members of an empire.

Exiles of the Gods. The third book in the series has an unlikely hero falling in love while defending Humanity against annihlation.

War with the Gods. The last book in the series unveils the enormity of the task facing Humanity if we are to survive.

All titles available as eBooks or paperbacks on Amazon.